ANNE ZOELLE

CAGE of SHADOWS

EXCELSINE PRESS

Other Books by Anne Zoelle:

The Awakening of Ren Crown

The Protection of Ren Crown

The Rise of Ren Crown

The Unleashing of Ren Crown

The Destiny of Ren Crown

House of Scepters

Cage of Shadows

Crown of Starlight

Tender of the Garden

Contents

SCANDI
DENMA
HELSGIR
OLBIA
YALENDII
TYRAS
ORSO
AXSAINA SE
MORU
LISSO
ANCYRA
MEDIT SEA
SHOUNE
RABA
ZAGA
SY
CARTHA
MEMFI
KEMET
LIBU
ERSINE
KUSH

THE FEHL EMPIRE
SCYTHIA
RSK
HELIP
TOMYR
CASP SEA
ZENURIT
ZENUSFT
ZENUFT
ZENUNI
ZENURE
HEIT TERRITORIES
DRA
LYNDEL
TEHRAS
LORAN
BAHRA
HERAT
TEHRASI
PARSA
FEHLAKA
CUIPSIN
HOSFURI
HLA
KROKOLA
NURFINE
FEHLA-DA
FEHL
SEA
INDI
T

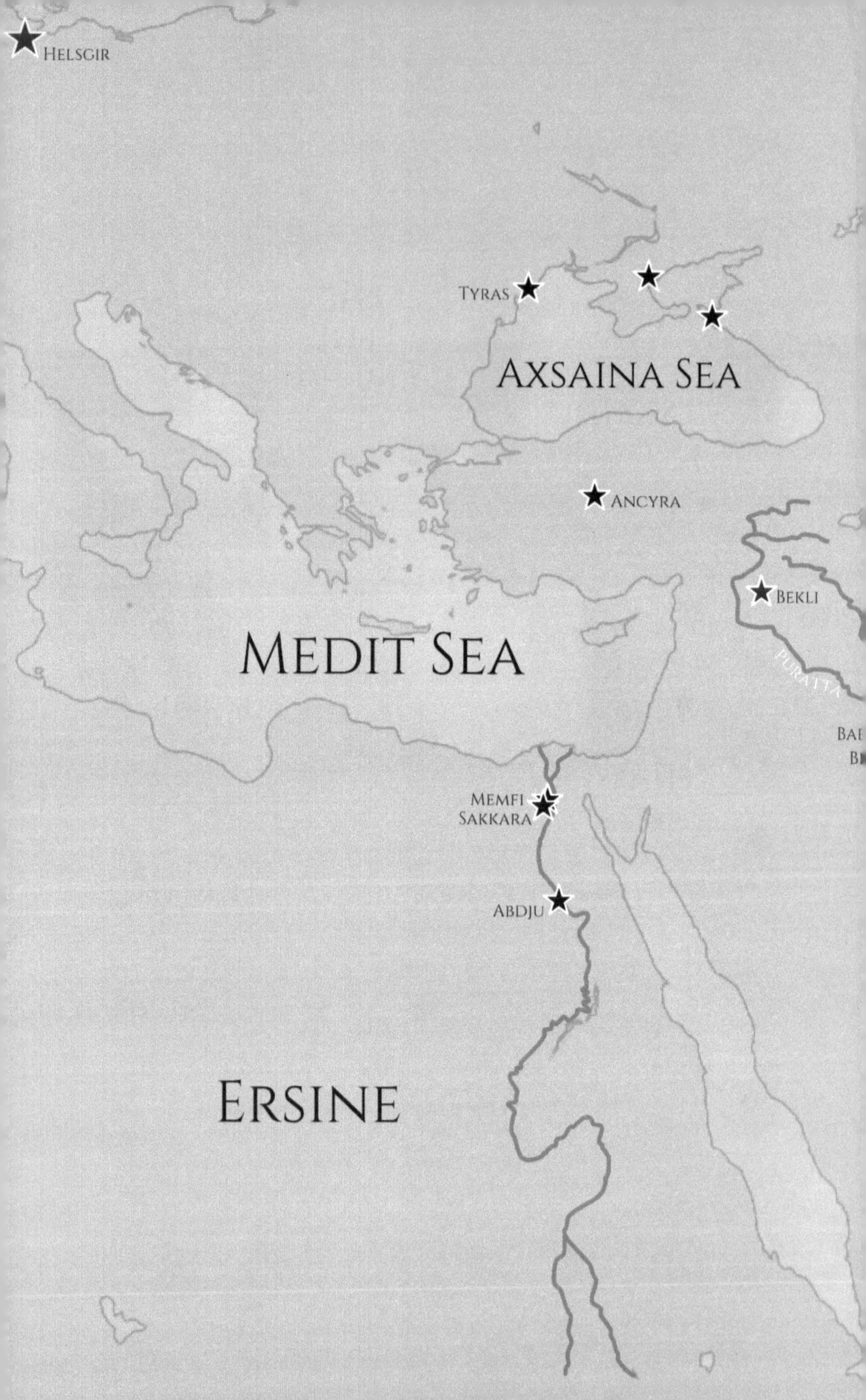

Helsgir
Tyras
Axsaina Sea
Ancyra
Bekli
Medit Sea
Puratta
Bae
B
Memfi
Sakkara
Abdju
Ersine

CHAPTER ONE
IMPERIAL MARCH

NINLI

(Imperial Palace, Fehlaka)

The Imperial Palace was as glorious as it was massive, unfolding into a series of magnificent rooms—each grander than the next—each taking Nin one step closer to death.

With senses on high alert, she noted everything around her.

Through the halls, soldiers marched, councilors strode, and servants scuttled. The staccato movements of the service workers were in stark contrast to the beautiful women draped suggestively across opulent lounges, the favored men smoking from long pipes, and the royals dining on delicacies from kingdoms afar.

Palace rhythms moved around Nin as she silently trailed behind the man she was bound to for the life and death of a moon.

Taline...Rone...be safe. Please.

They had fallen to the non-magic world and there was nothing she could do for them. She could barely hold her own head up after the massive amount of magic she had used.

Kaveh ul Fehl strode into an overly sumptuous room, his magic flying on visible wings—searching for listening spells, then flaring to encompass her in an invisible shroud, hovering millimeters from her skin.

She could move—the flicker of shadows shifted when she did—but she had nowhere to escape. Her oath and lack of magic was as much a prison as his cage of shadows.

The room's gold craftsmanship glittered against the richly patterned fabrics with their vibrant tones, as she shifted in a slow circle on cat feet, searching for hidden danger. She was keenly aware that her companion was also scrutinizing the room. Dark, swirling lines zipped through the air.

A guard stepped inside. "Your…Imperial Highness." The guard audibly swallowed. "His Imperial Majesty has been informed of your arrival and is on his way."

"Leave."

The man bowed and closed the door as he swiftly retreated.

Nin's gaze searched the corners for anything Kaveh's shadows might have missed. "Dismissing all guards," she said. "You will be assassinated, with hubris like that."

His half-empty well of magic—a consequence from the ritual at the scepter temple—pulsed. She needed to learn everything she could about the man she was now connected to.

"Even at a tenth of my strength, I'd like to see them try."

Nin flexed dirty fingers. She wished she were even close to a tenth. Even battle worn from the temple, he looked like he could conquer vast cities. So far, the stories hadn't been exaggerated. "What are you going to tell the emperor?"

"Well, I have a bit of a problem, do I not?" he bit out. "I'm not allowed by the vow to reveal any secrets I knew about you before the oath was in place or any confidences that I learn during the period of the oath that you negotiated through duplicity."

He had shown no overt surprise at the revelation of her eyes. That meant he had suspected who she was before her eyes had revealed the truth—that she wasn't a palace servant to the Carres, but a false idol bred from a palace of lies.

She stood motionless; chin lifted. "There was no duplicity. You thought we would get the scepter immediately, as did I, but I put a buffer in—"

"Let's get this straight, Ninli. You have three weeks until the oath is deemed unfulfilled. Should your sister bring forth the scepter, you will have a month from that day to run from me. But your freedom will be a moon cycle's myth. It is best you come to terms with that now."

She steadily held his gaze. "I've lived life in two cages, even if the bars of the latter were of my own making. Freedom is a gift to those born to other circumstances. But make no mistake—every cage has a weakness."

"Born like your sister?"

"A sister of my second life's heart. Taline is not of my blood." She needed that to be perfectly clear, so he didn't think Taline another piece to be used. "You need not concern yourself with her once you have the scepter."

"You deceive yourself to think she and the marked prince will show up with the relic to save you."

"I hope for quite the opposite." The vow shuddered and the ribbon constricted around her wrist. "I will accept the death of my second life and be grateful that the death is mine and not theirs."

Never again. Never again would she let others be sacrificed in her place.

Fury strummed through the bond, then sudden calculation. She held herself stiffly as he rifled through her emotions and his gaze switched between her eyes.

"You will rue this oath," he said.
Harsh, militaristic footsteps echoed outside, announcing the arrival of the emperor's procession.

"I will never rue saving those I love."

"A fool's notion."

Echoed hails to the emperor called forth from the hall.

Nin closed her eyes and held herself motionless, allowing herself a last moment. She didn't possess enough magic to complete the spell to transform her eyes, and she knew what they would reveal to the emperor.

Eye colors were varied and numerous in the multi-cultured people who migrated around the Casp Sea, but red...red was singular and specific. The Carres had magically cultivated their poisonous red eyes to match their bloodline and stand as warning.

Beware the bloodthirst of the Carres had always echoed in their gaze.

And this was it. The last gasp of the Carres.

"Aren't we all fools, in the end," she murmured.

The doors began to open.

A spell whisked over her face and an enchantment descended with a suddenness that stole her breath and made her blink. She didn't know what shade her eyes were now, but she knew they weren't crimson.

Kaveh turned his back to her, muscles tight under the straps that crisscrossed his chest and back—his conjured cloak draped across the back of a chaise, his real cloak lost to the non-magic layer with Rone and Taline.

She stared at his back, uncomprehending, but quickly fell to her knees as the hallway opened to view. Her neck stiffened with refusal, but she forced it down, watching the procession only through the top of her vision.

The great gilded doors parted inward and guards ten deep straightened along the hall. She could see the ghostly shadows of other guards arraying themselves outside the windows, hemming them in, assuring no escape.

The emperor, alone, strode into the room. The doors shut behind him, leaving the three of them without personal guard.

It was a show of absolute trust from the emperor to his warrior son—or an action born from the same hubris that his son maintained—a hubris that spoke of the ability to fend off any attack without aid.

"A gift?" The emperor's voice was warm and deep. His flowing robes of rich blue brushed along the intricate stonework like shadows over flesh. Her gaze pulled from the hem of his robe up his frame and to his face. His eyes narrowed suddenly on her.

The room tilted. What did he know?

A hand wrapped around the nape of her neck and squeezed. Feelings of forced calm pushed along the fledgling bond. Only then did she realize her breath was releasing in stuttered pants and her vision was tunneling. The clamped hand wasn't soothing, but the warning squeeze was enough to snap everything back into sharp focus.

Kaveh's rough fingers fell from her skin and he stepped forward to greet his father, bowing his head.

She found herself unable to do so again.

"Your Imperial Majesty," Kaveh said.

Crelu ul Osni had set the chain spell that caused the deaths of her family and loyal servants, and Jisarek Carre had been the root cause of it all, but Sher Fehl had created the stage. The man who stood before her had made those executions possible. In his own revenge, Sher Fehl had given Osni the means to wipe the Carres from existence.

Handsome, charismatic Sher Fehl with his rich, dark hair and sunlit brown eyes, stood resolute before them. His features weren't as sharp and otherworldly as his son's, but they were as uncompromising in their expressionless set when he wasn't trying to project charm.

She had seen him before, from afar. The emperor of the Fehl Empire, or as he preferred—the Sunlight Empire—had frequently visited Tehras in the first few years post-conquest. She had seen him from the streets, waving and striding forth with a glittering smile—a conqueror proud of his newest gem. From a distance, she had been able to look at him with a detached focus.

It was harder to compartmentalize her feelings when the man stood before her. It was harder to compartmentalize what it meant to love someone who did unspeakable things—her family's tyranny as the enemy of the people they served—when forced to see those things in bright light.

It was hard to feel ease with a new ruler when you could see that same iron control in his eyes. His eyes lightened a fraction when they landed on his son, then hardened again infinitesimally.

"There is a scar upon your magic, Kaveh."

Kaveh inclined his head. "A sacrifice was needed. My power will return."

The emperor perused him silently, his unreadable gaze catching on the husk of shadow curled in Kaveh's conjured cloak. "Is it dead?"

"No. Ifret will revive with care and rest."

For the briefest moment, an odd combination of relief and consternation crossed the emperor's face. "I'm sure Irsula will be glad to hear it. A sacrifice of magic—you found the temple, then."

"And the scepter." Kaveh looked straight at the man. "The Scepter of Darkness was found and lost again, Your Imperial Majesty."

Nin fought a wince at such directness. Lengthy word games couched in conciliatory tones were the natural address to those higher in status for a reason.

The light in the emperor's eyes died completely. "Explain."

Kaveh did, in clipped tones and short sentences. He adequately summed up the temple journey and battle until he reached the end. She found it strange, though, that he didn't label the men who had attacked first and been killed by Osni as pentalayerists. Perhaps Kaveh felt them insignificant—they had been insignificant other than in raising the initial barrier.

Or...perhaps he didn't know their label. He seemed to regard most people as beneath his notice. She tucked the information away.

"Osni slipped through the closing gate." Kaveh tossed Osni's toes to the floor. "He did not escape unscathed. Ifret poisoned him. He is a traitor to the empire, but the scepter will not be easy for him to gain, as near to death as he is. I would only trust seeing his death with my own eyes, however."

"And the scepter?"

"The scepter fused to the hand of Taline ul Summora, a low-level magi, who will try to return it to our grasp. Rone ul Valeran proved that he is not to be trusted by the empire. However, it is possible he will be swayed by the girl enough not to kill her outright. He is weak to her. And the scepter cannot be underestimated as a beacon now that it has a magi to use. If she touches a marked site in the non-magic layer, we will have its location."

The oath protections for Rone had been extinguished by his actions at the temple. It was why Kaveh could disclose his duplicity. Rone would not return to the empire. There was only death for him now.

"How...disappointing." The emperor's hands fisted, as if he were stopping himself from casting a spell. "Oralia's child truly is a disappointment. Crelu ul Osni will rue his betrayal, as will my wayward spawn."

Discipline kept Kaveh's face impassive—but she could feel the coiled tension beneath. He was readying himself for whatever spell was running beneath the emperor's skin.

The emperor's biting gaze slid to her. "And this girl?"

Her head should be bowed. She knew she should bow. She felt Kaveh's frustration and unease. But her neck refused the instruction a second time. She couldn't look away.

"A healer from Tehras," Kaveh said.

Her shock echoed Kaveh's own at that description.

"Is someone ill?" the emperor said with the slightly caustic cadence of a person who knew when an introduction was obtusely incomplete. His flat, angry gaze never left hers.

"Ninli ul Summora," Kaveh said. She could feel the pull within the bond—the oath vying against his devotion to his father. Rage gathered in him at the struggle, pushing against their bond in hot, angry swirls. "She is the sister of the one with the scepter, but she is the one who retrieved it."

Hard eyes just like his son's narrowed on her. "Did she? How?"

"She was a denizen of Carre Palace before the fall."

He could not reveal her secrets, even in subterfuge. But he could tell truths that hid deeper truths. Truths that could lead back to the root.

She could feel the pulse of magic with every step the emperor took as he strode toward her—like a drumbeat that echoed beneath her folded knees. The beat pulled in abruptly—sucking the energy from around him—then beat again.

She pressed down on a shudder. She knew what the emperor's power was. Everyone did.

It was as rare as hers, but far more personally devastating. Whereas her power opened pathways between places, the emperor's skills magically sucked a person or space dry, locking the magic in a way that was impossible to overcome.

Even Etelian ul Fehl, who had the slightest wisp of a stripping ability, couldn't undo the emperor's locks.

The emperor observed her coldly, the way one observes an insect while the decision is being made in how to kill it. "I am very displeased by your tale, Kaveh. The Scepter of Darkness exists, and two traitors are in possession of it."

"Taline ul Summora will bring it to us or die trying. If the scepter is not brought here by the next moon, her sister is mine."

The emperor's cold gaze swept over her. "I suppose that, too, explains the state of other things. That band around your wrist, for example. Partnership? Trust?" He turned dark eyes on his son. "It's like I'm looking at someone I do not know."

"Finding the scepter required it." Kaveh's voice was emotionless. His feelings were not. "The plan was working until Osni interfered. The scepter fused to Taline ul Summora against her will. If she survives and returns to our world, she will bring the scepter to us. They are loyal to each other."

The flare of fury in the emperor's eyes made Nin instinctively lean back.

"If she returns? If the scepter to rule all scepters is lost to us, it must be lost to all."

He motioned sharply and Kaveh dropped to his knees beside her. "I will see it done."

She hadn't known the Shadow Prince long, but it was surreal to see him coldly on his knees and feel the cocktail of emotions fighting inside him.

"I am disappointed." The emperor gripped Kaveh's chin. "And I am unused to such a state with you. I know not what to do about it." Magic rippled over both of them and the emperor's fingers tightened. Tension screamed through her.

"It wasn't his fault."

The scene froze, and Nin did, too, as she realized the words had come from her.

She could feel Kaveh's horror, though he self-identified the emotion as fury in a quickly caught wisp of internal swearing shared by the bond—an interesting observation to unravel at a time when she wasn't about to die.

She firmed her expression. "It wasn't his fault."

The emperor dropped his grip on Kaveh and grabbed her jaw instead, his fingernails digging into her skin. It was a far less kind hold and she strained upward from her bent knees. "I don't remember speaking to you, girl."

"You did not, Your Imperial Majesty."

He squeezed tighter. "Foolish. Brave. Honest. I would have pegged you from the stables of the House of Carre for exhibiting the first characteristic, but never for the second, and definitely not for the third."

Magic yanked from her—through her jaw, her teeth—and she strained against the desperate urge to flee. Unlike the scepter protections, when the emperor took your magic, it didn't return unless he wished it. It was locked away in a state only one with the same skill could unlock.

Magic tore through her, scorching pathways that she could not fix.

"Osni dabbles in necromancy," she said, panting, trying to stay still and compliant as her magic was ripped from her. She had been bred by predators. She knew what predators did to those they saw as prey. "He raised revenants. He used his ceremonial scepter to enact a sunlight barrier." She kept her gaze steady on his. "The scepter you allowed him to keep."

"I will destroy you, little girl." Another pull of magic was ripped from her—veins pulled free of her flesh.

"You will not get your scepter that way," she said. "There will be no reason for anyone to save a girl already dead."

The emperor smiled coldly and roughly released her jaw. Her mind spun and her body ached, but she had been tortured before—hurt far worse by those who shared her blood. She steadied herself on her knees as the room spun. With so much already broken within her, she couldn't calculate how much magic he had taken. Two levels, maybe? She swallowed. She wouldn't mourn their loss. She had more. He also didn't know that she was more depleted than Kaveh. He had taken only a fraction of a fraction of magic, when he had probably thought he was removing a percentage far greater.

Metaphorical fingernails had been yanked away, but better than a hand lost.

"You survive only by my will and whatever ignorant bargain has already been made. I see what you've done to my son." His gaze passed across Kaveh's covered wrist, then Nin's. "And I know the look of silence and secrets. If you were attached to any other person, you would already be dead on this floor."

There were so many things she wanted to say—about Etelian ul Fehl, about how the emperor had allowed Osni to live, about the emperor's hubris being his downfall.

But she would die at his hands for expressing further thoughts.

At her silence, he dismissed her from his attention.

"Disappointing. Perhaps I must adjust my view of your usefulness, Kaveh."

None of Kaveh's roiling emotions showed on his face, but she could feel his fury. An internal fury—inwardly directed. She curled her fingers into her palm, cutting into the skin.

"In your absence, evil has been breeding along our borders," the emperor said. "Either that, or I've mistaken luck for competence, and your exploits are petty indeed."

Kaveh did not break eye contact. "I will not disappoint you again."

"We'll see. I will send someone more competent to find the scepter. Silence the rumors on the front. I will call you when I have need."

"As you wish."

She could feel Kaveh's emotions. The anger. The fury. But his face was expressionless.

"What I wish is far from this." The emperor grabbed her face again. "This baggage, this drivel, this parasite."

Her stolen magic unlocked in a horrible grinding sound that gave way to pathetic relief even amid the pain.

He yanked her toward him by her jaw. "I will make you a magicless crouel next time, dead girl, regardless of the shared pain."

The emperor let go of her in a forceful push and strode from the room in a sweep of robes and bitterness.

She stared at the tiles under her hands and licked cracked lips as droplets of blood dripped on the ceramic. Everything hurt within her, and yet the leaking bond from Kaveh was the most devastating.

As soon as she thought it, he buttoned up his emotions so fast that she could have experienced them as a fragment of a dream. She leaned back on her heels and silently watched as he rose, mask back in place—dark and searing.

Kaveh hadn't disclosed her identity, not even in the midst of devastating disappointment. No hints or excuses for his failure to bring back the scepter. The oath was a smothering blanket upon them.

For now.

Once the emperor knew she was a Carre...

She shuddered and pressed a hand to her mouth to wipe away the blood.

Kaveh secured his conjured cloak, taking care not to jar the creature inside. He flicked his wrist briskly at her and strode from the room in a reflection of the emperor's exit. She hurried after. People in the hall scurried to get out of his way—bowing in awe and terror. But even those who didn't bow—those dressed in highborn garb or children of the emperor born to mothers from countries far and wide—watched him pass with tilted-down heads and wary eyes.

Those gazes quickly darted to her, narrowed and questioning—taking in her bloodied mouth, blanched and sweating skin, crescent-bloodied cheeks, and hurried position behind the Shadow Prince. Her general state of dress, and the slightly lighter brown skin, fuller cheeks, and accent that identified her as Tehrasian would require a second impression, but they would be all too obvious when she wasn't hidden by blood and trauma.

And palace life was all about observation.

She wouldn't be able to keep her real identity hidden in such a place. Not in a place where people were looking for secrets to use.

And in the studied familiarity of the bowing and fear—she could see that the prince wasn't a stranger to the imperial palace, regardless of his preference for the battlefront.

Nin hurried to stay within the long, unnatural shadow Kaveh cast as his conjured cloak whipped out behind him. His presence pulled attention like a windstorm lifting and shoving objects and she knew this dance—she simply needed to be the beetle who was too small for notice.

The corridors cleared as their destination became obvious and word spread—allowing people in the distance to flee from his dark path.

It wasn't until she saw the shimmering courtyard gate that she voiced the question left by the emperor's departure. "Are we really going to the battlefront?"

"You think I am going to disobey a direct command from the emperor?"

She increased her pace until she was alongside him. "Your power is only at half."

"Are you concerned for me, sparrow?" His voice was steel.

"I'm bound to you. It seems a prudent gesture."

"I can conquer a territory with nothing but a sword," he said scathingly, never breaking stride. "Losing half of my magic for a few days is hardly going to put me in mortal peril."

"Hubris," she murmured.

"You would know, Hand. Worry about your own tenth reserves."

They walked to the gate and she felt the magic reach for her—as every gate did—but she pushed the feeling away. With so little magic thrumming through her, it wasn't hard for once.

The gate opened to Parsa, the city of a dozen great gates. One gate would take them to another, then another to the battlefront—through the vast interlinking gates of the empire.

"I'm not a soldier," she said. The distance restriction demanded that she be physically close to Kaveh, and everyone knew the Imperator General didn't sit in a tent while his forces fought.

"You will learn to be." He grabbed her elbow and they walked through the interlinking gates and into war.

CHAPTER TWO
DISTRUST AND DOMINION

TALINE

(UNKNOWN REGION, FIRST LAYER)

The murmur of low chanting voices echoed along the crude stonework halls of the cavernous temple as Taline followed Valeran. The temple was decorated with earthy stonework and carvings and quite exceptional in that it had been completed without magic.

Taline looked at a few intricate Sanskrine glyphs and carvings tucked into the awnings. Someone—likely a Carre—had placed ward seals to nullify the scepter's presence, then disappeared back through their gateway, taking their ripgate with them.

Depictions of the scepter, sun, moons, madness, bloodlust, and death were painted in zealous strokes, endless ochre spewed across the walls. The drawings proceeded them, growing bolder and gorier—a tale of calamity and tragedy.

Nin.

Taline unwillingly memorized the drawings that ended with a blood moon—as the crowd of worshipers followed them through the increasingly cramped corridors. She limped stiffly behind Valeran toward a large beam of sunlight. Quick hands darted out to touch them from stone windows and bodies tucked in awnings.

Valeran cut his knife lazily through the air in warning.

The hands retreated, but the close press of bodies remained.

She had to force the tightness from her shoulders. If they tried anything, she had no internal magic to aid her, and the temple itself purposely held no magic that could reveal its location—but these were non-magic humans, with regular hands and superstitious beliefs.

She could handle regular humans. She had handled sadistic magi even when she had been forced to non-magic levels. She gripped her fingers around the scepter. He couldn't get her here. And if he came, she would show him the consequences of fighting on an equal level.

A magi had to be able to pass through the world layers to get to the non-magic lands, and finding people, relics, or places that could do such a thing was exceedingly rare. Nin was rare. The Fehls had control over Nin now, but her oath with the blasted thirteenth prince would protect her until the dark moon.

She looked at the metal pole fused to her right palm.

Taline had one month to escape the non-magic lands—lands described in dire minstrel tales—for if the non-magic humans didn't kill you, the guardians of the layers would.

She had one month to find and free Nin, then run.

The problem with minstrel tales was that Taline was far from the champion of the story—and the champion would be chained forevermore unless the mouse beat the lion king.

She flexed her fingers around the metal stick that was melded to the center of her palm.

"A middling magi with more brains than power," Valeran drawled. "Taline ul Summora now holds a relic that makes her, quite possibly, the most dangerous magic user in all five layers of the world."

"We are in a place without magic. I am as useful as ever," she said bitterly.

"Still unable to activate it?" he asked idly as the corridor split before them.

"If I could, you'd be a stain on the stones."

He raised lazy brows. "Lies."

She bared her teeth at him, and the crowd immediately started chanting in a tone that was akin to a plea for mercy. A woman was pushed forward, head tilted back, and neck exposed. A priest stabbed a knife toward the woman's bared throat.

Taline's right hand shot out and the scepter blocked the knife's path with a clang. The man stumbled away, murmuring a prayer or a curse. The glassy-eyed woman stared at Taline in confusion, shame, and fear.

Taline's lips tightened and the edges of her mouth pulled down. She didn't have to wonder what the Carres had demanded of these people in the past. Sacrifice had been their favorite first course.

Residents of Tehrasi, even ten years later, still expected the axe to fall on festival days. It was without question that the non-magic lands of the Carres would expect sacrifice as a matter of course.

The empire didn't overly interfere with the local populations of captured territories in their layer other than to institute their imperial ideals and introduce their technology, but Tehrasi had always been different, and Sher Fehl had banned sacrifices there—stating that the sacrifice of the royal family had instituted a hundred years of prosperity for the land.

It had always made Taline nervous, for what if Tehrasi fell—what if Nin was uncovered?

Nin would be the first sacrificed, if the populace converted from their fervent sacrificial tendencies to the crown to the desire to see the sacrifice of the crown. Like people who pledged allegiance in meeting rooms, then stuck knives between ribs in dark alleys, there was no trust in a single decade's change.

And in the non-magic lands, the Fehl Empire was completely unknown.

The woman in front of her began babbling foreign apologies and casting fervent looks to a stone window and the jungle vantage beyond—a place from which to cast herself through.

"No," Taline said harshly. She pointed the scepter at the woman, then drew a circle to shape the sun lifting into the air.

The woman's eyes went wide, lighting with inner fire and adulation. The woman turned and the crowd readily accepted her within, bowing to the woman—their eyes lit in sacred fervor as well—as she fled back into the temple.

"Nice work, Summora. Now a vestal virgin will tend the closest temple of the sun for the next five hundred years."

Taline gritted her teeth. "What did you want me to do? Bathe in her blood?"

The crowd murmured, staring at her in increasing awe as the enchantments continued to fade around her. A fearless man extended a hand toward her face.

"No." She grimly blocked the man's hand, but the looks of the crowd grew in wonder.

She could feel the last enchantments on her face fading, drained by the lack of magic around them—the world layer greedy for the magic it had been denied for the past five hundred years. To the people, her appearance would be a revelation.

Valeran swiped glittering gems from each offering plate into his satchel.

"Stop thieving, Valeran," she hissed.

"A thief belying a thief?"

The crowd murmured, not understanding their words but reading their displeasure, and the head priest motioned sharply with his staff to them, then back to the cavern.

More jewels in another chamber?

If Valeran turned back, she was leaving him.

Gaze distant, he tapped a finger against his thigh, then continued toward the light.

Similar to the temple entrance in their layer, this exit was nondescript. Symbols of death, resurrection, and the eclipse of each were hand-carved into the edges, hiding what was inside. For all their flashy and cruel excesses, the Carres had been magnificent at keeping their secrets.

Taline looked out at the jungle landscape extending from the temple, an area overgrown with wild tangles of vegetation and dense areas of plants. Heavy moisture clung to each surface. It was an entirely different climate from the woodland forest surrounding the connected temple in their own layer. Even the river that flowed along the base of the rock face and the crudely crafted steps were different.

She looked back at the temple that was cut into the rock face and extended high above.

Worshipers were melting into crooks in the stones.

The men and women had the look of Indi, with their slightly darker skin and features. In a world with magic, travel was easier, migration was common, and cultures mixed far more frequently—but the core pockets of ancestral inhabitants that existed before the split remained the same. It made it easy to at least identify basic territory.

Which meant, they were likely nowhere near the Casp Sea or Telb Mountains. They weren't even in this layer's version of Tehrasi.

She didn't know where they were, and she had only one month to find her way back home.

Nin.

Landscape equivalents aside, the lack of magic flowing through her was the starkest reminder that they were not where they were supposed to be.

Valeran had kicked her through a layer ripgate, and now Nin was somewhere in another layer of the world, chained to a man who would use her and cage her. Chained like Taline had been before her sister had saved her.

Her skin began to burn around the scepter, but the scepter did not light. She stared at it.

Get me home.

Her skin burned. She closed her eyes.

Find Nin.

The heat stopped.

A ragged sound escaped her throat. The most powerful scepter in existence was fused to her skin and she could do nothing.

Useless.

"All well there, Summora?"

"Nothing is well, Valeran." Taline took another ragged breath and straightened her shoulders. Get it together. Breathe.

Powerlessness was an old foe—a weakness that said, hide, be silent, say nothing...embrace me, and I will always be here for you. She knew how to treat that kind of enemy.

She set her jaw. She didn't have to be powerful. She just had to be strong in belief and clever enough to see and take advantage of opportunity. Nin had taught her that. Nin had allowed Taline to be part of her life in whatever capacity Taline had desired—she had allowed Taline to be free.

Information. Decision. Action.

She swept cold logic over fear. She went over the oath parameters in her head. She had made Nin painstakingly list them. Kaveh ul Fehl couldn't kill Nin or reveal her identity for the period of the oath. There was time to save her sister—as long as the emperor didn't discover Nin's true identity on his own.

There would be time. She would make it so.

Valeran was examining the landscape in micro detail.

Information. Gather information.

"Do you know where we are?" she asked tightly.

Not many people had traveled through the non-magic lands, and Taline put little stock in the stories told in Vanichrest and Caire's twisting gambling caves. But she put stock in Nin. Nin had mentioned more than once that Valeran had been to the non-magic lands. That meant Valeran knew how to get home.

Valeran looked at the sun's position. "The nature of the language paired with the terrain, people, and dress... I'd tentatively put us in Magadha, the equivalent of Midwestern Indi in our layer."

The confirmation did little to ease her tension. Dense jungle, large cats, and no magic—with zero idea of how to get home.

And, Sehk, she needed help, but she couldn't trust him. He had put her here. He had kicked the scepter from Kaveh ul Fehl's reaching hand. She didn't know why he had done it, but Valeran's actions signified he didn't want the scepter in the empire's hand. He would never allow the scepter to be given to the empire in exchange for Nin.

If Taline could pick anyone to trudge through the jungles of the non-magic lands with, it wouldn't be Rone ul Valeran.

Still, if anyone could get her to where she needed to go, it was the man in front of her.

A seasoned adventurer and trickster, Valeran's relic hunting skills were unparalleled.

She searched for what she had to aid her. Magical items still worked, and they had enough left in their bags to lend a hand. Magic could still be used, aided by trickery and subterfuge.

With trickery and subterfuge, Valeran could build his own empire here.

"Or I could take over Kūruš's empire, which has been pushing borders across the same space as the Fehl Empire." Valeran's words jolted her, making her realize she had muttered her last thought aloud. "If Kūruš still remains. The leadership of the non-magic layer is as bloodstained as ours, so it might have switched to another in the year since I've been here."

"I care not about the empires in this non-magic world," she said in anger and embarrassment.

"No? Well, there is always the option of finding the lands of the beasts, or those of the magi who look the same but who have terraformed their kingdoms with magic differently than ours. Or the truly mythic land where all is ever changing."

Five layers of the same world. Five worlds built upon the same lands. She looked at the scepter, which was capable of transporting someone between the five layers—or of collapsing pieces and combining layers…if she could work it.

She needed magic—or at least a place holding enough to siphon off. She had a bag of empty containers. She could make something work. She just needed opportunity.

Nin had created a long, thin canyon gate between the five layers only accessible by khursifa and direct knowledge of the spot in the cold lands two years past. Taline could get there by khursifa with a wind director in hand. And though she had both khursifa and director, both were useless in a world without magic to ferry a steady breeze or guide a spellbox.

She firmed her lips. "And where are these gates to the other layers?"

A gate—a permanent fixture as opposed to the temporary nature of a ripgate—between two spots in a single layer required a relic or gatemaker to connect its points of permanence. Gates between layers required added complexity and far more points. Only a few magi in every generation were capable of it, and even then, creating a layer ripgate put a magi like Nin out of commission for days. Creating a layer gate would require far more.

They had made forays to the non-magic lands in order to deliver people who could bear their world no longer, but only after careful planning. Nin could do little after opening a ripgate between layers.

Valeran's eyes were heavy-lidded. "That is the fundamental question, is it not? The layer purity zealots collapsed most of the set ways to get from layer to layer hundreds of years ago. The pentalayerists exist in smaller groups than their founders, but smaller groups hold fiercer numbers, and they are always looking for ways to seal layer gates and destroy items of overwhelming power to keep the layers separated and clean. They hold the breaking of the earth into five layers as the most sacred of actions. And they will kill any who oppose that view."

She gripped the scepter. "Or any who hold a world-breaking weapon in hand."

"The relic that can open ripgates between worlds at will? They will do anything to destroy the Scepter of Darkness, and they cannot see beyond their aims. They have probably known where the temple entrance between our layers is for a long time, keeping an eye on anyone who approaches. They skulk around in the dark, quietly killing worldchangers and powerful gatemakers. The Carres were isolationists for multiple reasons—their need for worship and their need for safety. They made a bargain with the pentalayerists long ago. Though, if you think the pentalayerists had nothing to do with the fall of Tehrasi, you are a fool. They long desired the death of the Carres."

"And you let them follow us," she said bitterly. She didn't need confirmation of who had allowed the men to follow them. She knew. Valeran had looked entirely too interested in the footpath Nin had laid—and that small silver ball he had twisted before the ritual opening—she had known something was off.

"You left a trail for the pentalayerists. People who would gladly kill Nin. Were you going to hand her to them as well?"

"Ninli is too damned, and too lucky, for the pentalayerists to catch. They will never get her."

"No thanks to you."

"I've known her for half her life, narsumina—the half spent in alley shadows. They would never have caught her. It is your skin the pentalayerists will now try to flay. The skin attached to that thing." He motioned to the scepter.

"Nin had no magic left! Who knows what has happened to her! You killed her."

Something dark and furious rose in his eyes, but it was gone a moment later, as if it had never existed. "Ninli can handle herself."

"She let herself be drained," Taline spit. "She had nothing left. I know that because she is not here. And yet you allowed forces who wanted to kill her—you let Osni—follow and disrupt the plan. Crelu ul Osni might have killed her as soon as the ripgate closed!"

"Calm down, Summora." He looked at the scepter attached to her hand. "You do not comprehend the danger of what you hold in your fury."

"I comprehend the danger just fine. Nin is bound by Kaveh ul Fehl. And the emperor doesn't have his toy." She lifted her hand and shook the scepter angrily. "He will kill her."

Valeran had done this. She felt something monstrous stir in her, and heat gathered in her fused palm.

A slew of language assailed them, and Valeran's eyes shifted and narrowed to decode the temple priest's words and motions.

She tore her gaze from Valeran and the feeling building inside her abruptly ceased.

"What's he saying?" Taline asked, trying to interpret the motions and rhythm of the words. She didn't want to rely on Valeran.

"Reverence. The sun. Light. Terror. Darkness. Renewal. Balance."

Valeran was cocking his head in a way that said he was understanding more than what he was translating. His eyes slid to her—telling her more than she needed that something referenced her—and she gripped the staff. She hated him.

The man bowed repeatedly, pointing to the temple, and set a candle down on the grass. The priest bowed continuously as he moved backward.

Another man motioned in a completely different way, causing Valeran to stiffen.

"What's that one saying?" Frustration and anger caused Taline's voice to sharpen.

"Someone came through after us," he said slowly. "Whoever it was, just roused."

Taline looked sharply at the temple and started to return.

Valeran grabbed her arm. "What are you doing?"

"What if it's Nin?" She shook herself free.

"What if it's not?"

"You think it's the Shadow Prince?"

"No."

Above them, high in the temple mount, she saw a burned and bloodied man scuttling into the jungle. The blood drained from her face, from her hands and feet—as if her body knew that it needed all available sustenance drawn inward to keep her heart beating.

The man disappeared from view as abruptly as he had appeared.

"Osni," she said stiffly. They couldn't catch him from here. They would have to wind their way back up through the temple, and Taline wasn't certain she completely trusted the hungry looks in the eyes of some of the worshipers.

A throwing knife twisted through Valeran's fingers. "The trail was for the pentalayerists, not Osni. If I'd known he slipped through the ripgate, I would have finished him the non-magic way," he said roughly.

Osni would have known that, too, and in his desperate physical state he must have remained hidden while the two of them had been focused on each other.

"How is he still alive?" she asked tightly. "I've never heard of someone surviving the Shadow Prince's monster." She wondered whether the monster had survived as well.

Valeran's gaze dropped to the scepter in her hand, and she understood his thoughts—Osni had a scepter, too. She gripped hers. Of what was his capable?

"We need to be careful," Valeran said.

"There is no we in this."

"I'm hurt," he said casually, gaze carefully tracking the brush. "Would you rather make a deal with Osni to get home instead? I'm certain he will be open to negotiation."

"I trust you as much as I do him."

"You have always had excellent sense. So what are your terms, narsumina, of Narsum's Bane?"

She hated that jab at her looks. At the reference to the vestal tenders of the divine ruler of beauty, age, and time.

"I don't need you, Sehk's Scourge of Chance Wielders—the face of trickery."

Valeran looked out to the jungle—a landscape teaming with life but dead to magic. He motioned forward. "Off with you then."

"I don't need your permission either," she hissed.

She grit her teeth, clenched her muscles, then shook her stuck palm. Activate.

Nothing happened.

Home.

She looked at the scepter, trying to communicate her need, and tried it again.

I need to get home.

Nothing.

I will die if I don't get home.

"If you are going to activate that scepter," he said lazily, "you're going to have to put your back into it."

She tore her gaze away from the scepter. Valeran had moved to sit on a stone wall, chewing a dried strip of meat from Ninli's pack. He wasn't trying to hide his dark satisfaction.

Taline reached out with her free hand and ripped the pack from him. "You do not get Nin's supplies."

She made no move to take the Shadow Prince's discarded cloak, lying next to him.

"How impolite." He laid back on the stone shelf and put his hands behind his head, looking up at the sun and clouds with one knee bent. "There is some truly excellent cloud watching to be had. The foliage seems to lean instinctively away from the temple. That looks like a rat-beetle, don't you think?"

"Stop talking," she hissed.

She took a quick view of the sun, falling from the midday peak which they had needed to place the totem, and at the angle of the cast shadows, then stomped down the bank of the river toward north—a trail of worshipers following her.

She would do this alone.

CHAPTER THREE
ANOTHER LIFE

NINLI

(Shirsk)

Nin wiped at her face with fingers that felt disjointed from her body.

She was alone, but the screams still echoed in her ears.

Dirty and numb.

The tent was plush and warm, the lights soft and glowing. But Nin could appreciate none of those things. Not after what she had witnessed.

Not when she was soaked with blood.

Fresh fruits and meats were placed on the wooden platter to her right—brought by one of the camp workers. Out of sheer self-preservation, she had consumed the fare Kaveh had pushed into her hand on the battlefield—squares of densely packed meat and bread shoved and chewed quickly. Her hollow stomach said she should eat, but she wasn't certain she could keep anything down if she tried.

She felt Kaveh enter the tent before she saw him—a removed feeling that had only grown stronger the longer she had been at his side.

She stared at the smooth stone basin as gray and rust-brown water swirled where her hands dipped. She touched the water to her face and though she could feel the coolness upon her flesh, it was a removed sensation—the feeling that she was in someone else's skin.

"I'd have thought you'd be more used to death, given your heritage." Kaveh moved around the tent, discarding leathers and tucking away weaponry, but she could feel his gaze on her. "You look no better than a greenling after his first foray."

Nin watched the water hit the basin in fat drops from her cheeks. "It has been long since I've been unable to save."

She didn't remember the last time pure will hadn't allowed her to bring someone back from death. In the dark alleys of Tehras, no one died if she was near.

On a battlefield where thousands had perished in the first hour, and with her magic still creaky and shaken, she had lost more than she had saved. And Kaveh had pushed on, not resting once, like a storied hand of death.

In the non-magic world, armies relied on numbers. But here, massive armies hadn't been required or desired for a long time. A far smaller core of overpowered magic users, relics, and spellboxes had been preferred. Magi had learned to spread intent and enchantment. Like a virus in the magic, an oath in the waters, or a rippled curse on the sands. When extremely powerful magi Awakened, kingdoms either wanted them on their side or wanted them neutralized.

Tehrasi had used golems and revenants to fight for power and standing, then folded when one side was beaten. For to be beaten in a test of magic meant to be beaten in a war.

But with the coming of Kaveh ul Fehl, tactics had changed again. Magi who controlled golems died painfully from his shadows—a never-before-seen feat. A one-on-one magic duel with him was sure to fail. Therefore, physical numbers on the field had increased again, hoping to overwhelm an unstoppable force. And when the numbers on one side increased, the numbers on the other rose to deal with the underlings.

When Kaveh passed, there would be another wave of military advancement—what it would be remained to be seen.

But for now, he was unstoppable.

The Shirskens had surrendered. Of course they had. But not soon enough for Nin's tastes. Why had their commander allowed the slaughter to go on for so long? They had finally thrown down all arms as Kaveh had closed in upon their highest-ranking generals. Their leaders were captured and awaiting judgment. Their forces had been banded with activated imperial tags. All the usual things associated with a loss to the empire.

But the shadow of betrayal painting the faces of the Shirsken generals and leaders circled through her thoughts. Betrayal from whom?

Shirsk had been a territory ready to cede to imperial forces a week ago, according to camp gossip she had overheard as she had followed Kaveh like a wraith. But something had changed. There had been a surge by those in power against the insurgency of the empire, even when they had been on the cusp of defeat.

Something wasn't right, and even above the emotional devastation she felt, the feeling of wrongness persisted.

By continuing the fight, the Shirskens were sure to face the full wrath of the emperor. And she could say that was a position she had no desire to be in. She had no idea how things would play out for their people—sometimes the emperor made an example of those who chose to fight instead of surrendering immediately.

She ran numb fingers through the water. She hadn't slept since they had broken camp for the temple, and with the amount of magic she had used in the temple, she should have.

She wasn't certain how Kaveh was still standing, for she was certain he hadn't slept since the night before the temple, and perhaps a night before that as well. And his first charge on the battlefield... The amount of power he had unleashed had been staggering.

She shuddered as water lapped at the edges of the bowl.

Sheer fury seemed to drive him, though she could finally see his fatigue as he disrobed. He had tried to hide the strain at first, but he couldn't hide from the bond.

Neither of them could.

"Your power is returning," he said.

"Yes."

It was both fortunate and unfortunate.

In her initial crippling deficit, she hadn't been able to save many of those who fell around her. She wouldn't have survived the first phalanx charge either, had she not been wrapped in an impenetrable shadow. The death toll had been far too great.

Healers specializing in death and battlefield magic had swarmed through the squads, doing what they could, but they, too, had lost their own numbers.

Death came for all on the battlefield, and with her deficit, she should have died. But in the second charge by the enemy...

She squeezed her eyes together, as if it could somehow block the memory. The Shirskens had made the devastating mistake of trying to use life-force-draining spells on them. She and Kaveh had been peppered by the spells, but instead of batting them away, the shadow phalanx had inverted them, and she had not only watched the soldiers surrounding them screaming in agony as life was pulled from them, but their life-force had filled her veins.

She hadn't looked to see the devastation Kaveh had wrought from that. She had been too busy staring at her poisonously glowing hands, full of death and stolen power. Kaveh hadn't inherited the emperor's ability to drain and lock away power, but his shadows could steal it when it was aimed at him and feed it through to others connected to his shadow. Feed it to her.

"I need my secondary healing belt," she said aloud, staring at her murky, wavering reflection.

"And I need at least three more state heads on a pike in order to quench my thirst for blood." His voice was biting.

She stared at the water. Even now, the stolen magic oozed from her like a gluttony of sweets madly consumed—slowly seeping away and leaving a crippling ache behind. It was an ache bred into her bones and a well that demanded to be continuously filled.

She could not save the enemy as their magic had roared into her, filling her with the power of forcible sacrifice.

"It's in Tehras," she said. "In my rooms there."

Taline and Rone had her primary belt and pack, along with everything else that had been near the plinth, but her secondary belt also contained the glyph Taline had carefully stitched inside to stop the ache. Taline had been reluctant to stitch the glyphs, grumbling that they were unnecessary. But then, she thought only the best of Nin.

"No."

She gripped the basin. "I can open a ripgate. I have enough to sustain one now for the period of time needed to gather my things." She knew their rooms well enough to open a ripgate directly inside of them. It hadn't been worth the risk to return when Kaveh was chasing them around the countryside. She hadn't known the extent of his powers then—of whether he was capable of leaving shadows behind to bind or travel through.

She knew his powers better now. Her fingers tightened on the stone. All of the enemies' magic had been fed to his connected shadows on the battlefield—the great sweeping death of them.

"You aren't going to Tehras or anywhere in Tehrasi." He moved around the tent, movements finally growing more sluggish as each piece of the battlefield was removed.

"I don't know that I need your permission." Only numb fatigue kept her voice even.

"The oath you made says otherwise—or have you finally decided to show your deceit?"

"If I was going to leave, I would have disappeared within the first minute of battle, believe me," she said coldly. "If you are going to continue with such slaughter, I need my belt, so I can save more of your soldiers."

And to make it so she never consumed another. Her fingers shook. She couldn't let that occur again. Even now, her blood tingled with the remnants of it.

"You can make a new healing belt," he said dismissively. "List the items and I'll have someone bring them."

"And you can fight with a new sword—just pick up any one on the field." She waved a hand over the basin. "One is as good as any other, no tempering, balancing, or preparation involved."

She didn't bother looking up—she could feel his distemper, his unsettled irritation. She knew her words rang annoyingly true.

"A Carre relegated to life keeping. I still cannot fathom it," he said mockingly. "Tell me, Zehra, what would your family have thought?"

Nin watched the water surface break, ripple, settle, then break again. "That's not my name."

"It was the name to which you were born."

"Zehra Amanan Carre is dead. She died in an alley filled with trash. A girl in a different life."

"Born to the same parents, all the same. What would they have said about your baseborn exploits, your healing of the useless—in the country you were born to rule?"

"That I'm worse than a traitor." Water droplets fell as she slowly touched the water and raised her hands. Drop, drop, drop. Matter pulled away, returning to its source—forming again into what it once was, no escape. "But then, they are long dead. So there is little for them to say. Your game in their mention will gain no reward."

"You think this a game?"

"I am not the one with a strike tablet." Her fingers curled into the edges of the basin again, then pushed her upright.

She had given more than one enemy combatant last healing rites today—had held the hands of soldiers on both sides as they uttered final thoughts of loved ones, sorrows, and regrets. She projected the feelings outward across the bond.

Agitated movements edged her peripheral vision immediately. Good, she thought fiercely.

She straightened her spine. "I need my healing belt. It is a simple, temporary ripgate."

I do not need your permission. I can do this without you. She wanted to restate those words aloud, but she wasn't certain. There was a leeway in the oath for some things—and intention mattered—but neither of them had tested their boundaries on the battlefield to see whether anything had changed since the oath had morphed.

She could feel Kaveh's unease. He wasn't certain whether she could circumvent the distance limitation on the oath either. Wasn't certain she couldn't open a ripgate, hop through, then close it behind her.

She narrowed in on the doubt.

"You said you can track me no matter what oath holds me or does not," she said, challenging the hubris he wore like a second skin. "You seemed quite willing to take the challenge after the time limit placed by the oath expires."

"That doesn't mean I'm going to leave my post—the post the emperor commanded me to—in order to satisfy the whim of tracking you down when you are already here at hand. For a healing parcel, no less."

His voice was implacably dark. But there were other ways to defeat darkness.

She looked at the dark knot of writhing black coiled in the corner. Encompassed by the dense swirls of her brethren, his corporeal shadow was laid out on a pillow—carefully placed there by Kaveh when they had entered the tent.

"Your companion. Ifret, I heard you call her." The shadow had been inactive on the battlefield, silent within Kaveh's battle cloak, and from what Nin had previously observed, that was not the usual state of things. "She is not healing."

Night abruptly spread spiked fingers toward the side of the tent where she stood. She watched the way the shadows halted and felt along the path to his emotions at the same time.

"Trying to find a weakness to exploit, Ninli?"

"I have not selectively forgotten the lessons of my birth, regardless of the name I choose as my own," she said. "I was raised to look for weak points. You are correct in that I will use one, if I find myself able."

She expected fury, but the thread of amusement mixed with consideration was far more interesting. She approached the serpentine shadow slowly. It hissed, tense.

"I made the terms and I abide by the oaths I make," Nin said. "No matter what your thoughts on the matter, I will not alter them."

"Will you not, oathbreaker?" But there was a note of resignation. The bond didn't lie.

"I do not know what exactly Osni did to your companion, but sunlight kills shadow." She looked closely at the marks she could see. "Or casts it into stronger being."

"Osni will die."

On another day, when she was capable of non-survival emotions, she would feel fierce gladness at his statement. Today...

She stared at the shadow. The sickly shadow stared judgmentally back. Nin judged the distance between them and calculated what she had seen of the shadow's range. She let a current of air nudge the shadow's side. It was like lifting a wispy snake. There were patches of darkness that were hindered and broken—like mud, dried and crackled.

A knot of lesser shadows swirled around Ifret, as if asking for direction on what to do.

If one directly shot at Nin, she would have to rely on Kaveh to intervene.

"None of your others are like her."

"Ifret is a creature born of shadow, but not a shadow herself," Kaveh answered, pulling alongside her. "You think you can heal her?"

He wanted her healed. The emotion couldn't be hidden.

Nin used air to lift Ifret further. She snarled at Nin in warning, looking to Kaveh before returning her tense gaze to Nin.

"I don't know. I've never treated anything like her," Nin murmured. Ifret was beautiful in the savage, wild way of a beast driven by instinct. There was something familiar about

Ifret's magic, but foreign at the same time. "She is part of you?"

"She has been with me since birth." His voice was dismissive, but his emotions were not. Looking at him, one would never guess.

His eyes narrowed at the sudden compassion he could assuredly feel from her, and his emotions turned darker.

"Let me get my healing belt, Kaveh," she said softly. "I will hold to my oath." She held open the palms of her mind.

She could feel a surge of emotion from him that was quickly tamped.

"Open your ripgate then, gatemaker."

CHAPTER FOUR
UNWANTED PARTNERSHIP

RONE

(Assaka Region, First Layer Indi)

Rone didn't stop Taline when she left. A pairing between them would only work one way.

And if it didn't... He touched the scroll tucked against his back that he had taken from Ninli's pack while Taline hadn't been looking. If it didn't work, he would get creative.

Taline would be back. She didn't trust him, and she was absolutely correct not to. But Taline ul Summora was also practical—ruthlessly practical—and smart. She reacted like wildfire; inciting her was invigorating, but she also burned like iron—long and deep.

She would be back as soon as flames turned to embers—with a branded fury she wouldn't forget, but he didn't need or desire the deep trust the girls foolishly offered each other.

He waited for an hour—needing only to slice one man with his enchanted knife in order to establish his hierarchy and keep the others from trying to steal his items or use him for sacrifice. Confident that he had made his point, he laid back down and continued his vigil. Right on schedule, Taline tromped back, a contingent of worshipers trailing her.

There was the lightest feel of magic from her that made him tense. The scepter had activated in the time she had been gone.

"Giving up after only an hour?" he said idly. "That's no way to find your sister."

"When you die, I will dance."

He could hear her teeth grinding. He smiled up at the clouds and said nothing. Whatever the scepter had done had been minor then. Likely nothing more than saving her from similarly wayward hands like he had needed to do with his dagger.

But if the scepter started to activate in situations that weren't life threatening? Worse measures would need to be taken.

"I need you to get me to a city," she ordered. "Then you can slink off to whatever rock hole you plan to seek."

"I'm considering staying right here. These good people are in search of quality leadership, and I—"

"You aren't a leader."

He put a hand to his chest. "Hurtful."

"I'll pay you."

"With what?"

"Your life."

"I think not." He spread his fingers upward and peered through them. "That cloud looks like a glove. Look at the fit."

"You owe Nin."

"Do I?" he mused, ruthlessly shoving down all emotions of agreement. "I got you through the temple to the scepter chamber. I did my part to get that stick. My debt is gone."

"Does this look like what you were hired for?" She shook her fist at him, scepter waving wildly between clenched fingers. "Your debt is larger than ever. You will find a city."

"Why? Here"—he snapped his fingers and one of the worshipers hurried forward with a plate of berries—his enchanted knife had been convincing—"I can be king."

"You don't want to be king."

"Everyone wants to be king."

"I don't," she said darkly.

He looked at her through heavy lids. "We'll see what you say after having that attached to you for a week."

"My answer will stay the same."

He looked to the sky and laughed. "The wall always loses."

"What? Have you hit your head?"

"Many times. Against your fists."

She straightened imperiously. "I have never struck you."

No. Taline ul Summora spoke with words and deeds—of honor—not fists and fear. She wielded shame like a weapon, but it was always equally pointed at herself. It would take much for her to become the thing she hated.

The scepter glinted in the light. His gut clenched.

"Metaphorically." He roused himself, curling onto his feet. "I will get you to a city—in fact, I will get you in front of a gate leading back to our layer even." He would get her to a layer gate, but it didn't mean he would help her get through it. He held up a finger. "On one condition."

Her fingers tightened around the scepter. "I will not trade in earthly bargains."

"Repellent. No." He somehow kept his tone carefree, though darkness churned beneath. Killing the current Padifehl of Tehrasi would help even his score with Ninli. Yes, he would do that. "The condition is that we remove that thing from your skin."

Her fingers loosened immediately, and his chest tightened in an entirely different way. Regardless of her past, her base level of trust in him was that he would not harm her.

She didn't trust him to keep his word about the scepter, but that she trusted him at all was…madness. Where the previous darkness had been welcome, he wanted this feeling gone.

Remove the scepter, destroy the scepter, kill the padifehl.

Taline would live. Her beauty would likely tear apart kingdoms here, but she would survive. His vow would be fulfilled.

He would be done.

And so would the scepter.

"Nin will remove it," she said.

"Ninli is attached to a man who would murder you as soon as look at you."

Taline raised her chin. "Whatever will be. As long as she survives."

Blasted Summoras. It didn't matter what they had been born as—those who took the name Summora were all the self-sacrificing same.

"If you think Ninli is not a survivor, you don't know her at all," he said. It got the desired rise.

"You dare. The longer—"

"You can't get to her today. Nor tomorrow. Not even with my help. Not unless you can power that thing." He waved his hand. "The non-magic world requires...patience. And we have options."

He held up the scroll that had been in Ninli's pack. She reached out to grab it from him, but he held it above his head. "Now, now, narsumina."

"I'm not playing your games, Valeran."

"Then play your own, Summora. Think." He tossed the scroll in the air. It landed back in his hand and he flicked the end downward, unrolling it to reveal the detailed glyphs, moon illustrations, and calculations. "Separation. Strategy. How are you going to save your sister? How fast could you extract Ninli, if you have the scepter already disconnected and ready for transfer? You could throw it at the emperor, and Nin could port you both out then and there."

Taline stared hard at the scroll, empty left fist curling. He could almost see the vision of throwing the scepter at the emperor working through her rational brain. He could see the plans coil so willingly—how she and Ninli could disappear.

She trusted in Ninli's powers too much.

He saw her determination settle and he smiled, flicking the scroll closed. "All we have to do is follow these instructions, narsumina. Simple."

And if it proved not simple, he could run her around this world for thirty days.

"I'll allow you a week," she said, eyes dark as they switched back to him.

Triumph curled. "You dream. I get you to a gate by the thirtieth—"

"Twenty-five days," she said tightly. "We ride this moon to fullness then die with it to darkness and Nin's end. Twenty-five days more until the moon dies along with the oath."

"By the twenty-fifth day, then, but you go to as many temples as it takes to detach that from your palm."

She motioned at the scroll. "Only one temple is required—three moonrises can occur in any appropriate temple space."

Of course she had already read the scroll, because Ninli would have been unable. He pressed the irritation at their thoroughness down. "And if the first temple is broken? We continue, no matter how many temples it takes."

"You have ulterior motives. You always do." Her expression was cynical. "You want the scepter."

"Here I am, doing everything for you out of the goodness of my heart. I offer my services and provide a way for you to save Ninli and live, and you ascribe ulterior motives." He put a hand against his chest. "I'm wounded."

"You are anything but. You are the worst of selfish creatures."

He kicked out his legs and launched himself from the rock wall to land in the grass at a crouch. He rose with a smile. She tensed, then loosened again, and once more, there was that base trust. He covered his internal screaming with a larger grin.

"But those motives aren't to have the scepter myself. If I had wanted it, I would have lifted it with my own hand. I want it like you want the emperor's seat."

She examined him coldly, not rising to the bait like he had hoped. "You won't let the empire have the scepter," she said. "You said as such to the Shadow Prince. Do not befuddle your ulterior motives in your own mind, Valeran. You won't be able to keep them straight."

He let his facade drop and allowed steel to take its place. "No one sane would put the Scepter of Darkness in the emperor's hand—a man who can already drain magic itself. Do not tell me you do not think he holds the worst of magics? Do not tell me that you want Ninli anywhere near the emperor when he lifts the Scepter of Darkness?"

She looked at him, clutching the scepter fused to her hand, the unmitigated resolve on her face covering the tremors for her sister in her heart. Practical, smart Taline ul Summora. There had never been another choice but to seek his help, and they both knew it.

She lifted her chin. "Three temples and your oath not to interfere when I leave with the scepter in hand."

But she would make him pay. At some point, she would make him pay. He just had to make certain he had enough coin.

"Three moonrises in any number of appropriate temples and you give me an oath before you leave."

"Never."

He motioned to the river, the steep rock face, the jungle around them. "Good luck."

He meant it, and she knew it. He wouldn't follow after her like a lost lamb. And he would only trade an oath to her for one of his own—something that only a fool would make with Rone ul Valeran.

Taline ul Summora was no fool.

"Two temples and a functioning gate home." She gritted her teeth. "You have two days to find the first."

"We won't even find civilization in two days."

"One week," she said bitingly. "And as soon as this is removed from me, I go home with it."

"Three weeks, three proper temple moonrises, no oaths."

He calculated. There were ways. What's more, there was time. If he got that thing detached from her sooner, all the better. He could run her in circles freely afterward.

"Two weeks for whatever temples we find then no more, and one functioning way home."

Her sister was twenty-five days away from permanent enslavement or death—a woman who had saved his life more than once. But Ninli ul Summora was gone. Brown eyes had bled to red, and her name would have already unraveled to another.

She had given Rone leave to destroy the scepter by the very fact that she had known Rone's goal and given her blessing as long as he kept Taline safe. There was no need to feel guilt.

He swallowed any threat of it down—an action that had always been easy with anyone not named Summora. He would keep Taline ul Summora alive, fulfill his vow, and wipe Etelian ul Fehl from the earth, but the scepter would never end up in the empire's hands.

Ninli was already lost.

"As many proper temple moonrises as it takes, no oaths, and one functioning way home by the twenty-fourth day." He touched his mouth, eyes glittering. "On my word, you will have it."

"Your word is nothing."

But he had her. He had her.

"I offer my aid, my very heart," he said casually, letting his hand drop to his chest and his triumph curl. "I'm hurt."

"I thought I'd made it quite obvious," she bit out. "With a sentiment that has proved itself true. I don't trust you."

He smiled and headed north into the jungle to cover his sudden disquiet.

The problem was that she already did.

CHAPTER FIVE
POSSESSION

KAVEH

(RIPGATE TO TEHRAS)

Kaveh watched as Ninli ul Summora knelt and touched her hands to the ground. She was graceful, as only the most deadly magi could be.

Power filled her hands and she twisted them on the floor.

"You didn't have to do such a ritual in Tehras," he said. She had opened ripgates with the blink of an eye when she had been fleeing him.

"I didn't have to return to this exact spot then," she said. "Getting from one place to another is simple when I don't need knowledge to return. And I know the capital city of Tehrasi like I know my own magic."

She pulled upward in a graceful lift of body and limbs, parting the air with her hands as she did—pulling them outward.

"Ripgates do not require knowledge of a secondary spot to create," she continued. "But just opening the layer from one spot to another without knowledge of the other end invites disaster. Falling into a volcano, ending up in an ocean, falling into an icy crevasse, being swallowed by a monster—there are many undesired outcomes."

Through the bond, he could feel something in her settle as the space opened—whether it was seeing her rooms again or whether she had been unsure that she could still use her powers, he didn't know. He watched her, gaze focused.

"The emperor's scepter doesn't work that way when activating gate points."

"It does. You just don't see it as it happens." Her head tilted toward him. "The scepter given to the emperor reads a position set as it is activated and records the set as an endpoint. Ten sets of readings, to allow five gates."

"The emperor was displeased to note that the eleventh reading overwrote the first." The event had been well before his birth, but it was a tale that was oft told in warning of the emperor's displeasure and what was wrought therein. A city had burned in his rage.

The emperor had been nineteen. The world had taken note. Tehrasi had taken note. Jisarek had taken Nera two years later.

Nin smiled tightly. "My family wasn't noted for its generosity. There is also a safety mechanism inside wherein any knowledgeable gatemaker can modify or deactivate any of the gates contained within the scepter."

Kaveh's eyes narrowed. "Is there now?" Known to the Carres alone, likely. The Barrinis had never said a thing when they had toiled as the emperor's gatemakers. The emperor had thought the scepter keyed only to him.

"I haven't done anything to the empire's gates." And he could feel the truth of it in the cursed bond. "I am not your enemy."

"No? I don't see you rushing to aid the empire with your powers."

"That I am not your enemy does not mean you are not mine," she said, gaze held to his.

She turned and started to step through the ripgate.

The oath stretched tight. He saw her lips tighten. Good. She couldn't just open ripgates to Tehrasi and disappear through.

Not that he would let her.

She pulled her leg back. She rolled her shoulders and pushed outward with her hands, widening the ripgate. Turning, she took his arm at the elbow. He forced himself to remain still at the touch—no one touched him—then allowed her to pull him forward. The bond settled abruptly.

Moonlit shadows in the Tehrasian room pulsed at their arrival as Nin lit the enchanted lamps on the walls, throwing shadow and warmth across the main room in the tiny place she called home.

Shadows swelled and retreated beneath her wary, remote gaze as she quickly surveyed the room that he had filled on the same day she had fled the city.

She moved toward the leather belt sitting prominently on the front table. Her fingers traced glyphs carefully carved and set into the leather with spells.

Two shadows embedded in the natural valleys of the buttery leather slid to life beneath her questing fingers, and he felt dark resolve tighten along the bond. He wished her luck in expelling them—he wouldn't be doing so anytime soon.

"How do you still have any left?" she asked tightly.

"Do you think me limited?" He hummed and lifted a knickknack on a sideboard. "As soon as the three of you left the city, porting out of imperial boundaries, these premises were bound to me."

He had ensured that if she went back, he would know.

The bond spoke of her lack of surprise. "There was a reason we headed for Urshna for the glass we needed instead of returning here."

He had found them anyway. He saw her lips tighten—no doubt feeling the arrogance he didn't bother to hide.

"If you try to leave me now, Ninli, these shadows will seem a paltry few."

Her fingers curled around the leather. "In a few weeks, you will be bound by oath to let me leave."

"You are a fool if you count on Valeran having a change of heart."

Valeran would betray the other girl and show his hand to the empire, then die. But not before Ninli ul Summora was bound by the oath between them.

She didn't respond, looking at her hand with an intensity that forced him to rifle through the bond. Her emotions were muddled and unclear, and there were so many that it made him uncomfortable. He narrowed his eyes.

"Get anything else you need," he said. "Or I will force you back to the tent in thirty shadows."

She moved quickly through the space, not letting go of the belt and not questioning the dictate.

But then, so far, she had shown herself not to engage in pettiness. She was quick and efficient and realistic.

He watched her as she moved, gaze moving between the woman and her space, and the connection between the two.

The rooms weren't lushly decorated, but they were...warm. Browns and greens and deep blues offset with delicate roses and light-purple flowers indigenous to Bahra. The plants still survived beneath their care spells, but the Carre princess refreshed the enchantments as she passed by them.

As her fingers touched the soil of the light-purple plants, he could feel melancholy and fierce emotion rush through her.

He had no wish to name the feeling. He shut the mental path and continued cataloging the space while she quickly and efficiently made her way through the room. He double-checked each shadow already tucked between drapery folds and the draping fabrics that had been carefully arranged across surfaces with a loving hand.

A small space, nothing at all palatial about it, but it spoke of quiet comfort and happiness.

He looked back at her. The dichotomy of her birth chewed at him. With her eye color masked by spell, the prominence of Carre in her features was reduced to a sharpness that could be explained by any number of bloodlines. Without the red, her eyes were too...benign.

She was too...soft. All that power wrapped inside a benevolent package.

When he refocused, her head was tipped, and she was regarding him—curiosity and caution clearly brimming along their connection.

He straightened and reached out to take one of the extra bags from her, then extended his arm to her. They both blinked at the gesture, but she wrapped her fingers around his arm before he could retract it and she led them through the flickering ripgate.

She turned to close the ripgate behind them, letting her fingers slide from his arm. He felt some nameless discomfort at the loss. Unacceptable.

He flipped a knife from his belt and stabbed it into his left palm. Pain wiped everything else away.

She turned to look at him so abruptly that her ripgate stopped closing. She looked at his knife-struck palm, to his face, then back to his palm. Something that felt like sadness tingled along the connection, but with the pain bright in his mind, he easily wiped it away, too.

She let her fingers drop and the ripgate began to dematerialize behind her again.

She grabbed his left wrist.

The touch immediately recalled those strange, uncomfortable feelings, and he tugged back. She locked her fingers around his wrist and pulled him in with sudden, surprising strength. Power flooded from her, numbing his hand.

With the absence of the pain to concentrate on, fatigue descended—a feedback loop pushing between them.

Her shoulders wilted and she reached for her healing belt. "Consider it a test before I try it on your companion. Just...sit."

She pushed him to the two fabric-covered stools surrounding a folding acacia table and set the belt on top.

"I saw you heal people with a touch today." He watched her unlatch a pocket. The numbing magic flowed through him and he cataloged it—not that he ever planned to use such a thing.

"If you want the headache that comes with such an instantaneous cure, I will gladly provide it," she said somewhat tartly, but her fingers kept moving, withdrawing small rocks and vials.

Her ripgate winked out completely in the background with a starred twinkle, taking with it the show of power that she so casually wielded.

"How did you survive the palace purge?" Obviously, someone wearing her face had stood in her place. There had been no question that they were all dead. The spell had even ensured that no one in the room could be resurrected. But how had she not been pulled to the room with every blooded Carre? "You said yourself that the Carres were called by the First Scepter to the chamber room."

The shift in questioning paused her motions, uneasiness sliding back into the bond. "I was nine."

He allowed his pointed curiosity to skim the bond. Most magi accessed their full powers between thirteen to fifteen years past birth, but blood was blood, and the Carres would have connected their bloodline together, no matter the Awakening. "That mattered?"

"Carres take their scepter at ten. There's a ceremony. Awakenings are...forced. Three mere weeks until I would have held it in my hand." Her fingers curled, brushing against his skin. "I was disconnected from the regular palace magics a week before the purge on Farrah Osni's say... She said it would make a stronger connection to the scepter magic for a natural gatemaker to be disconnected for a full turn of the moon. I don't know if she..."

Her fingers curled into a fist. He directed a shadow to slip along her neck, trying to concentrate on her distraction instead of his own. He would know this uneasiness and the use of Osni's name. His wife?

Don't do this, Crelu!

The unknown voice spread guilt and pain through the bond.

Nin's fingers clenched, and he watched her push the memories back with effort.

So special. Zehra, the special one.

A different voice this time, but one that held a passing familiarity, quickly expunged. He had watched the Carres die. He didn't think that was the queen's sneering voice. Younger. Maybe t he—

Nin suddenly gripped the shadow and threw it from her neck. "That is cheating," she said in a measured voice, then continued stemming the flow of his blood, fingers moving through practiced motions.

He tipped his head in acknowledgment and let the shadow coil with the others instead of reattaching it.

"I wasn't attached to the palace magics when the empire attacked," she said, entirely too calmly for the state of her emotions. "A fluke."

No. He watched her methodically work. Not a fluke. He tucked the name Farrah Osni away.

"Your natural magic is gatemaking, but how did you learn to use your abilities, given your age at the death of any available mentors?"

"I ported at age five. Slipped-through magic, as we all experience. I was rigorously trained thereafter, in preparation." She mechanically moved through her healing motions. "I had been fed most of the Awakening potions in anticipation of the event. Experimenting was...encouraged."

Rigorously trained in the moments where her magic had sparked—he knew the drill well. Natural affinities showed up before Awakenings. Magic burst as the body prepared to channel magic, and it mimicked whatever a magi was going to be strongest at.

Which wasn't healing, no matter what she played at as his skin expertly knit back together.

"Can you create gates to the other layers without a scepter?" He asked innocuously enough, but she looked quietly back.

"I know the opening paths to many places in the non-magic world. Given an hour or two, I can create a ripgate there, especially if it is a place I've been before."

Coordinates to places of great sacrifice or easily gathered followers—the Carres had been notorious for their blood and power rituals. As the quietest and smallest—the beetle princess, they had called her—whoever had been wearing her face in the Carre extermination lineup had maintained little physical presence.

Having observed her and the watchful way she handled herself in uncertain situations, she had undoubtedly developed those skills early. She had likely been gifted with amazing amounts of information by listening and blending into the background of a family born to flamboyance and aggrandizement.

Coordinates for temples and abandoned sites would have been aggressively memorized and used extensively in her work as the Hand.

She really would make a fantastic asset. He had thought so in the alley, and the notion only grew stronger.

"But not to the temple where the scepter was kept. How fortunate for you." Her transparent feelings on the matter in the immediate aftermath of the temple debacle had marked the truth of the notion.

"You want to go after them." She steadily closed his wound, mixed feelings of anticipation and anxiety saturating the bond.

He had wanted to follow them as soon as the ripgate closed. But she had been all but useless, drained magically, and Kaveh had had no choice but to believe her statement that there were protections against the knowledge of the temple. Emotions weren't something either of them could hide now.

"If you think taking me to a place without magic will make me easy to kill, you are mistaken. I need no magic to kill."

"No," she murmured, cleaning his hand. "But you rely on it like you breathe. We were both bred in the belief that power is all. I wonder what you would do in the non-magical world."

He would not find out—not until all the magic worlds were conquered and he needed to conquer the non-magical world as well.

"Your friends are already long gone from wherever they landed. They will come, or you will be eternally bound." He looked to the corner where Ifret lay. "And after you have accepted your fate, when the scepter enters this world, I will rip it from whoever comes through."

The change in her was instantaneous. Tension, and white-hot determination. "You can try. I will stand in your way. No matter what bond you claim."

"I look forward to it." Predatory delight rushed through his veins.

He looked at her healing belt as the tent lamps cast it into sharp relief. Pockets and sheaths wound around the thick loop with frilled ties at the end that each contained a spell. Runes decorated the surface spaces and pockets, neatly carved into the leather. He touched an unbloodied finger to one, and knowledge bloomed within him—the seeds of how to use the spell he had touched, as well as a small reserve of magic to aid the enchantment.

"Your spells are easily known." He frowned at the belt, lifting the edge with one finger to peer beneath. "You store magic to share the knowledge of the enchantment."

She shrugged. "I can touch one to make sure it is the one I need. It makes it easier when I don't need to take time to deduce each if I change their positions."

"You can just create a coded glyph. Read what others cannot."

She didn't say anything for a second and he felt a strange combination of regret and rue mixed with determination. "A coded glyph is unnecessary. This works."

He raised a brow. "You cede your advantage."

"If more people are healed because I've shared such spells, then I will have done some good in this world," she said quietly.

As someone who didn't use her true power, this was an incomprehensible action given her position and status. "You will make yourself useless."

She looked up. "Would that that would be true. We could fix so much in our population if the general layman had my skills."

"You won't fix your own starvation—or that of your family—when you have no desired skills."

She pulled a bottle of liquid from one of the pouches. "No? Those who stand on my knowledge, and all those I've learned from, will be greater than I am. Knowledge will advance beyond me, and the more who can advance that knowledge, the better." There was an aching desire that was almost tangible. "The world made better will make things better for the people I count as mine, and all those who come after."

"One of those, are you? Fix the world instead of making everyone fix themselves."

"The empire is rich. But all those you conquer are not. Look to the people in the poorer countries or those under the worst of rulers."

"You reference the Postines. I see people who do nothing but complain about their lot. They birth more children, then they complain when their food stores run dry."

She nodded. "Yes. Why is that?"

"Because they are lazy."

"Is that it, do you think?"

He looked at her. "You try to play me into some gambit."

She nodded and poured a drop of liquid on his closed wound. "With the eyes of one's birth, it is hard to see anything beyond. Looking with eyes outside yourself, that is the work of colossus."

All signs of a wound disappeared. "Helping the indigent and impoverished. Perhaps you were switched with a sandsweep's babe at birth."

She looked steadily into his eyes—not something he was used to, even from those who shared a father with him. "It is because I know the alternative well that I find solace in such views."

He found himself leaning nearer. "Solace is for the dead."

"Then I will take it to my grave." She touched the area she had just healed with the tip of her finger. "You didn't even take a wound a quarter this grievous today."

"There are few who can harm me."

"Just yourself?" she murmured. "Untouchable otherwise?"

He rotated his hand around. Used to healing himself, he hadn't gone to a healer since he had turned fourteen. Everything felt...perfect.

"Satisfied?" she asked.

"Passable."

Her gaze slid to Ifret and his curiosity—already caught—switched to his companion.

"Can you heal her?" Ifret had only taken wounds so grievous once before—from the emperor himself. She would eventually heal on her own—or she wouldn't. But no one had ever offered to heal her before. To most, it was like offering to heal Sehk himself—the death and destruction half of the two-faced god of dominion.

No one wanted Sehk-Ra's darker half turned against them.

"I don't know." She approached the shadow cautiously. Her caution was warranted. "But I will try."

He leaned back, crossing his healed arms. "Worried that you will be bitten?"

"Everything in this tent bites," she said casually.

Amusement curled, unwillingly.

He rolled his body upward, walked past her, and lifted Ifret, ignoring the snapping of the shadow's jaws. He pulled Ifret against his chest, wrapping his palm around her head to hold her steady there. "Try your magic."

Nin said nothing for a moment, staring at him as if fighting some image in her mind.

Ifret snapped at his fingers, but he well knew how to avoid her bites. He had been covered by them as a boy. Wearing her like a nightmarish scarf had been a long process of bargaining and trust.

"What happens when she bites you?" Nin asked.

"Pain."

Her head cocked to the side and he could feel the press of her curiosity. "You are immune to her death bite? Or has she never bitten you with the intention of death?"

He remembered being unable to move from his bed for a week at age five—Ifret in the corner, snapping and hissing that it was his fault he was dying—stupid young, why aren't you already dead?

"I seem to be exempt from her brand of death," he said wryly.

When he hadn't died, their partnership had shifted. Ifret was...dismissive of weakness, and he had been quick to take advantage of his living state. Her bites had become less toxic over time—a combination of his own increasing immunity and their increasingly aligned goals.

There was only one thing they disagreed upon.

Nin took the opportunity to cast a scan while Ifret was snapping at him. Ifret glowed blue, then suddenly froze. Kaveh looked down to see her ghostly eyes narrow on Nin.

"I know," she murmured to Ifret. "I mean no harm."

The shadow hissed again.

"Diagnostic spell." Nin opened her palms. "Nothing more."

They stared at each other. Something strange passed between them—something he was exempt from.

Nin looked at her, calmly extracting items from her belt without needing to look at what she was touching, just as she had claimed.

"This cloth contains a basic healing elixir," Nin said to Ifret, pulling a bandage from her belt pouch. "I've used it on magi, beings, and creatures before. And your scan says that your biology is compatible to the enchantments."

With smooth movements, Nin affixed the cloth around Ifret's midsection and pinned it to itself.

Ifret was completely still, eyes tracking Nin's movements. There was death in her gaze, but also a strange sort of tension.

With a flick of thought, Kaveh lifted a floor shadow toward Nin's neck to read her thoughts, but Ifret pinned it to the floor with her tail and sent him an uncompromisingly severe stare.

Interesting. He turned to Nin. "What doesn't she want me to know?"

Nin didn't look up from where she was dabbing a gel onto a small square cloth that she tucked under the bandage. "That seems like it would be none of your business."

He raised a brow but felt some of the tension seep from Ifret.

Nin repeated the small cloth applications five more times.

Kaveh finally let go at Nin's nod.

The shadow, wrapped in flexible bandages like a living mummy, weakly shot up and wrapped around Kaveh's neck, hissing long and hard at Nin, at Kaveh, and at the tent in general.

Kaveh touched one of the bandages and got a bite for his trouble. He shook his finger. "How long?"

"The spells will regenerate all night—and they should work in concert. She should be better by morning."

His brows rose in disbelief. Ifret had been on the edge of death, tucked weakly in his cloak for two days, and would be well by morning?

"Quite sure of yourself," he said.

She looked at him. "Then we are well matched."

Indeed.

No matter what her friends did, she was now his.

CHAPTER SIX
FIGHTS AND FIRST TESTS

TALINE

(Assaka Region, First Layer Indi)

A tingling ran up Taline's arm and she jerked.

Valeran narrowed his eyes at her, suddenly alert in the way a large cat senses a threat. "Summora?"

She stared oddly at the scepter in her hand. "It's nothing."

Valeran's eyes stayed narrowed on her, but he continued on the footpath into the small town they had finally stumbled across two days into their bargain. Small, but it had a stable, an inn, and people.

Even better, one of the many small jewels Valeran had picked up from the temple was greeted with greedy eyes and eager hands in exchange for two bowls of stew, rice-meal juice, and supplies. Roughly shaped copper and silver coins containing symbols stamped at angles were exchanged for the remainder of the jewel's worth.

Determining their location was harder in a small town, though. Showing up out of nowhere and asking clueless questions in another language was a suspicious endeavor, especially with the feeling of other that all those born to magic provoked in those without.

They were lucky that shapeless, cloaked travel wear was consistent across lands. Her wrapped dress underneath was dissimilar to those worn by the women of the inn, but not wholly alien. The fabrics themselves were entirely different, but without intense scrutiny, both of them could pass, especially with their cloaks pulled tight.

Valeran sat down at a wooden table in the center of the inn's dining space. Taline kept her gaze down and her shoulders meek, but keeping a low profile was a challenge when you had a long metal stick stuck to your palm.

They had wrapped a cloth around the large, decorative head of the scepter and tied it, and a second wrap enclosed the staff below her hand, leaving the only open spots the peeking areas around her flesh, but the wrapped scepter looked strange and unnatural—even more unwieldy than a crocodile bat wrapped in linen.

She pressed the scepter head against her stomach, trying to minimize it along the lines of her body, and ate quickly. Not for the first time, she wished she had caught the scepter with her non-dominant hand.

Valeran ate at a more relaxed pace, keeping his eyes low to the table, and a ready smile at his lips. Neither of them spoke. The massive amounts of trade brought by the empire encouraged a loose understanding of dozens of languages in city dwellers, and a quick uptake for the rhythms of speech, but the faster a spoken dialogue, the harder it was to follow. As a traveler and rogue, Valeran had far more experience with this game.

She knew he was actively spinning games in his mind, working through the best ones—she had enough experience with him to know what his silence meant.

He had been silent quite a bit in the last two days.

Taline tried to follow his lead, but she found herself staring at him more than her food as her bowl emptied.

When she had started her trek through the jungle alone—but for the temple followers in her path—she had realized very quickly the absurdity of it. She had no notion of a directional way forward, no allies in whom to trust, no plan to enact that would return her home in anything less than half a year.

Two followers had tried to kill her as soon as the temple had disappeared from view. They had quickly realized their folly when the scepter had sparked and crumpled them on the bank of the river. And, though that was promising for physical safety matters, there were other ways to die—starvation, falling into a pit... And other far more painful ways that she held no desire to test.

But most importantly, walking aimlessly would not get her home in time to save Nin.

Valeran was her middle play.

The burning question remained, though—what was his end play?

His gaze pinned hers suddenly and she felt her heart spike.

"What is your game?" she asked, more aggressively than she wished.

He said nothing, gaze cool, before smiling. "We are definitely in mid-peninsula Indi."

"We have established that." She gripped her bowl. "I know we are in Indi. The landmass is extraordinarily large."

Indi, of the most storied festivals, and the most acclaimed revels. And here she was trekking through it on foot, with her worst nightmare.

They had neither time nor resource to spare in getting from this world's Indi to this world's Tehrasi, and without Valeran, her only play was to get to Parsa, where she could access the ancient site she knew bled between layers of the world.

A way guarded by more than magic.

Without a gate pass or Nin, the trip to Parsa would be incredibly long no matter where in Indi they had landed, and the way through would be treacherous.

She needed Valeran to fulfill his end of the bargain and give alternatives sites.

Valeran had refused to name any layer gates until they firmly established their position. He had just kept them moving north and west—directions she could find no inherent fault or complaint with.

She gripped her bowl. Trusting Valeran was something she was not equipped to emotionally accept, however.

Valeran casually glanced at the table next to them and the four men who carried satchels full of axes and outdoor equipment. Two had what looked like crude fishing poles sticking from the satchels at their feet. "They speak of two rivers and two seas. Water."

He reached into his pack and lifted something before pausing. He grimaced lightly, then his expression forcibly smoothed. She peered over to see a reed pen and papyrus scroll in his hand. He let both fall back into his pack and withdrew a slim piece of wood and a knife instead.

Valeran put on his most ingratiating smile, hailed the table next to them, then quickly began carving.

The men took long moments to stare at Valeran, whose skin, though influenced with some golden tones by his father, was paler than theirs, and whose hair—though mostly covered by cowl—was slightly visible at the front as he bent forward. One red and one blond chunk curled over his forehead—a color combination that, even in the magical world, was noteworthy.

Taline's medium skin tone was an advantage—one she had frequently used. A few shades lightening, or a few shades darkening, and she could be from dozens of places with the smallest of modifications to her features.

Without magical aid, her skin tone was slightly lighter than the faces surrounding them in the inn—hers being closer in hue to sections of the Indi territory farther north—but she didn't stick out like Valeran with his multicolored hair, ice-blue eyes, tall frame, and tanned, but northern-influenced skin.

In their world, the Valerans were well known, and this one better than most, and few would touch Rone ul Valeran without the dubious aid of drink or desperation. In this world, though, despite his lean fighter's build, he was clearly an outsider with no allies.

Because no matter how she might blend in at a stretch, she was female, and that was a clear disadvantage in this town. Without magic to aid or equip, power in the non-magic layer was often based on physical form. She could see it in the silence of the smaller men in the room who had no companions of greater size and in the meekness of the women—few though they were in the meeting space, even at noon.

It was the larger men who dominated here—or those who could hire the largest men.

And one of the brawniest was staring at her in a way she well recognized. She turned her eyes down and slipped a knife into her left palm.

Using broken words and nonverbal communication, Valeran asked the men for the best fishing spot, in each direction of their location—finger pressing down on his crude start of a map to indicate a starting point in a town surrounded by jungle.

Two of the men stared at the map, then at him—comprehending, but wary, distrustful. The third man's eyes were narrowed, serpent-like. The fourth man's eyes...were still on her.

Valeran let his moneybag tip to the side on the table and a few silver pieces slipped out in a seemingly careless movement. One of the first men licked his lips and pointed hastily to a place east of their location, finger indicating a river.

Valeran's brows rose in feigned surprise as he looked between the map and coin. Then he gave a small laugh and put the coin on the table in front of the man with a jovial laugh while he pointed in vague motions to the west, north, and south of the town starting point.

The other men immediately began pointing—their motions quickly isolating their current geographical position as their fingers moved around, indicating geographical features with the banter of a language she couldn't understand.

A small, satisfied smile curled Valeran's mouth.

Sehk, she hated him.

Valeran nodded magnanimously and threw out a few more coins, bowing his head a few times, before slipping the moneybag, wood, and knife into the pack he had consolidated with Nin's larger items—the ones Taline hadn't taken into her own pack. The Shadow Prince's cloak rested at the bottom of Valeran's bag as well—carefully not touched with bare hands.

He had offered to carry all the supplies, but Taline would carry her pack, and everything in it, until she dropped.

Taline rose with him.

A hand reached out for Valeran's money pouch. Valeran easily intercepted the motion, but the reed pen slipped from the bag to the floor.

Two of the men cocked their heads, and the serpent-like man reached down to lift it.

Valeran smoothly intercepted that, too.

She looked uneasily at the expressions surrounding them—a crowd had gathered to see what was happening, people hoping to grab a coin.

Surely reed pens weren't so uncommon?

Looking around the crowd, she felt her heart sink.

Magic enabled progress. It also enabled mass death. It was a fine line every country and empire straddled. Writing utensils were obviously a bit ahead in their world, judging by the expressions.

The crowd looked at her, finally, searching, and she didn't like these expressions any better. The greed stayed the same, but the intent changed. She knew what she looked like, especially with her enchantments gone.

Her face had never done her any good in any world.

A man with a strange set of tools and stranger coloring, accompanied by a woman of uncommon beauty? They would either be treated as supernatural beings come down to trod among humans or they would be stripped of all elements that were desired.

"I wouldn't," Valeran lazily warned the man inching closer to her. Another man grabbed the carving knife from where Valeran had tucked it into his pack and held it up with a sloppy expression of threat.

Valeran looked at it, features painted with boredom. "The utility knife? Tch. That's just bad judgment."

Valeran was already moving, wickedly shaped blades dropping into his hands. Taline pushed away from the table and sliced at the hand reaching for her.

Taking a knife from Valeran just meant he had nine left.

He slashed and the air turned hot beneath his burning blades, enchanted by fire.

The enchanted blades would eventually run dry of their inherent magic, but unlike magi themselves who drew and converted magic actively, weaponry and relics held a set amount of magic within them. Renewable, if one had a source or magic freely available. Useful, but with an expiration to that use.

Without the aid of drawing on the world's magic, Valeran didn't display the overwhelming force he could in the magic world—keeping his motions efficient instead of devastating. But his instincts were the same, his motions ingrained, and his knives no less deadly or enchanted for being in a world stoppered of active magic. His blades burned with both fire and frost.

The space was immediately overcome with madness and screams. Some of the men, who saw what Valeran's blades could do—and of what the man himself was capable—tried to get away. But those behind them pressed in, pushing the madness closer.

Hands reached for her and she used both ends of the scepter to pipe-whip anyone who drew too near.

The scepter itself did nothing—dormant in her hand. The unpleasant sensation that none of the men were trying to kill her and instead sought other things did nothing to ease her previous notion that the scepter was specifically attuned to keeping her alive but not necessarily whole.

Bodies started to pile up and people finally started stumbling from the inn.

"Overkill," she said.

"I will have to work on my efficiency." He sliced upward, then pulled her from a reaching hand. "Stay back."

"The scepter will save me from killing intent."

"That is my fear." A man's nose burst open beneath his hilt-filled fist.

His expression was as grim as when she had appeared back at the temple. He had known, somehow, that the scepter had been activated.

She gripped the scepter. If it could only return her home…

"It protects you from death. It does not protect you from itself."

She stared at his back as he finished the last man fighting—laying the man out on the ground. Groans issued around the room, fallen men shifting faintly in pain.

Valeran flipped his knives and slipped them back in their sheaths beneath his opposing sleeves. He brushed his clothes free of dirt then toed the men onto their backs—searching pockets and transferring items to his own.

Those still conscious did not attempt to stop him.

"You are the worst," she said as he freely looted whatever took his fancy. She looked at the men and women pressed to the walls or hiding behind overturned tables. None moved to stop him.

"They chose to initiate a thieves' fight. They surrendered their belongings as soon as they hit the ground unconscious." He looked her over absently, pocketing what looked like a fishing kit without looking at it. "You still in one piece?"

Taline huffed breaths and looked at the twitching bodies, then at the scepter. "It's dead weight, but still a weapon."

"Come, we can't stay here. But our options for travel have multiplied." He tossed a piece of leather into the air and caught it again.

His words made sense when they walked from the inn to the stable. There were four horses inside.

His lips curved. "They said they had traveled a day's ride from the river most full of fish. What a fortunate turn of events to not have met brigands traveling by foot."

She looked at him distrustfully. "Did you start that fight?"

He put his hand to his chest. "Hurtful. You were right there. How could I have possibly—"

"You did." Looking at the horses, she was certain. "I know you did."

That reed slipping from his pack... Her lips pressed together.

Valeran was insufferable, not careless.

"I did not throw the first fist." His air of innocence released to a cloud of grim certainty. "And the fourth man was never going to let us go. One look at you started that fight before it began."

She drew herself upward.

"Don't worry, narsumina." His grin was careless. "I won't hold you responsible for your face as long as you don't hold me responsible for mine. The question you should be asking me is—to where do we now travel, glorious leader?"

She hated when he called her narsumina—like her face was the sum of her worth—and she hated that stupid grin. That grin had always infuriated her. She opened her mouth to rip it away, but her jaw snapped shut as sharp energy crackled down her spine like lightning on an open field.

His careless grin.

Valeran was never careless.

Unease slid through her. So this expression, the one he wore so often...

A lie. Past interactions rose in blurred frames, one after another.

Unease with the sudden fluctuating state of something other buried beneath his facade made her wary. "You are the intrepid adventurer," she said carefully.

His head swung sharply His eyes narrowed on her. "I knew your admiration was mine."

But the deliberately incendiary words couldn't hide his initial reaction or surprise. He had counted on her responding as she had initially intended to respond.

He had deliberately tried to manipulate her to anger and dismissal over his careless disregard. He was trying to again. She could see it in his posture now that she was looking for it while not overcome by the fury he so often invoked in her.

Unease turned to pounding disquiet.

How many times, then, had her irritation with him been at his own design?

"You think of yourself enough for the both of us, Valeran."

His expression relaxed and her heartbeat spiked. Here then was the truth. He wanted her to dislike him. The man in front of her was not only what he portrayed.

Nin always knew who to trust. And yet how many times had Taline questioned her judgment about this man? He had always been the single exception. The one Taline couldn't accept.

A tingling grew from the scepter to her arm at the thought of Nin. She pivoted slowly. The tingling grew, moving through her body. She jerked her arm, trying to cast the scepter away, but it was an instinctive motion. The feeling dissipated and she brought her hand back toward her chest. The feeling grew once more. She held her arm out, orienting it.

"Going crazy already, Summora?"

She could see the glint of silver in his hand, the only motion in his suddenly still body.

"It's…" She pivoted in another slow circuit. The scepter pulled in the same direction. She walked forward and the tension in the scepter stayed taut.

"It's a powerful object telling you to do monstrous things?" Valeran's voice was lazy, but his eyes were not.

"The scepter wants me to go this way."

His eyes followed the path. "North? To the lands of barren waste?"

"Northwest. Far."

"To the cold-ridden isles where hope dies? We'll get there soon enough."

She pivoted, and the scepter head grazed Valeran's chest. Power slid through her hand and she gasped. The scepter pulled.

The world swirled to memory.

She was limping on frozen toes and wheezing around a broken rib. Ice and snow formed a winter wonderland around her, but all she could feel was death.

Small boyish hands maneuvered around a fence, a frozen garden, until she—no, this was not her body or her memory—until he reached the grand stone house. A wide expanse of windows and doors covered in spells to keep the heat inside stood before the eyes of memory she was seeing through. A small hand reached up to grip an icy branch so he could stand on tiptoes and look inside.

Couples danced. Men gamed. Women gossiped in clusters. People leaned together on chaises. The entire scene was of cavorting, in word and deed.

Hair of gold and red dominated—scattered throughout the scene. But one woman, specifically, spinning in the arms of a man of the north, held his gaze.

The woman was radiant, and the smile on her face—had he ever seen her wear such an expression? Freedom, happiness, satisfaction. No guilt, no degradation, no hate.

The woman inside the ballroom—lit from the inside in delight—was never coming back.

A vision of an alley replaced the ballroom suddenly. He looked down at his grubby hands. Out of the cold, they were quick, and his mind, even quicker.

No one on the streets pretended to care. They would sell him for a coin and expected the same from him in return. Always be on guard—once you learned that, it was always true. And the ones who didn't know it only deserved pity.

It was better to know sooner rather than later that you could only rely on yourself.

Taline scraped and tried to claw her way out of the memories that were not her own.

The scene broke into icy shards.

He will betray you.

The voice was not her own.

Valeran was staring at her, body tense, silver glinting in his hand—two long strides away from the scepter's touch. "Everything moonshine, Summora?"

"What was that vision?" Taline stared at him.

His eyes narrowed. "What did you see?"

She shook her head, not looking away. Valeran's memories? "I saw northwest."

He will betray you.

She swallowed.

"We head in that direction anyway." His half-lidded gaze narrowed in on her dangerously, head cocked. "Can you activate it?"

She wondered idly whether he would kill her swiftly, should she say yes. "No. It...it was just a tug. Like something in another land pulling its attention."

Like Nin. Who trusted Valeran.

Give me to the girl who carries blood in her gaze. Listen not to those of ice.

The memories might be Valeran's, but the sudden dark thoughts were from something else. She deliberately did not look at the scepter.

Valeran slid the knife away, as nonchalantly as if he had simply taken it out for a cleaning.

"What...?" She licked her lips and slowly sat back down, unwilling to look at the thing fused to her hand. The thing that had started speaking. "What do you think it...?"

"Could be pointing to a place of power, another relic, a gate. Could be three paces away or three thousand."

She examined him carefully. "You don't think that." His knife was stashed back wherever he kept it hidden, but that he'd had it out at all... She already knew Valeran trusted no one. She already knew he would betray her, if given the chance.

But Nin trusted him. Why?

The girl with the blooded gaze...go to her.

"Does it speak to you already?"

"What?" She asked, heart jumping to her throat.

"I take relics seriously. And all-powerful ones such as that have their own sentience. It knows what I mean to do." He tapped his fingers on the log he rested against. "We are heading northwest anyway. If things change, we will modify our directions."

She looked down at it finally, then back up at him. "You truly wish to destroy it? You sacrificed Nin so the empire wouldn't become a great evil? Rone ul Valeran, soldier of fierce heart?"

"There aren't any gambling halls to patronize when martial rule is imposed across the layers," he said negligently. "And unless you wish for one less travel companion, my intent is to deliver it to glory."

He will betray you.

"You watch me anyway, don't you, Taline." He watched her steadily, idly, and she stared at him through the shadowed light of the stables. "You don't need a relic telling you what to think of me. You already know. And I know the gates in the northwest lands."

"You hate your family." The certainty in her own statement shocked her. The vision from the scepter—what did it mean?

His lips curled back just the slightest bit before he shook the emotion free. "But I know their lands and I know where their gates stand. Know your enemy."

A coil of some emotion she didn't want to label slid down her electrified spine.

He absently tapped a horse's side and she could see his irritating mind working beneath his absurd locks of hair. He ran a finger along the horse's foreleg. "However they are too far to access by foot from here. We need to search the legends here, should you want to find the secrets of this land which will lead us further on."

"That will take too long," she said tightly.

"There are gates spread through the non-magic world," he said. "It is a matter of finding the right ones. The notable ones are hoarded by rulers we would be foolish to step before. But there are those set up long ago in the split, then forgotten by those without magic, sustained by those with only the barest amounts. Known only to those who seek them. If nothing else, the henge in the blighted lands of the north can be used at summer solstice."

Everyone knew of that place. "That henge is cursed."

He drew a hand down the first horse's leg. "So are we."

"A gate north of your mother's homeland?"

"There is a port in Ancyra—or the Ancyra of our world, though I believe the naming to be similar."

"A lovely choice. We only need travel forty days."

"Most of the pyramids are in this world, too, built as they were before the split. Memfi, Sakkara, Abdju… We could fight for our lives there instead. Memfi, changed to Memphis, then someday, to be named something else. It might even change in our world, if someone takes a liking to the new name. Always amusing what bleeds between layers, especially when someone from one world takes over a portion of another."

"Not that this isn't fascinating, but—"

"Perhaps your library will discover a spell to translate each place name as it is said, and naming will become personal. Sakkara—there is where you should build your library, narsumina."

She looked at him sharply. "What do you know of the library?"

He smiled without looking away from the horses. "You are not the only one who deals in information, narsumina. Good thing for you, in this instance."

She narrowed her eyes and decided to leave that argument for another time. "Ancyra is twenty-five days' by foot from Tehras." And that was with the aid of healing magic to the feet, at the very least. That would only give them five days to make it through whatever trials Memfi and/or the Henge of Stones would require.

And there was no way the Shadow Prince hadn't told anyone in the empire to be on the lookout for them. Valeran had actively burned his own path back to their layer. The empire would kill him as soon as he set foot back in imperial lands.

There were ways around the "protection" clause of the oath—and who knew what Valeran had done to their part in Nin's oath when he had cast them here—but Taline should still have some options.

"Which is why we take none of the power paths and find a secret way instead. A way that existed before the split—an ancient site that retains seeds of power. We exit this jungle and figure out where we are, then plan our next move."

The wind outside echoed with the eyes of the wary and plotting. How long would it take?

"It will take too long," Taline said tightly.

He shrugged. "If we could find someone of this world who could point us to mystical sites in Indi, such a problem would be lessened. Someone not stirred by greed, or at least only stirred by the silvered kind." He checked the other horses. "Such a list is thin, however."

Taline looked off into the distance. The scepter almost seemed to warm in her palm. Like Nin was looking at her from elsewhere.

"I know someone who lives near Anarta," she said reluctantly.

He looked sharply at her. "In this layer?"

She grimaced. "Maybe. If she is still in the place Nin relocated her two years' past."

"Ah, one of Ninli's charity cases."

"You are one of Nin's charity cases."

He leaned toward her. "A distinguished group since we have you as a member."

"Hardly." Taline would never count herself a member of a group that left Nin behind.

Valeran held out his crude block map. "Where?"

She reached over and touched a point. "Here. On the sea. Notable in geography." That each layer had the same topography made things far easier than they would have it otherwise.

He cocked his head and studied the position. "Two days by horse. An acceptable foraging journey."

She grimaced.

"Can't ride, narsumina?" he asked, mistaking the root of her expression. He switched attention to the sturdiest of the four horses, seemingly uncaring as usual at how his barbs fell. "Or are you just eager to be pressed against me?"

"I can ride."

He stopped unhitching the sturdiest. "Alas. I was so looking forward to having your body pressed to mine." The careless grin stole over his mouth again.

She narrowed her eyes at it. What did it mean, then, that grin? The opposite? And his pointed barbs—if they were to provoke distancing emotion in her, what was he hiding?

Uneasy with him pressing outside the spot she had assigned him in her mind, she turned her attention to the horses.

The horses here were different in build than the horses of her tribe, but they still functioned the same. The selection of mount would be no different.

She waited to see which ones he picked—to see whether he went for the showy-looking brown at the left instead of the hardy brown to the right.

In the end, he picked the two she would have. She compressed her lips together.

"Not up to your standards, narsumina-of-the-divine?"

Irritation curled. No matter why he wanted her to dislike him, she could still choose to dislike him. The thought comforted her.

"So few things in this situation are, Valeran." She unbelted one of her sashes and used it to divide and knot her skirt in a motion of long practice, then stepped closer to the horse that would be hers—the one she would have chosen on her own. She ran a hand along the rudimentary saddle cloth and sighed.

"No magic to affix you in place, narsumina. Need a hand?"

She leaped at the low wall at her right, pressed hard with one foot and vaulted left over the side of the horse, sliding the underside of her bent and stretched left leg across the horse's back and into a straddle as she gently caught the side of the horse's neck with her left palm. The scepter made everything more difficult—she didn't want to start a relationship with her mount through pain—but she had been born to horseback.

Valeran looked at her beneath lifted brow. He knew nothing of her previous identity, exactly as she liked it. "And here I thought you more of a sky rider."

"There is no sky to ride here, Valeran. Mount your animal."

He pulled himself smoothly into place, touching his horse's neck with a soothing hand.

They had no overt magic with which to soothe their mounts, but the energies of life still ran through everything. Connecting with those energies took simple concentration, attention, and practice.

"Do keep up, Summora," he said beneath lowered lids. "And try not to fall into hell."

CHAPTER SEVEN

NIGHTMARE OF THE EMPIRE

NINLI

(IMPERIAL BATTLEFRONT, CONSTANTLY EXTENDING NORTH, WEST, AND EAST)

Nin was in hell.

One battlefield turned to two, then to three. One country turned to four. Red ran across the Ominous Sea.

Screams echoed in the scattered dust of prophecy.

"It's the Nightmare of the Empire! And the creature! They said neither surv—"

"The Terror of the Battlefront! Run!"

She tried to keep her chin above the tide of blood.

Nin had thought nothing could be as awful as the screams of her childhood—watching unwilling sacrifices die in the deep caverns and catacombs of the palace. But with a complete night's sleep and renewal potion, the absolute enormity of death that surrounded her now was overwhelming—the shrieks as bodies were rent and souls were shed—and it was starting to overwrite her memories with fresh new horrors.

In the middle of it all stood Kaveh, dark as death, surrounded by a black mass of shadows swirling out and piercing through bodies like a smith punching holes through metal. He looked untouchable in the middle of the chaos. The eye of the devastating storm.

And Ifret, healed and furious, raged alongside him.

Hardened soldiers fled in all directions as they advanced. The battle raged around them, hundreds of thousands strong in flesh-and-blood soldiers, spell weavers, and enchanted golems. Healers and spell collectors darted through the chaos, reviving the fallen or collecting spellboxes and enchanted tokens to take off the field of battle and add to their own coffers.

At some point, the healers wouldn't be able to keep up with the high-level dead and one side would call a retreat.

There was no doubt which side that would be.

Nin knelt next to a Third General and dragged her fingers over his face and aura, restarting his heart and securing his mind, then setting his magic to fix his internal trauma. His heart heaved on its own, pumping blood to his brain, then sending out the first signals. She moved onward to the next body—a boy in ill-fitting garb.

She had been given explicit instructions to revive all members of general level and above, and to leave the lower level soldiers to others.

She grimly placed her fingers on the boy's blood-and-dirt-streaked face, and he breathed in a gasping breath that became a heave. He stared at her in fevered wonder as his body knit itself back together at her command. The young were both easier and harder—their bodies were quick and eager, but they needed a more deliberately shown path than for those in their prime who knew their bodies well. Healing was always a two-way process. It was the strength of the healer to show the correct path.

The boy coughed up blood as his gaze shifted to look around them, eyes growing impossibly wide. His temporary awe turned into something more permanent as he looked back at her as the epicenter of the maliciously circling cloud around them.

She firmed her lips and fixed his lungs, knowing what the boy was seeing. Kaveh's immense power surrounded her at every moment, whirling in a wispy, dark circle of death across the battlefield, like the edges of Death's robes flared about her in a storm of destruction.

"Goddess Ferra?" the boy whispered. "I'm Akel. I will forever serve you."

"No, Akel. I am just a healer, but I do need your help. Listen to your heart now, listen to her beat." She pushed his magic into the flow of his internal organs, circulating the path while holding a thread of his mind, forcing him to concentrate. "Patch and smooth like this. That's right. Now your liver. Another pass."

He followed her instructions, but his stare didn't lose its glossy awe. "I will fight for you."

"No, I need you to fix your friends and allies in this way." She moved his magic along the path again, tweaking his undamaged brain again so that he was forced to memorize it. "After I revive them, I need you to patch and smooth. Will you help me?"

"Yes, anything," he said with fervor.

She brushed remorse away—there was no time for it in the festival of death.

"Stay in the circle." She motioned to the dark, deep shadows surrounding her.

He scrambled up and, though his face crumpled at the sight of the pile of broken boys he had been laying upon, he immediately began following her dictates.

After the first, they quickly fell to a rhythm—she revived a boy, passed the healing strings to Akel to finish healing, then moved to the next body. Revive, pass; revive, pass. The only interruption was when an undamaged and ready mind showed itself during the revival. She replicated in each a copy of Akel's motions and their numbers drastically increased.

Five boys no older than fifteen trailed her like puppies, patching all those in their wake; then there were twenty, then forty. Revive, pass; revive, pass, show...

When one ventured too far beyond her circle of protection, they almost immediately found death once more. Nin firmed her lips and tried not to think about numbers and ages and bloody conquest. Do, do, do, fix, fix, fix. Thinking and lamentation was for the darkness of night.

When the group finally outgrew the circle of protection completely, she slit her palm and created a pocket-well into which she pushed the youngest and most vulnerable, sealing the earth over their heads.

She did it again when the numbers once more grew too vast. Twice. Three times.

Forced to follow in Kaveh's wake, she was privy to the deadliest and messiest bits of battle and bloodshed. Forced to bypass torn bodies and irreparable death, she concentrated on those who could be revived.

Figures who did not burst to black dust as the denizens of death swarmed them.

The sheer death toll of the last strike caused her to falter. She looked up and watched Kaveh flex his shadows. Ifret opened her mouth and screamed alongside him—agonizing death spewing from her jaws.

Nin tried not to feel she had done something terribly wrong in healing the shadow.

The taking of Shirsk—followed by the taking of all the territories around it—energized the imperial forces with the absolute devastation left behind by their Imperator General. A herald from Sehk-Ra himself as to the legitimacy of the empire.

She was the only one on the battlefield who could feel Kaveh's emotions, but everyone knew his wrath.

KAVEH

Kaveh sent another blast.

He could see everything, feel everything, anticipate all. Shirsk had fallen. Then Helip, then Rasse, then Yalendil.

A fifth country conquered in half as many days. He would make them all bow. Scrape to the empire.

This is where he ruled. Where he was executioner. Where he could forget about the emperor's disappointment, and when he couldn't, he could pass that feeling on to his opponents, before destroying them.

Screams and panic. Ifret flowed alongside him and he could feel her satisfaction—her zeal.

It was as if the girl had revived them fully, in a way they hadn't realized had dulled. Each night, she patched invisible wounds only she could see and find.

He watched her move through piles of death, reaching out one hand then the other to heal. He could feel her energy lag after ripping someone from Death's jaws, could feel when she pulled more power from within, not letting herself fail.

An army of useless soldiers stumbled in her wake, helping her heal at forty times the speed she could do on her own. Surrounded by an impenetrable force of his shadows, they huddled together over the fallen, light spilling from their palms, reflecting the power that came from her.

Weakness.

He concentrated a burst of needled shadow forward, piking bodies in a continuous row down the front line. He cast a quick glance toward her as she healed a boy of, at most, thirteen, wearing the colors of the enemy.

Weakness.

He rent apart a squadron that was eyeing the healing knot around her. Then another who had begun to concentrate fire at the shadow-soaked group.

He ripped limbs from the torsos of those who approached her with malice. The girl finished healing the youngest members of the other side and began working on their own forces again. Healing, not destroying.

He should have terminated her in the first darkened alley. Or in the desert town of glass.

Instead, he tore apart everyone who approached her.

With her power, she could be destroying their enemies in dozens of ways. Opening ripgates behind and letting his shadows stab through—the possibilities were endless and enormous. He shivered at the thought of her dealing death alongside him.

He watched as the wet-behind-the-ear soldiers trailing her like eager puppies disappeared into the ground when their numbers grew too large to keep safe within the cage he had constructed to protect her.

Saving useless pests with her power. The power that touched him each night.

He surveyed the battlefield and saw one of his generals miscalculate the angle and propulsion of a spell package, taking out a squadron of their own men. He grabbed the man with shadow and snapped his neck.

Weakness. He had no patience for weakness.

The girl moved just out of range of his shadows and he pulled abruptly from his surge forward to expand the protective net outward. The tendriling shadows surged and wrapped around her form.

In response, he overused his power and destroyed half of the force in front of him. The rest immediately dropped their weapons and locked their hands together skyward in surrender.

Power surged through him.

No one could kill him. All who dared, died.

CHAPTER EIGHT

NIGHTS IN DARKNESS

TALINE

(Assaka Region, First Layer Indi)

Another tingle ran through the scepter and down Taline's arm.

"Nin is making ripgates."

The scepter seemed to recognize it—the type of magic that could split layers—and each recognition vibrated through her. The tingles had been occurring for the past two days.

Taline would kill the Shadow Prince.

Valeran withdrew five cylindrical pieces of stub metal from his pack, his gaze entirely too lazy as he lifted a metal stub and a tool. "She is a tool of the empire now."

She narrowed her eyes on him, recognizing his motions and the magical tool in his hand. "What are you doing?"

"Making us rich." He peered at one of the coins they had collected, traced one of the five designs on it with the tool, then carved the design into the metal. The metal around the carving hissed and burned, then melted back to create a stamp in the shape of the carved design. She recognized the carving tool and metal stubs. Beyond illegal to possess, they burned with duplication magic.

At home, the reproduction of currency was an action punishable by death. It didn't surprise her that Valeran possessed such tools.

"It means losing a hand and eye to be caught with any of those."

"That's why you don't get caught." He examined the next image in the design, then chiseled and inverted it into a second stamp on the next stub. "The empire uses a nearly foolproof method of ensuring the legitimacy of their coins. Unlike the legitimacy of their children," he muttered. "But places that the empire has yet to touch?

Well, there are many paths to riches for an adventurer with...flexible morality."

He turned the coin and made another mark. He held up the second stamp for closer inspection, then began a third.

Taline looked at the scepter. "The Shadow Prince is going to bind Nin to him permanently."

"He would be a fool not to."

Taline gripped the shaft, hands shaking. "I will raze the empire, if he does."

Valeran's brows slowly lifted and his posture visibly relaxed—which meant a knife was slipping into his hand beneath the tools already there. "What a lovely thought under such an innocent spray of moonshine."

"I will." The scepter warmed. She looked down at it. "It will help me do so."

"Of course it will." Valeran's voice was easy, but his gaze was not. "The scepter thrives on power. On conquest." He leaned back, crossing his legs. She couldn't see it, but she knew both of his palms were full of steel. "Now imagine such a weapon in the hands of the emperor or the Shadow Prince."

"He'll bind her no matter what."

"You'd be a fool to delude yourself to any other way of thinking."

"I'll kill him first." Taline swung the scepter back and forth to get used to the weight and timing of the swing.

Valeran returned to his illegal stamping. "Best figure out the ideal moment for that, narsumina, in your suicidal plan."

If the Shadow Prince died by Taline's hand before the oath was fulfilled, Nin would die, too. But if the Shadow Prince died from someone else's hand... If the scepter read her desire and just...did it...

Kaveh ul Fehl was thought to be unkillable—a beast born of shadow. But nothing that had been made could not be unmade. And Nin would know his weaknesses soon.

As long as Nin remained unbound, she could be saved.

Taline gripped the scepter and swung.

She would try Valeran's temple solution first, and the three moon ritual Nin had found. But she had secondary plans as well. Ancient sites and temple iconography often included pictures or codes to other sites—information that could give her ways to leave Valeran behind and find her own way forward.

But even if she and Nin escaped the empire, the Shadow Prince would chase them. Other plans would need to be enacted, and the Shadow Prince's continued ability to draw breath was priority number one.

Another tingle ran through her.

She couldn't bear thinking about what was happening in their world. She had been separated from Nin for four days.

She forced herself to think of their current path.

They had followed the river north of the post town west to the coast and flatter land, before turning north again. Traveling hard meant little time to speak, which was just fine with Taline. But as the sun set and traveling on horseback became more dangerous, they were forced to set camp.

The long ride had given her a long time to think.

Valeran would try to betray her—of that she had no doubt. She needed him now, but she would be ready when the time came. She swung the scepter in a pendulum motion—like an ancient irrigation tool—feeling the motion through her arm and identifying the moment she could release the force. She would be ready—she would make certain of it.

Valeran smiled up at her, his eyes sparking with firelight, his expression saying he knew exactly what she was thinking as he used his ill-made stamps on the coin blanks he had amassed or created. "Temporary alliances are always fraught with distrust."

"It is hard to trust a man who will see Nin dead in order to justify his aims." She bent her wrist back and forth, swinging the scepter again, then making a striking motion toward the dirt with its dangerous, circular head.

"Ninli's goals have always been greater than any value for her own life. You can't have missed that in the past four years you've clung to her."

"And you can't have missed me trying to convince her otherwise." She let the end of the scepter hit the ground and lifted a stick to poke the meats strung above the fire. "I was close to doing so." So close. "I will never forgive you that."

"The empire will never stop chasing her."

Taline viciously stoked the fire and skewered meats, while Valeran, finished with his first round of coin making, switched tasks and used one of his blades to slice and shape large pieces of flat wood he had gathered.

"I'll deal with the empire."

"You'll run for the rest of your free lives."

He shaped the wood—molding, joining, and searing it quickly into a candle flame shape that could be fitted over the scepter's tip. Valeran was nothing if not clever.

"Then we'll run," she said. "Without you."

He smiled. "Unlike you, I've never required anyone at my side."

By the time she finished serving the first part of their meal on large flat leaves—movements awkward with the scepter still fused to one palm—he had fit a long stick over the staff and head, turning the scepter into a crutch. A cloth-wrapping hid the decorative parts of the scepter from view around her affixed hand and pulled the old and new parts together into a dull, less noteworthy whole.

She swung it, gauging the change in weight, shape, and dynamics, and the compensation it would require.

She looked at the additions. "Even as a walking staff, it will still be noteworthy since I can never put it down, even when seated."

"Limp more." He shrugged. "We can pad your middle as if you are carrying a child late in term to deter questions."

She grimaced but nodded.

A tingle raced through her again. Taline closed her eyes. Nin?

No one answered. Taline blew out her breath, inhaled deeply and clutched the dead stick in her hand. Work, she demanded.

Wind swirled around her. She opened her eyes and saw Valeran stiffen.

Yes! Work.

The wind ceased. So did the tension in Valeran's spine.

"Not enough of your back in it yet, narsumina," Valeran said, lightly, taking another piece of meat. "Goodness, it might take years."

She bared her teeth. "Valeran—"

But he was already leaning back. "Did you feel something? Does it feel like you can use it?" he asked casually.

She hesitated, flexing her fingers around the shaft joined to her palm. Despite her inability to activate it, she could feel it doing things to her—incorporating into her being as if nestling in there, as if telling her brain that it had always been there—that she had another limb.

So alien on the first day, it was slowly starting to sink its roots into her, but it provided no answer to her endless desire to get back to her sister.

"I can do no more magic than when we arrived. With or without it." It was an uncomfortable reminder each time she absently tried to execute a daily spell. Each time reminded her of memories she had firmly put behind her.

He hummed and pulled the skewered meats to serve the last part of their meal. "The non-magic world takes some getting used to—having no access to magic."

She had helped Nin send people here. Those looking for a fresh start in a new world or those with little magic to sustain identity spells. The latter usually embraced the idea of living freely, with their own faces, somewhere they couldn't be found.

For Taline, the danger was opposite.

"I know the feeling well already," she murmured, chewing a meat strip. "It is not something that I want to get used to again."

Taline looked at the henna dots on the backs of her hands. Along with the others tattooed on her body, they were the only remnants remaining of the anchoring spells that had once secured her anonymity and freedom. There was nothing to sustain the enchantments anymore. She touched her waist and the empty spellbox that normally held her facial enchantment set.

Nin had powered the box fully every feast day.

Taline was a dead woman in a living woman's skin. Or a living woman in a dead woman's skin. Whichever it was, Siran Bey was dead and Taline ul Summora lived on.

Nin and the spellbox were the only reasons Taline hadn't been found.

She closed her eyes. She missed Nin. She missed her indomitable spirit on a quest. She missed knowing Nin was safe.

And she missed her ability to whip up a ripgate to wherever they needed to go.

Moons. It would take moons to reach home. And Valeran had put them here.

"Why did you do it?"

He poked lazily at the fire after they had finished eating and cleaned. "There are so many questions that could pertain to."

"Why did·you kick the scepter to me? Why did you kick me through the gate?"

"Instead of letting Kaveh ul Fehl, already possibly the strongest magi in existence, have the scepter?"

"He would have given it to the emperor."

"Maybe." His gaze flitted over the scepter.

"You think the Shadow Prince would have kept it?"

"I think that no one can truly understand what having power like that can do to you until they have it in their hands. I think that either of them having it would be apocalyptic."

She looked at the scepter, docile and static, in her lap. "You kicked it to me because I am the weakest, then."

He looked at her and said nothing for a long moment. "Yes, that is why I chose you."

She frowned at the too-smooth way he said it, but anger was easier. It always was with Valeran. "I will become more powerful than all of you."

He looked at the scepter, then back at her, eyes unreadable. "I do hope that is not true."

She bared her teeth at him and narrowed her eyes. "Kaveh ul Fehl already has power. As does the emperor. Nearly unlimited power. What is a drop in the bucket more?"

"The scepter is not a drop. It was made by a magi with a power like those who split the worlds. Millions have died for such power. The Carres didn't keep their borders closed solely due to being scared of outsiders rising up in revolt against their brutal customs. They liked their populace docile, but they fought and killed to keep the scepters in their control." He stoked the fire. "Ironic, that they were betrayed from within. Their brutal customs, turned carelessly against those who they demanded loyalty from, was the thing to destroy them."

She looked sharply at him. "What do you know?"

"I've known 'Ninli's' secrets far longer than you have, narsumina, trust me."

"Why? You trust no one."

"True. Trust is a child's emotion." He twirled the knife he was sharpening. "I make bargains instead, and I occasionally stick to those bargains in order for more bargains to be extended my way."

"Nin has never failed you."

He examined his steel. "She kept you around. I can't say that wasn't a disappointment."

She firmed her lips. "Why are you this way?"

He smiled sharply. "Why are any of us the way we are? Experience? Learned lessons?"

"You usually run from your problems."

"I have survived this long by knowing when to flee."

"And yet, here you are. Curious. I know Nin," Taline said, bitterness creeping into her tone. "There was no reason for you to go to the temple after the Shadow Prince learned your identity. Nin would have freed you from any bargain. Why did you not follow pattern and flee?"

"I fled quite quickly from Kaveh ul Fehl's wrath."

"Are you saying that Nin did not tell you to leave the night before we reached the temple? When you two were whispering, as if either of you had any sense of subtlety?"

"You mistake subtlety for strategy."

"Valeran."

One brow rose in disdain. "She did," he unwillingly agreed.

"Why then did you remain?"

He pulled a skewer from the fire, rotating it to check the sear on the meats they would pack for the next day. "I don't know. Perhaps all your lectures finally took hold."

"I don't believe it."

"No." He smiled. "You prize steadfast actions and unwavering commitment too much to believe anything so mercurial."

She gazed steadily at him. "When you don't have control for most of your life, then are suddenly extended an infinite supply to wield, it is a heady thing. Both balm and curse."

"Ninli lets you set all the parameters in your joint ventures—except when she hies off on some harebrained scheme midway through. She lets you control your environment and hers. It works for both of you only because you would do anything for her."

Taline looked at the scepter. "I know what I have been given with her trust."

"Yes. It is one of the things I respect about you," he said. She looked up at him, sharply. "And decry."

She bristled. "You would."

"What are things, but things to be taken?" he said idly.

She viciously poked the campfire from her side. "I don't know what she sees in you."

"That's because you ascribe nobleness to her every action. She is human, like all of us. And there is a darkness in her that will always pull her to others of darkness."

Taline stopped poking the campfire and allowed a smile to wind the outside edges of her mouth.

It put him visibly on edge immediately. He expected outraged. It was time to turn many expectations.

"How almost astute of you, Valeran. The flaw in your comment is that she isn't drawn to every evil in the shadows. It's not conscious, but it's unyielding—her instinctive knowledge of who to trust. Undoubtedly built upon from being born to an environment where trusting the wrong person meant the difference between life and death for others. She is drawn to those who eventually use their darkness for light. In the four years I've shadowed her, only once have I seen that dark trust fail." She pinned him with her gaze. "You."

"Maybe I'm trustworthy after all, then." He flashed his teeth, his lids dropped, and his mouth curled. "You should find out."

She tilted her head. "You are the mistake, the lie, or the most hidden treasure chest of all."

"I am incredible." His satisfied expression couldn't belie the uneasiness in his eyes, though.

She smiled beatifically. "Then one day I will answer the question of why she is drawn to save you."

"You have already answered that—why is anyone drawn to me? I'm irresistible." He rolled his shoulders forward. "And I will destroy, I mean, deliver, the scepter to one who can wield it to glory."

She narrowed her eyes, but Valeran was already working on his next project.

"The emperor's aims are pure and true," he said without looking up. "The scepter will enjoy being in his hands, don't you think?"

Taline firmed her lips and refused to feel unease.

CHAPTER NINE

IMPERIAL HUBRIS

NINLI

(Shirsk's capital city on the Axšaina Sea)

A tingle ran through Nin. She absently rubbed her palm, gaze turning southeast, before focusing back on Shirsk's gatekeeper as he connected the city's gate to Fehlaka.

With Yalendil's forces obliterated and the rest of Shirsk's allies subdued, the imperial forces had secured the capitals around the stormy waves of the body of water better known as the Ominous Sea and switched the main city gate from a connection with its northern sister city to the gate in Fehlaka that was used for temporary links.

The seal for the Fehlaka gate, emblazoned on Reen cloth, contained all the coordinate information to allow the connection. The gatekeeper pushed his magic into the gate path engraved in the seal.

The connection flickered but held. Nin could see the thin lines of it—the tiredness of the magic from the gate, seal, and gatekeeper. The magic had flickered intermittently for the last hour, waiting for activation on the other side.

She tried to keep her gaze away, but it kept returning to the flickering magic.

"Hold the gate, keeper."

The gatekeeper's terror increased every time Kaveh spoke. And though the reaper blade held to the gatekeeper's throat was incentive enough not to fail, Kaveh's presence seemed to be more terrifying to the man. She wondered what powers the gatekeeper thought the Shadow Prince possessed. A reaper's blade expelled a soul. What could be worse?

Pressed against the man's neck, the blade ensured the gatekeeper could not betray the wielder. Should he choose to try, he would fall beneath the compulsion of the blade and for a precious minute his body and mind would be under the control of the man holding the blade. If that happened, Kaveh would make sure the gate held until it could be shut down, and he would expel the man's soul with a single slice.

The gatekeeper seemed to have a high desire to live and little loyalty to Shirsk itself, so the threat was likely unnecessary. But Kaveh never played games with the emperor's life.

Sweat rolled in steady rivulets down the gatekeeper's face. She felt pity for him in this time of terror, but he would survive. The man was a weak keeper—barely able to keep the single gate working—but prized enough for even that skill to keep alive. The man would be installed elsewhere in the empire—separated from his original territory, in order to keep loyalties in line.

Finally, the gate lit gold. The reaper blade dug farther into the gatekeeper's throat and Kaveh's shadows swept around his feet.

The gate opened and the emperor walked through with the Crown of Sunlight upon his head and the imperial scepter in hand.

"Kaveh." The emperor strode sinuously forward. Aros ul Fehl and four men in guard garb followed.

A contingent of high-ranking soldiers from the imperial army immediately took up position of guard—a changing of hands from the palace to the battlefield.

The emperor turned and touched his scepter to the gate. The Carre scepter given to him forty years ago in order to clean up the chaff in the southern peninsular territory that was now the Fehla-da province had become something far more in the hands of a clever and powerful man.

The gate connection firmed and resolved.

A tremor ran through her.

It was usually hard to keep her desire to interfere in check when gates were being manipulated, but with the emperor near, that desire was completely absent.

Kaveh removed the blade from the gatekeeper's neck, and the man dropped to the ground, his body shaking uncontrollably. An imperial guard quickly pulled the gatekeeper upright and shoved him into a chair, the motions practiced.

Kaveh held out the precious gate seals they had collected in each conquered major city. "The Axšaina Sea is yours, Your Imperial Majesty, as are all the territories along its borders."

The emperor took the five seals from his hand and inclined his head. "The Ominous Sea—swept stormily and finally into the empire." The emperor handed the seals to one of his retainers. "Walk with me, Imperator General."

He pulled his fingers along the imperial scepter, then he was striding down the hall with Kaveh and Aros to either side. The curt motion of Kaveh's fingers and the feeling in the bond told her she was to follow.

Aros ul Fehl stared back at her, eyes narrowing, as she did as she was told.

The emperor and Kaveh exchanged pleasantries as they walked through the hall—a practiced facade.

When they reached the designated meeting room, Kaveh's shadows leaped to secure the interior as the guards stationed themselves outside the doors. She was used to seeing Kaveh secure the tent every night but watching him do it on a larger scale was always breathtaking.

A nook to the side of the guard-lined hall beckoned and she stepped toward it as the men entered the meeting room.

A shadow whisked around her ankles and snaked into the room. Another wrapped her wrist and sharpened to a directional point.

Nin reluctantly gave up her nook and followed the three men inside, swallowing as the doors closed heavily behind her. She had experienced this scenario only in nightmares—to stand alone in a closed room with Kaveh, Aros, and the emperor.

She lifted her chin. Things could be worse. Taline or Rone could be alongside her. It was only Nin on the severing block. Nin forced the ripgate coiling in her palms to recede.

The emperor disregarded her after a short, cold look, then turned to Kaveh. "What have you found?"

All pleasantries were dropped now that the room was secured.

"Your Imperial Majesty," Aros said, staring darkly at her. "I don't think—"

"She stays, like the leech she is," the emperor said coldly, without looking at her. "And she will be dealt with like a leech in the end."

Aros's eyes narrowed in on her further, but in the presence of the emperor, Aros seemed to toe the same line as everyone else in the empire.

"Siru ul Teg was found dead by his own hand," Kaveh said, not commenting on the emperor's aside to Aros other than with an internal tightening down the bond. "Or a hand close."

The dead man had been the First General in charge of the northern section of the front in Kaveh's absence. He had been the lead point on Shirsk. Nin had been in the tent—with Ifret staring at her unnervingly—when Kaveh had received those reports.

"Siru ul Teg was a competent general. Treachery from him would be surprising."

"Ber ul Hon of the First Guard will be conducting the investigation," Kaveh said. "We will know the truth."

"And the uprising?"

"Crushed."

"Good. We have more significant problems. The knowledge hasn't been released yet—but Carsue is dead."

She felt Kaveh's shock, though nothing showed on his face. Her own shock echoed. Carsue ul Fehl had been the sixth blessed child of the emperor, and Padifehl of Moru. At thirty years of age, his death was likely not of natural cause.

Aros stepped forward. "The gate to Moru went dormant two days ago. There is no report on how that occurred." His gaze slid to her for the barest moment of consideration, an action that made her go cold.

She had opened a ripgate in front of Aros and Etelian. And though Etelian could be counted on to be too wrapped up in himself to understand what happened around him, making that mistake with Aros would be fatal. Terror churned.

Aros's gaze slid back to Kaveh. "Spies say the Moruvians reportedly took the gate failure as Sehk-Ra's blessing to kill the padifehl and reestablish their rule."

"A grievous mistake." The emperor smiled thinly.

Rebellions were unusual in the empire, because they were so ruthlessly dealt with. And after the news of Tehrasi had rippled across the lands—with the complete extermination of one of the oldest ruling families—transitions of power from independent countries to imperial territories had increased.

The emperor and his top generals had secured the cities on the southern edges of the Medit Sea through blood and death—and with Kaveh as their active hand. When Kaveh had taken lead position of the armies, he had expanded the empire twofold, knocking the rest of the territories down like a child's toy village.

Nin didn't know much about Moru, having never traveled that far west, but she knew Carsue ul Fehl had been integral in obtaining the rich peninsula on the ocean—the closing gate of the western Medit Sea strategically positioned between the two great landmasses.

Moru wasn't connected to the empire directly except by a single gate held at Fehlaka—so any normal imperial travel had to be done through enemy territory or by gate to Shoune, then up through the strait.

Carsue had strategically wielded twelve-year-old Kaveh and brutally conquered Moru for his own. Even as separated as it was, Moru had been a stronghold of the empire for a decade now, held under the iron rule of Carsue ul Fehl.

Once a great general, Carsue had relinquished his dour battlefield attire for the rich silks of rule when Kaveh had ascended to Imperator General. Carsue had claimed his most prized conquest lands to rule—ruling the western gate of the ocean-side lands, and the western bridge between the north and south great landmasses.

He had been known as a brutal tyrant to the people who sat at his feet. He had not been a beloved leader. But for the empire, he had been the best choice to hold embattled lands far from the center of their domain.

He had been held up as a strong power who would not be taken down by outside forces, and that had set well with the subset of people who valued the security of steady rule over liberties given by a leader more generous, but less powerful.

She had heard more than once that Kaveh was of Carsue's mold, but greater. Looking at Aros and how he looked upon Kaveh—with a strange edge of hunger and respect—she wondered what Carsue, a once great general, had thought of the thirteenth blessed child. She wondered what he had felt for a child magi with such overwhelming power—a child who had easily replaced and eclipsed him.

The empire had been won by the overwhelming dual hands of the emperor and Kaveh. Even at age eight, Kaveh had been depicted wielding a shadowed blade by his father's command.

"When do you wish me to leave?" Kaveh asked, no further discussion needed.

"Nightfall. Punish everyone responsible. Aros will deal with the authorities after you've leveled the soul of the palace."

"It will be done."

Something in the emperor's bearing softened at Kaveh's unquestionable acceptance. His gaze shifted to the shadow around Kaveh's neck. "I see that your companion is better. I thought it lost."

"Ifret survives on spite." Kaveh's delivery was free of all inflection, but the internal thread of fondness that was always there for his shadow remained. "Ninli healed the rest."

The emperor narrowed his eyes at her. Surprisingly, Ifret hissed low—a rumbling sound at the emperor.

Kaveh smoothed a hand down her back and she settled to glaring.

"I see her temper hasn't improved."

"Spite," Kaveh reiterated.

"A force of great power in women and men alike. Walk with me."

The emperor and Kaveh walked to the side of the room. They were immediately encompassed by a wall of swirling shadows, leaving Nin and Aros on the outside. Alone.

"I don't believe we have been formally introduced, healer." Aros's expression was mocking.

"Ninli ul Summora, Your Imperial Highness."

Aros hummed. "More accurately, Ninli al Six el Healer il Tehras ol Gomen ul Summora, isn't it? Interesting, that designation. You are as much a Level Six as I am." His gaze switched slowly between each of her eyes and it was all she could do to stop herself from double checking her spells. "Perhaps that isn't all we have in common, either."

She forced her sharply rising panic into something more useful. "We both appear to have been considered unimportant for whatever conversation is currently happening in the corner."

"And she has teeth." He smiled, revealing all of his. "You'll need them, Ninli ul Summora."

"I will hardly be present for much longer. I am simply aiding the prince in a task, then I will be on my way."

"Doubtful."

"As you say, Your Imperial Highness."

She had studied Aros. Needling him once would amuse him. A second time would not—and she still desired to draw breath.

"You are still alive, even after a week at his side. Curious. They call him Death's Master for a reason."

"The Imperator General seems to have many names," she agreed.

"Kaveh is the finest force of nature in this world." He paused and the faintest real smile touched his lips. "Second finest force of nature in this world."

She wondered at his smile, unnerved. Aros had always unnerved her, even from afar. He held himself just like Jisarek—charming, but with a ready knife to be slipped in the back. Her uncle had been fey and mercurial, cruel and charming. But then, the entirety of the Carres had been a bit mad.

"You are the first?" she asked as lightly as she could manage.

"Sehk-Ra, no." He smiled—a charming smile, just as unnerving. "I simply...sweep after the forces of nature from behind and remove myself from their direct path." His smile grew and there was something very off-putting about it. Covetous was the only way to label it. "The best strategy is sometimes to approach from the rear."

She smiled, trying to match her expression to his feigned, easy conversational tone. "As you say."

He seemed entertained by her attempt. "You amuse me. I think we will have fun, you and I."

"I will endeavor to be of aid, Your Imperial Highness."

"Oh, I think you'll aid me quite a bit, Ninli." She didn't like the look in his amber eyes at all. "Quite a bit."

The shadow cage broke, and the emperor and Kaveh emerged.

Kaveh's dispassionate gaze swung between her and the first prince, and she could feel his unease. He had felt hers. He had cut short his meeting with the emperor somehow in order to see what was happening.

She had never felt more relief at having the bond than she did in that moment.

The emperor looked coldly between them. "Pay no attention to gnats, Aros."

"I never do, Your Imperial Majesty," he said, smiling.

Nin's heart skipped a beat.

The emperor looked as displeased as she felt and turned to Kaveh. "I expect a report of success in three days' time."

"It will be done."

The emperor left in a swirl of robes and imperial procession, Aros at his side.

Kaveh motioned sharply to her and headed straight for the room he had temporarily claimed as theirs in the Palace of Tranquility, overlooking the mercurial waters of the Ominous Sea where selkies and sirens liked to play. It was eerie how silent the halls were, no matter what the name given to the palace. Those who had fought had not survived the claiming of the structure, and those still alive had been conscripted to aid and feed the imperial forces or had been secured in the holding cells underground.

Kaveh secured their room, but this time there was a screech. Nin winced at the veil of death that permeated the arms of his shadows for a moment before blinking clear. Someone had not survived the power backlash overwhelming their surveillance enchantment.

Kaveh's motions were sharp as he readied for bed, his emotions tight and dark. Ifret watched him with narrowed eyes from the pillow she had claimed.

Kaveh was always a dizzying mixture of extreme and repressed feelings, but the current mixture of his emotions was especially difficult to parse.

She watched him snap a clasp in two. "Do you grieve your brother?"

"For his foolishness only. Carsue turned soft. A weakness when asps hover." Nothing in his emotions gainsaid his words. "I grieve only the problems created by his death. Dealing with Moru—an already conquered province but with a northern border we won't fully control without a full onslaught—means stepping back instead of pushing forward. Conquering the western ocean will come, but our forces are better spent elsewhere at present. We would have been able to squeeze the western territories in a year on our current path."

"You will deal harshly with Moru, then, for their interruption of your plans." She girded herself. The emperor had said to level the palace.

"Moru will learn a lesson that will spread. With the extinguishing of the gate that let the empire ride to their doors, the Moruvians have determined they are free to reestablish their own rule. They will be taught otherwise. We leave at dawn to catch the gate to Shoune, then we'll push north."

The nearest gate to more death.

Nin rubbed the band around her wrist and headed for the full platter of meat, fruit, and bread on the table. "What will be done here, in Shirsk? With the people who merely served and survived the conquest?"

"That will be the decision of others."

"Helping the people here," she said carefully, running a standard poison spell on the platter, then choosing a figstee fruit, "would secure them to you."

He raised a brow. "They can help themselves or die."

"There is no choice in that."

"That is the consequence of losing."

She looked at her hands and the spot of red juice from the figstee slipping slowly down one finger. "The ruling strength of a throne isn't always gained through might."

"Benevolence is gained on a battlefield of blood and death." He undressed roughly. "Why do you care? These aren't your people, and you have might ten times over any of them."

"I need to care because others cannot."

A tingle ran sharply along her skin, causing her to gasp and grab her right arm. The power of the Scepter of Darkness ran along her skin—a siren's song in the touch.

"What is it?" Kaveh stepped sharply toward her.

She turned slowly, facing southeast. She rubbed her right arm, staring in the direction tugging at her.

Taline?

But just as abruptly as it appeared, the tingle disappeared.

Unease swept her. The scepter had cleansed something—burned through a restriction. Where joy should have been—proof that Taline was alive!—only uneasiness resided.

"What is it?" Kaveh asked more sharply—shadows extended.

She shook her head, gaze pinned southeast. "Nothing. It's...nothing." Even the echo was gone now—as if the tingle had never existed. Movement from her periphery caused her to sharply point a finger at him. "If you put a shadow on me, I will stab you."

He raised a brow, but the shadows settled. "You shouldn't eat that."

She looked at the fruit in her hand. "Is it poisoned?"

"It has no nutritional value."

"That's not why I was going to eat it." She gave one last look to the southeast. "What do we do when we reach Moru?"

"We raze it."

Death. No. Death to all.

She bit into the figstee, hoping the taste would give a moment's respite from the living nightmare. Years of carefully built protections, tamping down all the Carre remnants within her, stripped away with each day.

Taline, Rone, be okay.

CHAPTER TEN
EMBERS AND SPARKS

RONE

(Seaside, Assaka Region, First Layer Indi)

Rone watched Taline stare at the scepter as they broke camp in the hour before dawn.

Unease, a constant companion for the past five days, edged into something sharper.

She had remarkably shown few overt signs of being influenced by the legendary relic five days into their journey. Taline really was remarkable in her steadfast light. A snappish temper at too little sleep was expected and he did everything to inflame such irritation in her, but she swallowed even that irritation in quick fashion and kept her chin upright.

But the relic attached to her had been created in evil deed, and it was only a matter of time. He needed them to get to a temple quickly, before the scepter took real hold.

He thought of promises. Of attachment. Of the choices that would spread before him.

She remained quiet as they rode.

They reached their destination, a seaside town, as golden light spread across the Fehl Sea—or whatever the locals called it here. In their world, the borders of the entire sea touched imperial lands. To the south, the sea opened into the southern ocean—touching places the Fehl would eventually conquer and spread.

Rone dismounted, allowing his horse to graze on the hillside grasses as they looked down to the town below. The thoroughfares circled around a large stone fountain in the center of the city. "This is the town?"

"I never went through the ripgate, but I remember the fountain." Taline's expression constricted. "And the sea beyond. This is the place."

They waited above as the town awoke and opened its doors to morning. The town wasn't large. Finding someone in it wouldn't take long, even if they had to ask a dozen times. "You remember the woman?"

"I remember her," Taline said grimly.

He sighed. He hadn't known Taline before she had taken the name she wore like a badge of pride. But he had known her for four years since becoming Taline ul Summora. That tone meant nothing positive.

He looked at the scepter head, and the smudges of grime that had collected around the edges of the light wood he had used to cover it. He frowned. How had it gotten so dirty?

Taline's clothing and the wrapping around her hand on the staff were travel worn, definitely, but not the darkened edge of grime that showed on the edges of the wood. The grime almost looked like...burn marks.

He grimly hoped she had been dragging the covered scepter through tree sap. Anything else meant far worse things for them.

"Let's go," she said.

Rone followed behind with the horses as he let her take the lead. She limped forward with her "walking stick" into the small, seafaring town. Boats and nets littered the coastal edge and beach. Market stands were being laden with produce—the town large enough to do outside trade. Morning risers walked around the fountain square, exchanging greetings and setting up for work.

He idly watched the activity and gazes as they passed. The townsfolk were interested in them, but not overtly wary. With their horses' leads in his hand and a half-dozen points of easy egress, there was little need to think more about defense until they deduced whether their prey was here.

Still, with the relic Taline carried, he would need to be on guard until the blasted thing was gone. He cemented the layout of the town in his mind. Quick exits, routes with the least resistance, makeshift weapons that could be used or pulled from horseback.

Taline's gaze narrowed in on a figure finishing a purchase at one of the stands. She pivoted her direction to follow the woman.

The woman walked to a small house of mud brick, thatch, and stone. A small carving with a doubled fortune omen—one for wind and one for sea—hung above her doorway. The woman began setting her purchases into baskets by the door.

Taline maneuvered up the shell path behind her.

This was their contact then.

He tied the horses to a fence with a loose knot and a quick pat. He didn't need to ask questions as he followed. They might never have gotten along personally, but Rone and Taline knew how to work together seamlessly when a task was in both their favor.

Taline squared her shoulders, unconsciously pulling the scepter into her body.

A concern for another time.

"Birsa."

The woman startled and turned. She looked at Taline in confusion for a moment before something—maybe Taline's voice, maybe the hint of another face in her now unguarded features—clicked.

"Taline?" Her gaze darted and locked onto Rone, wary. She looked around at her neighbors' homes before her gaze skittered back to survey them once more. Her eyes narrowed. "What a...surprise. In many ways. Where is Ninli?"

"We were separated at a gate. She is...I don't know where she is. A layer away."

Birsa looked around quickly, then motioned them inside. "You speak a language not understood, and your face..." She shook her head.

Rone scanned the neighborhood, but other than a few curious faces, nothing was amiss. Taline was good at keeping her head down. He ducked inside after them. Answering questions would be a problem that "Birsa" would have to deal with. And though this was a seaport, a thousand ships could not be launched from here due to Taline ul Summora's face.

"Why are you here?" she asked Taline sharply, pulling the tarp into place as soon as Rone was through. "Why hasn't Ninli opened a ripgate?"

There were multiple questions hidden within that one. A survival instinct he respected. But then, Ninli's doves were usually quite resilient. Rone stayed silent while examining the woman. Resilient, or they found their resilience after prolonged exposure to a girl overflowing with the quality.

"She doesn't know where we are. We were separated by a temple gate. The exit was different from the entrance, and neither was of her own creation."

"What temple?"

"It doesn't matter."

Birsa stared at her, then at the "staff" in her hand, nothing in her expression welcoming. "What temple?"

"Nin's in trouble. We need to get back to our layer."

"What temple?"

"The Temple of Darkness."

The woman went still, and her eyes locked on the wrapped stick that Taline had still not released. Birsa licked her lips. "Is that—?"

"It matters not."

"Does it not?" Birsa's gaze didn't move from the scepter and Rone nonchalantly fiddled with the strings of his pack while sliding a knife into his other palm.

"No. It is little more than a decoration at present."

Birsa's gaze went to her. "You can't wield it?"

"No," Taline said. A stretch of the truth, but not one that Rone would argue. "We need to get back as soon as possible. Will you help us?"

The woman silently looked them over, most of her attention on Taline. "The last time I saw you… I believe your last words to me were—Have a good life. They were not said with a smile."

Taline grimaced.

Rone allowed himself a small bite of pleasure at her consternation and let his knife slide back into the edge of his sleeve—but not into its sheath—as he withdrew a packet of salted meat and leaf from the pack. Taline had a quick and vicious tongue. And she was fierce about those she felt were leaving Nin behind. He knew that better than anyone.

If the woman, Birsa, was expecting an apology, it wasn't going to come.

"And I stand by my words." Taline regarded Birsa with perfect posture and raised chin. "You want me to pay for my slights to you, I will. But I won't apologize for them. You got your second start—a good start, if your current health and home is anything to go by."

Taline gazed around the space, that though small, was replete with personal effects and comfort.

"Nin will never get that, truly. Especially not now." Taline's eyes closed. When they opened, they were filled with fierce determination. "So, yes, I will pay for my slights. You can revile me in equal measure to how I've treated you, you can layer me in filth, you can ask for whatever demeaning act you determine necessary. And throughout, I will continue to ask your aid in helping the person who helped you. I will beg you for aid, I will crawl on my knees through the streets. I will do whatever is required, because I ask not for myself, but for Nin."

And that was what made Taline so dangerous.

She stood by what she said and what she promised, but she also accepted her faults and strove to do better.

Rone grimaced as he chewed. For people who had the ability to trust, she was someone who could be relied upon.

The other woman said nothing for long moments, unreadable gaze pinned on Taline. There was no love or power lost between them in the nonverbal exchange. Taline had shown her entire hand. Birsa had to determine whether she was going to play it.

"You speak too much." Birsa rose and walked to the firepit and the pot hanging over the flames. "What is wrong with Ninli?"

Taline's fingers clenched around the scepter. "Nin is oath-bound to the Shadow Prince to retrieve the scepter for him by the dark moon. She is forever bound to him on the twenty-first moonrise from now, if the oath is unfulfilled."

From what little Taline had shared with him on their journey here, Birsa had arrived two years ago. She would know exactly who the Shadow Prince was.

The woman's eyes shifted to him.

Ah. More than just who the Shadow Prince was, then. He smiled. He didn't bother to soften the coldness of the curve.

"He owes Nin as well," Taline said. "He is helping."

"Is he?" Birsa muttered before shifting her attention back. "A binding oath. Why would she do such a thing?"

"She..." Taline's lips compressed. "Because she's stupid."

"Saved you again, did she?" Birsa murmured.

"She is stupid."

"It is her nature to save." And for the first time, Birsa's gaze softened as she looked at Taline.

Rone wondered whether the woman would still think the same if she knew the name of Ninli's birth. Perhaps, for sometimes specific actions were so overwhelming, they compensated for every pain before.

But Ninli never absorbed the things people said of her effortless kindness. She was duty-bound to pay for sins not her own—or for those buried so far in the past that only she remembered the flesh of their skeletons.

"You should not have lifted it." Birsa looked at the scepter in Taline's lap.

"I didn't."

"Why is it in your hand then?"

"I do not know the answer to that."

Birsa looked between them. Rone raised a brow and continued to chew.

"A dilemma, this." Birsa stirred her pot. "I'm not certain that I wish to see a world where the emperor controls the Scepter of Darkness."

Taline stiffened. Rone did not.

But then, he had been waiting for something like this the whole time—which was why the handle of his knife was touching the edge between his wrist and palm.

"Will you stand in our way?" Taline asked tightly.

"You will stand in your own way. You underestimate the trials you will need to go through in order to return." Birsa looked at the pot. "Twenty-one moonrises is a blink of time in this layer. Or an unbearable eternity. Magic is scarce here. Many who come do not realize the toll—all of the things one relies on to survive and thrive."

"We have spent five days in this land."

"And you have not used it in that time?" Birsa glanced at the scepter, then back at Taline.

"I...have tried. I immediately tried to get back to Nin."

Birsa watched her with an eagle's gaze. Rone ran his middle finger along his knife's edge, waiting.

"What do you truly seek, Taline?"

"A way back that doesn't include activating the scepter."

Birsa tapped the edge of her cauldron for long moments. "Magic is scarce here, but there are a few places where it can be found—places the pentalayerists haven't discovered, some they use for their own travel, and some they do not yet know how to destroy. Pockets. Temples. Long-forgotten keys to the other realms."

Rone relaxed his grip.

"Babil, Memfi, Tehras, Parsa." Taline's gaze darted to Rone. "The Henge of Stones."

Rone watched silently, not adding anything.

Birsa nodded. "Large sites. Known. Heavily guarded. But magic grows scarcer everywhere, even in the pockets where it pools, as each new day dawns further from the five layer split."

She stirred the pot and smoke curled toward the ceiling. "Activation of a dormant layer gate requires a solstice, lunar eclipse, or other sun or moon sign, but also relies on immaculate tracts. The movement of a single rock by the non-magicals can negate the power of a site and destroy the pocket of power, like a binding stitch ripped out of cloth."

She looked at Taline. "Rumor whispers that thieves have disturbed the gates in all but one pyramid in Memfi, and that the great sphinx can no longer channel its guard. It, too, shall be lost to magic's touch soon. The Henge of Stones has had more than one of its gates disturbed, but it is said that five still remain—two of which go to our world. There is an island in the Medit Sea with a lintel that is reported to have never failed a high moon and a gift of magic. Or you could try Antequere. The Antequere mounds, and its connected sites, are rumored to still be active and in...a less controlled area. Not yet ruled by the empire here, though they, too, seek to stretch to the western ocean like the Fehls, to the lands of Moru—of Carsue the Bloody—on the flip side of the layer cloth."

Rone narrowed his eyes at her knowledge as she listed off the mythical network connected to the Antequere mounds—knowledge that was hard to come by even in the magic world where spells and enchantments hid the gates and rituals to unlock them. A simple gathering of data about a home and world to which she would never return? Or something already known before she had decided to live here?

"The gate in Babil will lead to any of the other four layers, but the pentalayerists have long made Babil their center of control, and no place will be more difficult to breech. Kiš, Ur, Bilbat, Bekli—all are possibilities for failure or success—for the fertile valley brings death and opportunity."

"There are lesser known spots, though, places without gates...places to fill vessels?" Taline touched her satchel unconsciously.

The woman glanced down, not missing the action. Rone kept his arms loose as he casually ate, knives accessible in an instant.

"There is Kailāsa in the east. Reportedly, there is a great well of magic in the mountain that could aid you, but it is an arduous journey. There are rumored spots closer to places of which you are more familiar. Closer to the Tehras and Parsa of this layer—both of which have gates that were built to specifications seen in our world, though as far as anyone knows, they were never activated. There are tales of a broken promise from gods beyond."

"You think the Carres made a promise to the rulers here?"

"There is little way to identify truth from tale in this world without magic. All seems myth to those without magic. What was built before the split is knowledge key to the non-magic world—for all things built before have a possibility to still exist with their properties intact. Magi can change the non-magic world, but it is incredibly difficult. What was around before magic was split is what still has potential to activate when the right circumstances are put into play, so long as the sites aren't destroyed or even one stone moved."

"Solstice." Taline looked at him. "Pathways in the henge will be activated automatically during a total lunar eclipse."

Birsa's gaze slipped to him. He gave a casual smile in return.

"But we cannot await the solstice," Taline said.

"No. But little of this information matters anyway." Birsa spread her hands. Her head tipped as she surveyed Taline. "You will use the scepter before you reach the end. You will wield it and be taken by its power." Her tone was certain. "And it will carry you to the place, but not the end, you seek."

Taline gripped the scepter. "Then it will carry me there, if there is no chance." Her tone was just as grimly definite. "Will you help me gain chance to do differently?"

Birsa said nothing for long moments, her gaze straying to the scepter again before traveling up to meet Taline's. "I will help give Ninli ul Summora a second chance. Like she gave me. And if it ends in an era of darkness, then I will have rolled the dice of the gods again."

Taline's shoulders loosened. Rone's lips thinned around the strip of meat. Taline automatically believed in those who believed in Nin. She couldn't understand how others could not believe.

Birsa pulled out a scroll. A map was sketched on the fibers. Pulling a finger along the lines, she motioned to the marks embedded within. "Each of these represents a temple with a well. The ones with red dots are ones I've been to, and I've made notes of elements to watch for or bits of landscape to find. The black dots are rumors or information purchased."

She spread her fingers along the fibers. "Sarg or the stone tomb at Fash." She tapped the map in two locations. "Sarg is on the way to Parsa or to Ur and the crescent valley should you decide to do Sehk-Ra's work and brave Babil's endless delights and nightmare gate. They say there are underground caverns throughout the fertile valley open to those who know how to work stone and tame temple guardians. Should the well at Sarg be a myth, you will still be able to continue by foot to Ur or cross the sea to Parsa."

"Babil is a fool's undertaking," Rone said. "The undertaking of one who has even less to live for than a fool."

Birsa nodded at the map. "I recommend trying Parsa to access the lintel. Or Kiš to Ancyra. Then to Antequere, and from there to the Henge of Stones. At the henge, you will need the correct moonrise and altitude, and to pick the correct gate, and you will be home."

"Neither Parsa nor Kiš are close, even by horse." Taline's fingers curled into fists. "We need a closer point."

"The pentalayerists have closed most points in Indi. I wouldn't send you on a death's run—especially one through places I'm less familiar with in the magic world."

"I will take a death's run."

Birsa stared at the table for long moments, some momentous decision taking place.

"By water, then. A boat will get you to Sarg or all the way to Ur. Then foot or horse travel to Parsa or Kiš. Or a more perilous sail to Memfi, with more stops to refill the magic. You could go to Pyra and the great temple there. Or Sakkara. You might even win against the shielders there, but what might you lose?" She looked at the scepter. "The pyramid gates are well known and guarded. My advice would be to follow vaguer tales and try lesser myths." Her gaze swept to Rone and stayed there. "You will be well-equipped."

He felt the sarcastic urge to offer a trip to the Eternal Spring to her list.

Taline's brows drew together. "We have no oar capable of such feat, and we saw no boat with sail grand enough in the harbor."

Birsa looked at the scepter. "You are certain you cannot activate it?"

"Yes."

Birsa drummed her fingers on the table, sighing deeply. "Magic is not part of this world, although magic still influences this world. It can touch it, change it, move it. You simply need to direct it."

"Weather."

Birsa nodded slowly, gaze still drifting continuously to the scepter, but she caught Taline's change in expression. "You have magic with you? Weather capable?"

Taline withdrew one of the three boxes she still had left.

Birsa touched one of the glyphs Taline had carved into the side. "You are talented with wind?" she murmured.

"It is...eternal and free. Unable to be constrained."

"Never truly caged, wind," Birsa murmured. "And when one tries, the pressure simply builds to where it explodes against the hand that makes the attempt."

"But able also to stay and swirl in the valley it desires," Taline replied softly.

Birsa looked down, hiding her expression, then rose with great effort. She walked to a set of thick stone shelves. She lifted one free of its moorings, revealing an empty space behind. Reaching in, she withdrew a sealed, thin-necked container with ten arms of spiraled glass. She held the exquisite creation in her hand for a moment, as if she were death weighing it against a soul.

"Here." She held the absurdly complicated and lovely container out.

Stillness settled across the hut. Rone could see the magic swirling gently within the multicolored glass arms and belly. Could see the wind and sea glyphs etched into the arms and the tiny sealed opening in the long neck at the center. He said nothing as the stillness grew.

Taline carefully cradled the intricately spun glass in her hands. "You brought this with you?"

"The container, yes. The magic...I gathered. From a source five weeks' journey from here over a series of moonrises. Too long for you and Ninli." Taline raised her gaze to solemnly regard the woman. Birsa waved her off, stiffening. "It is nothing. I can gather more."

"Not in this."

"Ninli can return it to me, once you find her."

But the chance that Ninli would be in
the position to return anything—either from
Taline finding her or of her own recognizance
and ability—was so slim that even Taline's
mouth pinched in displeasure at the need to
address it.

"This is your livelihood," Taline said curtly,
unwilling to put anything else into words.
It wasn't a surprise Taline had put together
Birsa's trade between the sign above the door,
the shelves, and décor.

"I sell tokens of good fortune. This town has
tripled in size since I've come. They call me
Luriandur—Devotional of Sea and Storm. And
I will bless this town until the end comes for
me, or for all."

Who had Birsa been before coming here? The
notion struck him sharply, suddenly. What had
Birsa been before?

"You will find a boat for sale in the harbor
that has been thrice blessed by my winds. With
the vessel, it can get you to Sarg, where you
can obtain just enough magic to get you to Ur.
Or you can disembark north of where the sea
greets the gulf, which will set you on a path to

Parsa. For the price of your horses, the boat will be yours."

"We can't trade for the horses," Taline said. "We will leave them freely."

Rone's gaze slid to hers. She met it defiantly. "They aren't ours to trade and we won't put these people in danger should they encounter their original owners. We are in a fishing town."

Rone sighed.

"For the price of that sapphire, then." Birsa nodded at Rone's pack, eyes gone shrewd. He was mildly impressed. The jewels were well hidden. "And in answer to the question I can see upon your face, I was a seeker, young Valeran. Held enslaved by treasure hunters not unlike yourself who sought great fortune and were willing to do whatever it took to gain it."

She looked away, and for a moment, he didn't think she would continue. "Ninli ul Summora was robbing the two men who held my enslavement bonds—looking for some relic or scroll that they had gained—when she took one look at me, broke the oaths upon me, and spirited me away."

She looked at her hands. "It almost broke me, being free once more...I was tired," she said softly. "I...was so very tired."

Taline closed her eyes and her head dropped a notch. Regret tightened every line of her body. "I... I am s—"

"Such fire." Birsa's voice was wistful. "There is such fire in you. That fire was taken from me long ago, and I allowed it to be extinguished. You have made your fire yours, scraped from embers and sparks."

"I'm sorry."

"Living here by the sea among simple folk who care for a good catch and a bright sky makes me feel blessed. Blessed." Birsa closed her eyes. "I will lay my eyes to sleep upon this shore. And I will hope for a moonrise after you release that thing from your skin."

"Birsa—"

Birsa looked at her. "May the winds of Akkan bless your journey, Taline."

Taline looked at the beautiful container in her hand, then at the woman in front of her.

She stood. "May the great waters of Oceana continue to greet you, Birsa."

"May Ferra bless you, Taline ul Summora. You and Ninli and all you hold dear."

Taline bowed stiffly and walked to the door. But at the threshold, she paused. Taline placed her hand against the door and her face tilted back. "You too, Birsa ul Summora."

Then Taline was across the threshold and Rone was left alone to witness Birsa's shocked face, clutched hands, and watery eyes.

Rone ducked through the door and wondered whether he would ever understand the woman who clutched the name Taline ul Summora so close to her heart.

CHAPTER ELEVEN

SEEDS IN SHADOW

NINLI

(MORU, IMPERIAL PROVINCE AND PENINSULA OF THE GREAT WESTERN OCEAN AND MEDIT SEA)

Nin wondered whether she would ever understand Kaveh ul Fehl's drive for conquest.

She watched Kaveh from her pile of blankets and leathers as he stretched and went through the sequence of motions that he did after every battle. In the soft candlelight, he moved through his fifth sequence, and she could see the power surging along his bronzed skin, loosening muscles and opening pathways that had been compressed and soothing ones that had been too stressed.

Shadows pulsed from his skin with each movement, like silt pebbles vibrating over an unending earthquake.

Other shadows flew around him, growing smoother with every new sequence. Like a dance, he would repeat it in the morning, to wake those same muscles and pathways.

Then he would ruthlessly obliterate all who stood in his way.

They had taken Moru quickly. Too quickly, even for a force of nature like Kaveh. The situation left Nin with a feeling of unease. Why kill the padifehl if you were going to be overthrown again so soon?

The Moruvians turning against the empire and killing their padifehl had pulled the full press of the imperial army against them. The full press of Kaveh ul Fehl, the Imperator General, who everyone knew, by now, had returned to the front.

Shirsk and the other Ominous Sea nations could have been forgiven for the knowledge a week ago that he was still alive, given the rumors and his three-day absence from the field of battle while he had chased her.

But in the days since? In an imperial province where knowledge was traded like spell blessings?

Unease shifted through her and she looked in the direction of the palace where the emperor, six princes, and twelve council members were deciding Moru's fate.

Kaveh had abstained. Repetitive conquest and physical maintenance dominated his routine, leaving little room for anything else. Kaveh preferred being in the tent than in the palace, and it showed through the bond.

As he moved through his sequences, she could feel his power and purpose grow and settle in meditative trance. But his movements were done in a progressive manner, as if to fit the interior of the tent. He performed successive movements backward and sideways rather than always continuing forward as she had seen him do on the field.

"Do you practice in here rather than outside so that I cannot escape while you are gone?"

He hadn't been more than thirty feet from her side except when the emperor was involved.

"Are you plotting escape?"

"Indefinitely."

A thin cord of amusement threaded through his focused emotions. "Then yes."

It was a burst of sweetness in his otherwise dark mental landscape. She hungered for it in the way that someone denied a favorite food looked at a plate of it through a gated window.

"You do know that if I had wanted to escape, I would have done so long before now, on some battlefield when you were otherwise occupied."

"I would question your sense, if you tried."

"Yes." Cross-legged, she picked at the blanket beneath her legs. "You miss nothing on the field of battle, do you?"

"You least of all, now."

To their mutual chagrin, their connection was growing stronger. With the immense magic they both performed on and off the field, it wasn't exactly a surprise.

She wondered when the bond broke, whether any of that connection would remain.

Would those bursts of amusement stop for him? What would keep him sane when he was on another battlefield five years from now? Ten?

She looked at Ifret, bandage-free and staring at her from the edge of the blankets. No help from that quarter in the sanity department.

Ifret's attention was focused solely on Nin. When the shadow wasn't killing something, Ifret watched her without fail. One of these days, the shadow would decide what to do with her.

Nin reached out a slow hand and touched her back—surprisingly soft in texture but firm in composition, like a baby sandrake's hide.

A low, rumbling warning came from the shadow, but the warnings were becoming less dire and more habit as each day passed.

Nin took odd comfort in the continued existence of the dark, maternal warnings.

It provided an old comfort. Salare Carre had given the majority of her attention to Savvan and Lorsali—the crown prince and the jewel of the Carres, the two eldest and the figstees of Salare's heart—but a wrong hand or word raised against any of her children had resulted in an automatic loss of said limb and the perpetrator's family annihilated.

Salare had always been eager to spill blood. And she had brooked no outside interference in the lives of her children.

Anguish seeped into memory. A deadly comfort that Nin had avoided as she had realized that receiving evidence that her mother cared had a cost. Dozens of servants had been lost to sibling spats.

Kaveh paused in his sequence and looked at her questioningly.

Nin let the sad and worn memories pass over her and let some power flow from her into the spot where Ifret had taken the direct hit from the sunlight spell. It was the only place where the damage was still obvious. It would take another week or two before it too, was healed, but in the meantime, Ifret had shown no issue with fighting or movement.

In healing Ifret, Nin had, in some way, encouraged the death dealt in all the days since. She could only console herself in the belief that with Ifret and Kaveh on the field, their opponents caved quickly, cutting campaigns that would have taken weeks into battles that took days or even hours.

Unlike the regular shadows Kaveh used and directed in battle, Ifret was fully sentient and capable of making her own decisions. Kaveh's multitude of shadows gained temporary sentience from Kaveh's magic—but that sentience was released when their task was completed. Ifret, on the other hand, was her own being and there was an agitation in her that never seemed to cease—especially when the emperor showed for a status report.

Nin wondered whether that agitation was a side effect of Ifret's creation.

"Is she usually this agitated?"

"Sometimes." His voice was unconcerned. "But she likes you."

Nin thought that was a generous statement. They had come to an unspoken agreement.

Nin didn't try to harm Kaveh, and Ifret didn't painfully kill her. The shadow silently watched Nin when Nin wasn't healing Kaveh or Ifret—and she only hissed like a viper when touching was involved now.

It was a steady state that worked for all involved. "Liking" was another category entirely.

Nin finished her checks and picked through the plate of figstees that she had asked a camp cook for a week prior. He had been sending a plate every night since.

"You shouldn't eat those," Kaveh said.

She selected two and set one in front of the shadow. She knew it would be devoured once their heads were turned.

"You should." Nin bit into the other. "Has Ifret always hated the emperor?"

Kaveh paused. "Why do you say that?"

She felt along the bond to see whether he was serious. The uneasiness buried beneath his suddenly flattened emotions told an entire tale's worth of denial.

She finished her bite, deciding how to respond. Raised in a house of secrets, she had always valued directness in her second life. "You know she hates him, but you try to deny it to yourself. Why?"

"I don't—"

"You do. I can feel it, you know."

His jaw tightened. The rest of his muscles followed, tensing back up after loosening from the movements he had been doing. "No." He restarted one of his sequences.

She nodded in acceptance and ate another figstee. Strong denial sometimes required time and distance more than anything else to loosen its poison.

She watched him move, then touched where the bond was strongest and let her own energy cross it to run alongside his power, loosening areas that needed extra attention—or that had tensed again—as both an apology and a non-apology.

When he finally reached the end of the long sequence, he closed his eyes and let out a breath. Shadows pulsed, then the tent went still, calm.

"The shadows...know. Ifret knows. She knows my father bound my mother."

Quiet shock took her. Everyone knew about Irsula of Denz, certainly—it was part of the emperor's mystique that he had conquered her. There were many things the emperor had done that had captured the attention of the people, but the defeat of the Mistress of Shadows—and the son he had with her—were legend.

That it would engender hate in all bound to Irsula's kind was not an unreasonable assumption.

That Kaveh admitted it, was.

He was singularly loyal to his father. How had the emperor bound his thirteenth blessed and favored child so tightly to him?

"Has Ifret ever attacked the emperor?"

"Once. When she had grown strong enough to do so. The emperor spared her. We came to an...agreement on the matter."

Kaveh had a tremendous amount of control over Ifret, but Nin could not imagine what that agreement must have entailed that the emperor allowed the shadow to live after such an event. The emperor was brilliant, but cold, and although he highly valued his lineage, he knew how to watch his back.

No one had come close to assassinating the emperor in his three decades on the throne. No one.

It had been a good move, whatever the bargain had entailed. Ifret was part of Kaveh's lore—an unbeatable combination at the right hand of the emperor.

"You said she's been with you since birth," she said, testing out what else he was willing to share.

"Yes. But she grew far stronger when I turned five."

"You Awakened at five?"

"Officially? Yes."

"And unofficially?" Because she knew this song and dance.

"Unofficially, a portion of my power has been active since birth. At five, I unlocked something and both Ifret and I became stronger. The emperor said it was a Shadow Awakening. Ifret doesn't speak to me in words. It's more a sharing of feelings. It's...a little like our oath bond."

The outward discomfort in him when he thought about the bond was still strong—but there was an inner fierceness that was starting to overtake it.

It made her mind whirl. He had accepted their bond so quickly—like a man starving. He had already slotted her into a permanent spot at his side, a mere eight days after forming their oath.

Kaveh ul Fehl, the man who needed no one.

She didn't know what to do with her own shifting emotions, no less Kaveh's, which were impossible to measure in how fast they could travel from ice cold to passionately hot. But then, the heat was only ever reflected in his eyes—without the bond, would anyone think him anything but wintry?

"Ifret is very protective of you," Nin said, determined not to let her confused feelings get away from her.

"I was raised in the imperial nursery, same as the others who were cultivated deliberately. But I was always different. Dark. There's a darkness in me." He stared at her without regret. "You feel it."

She acknowledged his statement with a dip of her head, not breaking his gaze. She had known she was going to die by his hand the first time they had fought, and she had felt Taline's death in his outstretched fingers.

Remorseless deaths—predatory satisfaction, the only emotional component that would have been involved.

But she already knew intimately what it felt like to have someone plotting her death. Kaveh's emotionless and animalistic desire to kill her had been nothing compared to the red-hot passion of family trying to do her in.

"You enjoy the kill," she said steadily.

"It's something that has always been there. I've always embraced it, and little regretted." He raised a shadow to float above his palm. "People are always afraid. Terrified creatures, humans. And something surges within me at fear. A predatory drive."

Nin could feel it coiling in the air now—that predatory drive.

He looked at her. "Others can feel it. They always have. And when caregivers perished suspiciously without a mark upon them, the emperor simply hired more, and smiled. Some tried to get past their fear, but within a day of arrival to the nursery, no one ever touched me."

"Your existence terrified them and that fed your nature from birth." She reached out and touched the shadow. It swam around her palm. "You grew and lived within their terror."

A bad arrangement for all involved in it, for the caregivers' fear had been justifiable. Fear was an overwhelming emotion that was so very difficult to push past. And the emperor had been feeding his people to the developing killer in their midst.

"They used to dress me with spells. When Ifret gained true power, the deaths turned...bloody, and obvious. The emperor moved us to our own rooms and into the execution ranks. Gave us purpose. Death was plentiful. Control was easier after that."

Beware the Shadow Prince. He will take your soul and consume it, for he is always looking for something to fill his soulless state.

She had accepted that vision of him, same as anyone who came into contact with him. But that wasn't all that lurked beneath his veneer. Death, yes—the darkness was there, swirling and immense—but intense curiosity and drive threaded everywhere through the mass. Undying loyalty. Protective instincts. Instincts that were iron hard, but that hadn't been nurtured past the nuggets naturally extended. To the emperor, Ifret...

She wasn't certain there were any others. Maybe the empire itself was included in the set.

To those three, his loyalty was ironclad.

"Your mother—do you see her?"

Nin was no stranger to royal nurseries. She had been raised in the children's quarters, by her early handmaidens, and by Farrah. But she had interacted with Salare. The queen made certain to check in on her children, even if dispassionately and coldly. She had been strict with her expectations for excellence.

More than one servant had suffered over a perceived lack of progress in their charge. Zehra Amanan Carre had made certain to always succeed.

"I saw her once a year for my first sixteen."

Nin wasn't certain which would have been more surprising—that he had nothing to do with his mother or that he actually visited her mythic tower.

"What is she like?"

"Irsula of Denz is the first and only of her kind." He lifted a figstee from her plate. "Born of Darkness's desire to understand humanity. Darkness waited for a woman of dark desires who found her equal in a man. And when they coupled, Darkness took hold. Neither woman or man survived the birth of Darkness's spawn. Darkness delighted."

That told her little of Irsula herself. Nin looked at Ifret, who was watching her narrowly. "Did she help you learn your powers?"

Kaveh turned the figstee in his fingers. "She doesn't register human emotions in the same way as you. She is even more animal-like than I am in the way that she sees things. If she had the ability to break free from her captivity in the palace's highest tower, she would be as likely to eliminate me as any other." His emotions were flat and honest.

"Why visit then?" She pressed, trying to piece together the information she had. Ifret took a saber-toothed bite out of the figstee Nin had set before her, eyes boring holes through Nin.

"The emperor thought it fitting that I visit each Feast Day of Shadows—the day dedicated to all things in our power. She said little to me until the feast day after I took control of the imperial armies." He smiled coldly. "She said he had always had me visit on feast day to keep our power in one place while the shadows crawled, and that now that he had me firmly in his pocket, I would be allowed a longer leash on a too-short chain. She stopped responding to me at all after that."

He tossed the figstee to the plate and took a long drink of water. "I haven't been to visit her in six years."

"And Ifret?"

He looked at her strangely, trapping her in his gaze in the overwhelming way he had. "Ifret what?"

She could feel the shadow's gaze boring into her. "Did she like your mother?"

"All beings of darkness bow to the Mistress of Shadows."

She itched to ask more but promise held her. She rephrased her earlier question. "What is she personally like?"

He took a long time to answer. Long enough that she wasn't sure he would. "Cold. Bitter. Trapped."

Nin absorbed that. "And you don't...want the emperor to release her?"

"She would kill him if she were released. The emperor can never let her go. He caught her once, and once alone. He would never manage it again. He only cut her power successfully because she didn't know how to fight it for the eight hours in which he held her."

Eight hours... And here Kaveh was before her.

"You don't think...there is something wrong with any of that?" she asked carefully. It was a prickly subject—rebuking the emperor. He was the only one who pulled emotions from Kaveh that were out of his baseline disregard.

"He made an extremely poor decision, then did what he had to do in order to survive the aftermath. As far as I know, he has refrained from similar choices since. No more creatures of darkness, only princesses or magi of power."

"How did he capture her in the first place?"

"He took her power," he said casually. "But she isn't human. She is Darkness's desire to see itself in human form. She is half-human, at best. The emperor couldn't cut off her access to her power forevermore, and she won't be caught in his trap again."

"Useful, such regeneration," she murmured. Though it hadn't saved Irsula from her cage. "And you?"

"My power can be cut off, same as any other magi's." He flexed his wrists.

She remembered him girding himself during the emperor's disappointment. "You've had it done to you."

"Once. The emperor wanted to see if my power could regenerate like my mother's. He held mine for a week." Kaveh's flatter emotions twisted. He rose and restarted a sequence. "And he maintained it clearly the whole time. He was relieved."

"Of course he was," she whispered, watching him seamlessly slide through the motions to regulate his emotional state back to even.

Kaveh's answering smile was cool, but not angry, emotions already baselining again. "The emperor needs to reign supreme. My mother can defeat my father, but trickery ensured she will never be free. No one else has stood a chance. Trusting those with the ability to spell your doom is a difficult task. The emperor does what he must."

Oh, Nin understood exactly what the emperor had done. The emperor had neatly bound Kaveh to him—bound him intensely—for even now, Nin could feel his unwavering loyalty. But the emperor had also made certain if that loyalty were lost, his thirteenth son could be contained.

Kaveh ul Fehl's battle sense, tactics, vision, and power were legend. To lose him would be a blow to the emperor—to have Kaveh turned against him would be far worse.

No one had ever exclaimed or complained over the emperor's overwhelming kindness.

Nor had they for Kaveh, but...

Sometimes there was a dryness to his tone—a hint of dark humor she had seen a few times now, humor he usually kept firmly hidden.

"What drives you?"

His motions didn't pause, but she felt his surprise. His gaze shifted to pinpoint on her—a perceptible question in the bond as he continued moving and didn't verbally respond.

"Helip, Rasse, Yalendil, Orso—whatever country is next? What do you seek?" she clarified. "You don't do it for the glory, and you cannot say you are seeking revenge outside of Moru."

"I seek whatever is on the border," he said, body smoothly moving, voice dismissive, but still actively engaged in the bond. It was strange how accustomed she was getting to having his emotions floating in the background of hers.

"Next in line?" She drew her fingers across the blankets. "Is that all?"

"Is that not enough?"

She looked at his endless motions. "It doesn't appear to be so."

She thought of the boys. Of the hundreds who would die tomorrow and the dozens she might be able to save.

She had a spot now, easy to open, where she stashed them in a deserted southern Tehrasian oasis she had discovered long ago. Sometimes she couldn't save them a second time.

Something of her thoughts must have bled through—either that or he, too, was getting better at reading her.

"All you save your ducklings from is death tomorrow. Especially those spawned from the enemy. And all you create for yourself is conflict. You won't use your powers offensively. You won't use your real powers to aid the empire. Yet, you open ripgates and slip useless soldiers through from all sides. Someone will comment on it eventually and word will reach the emperor."

He said it calmly. It was one thing he had not asked of her—to use her real powers in any way. He followed the rules, when there were rules to be had. He seemed determined to stick to the letter of their oath, and that included a month's grace period should Taline and Rone actually return with the scepter.

That grace period would be lost to the winds should the emperor find out about her powers or lineage. She had no idea why Aros hadn't already given her away.

"I do it because I must."

"You risk yourself for waste."

She closed her eyes. "Do you know how old those boys are?" Just awakening their powers and put on the field to die.

"Does it matter?"

"It should always matter."

"They signed up to fight. Their wages support their families. Their death marks earn them a generous settlement."

His emotions matched his callous expression and words. There was no malice to them, just a total disregard for the lives of which he was speaking.

She changed tactics. "Why are such young forces even necessary for the empire? I saw you on the battlefield. You handled nearly the entirety of the Shirsken forces by yourself...the same with Moru, Helip, Rasse, Yalendil, Orso... The boys were but fodder for the forces who hadn't yet died by your hand."

"Shirsk had been a neutral threat a week before the uprising. I wouldn't have even been there had the Shirskens not been driven to rise. As to the other fields, the generals are in charge of their segments and the individual forces beneath. That is why I told you to raise the generals, and by highest level first," he said pointedly. "They take care of those beneath them, and those beneath do the same. A chain—not a single thief rummaging through the streets."

"I've seen those generals. Not all of them treat those beneath them well." She had been hard-pressed to rouse one leader in particular when he had fallen. But she had done so. "And the generals above care not either. You do not."

"If I care what happens to a single bit of fodder, I will not win the war," he said dismissively.

"The fodder are your people."

She stared at the blanket clutched in her fingers. So drowned in feeling, she startled when his fingers touched her skin. He had been skittish of touch when she had first started healing him—almost disgusted by it—but over the past week, with her healing his minor wounds each night, he had initiated contact three times.

It was a shock, each one. And it lit the bond between them each time.

He turned her chin up to him, making her fingers clench the soft fabric further, and she could feel the simultaneous clench in him—so unused to touching anyone else except to kill. "Do you know what the Orso do to their young?"

She had seen the marks on the battlefield. Old marks. She knew what they did.

"You do know," he said calmly, without waiting for an answer. "And you don't want the empire to overthrow them?"

She couldn't look away. His eyes looked black from far away, but she had been surprised to find they were actually flecked with golden brown, mesmerizing when seen so close. His eyes seared against hers, seeking agreement.

"Then onto the next battle, the next country, the next front?" she asked unsteadily.

"Yes."

"And when will it end?"

His eyes hardened. "There is no end, until we come full circle back to our border again."

"The whole world? Then the next?"

He stared at her without response, but she could feel his emotions, his hard certainty, even as his fingers slipped from her skin.

"Why?" she asked.

"Because it will be next."

"Because the emperor asks it of you," she corrected tightly, watching him tense.

"I do as the emperor wills."

"The emperor needs to take care."

"The emperor is ever careful."

"Of his empire," she clarified. "I watched my family not care about the populace they ruled. And I watch as your empire does the same."

"The emperor—"

"The emperor cares about his advancement and the advancement of the empire. Always for what is next. He cares little for what is behind." She thought of Akel and the other boys. Of Rone. "All you have to do is see those who are born to him upon the streets."

"He seeds and unites the lands," Kaveh said tightly.

She watched his fingers curl.

Kaveh ul Fehl was terrible at debate. He wasn't used to people arguing with him. She knew that well by now. He often had no idea what to do when she argued with him.

It was a singular situation. He couldn't hurt her. Couldn't throw her to the wolves. The oath was adamant.

And for all the consternation it seemed to cause him...she could feel that he liked it when she argued. There was always a sliver of pleasure under his irritation. Whether it was because no one else dared, she didn't know. But it made it easy to push. Each argument made him open up more and so, push she did.

This man—if rumor, Aros's expressions, and the emperor's glances were anything to go by—was the heir apparent to the empire. She would never get through to the emperor. But to the man before her?

"Uniting the tribes and kingdoms, bringing technology and steadier trade routes. There are good things that have happened under the empire," she agreed, stretching her fingers and using a pacifistic tone. "But how do you regulate lands on the other side of the world? Where does it stop? Your father knows much about conquest, as do you, but he puts too much emphasis on power."

"Rich talk for a Carre—the pull of power. Your family were isolationists because they couldn't give up their pleasures and control."

She nodded. "Isolation keeps the populace under control. That is something your empire will continue to struggle with. Your father leaves seeds of greatness, but he doesn't nurture those seeds. He leaves them scrambling to survive."

"Greatness is begot from survival."

"And sometimes greatness requires a helping hand," she said quietly.

"A helping hand? You are a Carre. Your family slaughtered thousands in the festivals. You had a festival called the Festival of Blood. Your family were crooks and thieves, securing only the best bargains for themselves and ruining any who stood in their way. You think to lecture me on people under Fehl rule? A thief in blood and present deed?"

"Yes," she said. "A thief I may be, but one who knows the hand from which I steal. My family is dead. Yours will follow if you don't heed the lessons of the past."

"You have no leg to stand on in any argument of this kind," he said harshly.

"If you define my actions by those of my family, I have few limbs to call my own." She curled her fingers against her chest. "If I'm always to be haunted by their past choices, then I never will gain leg. But if I choose a path—be that the same path as those before me, or a path as different as starlight to the sun—then that choice is purely mine. And I ask that you judge me on it."

She looked at him. "I choose a different path than those who came before me," she stated softly. "What path will you choose, Shadow Prince?"

"I will choose—"

A pulse split the air—like the displacement of a ripgate—a feel that every red-eyed Carre knew.

Nin jumped into a crouch and a pitcher of water splashed to the colorful soft carpets in the glowing tent as she threw a blast of wind at the source. Wrapped head-to-toe, the figure sidestepped the spell and surged forward.

Ifret lunged from the side and clamped venomous fangs around the figure's forearm. The assassin screamed—a gut-wrenching, horrifying sound. She couldn't see Ifret's black poison visibly constricting the man's veins—the shadow was wrapped too tightly around him—but she had seen the results on the battlefield hundreds of times now. The assassin dropped to the floor an instant later, dead.

From behind Ifret, a spelled knife fell.

Nin held out her hand and pulled. The second assassin's knife stabbed into the bedding. This assassin was better—he didn't freeze or wait, already turning to meet Kaveh's attack. But Kaveh was no average opponent, and the front of the assassin's throat ripped free of his neck.

There was a cracking sound, then toxic smoke filled the tent. Nin lifted a hand to wave the fumes away with a spell, but Kaveh's shadows were converging from the sides and ceiling—diving into a knot and consuming all the toxins in a frenzy of ingested air.

The third assassin, and the fourth, fell with the knot, but it was the fifth who was the real threat. His figure appeared out of nowhere, as if a ripgate had opened from the fourth assassin's pocket in the fall. The man lunged through the swarming shadows.

Nin reacted automatically and grabbed the knife by the blade as it struck toward Kaveh. Blood spurt from her palm and fingers. Kaveh's shadows burst through the assassin's body, ripping him apart in chunks of cloth and gore.

The blade, with its hilt still clutched in the assassin's detached hand, was stuck through her palm. She took a deep breath and pulled it free. Black tendrils snaked across her skin.

She paused the knife's poison before it reached her wrist and used her other hand to form a spell cleanser. She clasped her hands together, pressing the spell to the wound, then drew the poison outward, flicking it into a conjured container. It was a laborious process but was made easier by not having to fake her skill level.

There was nothing revolutionary about this particular toxicant—it was a familiar one.

The Carres had used poisons as frequently as they had used beauty enchantments. She had known how to create a poison long before she had learned how to remove one.

And she well knew this poison. Coupled with how the fifth assassin had appeared...

She looked at the fourth body and the glint of gold spilling from a pocket. A colorless stone was cracked and smoking—melting into the blanket beneath. An amulet? Designs were embedded in the gold. Glyphs, incomprehensible as always, covered the fine metal and curled around its sides. She leaned forward to create a mental picture to suss out, letter-by-letter, later.

Before she could, shadows swarmed the five dead bodies, consuming them in darkness. When the dark swarm lifted, the bodies were gone, along with the gold piece and ruined blankets.

"Your fingers."

Warm hands touched hers for the second time that night.

She looked down. Unlike her palm, the ends of her fingers were still burnt and crisp from where she had touched the blade. The poison had been removed, but the healing was incomplete.

Kaveh's fingers closed over hers and the burns went numb. Her skin began healing without her aid.

Shock took her. "You know how to heal someone else?" There was a huge difference between healing oneself and healing another.

"No. But you've used that spell a thousand times on the battlefield."

She examined his face, then the bond, for a lie. "You need to have an in-depth knowledge of human organs, in general, or an intimate feel for another's body."

"I've felt you do it a thousand times now. Watching a thousand others perform it would give different results every time, but the feel of you is always the same."

"We share emotions through the bond. Not physical knowledge."

He touched her fingers, healing each burn with the intensity of a heart transplant. "You've had knowledge of countless people. To you, the bond is probably just like any other foolish relationship you participate in—one of many that have floated through your mind. I have only you."

She stared at him as he finished. She could have removed her hand at any time and finished healing herself. It was a simple process.

She stayed still.

Ifret coiled on her favorite pillow again, gaze focused intently on Nin.

"Why?" Kaveh asked as he set her hand on her lap.

"Isn't that the question I should be asking you?" she murmured, watching him.

"The oath ends should I die by a hand that has nothing to do with you," he said evenly. "You would have been free had that knife fallen."

She examined him as carefully as he was examining her. "You would have killed those assassins without my aid. Maybe I was trying to gain favor."

"You moved immediately. No hesitation. And I feel your lie. You did not do it to gain favor."

"I would heal anyone who needed it." It was true. She threaded her healed fingers together.

He tipped his head. "Yes. But that's not why you moved as you did."

"A product of the bond, then." She stared straight at him.

He leaned forward, tilting his head curiously, like a dangerous, wild animal. "No. You are intrigued by me."

She swallowed. "You would intrigue anyone."

"You don't fear me."

"You kill without regret. You admit you enjoy both the chase and the slaughter. I've seen you kill countless people in a nearly endless loop of battles."

"You don't fear me."

She licked her suddenly dry lips. "No."

"You trust me."

He was dangerous; Sehk, was he dangerous. And his darkness wasn't a mask. It was a deep core attribute. But the things he cared about—it made him easy to anticipate.

"In some matters."

"Why?"

"I... Maybe I understand you," she said in a voice that suddenly felt too breathy and thin.

He regarded her, only the intensifying feel of the bond giving away anything other than the same bone-deep curiosity he had been sporting.

"You have bloodlust within you. Buried deep."

"I'm Carre-born." She swallowed, picking at the blanket beneath her fingers once again. "We aren't the most stable of souls."

"You put that soul into healing the poor and useless, when you could be a queen." Shadows shifted around him, as if in question. "You were made to be strong, born with the blessing of the gods."

"Maybe I was born to bring change, to be the agent of the people."

"You were born to power, as was I."

"We were born with choice. We don't have to be defined by the gifts, or lack thereof, of our birth."

His fingers circled her chin and his other hand waved over her eyes, canceling the enchantment with bruising ease after watching her cast the spell so many times. "You are a princess. Zehra Amanan Carre. You have the forces of the gods themselves at your hands—the ability to slice worlds."

She stared straight into his dark, speckled eyes, knowing hers were blood red. "I am an orphan. I was born with the forces of the Carres, and I have chosen my path. I am Ninli ul Summora in deed."

"You will change your mind."

She picked up a figstee, then lifted a second and put it in his hand. "Or maybe you will change yours."

~*~

They received a new, clean tent, blankets, and the news that Urful ul Fehl, Padifehl of Shoune, twelfth blessed by the emperor, had been assassinated in the country just south of their position during the night.

CHAPTER TWELVE

WINDSWEPT MADNESS

RONE

(The Fehl Sea of the First Layer)

As Birsa had said, a sapphire had gained them a boat thrice blessed. An easy breeze had set them off from shore. And when they could no longer see the coastline, they unsealed the container.

The spiraled glass was designed for precise control. Curving glass arms held different weather glyphs upon which to press, and the tiny mouth exerted pinpointed streams of magic. They wouldn't need to worry about a sudden gale that might whip them somewhere farther from home.

With a main sail, two oars, and two fishing nets, there was only enough room for the two of them and their packs.

Rone watched Taline as she steered their small craft toward the setting sun. Even with the scepter unforgivably attached to her palm, she managed to use her fingers to stroke the glyphs and part the wind flows. With her feet pressed to the shipboards and her long hair blowing in the breeze, her eyes fiercely watched the waves that could potentially overwhelm them.

They had set the horses free instead of negotiating for more supplies. And they had given a warning to the townsfolk that the horses belonged to men who might seek their return, in case the townsfolk decided to chase the animals down.

Rone had not been a proponent of that plan. Damn Summoras, always giving away their valuables.

They rode the waves quietly for hours as the sun slipped down the sky. They took turns with the weather spells, sending the small craft soaring and skipping over waves in the gentle hand of manufactured wind. The glyphs in the curved glass served to use the currents flowing past the outer arms at the same time, an ingenious way of ensuring that once they were underway, they would stay that way.

Rone examined Taline as she guided them over a long set of swells with an easy undulation of her free wrist.

She looked at peace as she steered the craft around the great desert peninsula. There were still lines of tension in her body that would likely not release until her sister was safely tucked beneath her wing again, but he wasn't certain he had ever seen her face look so serene.

In contrast to her serenity, uneasiness claimed him as a strip of power moved from the scepter through Taline to the glass and back again. She seemed entirely unaware, but it was the third time he had seen it happen.

He started to rise. "I suppose it's my turn at the helm," he said, injecting just the right amount of boredom to his voice.

"You worry loudly, Valeran," she said, without taking her gaze away from the horizon. "The scepter's power is passive only—tasting, testing.

I can handle it. Twenty more swells and you can take your turn."

He sat back again, but kept an eye on the scepter. Taline was one of the most stalwart magi he had ever met, but the scepter was an inhumane temptation. "I worry not. Even I can acknowledge you are talented with wind and device."

"I do love working with the breeze," she said softly, wistful. "A changeable, flexible element that can never be truly snuffed or captured—only gently steered."

He closed his eyes, concentrating on the undulating waves beneath the boat and not the longing in her voice or the way the breeze caressed and knotted her hair.

"Nin would love this," she said, the wistfulness turning the slightest shade sad. "I wonder how she is?"

"Skirting a cage, undoubtedly." He looked at the setting sun in the west.

"I won't allow it." The darkness in Taline's voice vied with the fey vision of her at the helm.

"She will never be free, narsumina," he said tiredly. "No matter if you get that scepter to her or not, no matter if you make a clean escape, she will always be hunted. You understand that?"

Taline didn't reply.

He leaned his head back against the wood. "For all the overwhelming things she's been able to accomplish, she will never again lead a free life."

A small spray of sea splashed across the bow. Taline's eyes remained focused on the swell, lips silent.

"If you deliver the scepter to the Fehls, narsumina, it will stay her death, but they will never let her power go. She will never again be the thief in the night, righting wrongs—the Hand in the darkness so others can live in the light—she will never be the same."

Taline hefted the boat farther up the swell, then let it fall forward to ride peacefully with the reduction of power. "She will still be my sister."

"She will never be the same."

"You speak as if people never change. As if we all exist in a slotted space with a child's preassigned role, unable to fail and grow and move forward."

He crossed his ankles, absently picking at the strings of a net as he surreptitiously monitored her continued usage of magic. "Life preassigns us all."

"Does it, Valeran?" She pushed the craft over another swell. "You said I have talent with wind. I wasn't always a low-level spellkeeper. I was studying to be a windchaser for the horse tribe of the Ameni. I would have been a Level Six—good enough to wield for any city guild, but far less useful in our tribe. As the use for horses dwindled and they were replaced by other, faster means of general travel, my father refused to lead the tribe in the progression. He insisted horsemasters would prevail as long as the guild held firm and didn't change. He believed they just needed funds to survive a little longer. So I was given as gift to satisfy my tribe's failing occupational legacy. Repeatedly crippled to a Level Two—just enough to allow minimum healing—by my purchaser, a man who wanted to make certain I could never run. I thought my dreams as dead as I. And yet,

I lived on. Endured. Until I met Nin. Until I saw someone who hadn't just endured but had succeeded."

"You were given to Etelian ul Fehl." Rone had suspected. The clues were all there. Etelian's household was notorious for its high turnover and the hushed rumors of what occurred within.

But Rone had never wanted to know Taline's past. Knowledge was power, but sometimes knowledge was damnation.

Taline ul Summora was far easier to keep at arm's length as the brittle general of Ninli's crusade, instead of the damaged right hand who had to be brittle to hold things together.

"It was quite an honor for my family." She smiled strangely and the scepter sparked. "My sacrifice earned them respite. They received enough from their gift to keep their failing business going ten years more. I've yet to see them do what is necessary to succeed past those coins' end, though—they look only to the past and bitterly complain about the future."

"Such is humanity."

She said nothing for a long moment. "Nin has shown me there are those who strive for better."

He watched her. "The only way one leaves Etelian's service is in a box."

"It was a very nice box." Taline hummed, and a smile curved her generous mouth. "I feel the need to describe it. A closed chariot with generous gold embellishments, and a lovely underframe of wood. He had left me completely stripped of magic, internally bleeding, and with five broken bones—not the face, of course, never the face—while he ventured inside District One's diversion hall to purge the rest of his anger. Trapped within the excess he so loved, when the fire caught hold, the flames were soothing against all that interior gold."

The wind caught a lock of hair and pulled it along her cheek, caressing her skin.

"Nin saved you from the fire."

"She had planned to rob him. Her face was quite startled when she looked inside and saw me."

"How did the chariot catch fire?"

Her smile grew. "After Nin saw me, she lit the chariot on fire."

He sighed. "You are, all of you, mad."

"Yes. Mad." Taline's voice went faraway. "She told me to trust her. She was a complete stranger—a tiny girl who looked like she hadn't eaten in days. Then she...touched me." Her fingers slid slowly to her cheekbone. "She put her palm here and told me that she would not leave me. I...believed her."

And that was why Ninli ul Summora was dangerous.

Damn Summoras.

"So she saved you with a ripgate, I assume. Then viciously disconnected all your oaths and made it appear as if you died in the fire, forged you a new identity, and in return, you guiltily stayed by her side to lead a vigorous life of crime together."

She visibly shook herself free of her memories. "You deal in guilt, Valeran. Selectively, to be sure, and I suspect only with Nin. But you believe in a bargain system because you can trust nothing else. Which is why guilt is my most potent weapon against you and most of the others. But that is your curse, not mine. I do not stay because of guilt."

He smiled carelessly. "Ninli has enough guilt for both of you, I suppose. You stay because of pigheaded stubbornness."

She tilted her head, her hair blowing free of her cheek. A moon divinity given life. "Yes. Stubbornness. We were speaking of assignment and life before you asked about Etelian ul Fehl—as if change doesn't befall the most rigid of us." She looked at her hands—at the vessel in one palm and the scepter in the other. "Nin healed the physical damage Etelian caused, but there was nothing to be done about the continuous draining of my magic levels over years of wear. Etelian didn't like his property to be able to get away, you see, and an empowered magi is a magi who can run. And, though his power is nothing compared to the emperor's, continued application does take a permanent toll."

Bile rose in Rone, black and festering.

"I had to learn to be creative and invent ways to be useful as I scraped my magic back to a bare

Level Five. And I did. I looked at Nin and what she was accomplishing, and I wanted to endure. If you put complete stock in what you have at any moment, you won't be able to endure when things change. And they always change. Life moves. Like the waves."

She looked ahead, focusing on her motions. "Some things wear more slowly, though. The rock in the river. That was me. The water rushed, and I endured. The salmon in the river, that's Nin. She darts and the river shoves and pushes, and she goes forward. And it is hard to be the rock when your companion is the salmon. It is hard not to grow flippers or fins or feet. And one day...you have to choose. The salmon goes farther upstream and the rock remains. And the question becomes—do you remain the enduring rock, or become the intrepid salmon?"

She looked back at him. "So I chose. And as I go—as I keep going—I grow stronger. In here." She touched her chest with her sceptered fist. "That's why I keep moving. And that's why I care not if Nin needs a different existence when we return. We will move forward, forge a new path, together," she said quietly along the wind.

Damn Summoras.

He observed her, the enduring strength of her body, the wind catching her hair, but not moving her from her stance. "You are not the salmon."

She gripped the glass vessel, lips tight, and looked back out over the waves. "No, I suppose not. Some bedraggled hagfish, then, flopping about in continuous mortal peril as she tries to keep up with the sleeker fish of the school, then."

He looked at her standing there, accepting her supporting role and yet always fighting, never breaking. He thought of her indignation at Birsa and the others who had left Nin. He thought of Taline's quiet semi-acceptance at the end of their visit—understanding Birsa better, but yet never doubting her own choices in following behind her savior.

"No. You are the rock that moves upstream," he murmured. "Defying all."

The boat missed a wave and water crashed over the bow as she looked at him, startled. "What?"

Water dripped down her face, but did nothing to dim her inner fire, even in surprise.

"You protect her tail as she weaves around dangers. Shield her when the currents become too fierce. Hide her when there are jagged rocks. You will never be the salmon. But you move because your will is greater than the river's. And it will always be."

TALINE

Taline stared at Valeran, lips parting. He stared back, an unusually serious expression on his face for once.

She thought of Nin, of Valeran, of Birsa and all the others in the stream. She thought of loyalty, power, and magic. She looked at the man splayed at the side of the boat. "Valeran—"

Something clicked within. The scepter lit, the glass container shrieked, and light burst everywhere. Birsa's container shook with screams. Black clouds roiled across the sky, pushing the setting sun into darkness.

"What—?"

Unbridled power ran through her.

Birsa's endlessly spiraled glass container connected to the scepter, then that power screamed outward. The covering atop the scepter's head blew apart and the power continued unimpeded, opening a ripgate.

But it wasn't a ripgate like any she had seen Nin create. Nin's were small and personal with the warmth of Nin's magic. This was a rip in the air ten feet tall—dark, cold, and perfectly edged. A wave crashed around it and the water sliced against the edges—a doorway parting the sea.

Inside the doorway, she could see Birsa, Osni, and the men from the inn.

Birsa was fighting against five of them, and without magic to aid her, she was losing. The look of the men was one of anger heightened to the extreme. Unnatural.

The unnaturalness was perhaps explained by the other man in the room—and the ceremonial scepter he held in his hand.

Osni flung himself around to face the rip in the air, as if compelled by the feel of the scepter Taline held—his own scepter glowing in response. Hungry, maddened eyes traveled between the two scepters—locking onto her lit palm—and Osni limped forward, scepter hand extended, the other gripping the locket around his neck. "It will be mine! And I will have her back! And we will rule all of—"

"Taline!" Birsa kicked Osni hard enough that he fell to the ground. "Don't—"

A man grabbed Birsa, yanking the rest of her words from her lips, his hand dipping low. "We are going to have fun, you and—"

The world went white and black around Taline—the white silhouettes of the figures existing in cutouts of darkness. The world didn't need these men.

She pushed the doorway forward, slicing through sea and hut. Those standing nearest to the edge faltered, then fell. Osni seemed oddly unstable on his feet and he couldn't stop his sudden forward momentum, as he, too, dropped into the churning sea between Taline and the door. Two men still inside the hut scrambled, screaming, and tried to run. Taline rotated the doorway a quarter turn forward, then dipped it into the ground. The running men tripped and fell into the sea on the other side of the flattened, rotated gate.

Birsa and the man who held her were the last. Only their upper halves were visible, with the doorway all around them. A wave crashed over the top of the doorway, drenching them. The man tightened his grip on Birsa, violently tugging her to him. Taline pulled the outstretched scepter slowly back toward her chest.

Birsa's eyes went wide and she ceased struggling, letting her body drop with sudden weight. The man holding her fumbled his grip as Birsa collapsed to the ground—falling beneath the flattened doorway and out of view—leaving only the upper portion of the man above the gate over the sea. Taline pulled the scepter. The doorway swiftly followed the motion, slicing the man clean in half.

She rotated the doorway upright and the upper half of the man fell into the sea. The men below screamed and started swimming against the churning waves.

Birsa kicked the rest of the man through, then slumped to the floor, looking through the perpendicular gateway with impossibly wide eyes.

Birsa's gaze never left hers—equal parts awe and terror—with the reflection of an overwhelming white light.

Taline opened her mouth to say something, but a sharp tug turned her toward the churning waves.

Osni's scepter was pointed at her and he was chanting. Madness exuded from his eyes.

"No," she said calmly.

She lifted and spun the doorway. Vast landscapes swirled within—quadrants painted in possibilities—before settling on a seething vista full of giant, snarling beings with fangs and wings. She pulled the door forward like a ladle and scooped every last man—and body part—inside. Osni yelled furiously as he was poured into the other world.

The beings on the other side opened their mouths and shrieked in delight as one after the other fell within. Osni managed to dodge the maws, but she couldn't see where he fell.

"Sehk's Gate," she heard Valeran swear.

Power like nothing she had ever experienced surged through her. The lust of dominance and dominion. Of revenge. She could do anything.

She spun the gateway again, looking for another world. There were others she could punish. Others who deserved—

Papered fibers suddenly wrapped her right arm. The power flowing through her abruptly ceased and the world spun wildly. The press of firm fingers and blocking spells coiled around her skin.

Burn this hindrance through.

She raised the scepter. She would kill all who had created such a block.

"Narsumina." Palms framed her cheeks and she prepared to open another ripgate to cut the man before her in two. "Narsumina. Taline."

She blinked. Exhaustion rippled violently through her. The last of the magic collapsed.

She fell. Hands roughly caught her and lowered her into the wooden belly of the tiny craft. She couldn't catch her breath. She was going to die. Then arms were around her. Awkward pats. Not like Nin's all-encompassing hugs. But still an ember of flame in the midst of the ice crawling toward her heart.

She latched onto the flame.

Ice turned to water, and water to steam.

She was adrift in a suddenly stagnant sea. The sun slipped below the horizon, freed from its temporary darkness, and its last gasp echoed one last blast in colors around them, lighting everything in reds, oranges, and yellows.

"You in there?" a voice hesitantly asked.

She blinked at Rone ul Valeran, who veritably shone in such colors of light. "Why is your hair so stupid?"

He slumped above her and closed his eyes, like a great relief had taken hold of him. "You're in there."

"Like it's on fire at sunset."

"As opposed to yours, dark as midnight and flying in all directions a few moments ago. Anything else to add?"

"You are stupid. Like your hair."

"One of us is. Definitely."

The scepter was dormant in her palm—once again a decorative piece. But the power... What she could do with this power...

"So...the scepter works." Valeran looked over the side of the boat and grimaced at something floating in the water. She must have missed a piece. Hysteria crept up her throat as he continued speaking. "Unfortunately, just as described."

"They were going to—"

"I know."

"And Birsa—"

"I know." His hand hovered above hers for a moment, before withdrawing. "Do you know where you put them?"

"In the world of beasts, I think."

"No, truly?" he deadpanned. "I meant where in the world of beasts? Their world is a duplicate of ours. If we can—"

"I... That information was not given to me."

Location had never been her strong suit. Knowing every trade route around the Casp Sea? Yes. Knowing every secret route in Tehras? Yes.

Knowing anything about the world's land spaces at large? No. She had never been outside the Casp nations unless it had been through one of Nin's ripgates.

There were five layers. Everyone knew that. Five layers that had been split five hundred years before. Each contained a copy of the same lands. Two contained people of magic forging their own kingdoms, one was full of beasts and bestial beings who were born of and thrived on magic, one was an unstable wasteland full of endless trials, and one—the one they were within—was for people and creatures without magic.

Layered copies of each other—a well-traveled person would have been able to guess at a location.

Someone like Valeran, who had traveled their own world as well as the others, would have probably known immediately through the feel alone.

"Could you tell?" she asked.

"Those beasts were despiers. They are nomadic, unfortunately, so knowing what they are still makes pinpointing a location hard. They consume all and move on—a ravenous plague upon whatever new place they seek to overtake."

She shivered. "Osni is dead." Along with the others. She closed her eyes. *Nin, you never wanted me to become a murderer, but it is one.*

"Did you see Osni die?" he asked carefully.

Her eyes snapped open. "He could not have survived."

Valeran looked grimly at the too-calm sea. "Never underestimate the power of a scepter.

He has wielded that one long enough to guess its secrets."

"A single scepter—"

"You hold a single scepter."

She looked down.

The power...

She shivered. "What did you...? How did you...?"

Valeran hesitated for a moment, then held up a stack of small papyri rectangles covered in glyphs. Seals.

Taline touched the one sealed around her arm with a ribbon. Nin's magic pulsed inside, and so too did Valeran's. The three of them had made these. They had made them to hold a magi of Nin's caliber.

They had made them to hold Nin.

Out, off!

Her hand automatically moved toward the sky to try channeling the power to break the seal around her arm, but Valeran's palm pressed the papyrus wrapping her.

"Don't," he said harshly.

But she could break this seal. She could break his hand.

"You said I had to put my back into it." Her voice felt so very far from her body. "That will work now, don't you think?"

"If it does, you are as likely to slice your sister in half as to call a plague upon Tehrasi," he said grimly. "Is that your goal?"

"I wouldn't let it."

"The scepter doesn't answer to sanity," he said, unrelenting. "It answers to madness."

"We are, all of us, a little mad."

"Which is exactly why no hand should wield such an instrument."

"Nin could wield it," she murmured.

"Ninli would be a dark goddess who would shine the vengeance of the scepter upon the world."

Taline laughed grimly. "You are mistaken if you think she is the only one laden by vengeful desires."

"Yet you have learned to control that desire. To put it off. To continually put other things before yourself."

"Nin does that as well. She could have controlled herself and the scepter. But you never planned to let her hold it, did you?"

He didn't say anything for a long moment. "Perhaps I owed her after all, not to see her fight that urge."

After days—years—of quips and misdirection from him, she finally believed something Valeran said. She would give her own truth in return. "I'm afraid I won't be able to save her."

"Saving her means giving the scepter to the empire."

"Nin believes the empire could be good for the people as long as there is someone else on Tehrasi's throne."

"You don't."

"I find trust difficult. Without Nin... Well, she pulls people to her, doesn't she? And I found myself relying on other people without realizing it." Larit, Qara, Birsa, hundreds of other faces...

"That is Nin's real power. She is what she wants the world to be."

"And you are what she wants to protect."

She closed her eyes. When she opened them, she was still in the middle of the unnaturally calm sea. The covering Valeran had made for the scepter was burned to ash. The boat was slowly filling with water.

"We are sinking."

"Yes."

"I can move us somewhere else. Possibly." She could feel the scepter slinking through her thoughts and veins. If she asked...

"Possibly, but at what cost? Are you willing to pay?" His voice sounded far away.

"It...it is heady." She swallowed, clutching the scepter to her chest. "I want to feel it again, that power running through my hand."

"Such is the curse of power."

"You don't understand. The feeling—"

"I know what it is, to have power," he said bitterly, leaning back on his heels on a bit of upraised wood that was sinking with the rest. "And to suppress power blacker than night."

Her limbs loosened and her mind refocused. She looked at him for a long moment. The Valerans were well known for their ice powers, but she had seen him use those before. Ironically use them, usually, but still, he had used them. "What power of darkness do you not use?"

"The kind that would set you screaming from me in terror, Taline ul Summora. The kind that would make you shrink from me in fear as it dragged your worst memories into nightmare."

"You do not scare me, Valeran."

He looked at the remaining seals in his hand and tucked them away. "That's because you know me not at all."

They stayed there for an immeasurable amount of time, sinking, with Taline staring at Rone ul Valeran as if she had never seen him before and Valeran staring back in a jaded way that spoke of truth.

He looked into the distance. "This adventure has gotten us to port faster than anticipated, though not the correct port. Madness gives before it taketh all."

She followed his gaze to see shore.

"Come, narsumina. We can patch the boat with our leftover spellbox magic and float or take our chances in a last breeze. Let's see if that stick lets you live through the night." He stood and lifted the nearly empty wind container from the boards. He set a dwindling breeze to their sail and a slighter draft to sweep the water from the boat.

She slid into a seated position on the boards of the boat in the unnatural calm of the sea. The seal slowly started to burn from her arm.

"What power do you have, Valeran?"

Lit by moonlight, he gave a careless grin. "The power of nothing at all."

CHAPTER THIRTEEN
QUESTIONS OF POWER

NINLI

(THE WRECKAGE OF ZAGA, A ONCE GREAT NATION)

The Scepter of Darkness had been used. Somewhere, it had opened a ripgate.

Nin reached out for Taline, but her sister felt no closer than before. Nin had not had time to think on the battlefield, for Kaveh had not hesitated to use the power backlash from the scepter that had swept across their layer. His shadows had eaten and converted the thunderous roll, then released it into an even greater power.

Nin closed her eyes for a moment, so she didn't have to view the decimation left behind—the absolute nothingness of the lands they had traveled. Zaga's countryside had been destroyed—entire ridges and hills flattened, and vegetation turned to dust.

Focused power was always a greater force to be reckoned with than distributed chaos. She had grabbed onto the power backlash as much as she could while still staying by Kaveh's side. She had let the backlash eat away at her mind—at the pinpointed knowledge of where Taline and Rone were.

Then the connection had been lost—encapsulated by glyph paper—and she had let her knowledge pass with the connection.

Thank Sehk. Thank Sehk she and Rone had made those papers in the days when they had been refilling their supplies.

When asked by Kaveh, she had let the bond reach inside and grab the truth that the scepter had been in the Fehl Sea, but she had let the connection go before determining which direction they were headed.

Kaveh had not been able to argue, for the spike of power—the thunderous roll that had overcome the field of battle, then rocked through half the empire three days' past—had enhanced his own powers to the point that he could not recall half of what had occurred afterward either.

All that was left was the destruction he had wrought with the borrowed power.

On the battlefield, she was direct witness to the dark side of conquest. She was witness to what the emperor could do with the Scepter of Darkness in his hand and Kaveh at his fingertips.

And she knew what he could do with her at his fingertips.

She shuddered and looked at her palms. The scepter was a gift of madness and Taline had used it. What did that mean?

She clenched her hands into fists. It had been no surprise when Kaveh had received word that the empire had sent assassins to the non-magic world to recover the relic. The emperor had deliberately let her overhear the report, smiling all the while.

Nin watched the energy run through her fingers. Her abilities were running at peak after continuous high use over the course of the last ten days. She had never used her abilities at such a high level for so long. She could wipe a hand in a general direction and revive a group—or decimate them.

So far, she had refused the latter option.

If her family had survived, and she had properly Awakened in their grasp, she would have had to do far worse.

What could she do to aid Taline without putting her in more danger?

Nin had been careful to disguise her ripgates as illusions created from enchantment boxes. The boys had been quite vocal about the "Djinn lamp spaces." She was long past hiding her strength but using her powers without forethought was asking for the emperor's notice. Kaveh was right.

In the past, knowing she could do something required that she figure out how to accomplish it at a lesser level. She had needed to be clever.

Kaveh kept urging her to release that might. Leaving her powers unchecked, she could do anything, if she chose. It was a heady, terrible power—and she had always enabled a safety block within to shut her body down temporarily when she neared that feeling.

A self-protection mechanism. A fatigue and dizziness that was self-induced. She couldn't, couldn't be like her past—or what the past had wanted her to become.

Unease traveled down her spine. She slid a finger under one eye, checking the spell there.

Taline would be okay. She had to be okay. And Rone would keep her safe from the scepter. Nin needed to protect the people around her in the interim.

Those deemed responsible for the assassination of Urful ul Fehl, along with entire towns, had been razed across three territories, pushing a renewed vigor into the armies Kaveh had sent back to the northern front to push in that direction once more.

The mountain and desert country of Zaga, south of Shoune, had been directly implicated in Urful's death and Kaveh had taken it upon himself to extend the empire south, flattening their armies and pushing the empire farther into Ersine.

Raba, against the western ocean, had been swept alongside their Zagan allies.

The countries hadn't stood a chance once evening had begun its setting descent across the continent of Ersine, sweeping death over Zaga, and stabbing Raba by twilight.

After the Axšaina Sea nations had fallen like karogi tiles, no one in their right mind should have challenged the empire. Did they think the army weakened after the campaign?

It was as if someone was testing Kaveh. Wind users, water users, sand slingers, and sun catchers had all appeared on the fields at some point, trying to maneuver around Kaveh's shadows. But a challenge to the empire couldn't be born from any direction. Kaveh was relentless. He never grew tired, but Nin...

Blood under her nails... Blood behind her eyelids... Power in her hands...

Kaveh did this every day, and she knew the strengthening of his expectation—each night it grew in size—that this would be her new routine, too.

Each day she trudged through death and despair, and each night she joined her magic with his during his sequences and her meditations. The quiet and ease increased, but so too did the tension and stress.

Actions had consequences. So, too, did connections.

You will change your mind.

Unease swept her as she looked over the field.

The boys—and a few girls now—were all staying within the containment bounds, checking on the dead and dying, lining them up in rows. Their little troop had become quite efficient.

She let them finish their tasks as she used her power to sweep the newest row of fresh bodies that they had laid out for her to mass revive. Time was sacred to perform revivals, and they only included bodies within ten dial ticks of death. No one wanted revenants to rise. Small bodies darted in to help the newest revivals—healing smaller wounds and positioning the recovering magi in the massive swath of devastation trailing behind the advancing form of their Imperator General.

Unease crackled again, causing Nin to narrow her eyes on her surrounding pack and to make certain they were all inside the protective barrier. She would have to open another ripgate soon.

A shadow pulled along her shoulders, the bond hummed, then the shadow was gone in the swirling mass that constantly surrounded her on the field. Her disquiet eased. Battlefield worries. She should be used to them by now.

"Please," came a choked voice outside the shadow-encased circle.

Nin looked over to see a woman dragging herself along the ground, one leg bent oddly, fingers reaching out as if they would grab at the hem of Nin's sullied cloak. A flicker of red glinted at the woman's throat like all the blood of her body had been captured in a single, sparkling unit. The woman wasn't wearing the colors of either side, but instead the garb of the local villagers.

Nin took a deep breath. Here was the outcome they wrought.

One of the boys reached for the woman, to heal her, but tears pushed out from the woman's eyes. "No. Please, please." She reached toward

Nin, and Nin could see a paper clutched in her hand.

Nin walked over and leaned down, stretching out a hand to scan the woman's injuries. From where had the woman crawled? How had she survived the onslaught at all?

The woman lunged suddenly upward—her broken leg straightening as an enchantment cracked and fell like too-heavy ice from a branch. The knife in the woman's other hand rocketed upward in an arc. Nin was already reaching to block it, but a second figure rose from the woman's glinting throat—like some ancient monster ejected from her flesh.

This one had a blade as well, poised to strike upward. It formed, wraithlike, as it grew from the woman's throat and chest.

Before Nin could complete her block, an arrow of black pierced the woman's back and stomach, then thrust upward, piking through the second figure's chest, suspending it in a rictus upward lunge and spraying Nin with blood and shredded organs. The black arrow twisted, then was yanked backward, creating an even larger spray of ripped, internal organs over the battlefield.

Agony froze the woman's dead expression as she fell. The other figure dropped in masked silence at her feet.

Nin slowly wiped the spray from her cheeks, and said, without looking away from the woman and her accomplice, "You didn't have to do that."

She had realized quickly that some deaths that Kaveh wrought could never be healed.

Kaveh was already redirecting his shadows to another area. Screams echoed as he did. Ifret rounded Nin in a swirl and stabbed through a second flank of men. Nin's unit of children darted around, suddenly double-checking dead bodies on the perimeter.

"They were going to kill you," Kaveh said. "Pity them not."

"I am the enemy." At this point, with ten days at his side, all had seen "the wraith" of the Shadow Prince, surrounded by his darkness. Nin had heard the whispers as she passed that she was the incarnation of a shadow itself, which would have been laughable if she wasn't starting to feel that way in truth every time she stepped onto a battlefield.

"They have brought this upon themselves. The woman showed strength in her cunning. Pity her not. Pity the fools who flee, for they won't even be buried in their ashes."

In the distance, she saw the black cloud of destruction rise up and swallow all those fleeing. It was a massive, monstrous power that he wielded. A devastation only few in history had been capable of.

The glint of red caught her attention again and she knelt next to the dead woman. Carefully brushing the woman's hair from her throat, a cracked ruby amulet was revealed on a heavy chain that had pooled in the cavity of her neck.

Nin frowned, carefully maneuvering the amulet into better view. Not only was it similar to the one from the tent, up close there was something increasingly familiar about it—and there was a rotten familiarity in the way the second figure had appeared.

The battle raged around her, Kaveh handling the situation as he always did, while thoughts whirled through her head.

"Do you need to rest?" he asked, and she realized belatedly that he had stopped pushing forward and stood next to her, eyes on the field, still fighting, but holding the line instead of pushing on.

She wished she could dredge up a feeling of disbelief, but excess emotion was hard to come by on the war front.

"I'm fine."

He examined her, then accepted the half-truth, turning and flinging darkness in a wide arc.

Then again, the bond let him know exactly how she was doing—just as it did in the reverse. She could feel that he needed rest, and yet she knew here on day ten at his side—the eleventh of the bond—that he would continue on until the bitter end. Until they decimated this field and moved onto the next.

Then the next.

It was unnerving being the one who might crack first. She had never assisted someone who could match her in power. Even the single Level Nine healer in the guild couldn't match her, though Nin had soaked up everything she possibly could from the woman. Rone would never use his full power, and without doing so, his power would always be close, but not quite equal to hers. But Kaveh…

"Come. The stacked bodies make this a less optimal shielding spot. No one can touch you if we move two paces west." He waved a hand and took out five beasts charging forth, then looked back at her somewhat hesitantly. "One more hour, then your figstees await."

She looked at the cracked amulet for a few seconds more, then carefully gloved her fingers and unhooked the chain. She enfolded the necklace into a spare piece of fabric and tucked it into her pocket along with the note in the woman's hand, then rose.

Questions and plots were to be asked and unlocked later.

War awaited at Death's side.

CHAPTER FOURTEEN

A BRIGHT DOOM

RONE

(Sarg of the First Layer)

It took two and a half days to travel from where they had washed ashore on the desert peninsula up the coast to Sarg. They had started by foot but had managed to purchase horses from a traveling tribe halfway to their goal.

The damaged thrice-blessed sails of the craft had been removed, rolled, and attached to Rone's pack. It was not ideal to carry them, but they contained magic and could be used for both land shelter and sail on a future water craft. They had agreed to retain and tote everything that might have the barest amount of magic that could be siphoned at a future time.

The extra time spent traveling did neither of them any good. With every human and hoofed step, and irritating terrain detour, Taline's shoulders grew tighter and her sentences shorter.

They stole cloaks and cloths from drying lines, and Rone continuously looked for anything that might cover the scepter and last longer than a press of sunlight.

By the time they finally reached the wave-washed port of Sarg and turned inland to locate the secret stores, Taline had lost some of her perfect seat and posture and was hunched over, as if the weight of the scepter had grown.

That the scepter was not allowing itself to be covered for any period of time longer than a few hours showed its increasing influence as well. Each time it burned through its dressings, Taline's expression grew more pinched.

They dismounted on the hillside crowned by a three-stone statue that Birsa had pinpointed on her map.

"Well, Valeran, this is where you impress me."

His gut tightened at the tired sound of her voice and the moisture that had gathered along her brow.

He casually flipped a thief's blade. "You wouldn't be able to stand it if I tried, narsumina."

"You wouldn't be able to stand at all with my paring knife embedded in the meat of your calf."

"Stop trying to excite me." Their quips had become almost rehearsed at this point, though. Both of them sought some level of normal in an increasingly dangerous situation.

That the scepter was taking hold of Taline was a point neither wanted to acknowledge aloud. Rone needed the moon ritual to commence. Time and opportunity were slipping through his fingers.

He carefully examined the landscape. Knowing which rock to move and where to seek entrance was the key to any hidden place.

He analyzed how the land joined and receded, slowly walking the area to examine where the weeds and flowers grew—and where they didn't.

He looked at the position of the heavens—slightly off from initial calculations of their arrival. They would have been here two days ago, if Taline had not tried to channel the gods.

Not that either of them could regret the saving of Birsa. The woman had helped them get here; the scepter was safe and not in enemy hands.

An extra two days traveling would have been a boon, if only Taline hadn't used the scepter.

He surreptitiously glanced at her. The usage had cost her. It wasn't just the weariness of her posture and darkness beneath her eyes. He couldn't pretend Taline's continuously itching fingers on the scepter's staff were from holding it too long.

He crouched and ran a finger along a flat stone. It looked like any one of the others on the hillside but for a small notch worn by repeated friction. The ground surrounding the stone was more even to one side of the stone than the other.

He touched the notch and ran his finger underneath, following the smoothed path.

Magic was pulled from him—passive magic that ran through his blood—a tiny sacrifice of internal magical tribute, and a safety measure to keep away any who lacked the ability to use the stores inside.

"Valeran—"

The even side of the ground began to sink.

He stepped to the side as the ground tipped downward and slid inward, forming a ramp to a dark corridor below. He stepped down the ramp and lifted the torch at the right side of the base. A dip of the torch's head into the basin at its side lit the torch and the corridor in blue flame shadow.

There would be traps—if not those built specifically by the builders, then by those who wanted to keep the stash secret.

"Try not to touch anything this time, narsumina, yes?" he said, deliberately careless, as she descended behind him.

She growled. Satisfaction and tension coiled inside him. Rone needed her to concentrate on his careless words instead of on the scepter or on his intentions, but he was finding it less and less easy to utter those words as the days slipped by.

He disabled four traps and two snares before they finally reached the sanctum.

A still, gazing pool sat in a raised octagonal stone coffer in the center of the sanctum. The sunken geometric panels connected into a basin that held what looked like starlight.

"A living well." Taline's relief was obvious.

"One hooked into magic." He flipped his knives and laid them in the basin's center, pressing against the glyphs on the handles and letting the magic overwhelm and renew them quickly, not caring about the overflow that lightly burned his skin. It was a relief to have weapons he trusted back to their full potential. The knives would lose their charges again with use, but for now they would be at peak.

He touched his bag. If only he had brought more containers. But he hadn't needed them in their layer—he never did. Their natural world provided enough magic.

Taline stepped to the well, touching one of the glyphs at the side of the basin then setting

Birsa's container inside. The inner magic of the well lit with ghostly light, then the five glyphs on the container's sides glowed blue, activating the connection.

She unearthed five additional containers from her pack as the first filled.

Rone leaned back and contemplated Taline as she competently refilled the first container, capped it, then began filling the second. He looked at the handcrafted containers and watched how each carefully extracted magic from the well with little waste. He kept tabs on the girls whenever he was in town, so he knew Taline had made these. He knew the time and care she had put into each one.

For all her lack of power, or perhaps because of it, she knew exactly how to use as little as possible to achieve an end. She was always prepared to be without.

Ninli and he would never have packed five containers, too used to relying on endless internal stores and the ability to draw far more magic than the average magi. Kaveh ul Fehl probably wouldn't know how to take breath without magic to call.

Taline, on the other hand, had to use immense cleverness and forethought to keep up and aid Ninli in a world filled with magic.

He respected that more than he would ever let her know.

She twisted her hand with a little sigh, using a bit of the magic in the well to aid her in going faster. She used the exact amount of magic—no more, no less—controlling the container with precision.

Less effected by the lack of magic in the environment and knowing exactly how to compensate—Taline really could rule nations here.

He watched her touch Birsa's vessel again—as if to reassure herself that it was still intact—and shook himself free from the weird spell that had descended over him.

While she finished with the rest of her containers and tools, he walked through the room, using the torchlight to inspect the area. Whatever additional contents the room might have contained had been pillaged long before, but the stones and carvings had survived.

Some of them were very old—existing in a time when all had been magic—when beasts, creatures, beings, magi, and non-magic humans had fought for control of the world.

The non-magic humans had not fared well. Their memories had been modified to myth for their own sake.

He traced a pictograph and one of the pointing figures lead him to a second set of images with pyramids, gates, totems, and markings.

The two reaching rivers were all too familiar. He pulled out the map that Birsa had given them. He traced two of the locations that matched others he knew from experience and existence in their layer—sites from before the breaking.

The grandest sites had either been robbed of their power or destroyed. The remaining large sites were heavily guarded and used for the pentalayerists' own travel. Those sites, they guarded like dragon scale flame in all layers.

The crescent marked by the two rivers curving up from Ur to Bekli then over and down toward Memfi contained their best opportunities.

Memfi and Sakkara were the opposite of clandestine, and Babil was completely out of the realm of reason. They were the most well-guarded areas of the ancient world, back when five layers had been one. The price to use any site there was far too high, for they would have to use the scepter to get through and trying to separate the scepter from Taline would be for naught.

But the other sites...

He traced the largest marking within the closest range of their current location. They could be there in another day of horseback.

"It is done." Taline carefully stoppered the last vessel. Her face glowed from the pool's reflection. "To Ur?"

Deciding between Ur and Parsa had been a difficult decision, but the crescent was dense with possibility—both tapped and hidden.

Rone tapped the stone. "Here first."

Sharp brown eyes took in the picture, then turned his way. "Ur has a nexus I can use." She gripped the scepter. "I need to get to Nin. She is in trouble; I can feel it."

"Ninli is always in trouble. Stopping here first will not add much time. It is in the right direction of all else. Easily a day trip."

"I can use—"

"Ninli wanted you to be separated from it."

Taline gripped the scepter harder, and small lights wound around her hand. Her face began to glow, even away from the pool.

He swore internally at his own words. The scepter had a certain sentience, and it wanted to be used. After a week without magic, he hadn't thought about how touching the magic of the well might affect Taline.

Stupid, stupid. But the knowledge that Taline hadn't activated it yet allowed him to paste on a careless smile.

"Are you going to use it anyway, narsumina?" he said casually. "See if it can get you back without slicing your sister in two?"

"While you plot your own schemes?" There was something cool in her eyes—an otherness that was not her own. "It seems fair to examine all possibilities."

"It is always good to keep an open mind." He kept his voice offhand while internal swearing looped his thoughts. "But you promised to try Ninli's way and this temple isn't far. I will take you to the endpoint as promised."

"You plot, magi." Her eyes glowed unnaturally.

"It is my nature. But I also keep my promises—ask the girl within. Come now, narsumina, look at our resources." He swept a hand across her full pack, willing the determined girl beneath the scepter's influence to emerge. "You will be back in the magic world in no time. There might even be a working gate within one of the temples—who knows what might be found."

Brown eyes painted with a multitude of different hues stared at him. It was as if every brown shade known to magi had vied for prime position in her gaze and none had won—so instead the shades had worked together to pattern a lovely whole. His heart beat faster.

Where looking into her lovely eyes normally made him uneasy for personal reasons, the strange light glowing in the depths of brown made him downright apprehensive.

For a long moment, her endless eyes stared with that unnatural light, then it died beneath the lovelier hues of steady brown.

"To the Temple of the Rising Moon then, Valeran." Her hand twitched upon the scepter.

To a bright doom.

CHAPTER FIFTEEN

THE ARMS OF TRUTH

NINLI

(THE TENT OF THE IMPERATOR GENERAL, BATTLEFRONT OF THE NORTH)

Servants bustled through the tent, removing plates and bowls from their nighttime meal. Nightfall almost always meant a cessation in fighting and a conquered field. No one in their right mind tried to initiate a fight with Kaveh ul Fehl at night, and any who lasted that long, failed once darkness drew wings across the ground.

Night was a safe haven from endless death in her new existence.

She turned the amulet in her hands. She had removed the touch-based curses. They had been familiar curses with a familiar enchantment style. That it was the second such piece in twice as many days that had hidden an assassin inside was more than familiar, it was concerning.

The gem and scroll work around the edges were design elements meant for power and magnification—easily interpreted. Tiny glyphs of writing circled the edge of the amulet, though, as incomprehensible as ever.

She stared at the inscription, willing it to make sense and confirm her reluctant theory. The inscription was long and detailed—and detailed, unfortunately, meant each word spared no marks. The amulet held answers that she couldn't grasp without spending hours of letter-by-letter work.

As always, there was a blank space in her mind where knowledge refused to connect.

It was a certainty that Kaveh would ask her what she was doing three hours from now when she was still staring at the same object while painstakingly having translated four words.

She took a deep breath. She relied on Taline's eyes, or on all the small aids that were in the bag Rone and Taline now carried in the non-magical world.

Nin couldn't mourn the loss of her bag. There were things in there that would keep Taline and Rone safe.

She waited for the last servant to leave, took another deep breath, and put the amulet on the desk. She slid it toward Kaveh. "What does this say?"

What difference did it make now, giving him information he could use against her later? There were far worse things in play, and she needed to know what they were.

Kaveh looked up from the emperor's bound papyri instructions. His brows creased in the way they did when he was interrupted while intensely focusing—or at least the way they creased when she interrupted him. She had never seen the servants so much as take a breath in his direction.

"What does what say?" he asked.

"This." She tapped the inscription.

He slid the amulet from under her fingers, eyes skimming the glyphs before focusing sharply on her. "They are standard glyph coils."

She looked back at him, steady. "Yes."

One of his fingers rubbed the metal edge and she could feel him probing the bond. His feeling of realization was calmer than she had expected. Nothing on the battlefield or in the tent had required her to decode glyphs, but he had to have suspected something odd in the temple when she had needed Rone and Taline. And he had wondered at her belt spells. Yes, they were mostly for others to use now—she could do most healing spells without aid—but they had started as ways for her to keep enchantments straight.

"You can't read."

"With great effort and time, it is possible for me to decode the words," she said. "But I don't always do so accurately, especially with long words. I'd rather not gamble with this."

"I've seen you write. Are you trying to say—"

"I can write any glyphs that I learned as a child. I can't read what I've written. I lost that ability. I will not tell you that it makes sense to be able to write but not read. I know what I am." She lifted a figstee and placed it in her mouth, closing her eyes as she savored the taste—a moment of freedom in a small, wrapped fruit. "A broken bird in a broken cage."

He said nothing for long moments, but she could feel a second probe along the bond. "You lost it how?"

They have breached the inner sanctum...Live, my beetle. Be finally free.

A shut door. A release of trash. Pain and darkness.

"My handmaidens and the kitchen staff saved my life the day my family died, but it wasn't without consequence. I fell three stories, headfirst, down a chute that was not meant for human bodies." Nin ghosted fingers over the back of her head. Consequence. "I woke to life when all those I had cherished were dead, but I was unable to move, broken for days and trying to piece my body back together. Some things could not be fixed. One of those was losing whatever mental connection exists to the written word," she said, as simply as she could.

It had been such an...unexpected consequence. And it had hindered her greatly for a while. She had always relied on reading to increase her knowledge. And after her Awakening, when she had needed to access a greater store of knowledge...

She had made do.

"Why have you not healed it since? You are clever. On the battlefield, there is not much you're incapable of fixing."

She smiled without humor. "Only the activation of magic allowed me to survive the fall. The irony has never failed to elude me. The lack of magic made it possible for me to escape, the activation to survive. I was lucky. But I had no notion of, or skill in, life healing at nine. And even less without anyone to trust or anything to read. It was...a painful process over those three days to even heal myself to a level where I could crawl away. There was bleeding in my brain that I could not stop."

"You can't heal it now?"

"No," she said simply. "That tissue is dead. Those paths are gone. And I have no tears to shed on things such as that. I learned other ways to cope and compensate for what I lost. I can work out glyphs with great effort by breaking them down into individual slices and reassembling them in other ways. If you'd like to wait a few hours, and invite errors, I can do so."

She stared at him with unfeigned patience. She wasn't going to apologize for things she had not chosen and could not change.

He narrowed his eyes, studying her for far too long. "You give away vulnerabilities too freely."

"I am bound to you, first by oath, second by recognition to give you the scepter. I have nothing to gain by not putting my trust in you on this. You have already shown yourself trustworthy."

Complicated emotions ran through the bond. Derisiveness most prominently, but there was a softer, more skittish emotion beneath that was quickly squashed. She nodded in acknowledgment of the unease they both felt at how the bond had started to slip outside the parameters of the oath to encompass far more.

His lips tightened, and he looked down at the amulet. "Three poisons and one soul cavity can be contained within, according to the glyph scripts in the center. The second assassin leaped from this," he said, without needing her to cue the knowledge. "One of the indicated poisons was likely coating the blade she and the other carried. There is a declaration of intent extensively documented, with the final inscription emblazoned—the Arms of Truth." He turned the amulet in his hand.

Cold suffused her. "The Arms of Truth—you are sure?"

"I have never suffered a head injury."

"The back?"

"There neither."

She blinked at him. His attempt at a lighthearted jab was appreciated. Still, this was too important for jest to consume. "The emblazoned declaration. Read it, please."

"The Arms of Truth. The Hands of Pain. The—"

"Legs of Fear. The Heels of Glory," she whispered.

He looked at her, head tilted, and passed the amulet back to her. "You know it, then?"

"You don't?"

"Should I?"

"It's a child's tune. An oft-told tale."

"The tales from my childhood encompass blood and the best way of draining someone of it," he said simply.

Nin gripped the amulet without taking her gaze from his. "I'm sorry."

"For what?"

"Sometimes I wallow and forget my fortunes."

"You were raised by bloodthirsty ghouls, given brain damage, then forced to live in poverty," he said sharply.

Be finally free. "No. I was raised by a cadre of servants who were kind in their sharpness and fear. And I became...free. I achieved freedom, for a little while."

A weird feeling of constriction tightened along the bond.

Then amusement curled in him so strongly it was jarring. "The struggle felt by the Investigore of Tehras becomes easier to understand."

She looked at him, mystified. "The investigore? What struggle?"

"He is quite taken with you."

"The investigore?" Had Kaveh done something to him? "I am a thorn in his side, but he's a good man."

Kaveh leaned back. "He is still alive."

"That is good for Tehras."

"And you only care for the good of Tehras."

"That would be easier," she murmured in response. She looked down. "This...is the mark of a pentalayerist group—specifically, a group of assassins who used to be active in Tehrasi during the reign of the Carres. 'They come for you. Late at night. In the shadows. The arms of truth, broken and torn. The hands of pain, stripped of flesh. The legs of fear, shattered to dust. Heels of glory—the dead cannot run.'"

"Pentalayerist assassins."

She turned the amulet in her fingers, and the fractured ruby flashed in the center of text that was as incomprehensible as it had been before. Only now she knew what she held. "Ones who target gatemakers, worldmakers, and worldbreakers. They moved on from Tehrasi with the death of the royal family. The last I knew, they were searching the northern seas for makers."

"You think they know who you are?"

"No." She considered the ripgates she had been creating. "I've been careful, and I don't think I was the primary target, even today. I'm ancillary. You and Ifret were the targets in the tent, and I think one of the assassins carried a similar piece. It was destroyed with the body."

"The man appearing from nowhere." Kaveh shrugged. "This group will have no more luck than any other." His emotions reflected his dismissal. He was completely unconcerned about the possibility of being assassinated. "They are the ones who need take care."

Two dead padifehls and a relic that lit the world on fire.

"The group Osni killed in the temple—those were pentalayerists. Taken together, I have to assume they were of the Arms—that they are chasing the scepter."

She could feel Kaveh's disregard sharpen. "Then I will exterminate them."

"They will already be chasing the scepter," she murmured. Taline. "They have cause to think you know of it, if they are targeting you. They will come in greater numbers. They believe in nothing more than the separation of the layers and the worlds within. They will do anything, accept any death, to ensure the scepter is not held and used."

Two dead padifehls was a strike that spoke of a larger hand, though.

She stared at the amulet; thought of the gossip from the boys. The group of enemy child soldiers her group had recently saved had uttered the same litany as had previous captives from other conquered countries: orders and tides had recently turned.

"Why were we in Shirsk, Helip, Yalendil?" She turned the amulet in her fingers.

Kaveh looked at her as if she had suffered another permanent head injury and he was contemplating whether to put her down in order to end her suffering. He didn't answer.

"You had either conquered those territories, or they were near capitulation," she clarified. "In fields where the forces were previously ready to surrender, the leaders suddenly turned against the empire. Why?"

"You think the padifehl assassinations are connected with the recent churning across the landscape," he said without surprise. "You think the assassination attempt was meant for me, like the other children of the emperor, as a connection to something greater."

"Someone invigorated the front in the days you were absent—and rejuvenated the countries who were next in line to be consumed. I'm not telling you anything you don't already know. But the why..."

"Assassins from Tehrasi. You think Osni used them—that he set a plan in progress."

"I think it's all...suspicious. He had to be aware of the two pentalayerists working for him at the temple. He followed and destroyed the group led by them too easily."

"It would be to our advantage, if it is Osni. He is dead—or as good as dead. Any orders he had given will wane with each passing day."

Nin wiped her hands slowly. "You dismiss him too quickly. Osni will attempt to gain the scepter while Taline and Rone are without magic."

"Osni was half dead. He left behind two toes, and who knows what might have been removed on the other side. If they lost to him, I will have underestimated Valeran."

"You already underestimated him," Nin murmured, rubbing the amulet, brain only half-engaged. There was something...

"No. Circumstances were such that I had no choice in the matter in whether to engage Valeran." Kaveh's voice and emotion indicated that circumstances would be different when their paths next crossed.

Nin didn't argue. Watching the two of them fight would be...a spectacle. Because for all that Kaveh was without peer on a battlefield, the secret was that Rone hadn't needed her to save him when he was twelve nor any of the times thereafter. What she had saved him from was exposing his true powers—bitter tears running down his face as his fingers lifted against the guards coming to remove his hand. She had felt a wisp of his power building and understood the consequences.

And she had taken care of it. She had knocked the guards out and subtly shifted their memories to account for the "dead" prisoner in cell four.

She had understood secrets and hiding one's power only too well. Rone had little ability to trust—his childhood had been different from hers, dark in different ways. Whereas she had people who had almost loved her—even in the midst of the madness and carnage of the Carre household—Rone had only the streets and a mother who bitterly resented him.

He had disappeared soon after Nin had healed him, but not without spilling his secret as though it burned a hole in his soul.

She had made sure to keep an eye on him and shield him thereafter. She was never certain whether Rone would choose death over exposure.

She was the keeper of that secret now. And she would take it to her grave.

"You underestimate Taline," she said instead.

"I know little of your self-proclaimed sister except that she is weaker than you."

"Not in spirit," Nin murmured. And the scepter was an object not to be taken lightly. It gifted and cursed. "She is strong."

She was. She was going to be fine. Nin had to believe that.

She nestled into the blankets and closed her eyes, pulling the amulet through her fingers and searching for connections in her mind.

"Then you should not worry for them in regard to Osni."

She allowed a bitter smile. "Crelu ul Osni has a thirst for revenge, the type that can never be quenched once begun. It has chased him to madness. Never underestimate the maddened."

"And your thirst for revenge?"

A slew of faces memorialized in memory—Farrah, Heba, Reyi, so many others—crossed her mind in rapid succession. "I want justice, not revenge."

"Justice is the justification of revenge."

"The line is so very slim," she acknowledged, opening her eyes. "And I know the consequences of crossing it, of the madness of the path—the madness of revenge. Should I fail and cross, I will accept my own death as due, rightful consequence. But Osni... No matter what happens, never count Crelu ul Osni out."

"Destabilizing the empire won't aid Tehrasi."

Nin looked to the ceiling of the tent. Sadness and anger suffused her. "Osni has not had Tehrasi's interests at heart for a long time. For years, I've waited for him to kill Etelian. He's worked beside him, but he has yet to lift the knife. I've waited for Aros to be disemboweled on the palace steps, but the eldest prince is careful in his comings and goings. I've long wondered if Aros knows the danger of Osni. Any of Nera's spawn are in mortal danger from Osni, but Aros most especially."

She could feel Kaveh poking at the bond, trying to divine her thoughts. "Osni is oath-bound to the emperor and also to Etelian as padifehl," he said. "Even if he manages to return here, he is bound by his oath. He can't kill a blessed child."

Nin pulled the amulet chain through her fingers and said nothing.

Kaveh leaned forward. "What aren't you saying?"

"Farrah made all things possible," she whispered. She could feel the probe of shadow along her skin, seeking access to her thoughts. She brushed it gently aside.

"Farrah Osni was a casualty of the palace battle," he said. "I looked her up after I read your memory."

"The first casualty," she said softly. "The key to getting Crelu Osni, as he was known before the empire, out of one set of oaths and into position to wipe the Carres from Tehrasi's lands."

"He killed his wife." It wasn't a question, but there was a realization in his words.

Nin focused on the amulet, unable to look elsewhere. "In order to elicit his revenge, he had to get out of his oaths. Only the darkest magic can erase a life-force oath, though it leaves a permanent scar behind. The severance of one's own heart—a death of self that can never be recovered. Farrah was the most precious thing to Crelu besides his son, Bilen."

"The rolls said the son was executed."

"My family killed Bilen Osni for treason when I was eight," she said, voice strained. A mere year before the empire conquered Tehrasi. "It was in response to a coup. My father made Crelu perform the execution in order to test his loyalty—and to make certain he hadn't been part of the coup Bilen had been leading. If Crelu hadn't executed Bilen, Crelu and Farrah would have been killed alongside their son. Crelu severed his son's head, while plotting my family's demise behind a penitent face."

Nin took a deep breath, trying to keep her turbulent emotions from overwhelming her, as they always did when she thought of such things.

She could feel the tilt of Kaveh's emotions—cooler against her own. "You thought well of Bilen Osni."

"Bilen was...a good man. Kind, strong. Jisarek's continued maneuvers to kidnap Nera again, to claim her firstborn, and to tweak the emperor's nose were making enemies of the generals. A faction rose. They knew jabbing the growing Fehl Empire was a tactical misstep and sought to neutralize Jisarek. They failed. My father doted on his brother to an unpleasant degree. Trying to kill Jisarek was a death sentence of the worst kind. Bilen's death at Osni's hands filled Osni with madness. Farrah's death by those same hands made that madness permanent."

Osni had been a victim of the Carres, but he had become a villain in his grief.

"You knew her well?"

Nin could see Farrah in her mind—she could feel the memory like the softest linen wrapped around her neck. "She was my teacher. Gentle, kind, giving. She was a gatekeeper—permanently stationed in Tehras, but without active gate duty. She instructed in gate duties and tasks, but when Bilen entered the soldier corps, Farrah sought other children to nurture further. She took the four youngest of us—Allit, Memni, Jolan, and me—under her wing. Nursery teaching, early training to ready us for when our powers came in. She opened our pathways, readied our bodies and minds. Mental training far in advance of our elder siblings—though only later experience made me realize that. It was no wonder that Bilen was the best soldier and leader in the Tehrasian armies."

"The Carres kept their gate secrets close. It amuses me they could be bested by a mere keeper in training."

"Lorsali scoffed at all of it." Nin smiled without happiness. "The boys developed individual interests and wandered off to engage in them once their powers bloomed. But I stayed. Farrah was a cultivator—plants, people, animals, anything that could be nurtured—and was so very, very wise."

"I can feel your regret." He tilted his head. "You loved her powerfully. And in one such as you, who views such emotion as a strength, that says something. What do you regret?"

Breath was always so painful to draw, when thinking of it. "I was always in her rooms. I shadowed her like a leech. I...overheard Crelu ranting madness to her behind closed doors more than once." Nin looked away. "I never said anything to the others. I knew the consequences if I did. I saw Bilen die. I saw what they did to bind his soul. The palace floors ran red most days. Death and dismemberment were doled out for the smallest of infractions. Crelu's words would have killed them both. I didn't want anything to happen to Farrah." She gripped her hands together. "My silence killed her anyway."

"If Osni is alive, he will show when the scepter does."

Nin's hands tightened. "He will."

He crouched down in front of her, arms crossed over his knees. "And I will kill him for you."

She looked at him—so close she could feel the heat of him.

Kaveh tilted his head toward her. "I would see Osni dead with or without the oath binding me to it. He earned his execution mark as soon as he entered the temple and doubled it with Ifret.

Justice or revenge, I only care for his death. But I will make sure that I am the one to do it."

Nin swallowed. "The assassin's group... The pentalayerists being from Tehrasi... I do not want Tehrasi to suffer."

"Whether it is Osni or someone else, I will find out who is trying to undermine the empire. Join me. Fully." He leaned forward a fraction further. "And your province will thrive."

"I will be the bait that buys my country's freedom?"

His fingers curled, then extended. "Yes."

As long as she continued to be useful, he would continue to rely upon her. As long as he continued to show the cracks in his otherwise impenetrable armor of darkness, she would continue to be useful. A circle that would either lead to something unbreakable, or something that shattered in disappointment and death.

It felt so temptingly as though it could be the first.

She put her hand in his.

CHAPTER SIXTEEN
TEMPLE OF THE RISING MOON

TALINE

(Temple of the Rising Moon)

The Temple of the Rising Moon was hidden in a landscape of rock. A stone door inset into a boulder thirty men high was otherwise hidden by a landscape empty of vegetation or scenic diversity.

"Clever," Taline murmured. "Well, then"—she turned to Valeran—"you said we needed to be in the chamber at moonrise. We haven't much time."

Though that wasn't quite true—moonrise on the waning shape that would light tonight meant an early evening rise; a stroke of good fortune. Two days before the full moon, the Temple of the Rising Moon would be near its peak power. A good temple choice indeed. Not even the scepter seemed able to fault Valeran's choice.

Its presence buzzed beneath her palm.

Valeran rolled out Nin's scroll and scanned the vague depiction inside. Taline already knew it by heart. The Ritual of Three Moons said that a scepter positioned correctly at moonrise would free or bind whatever object it came into contact with—in this case, Taline's skin.

Over the course of three moonrises, it indicated that an object touched by the moon would be free or bound completely. Moon temples were often connected to each other, so if they gathered the appropriate coordinates or struck luck, they could travel and gain multiple moonrises on succeeding breaths of time. How the temples were activated was a secret guarded by disciples of the moon, unfortunately.

The scepter vibrated beneath her palm. She pulled it closer to her chest. She had been trying to keep the scepter's increasing wishes secret from Valeran. But by the frequent glint of steel in his palms, she didn't think she had managed well.

"Valeran, you are sure the Scepter of Darkness answers to the moon?"

He rolled the scroll and stowed it in his pack again. "Ninli was."

Taline nodded. The scepter sparked.

She turned away from him and tried not to think of the depictions of doom she had memorized in the scepter temple while Nin and Valeran had worked. Warnings were common in any temple that wanted to protect its treasures.

Not all warnings were true.

Detaching the scepter would be easier in the non-magic lands than in ones with magic. The scepter would fight tooth and nail if magic were available. How hard could it be here, in a landscape scarce of magic?

He will kill you.

Taline took a deep breath. Valeran hadn't killed her yet, no matter what the scepter whispered. If he had wanted to kill her, one of them would already be dead.

He will kill you after I am no longer able to save you.

"You still there, narsumina?"

She turned back around, stretching the placid smile she had perfected in the palace onto her lips. "Vaguely."

His features tightened, but he nodded.

If she had met this Valeran four years ago... But he was moving past her, and she couldn't think such thoughts.

He will kill you.

So too might the temple, if she didn't pay attention. She pushed the scepters' whispers aside.

The moon temple was similar in appearance to the Temple of Darkness. A series of puzzles and gates stretched before them—solve one, enter, fight, travel, solve the next, repeat the process. Valeran barely drew breath as he finished one, then the next—muscled arms, liquid figure, and sharp brain working through each. She had reluctantly admired his cleverness before. She found herself less reluctant now, but more on edge.

If she had met this Valeran four years ago, indeed.

They reached the last obstacle. A stone door and metal mechanism stood between them, the main chamber, and moonrise.

The scepter grew excited. Unease ran through her and she gripped it tightly.

A wave of energy ran through her—making her feel physically better than she had since the morning following the activation of the scepter. The scepter knew they were trying to disengage it. Excitement meant nothing good.

Valeran withdrew gloves from his pack and pulled them on, carefully adjusting them as he did. She narrowed her eyes.

He twisted one finger of his glove and a small bladed tip extruded. A twist of a finger on the other hand produced the same result. He carefully inserted the tips into the mechanism and fiddled for a second—pushing up and right, then left—before a sound indicated the give of the latch disconnecting.

The door creaked open to show a large chamber filled with dust and sand. Cleverly removed bricks staggered haphazardly across the dome showed the open air beyond. The falling sun spread through one opening and motes drifted through the air, glittering in the glow. As the sun fell, another opening half a step down but far to the right lit. Then a third one lit far to the left.

The openings in the dome were staggered and, in no foreseeable order as the sun fell, different ones throughout became beacons of golden light in a checked sequence.

She checked the position of the light and the slope of the sun. They had to wait a half rotation of a standard sand turner before moonrise. Valeran looked around the chamber, but didn't step inside, and she followed suit.

A large, dull golden staff with an open, diamond-shaped head was positioned upright in the floor. Dust and webs obscured any ornamental details upon it.

A small empty well was inset into the stone wall near where they stood in the entrance.

Valeran motioned and Taline grimaced but unearthed a container from her pack and fed the tiniest bit of magic inside the well. The well sucked it inside and the chamber creaked to life. A breeze swept through the room and out through the openings in the ceiling.

The room suddenly stripped itself of age and wear with the flow of the magical breeze.

The staff, cleared of webs and dust, stood without adornment. Glyphs and circles of dormant power spread beneath.

Valeran walked to the edge of the outermost circle.

Taline could feel the faint shimmer of magic from the center circle—running up the core of the staff. A well was located somewhere beneath—a pinpoint of power awaiting true release—waiting to feel sunlight or to feel its absence, depending on the position of the staff.

The moon and sun moved in predictable ways, rotating in a dance that was always able to be derived.

Taline had read the ritual text. The great stick in the middle had to be turned to compensate for the moon cycle and day—the exact day. Full moons were ritualistically easiest—rising at sunset and setting at sunrise—making it ridiculously easy to estimate times as compared to other moon phases. It was one of the reasons full moons were used so often in rituals. Dark moons, with the opposite rise and set, were easily second best—though there was less visual aid to assist.

"We are waxing four—four from full." Taline looked at a small moon compass in her pack. "Or three from three, if you use the old standard of not counting your positional nights."

"Look at you. You'll be a site robber soon, Summora."

"Get working, Valeran." But she said it almost fondly, without her usual sarcasm. The scepter twitched irritably in her hand and she clutched it tightly.

He stepped carefully inside the center circle and rotated the staff so that the diamond head was aligned with the opening above that would reflect the sunlight of a waxing four moonrise.

Taline took a deep breath. The sunlight continued to cut across the openings above them. They could do this.

Nestled into the floor, small, inscribed bowls awaited the temple's magic.

Valeran inhaled and pointed to the appropriate bowl, motioning Taline there. The drawings in the scroll had indicated that the magic would need to hit the affected area.

"Once the light penetrates the diamond of the staff, put the head of the scepter under the beam first. If that doesn't work, let the beam strike your palm."

"If it slices off my hand, I'll be seeking recompense."

"I'll always pay you with flesh, narsumina." But his gaze was too casual. "How do you feel?"

She could see his fingers twitch against his sleeves. Steel would not be far from his palms.

"I feel fine. No need to exterminate me yet."

A hint of a real smile tickled in the lights of his eyes. "And the scepter?"

"Is...cautiously eager."

He grimaced and they both turned as the sunlight shifted to the next opening. The beam of light slivered, then slid into the hole of the dome they had identified. The beam of light hit the diamond head of the staff and gold immediately glowed in shining light, inching toward her palm, the scepter, and the basin beneath.

"Sehk, I hope that scroll was correct," Valeran muttered.

"Dammit, Valeran—"

The beam fully slid to fill the moonrise opening, then shot through the staff's diamond opening and directly at the Scepter of Darkness.

Burning. Pain. Taline let out a guttural sound that increased into a scream. But she held firm, and it was in that moment of resolve that the scepter jerked in what she could only describe as horror.

Move! Stop! The scepter shrieked.

But she knew such whispers. She knew pain. She knew determination. And Taline held tightly to the feeling of decay in her palm.

Detach! she screamed at it. The scepter head glowed with gold-on-black light. Her palm smoked.

Pain, worse than before, shot through her. From one moment to the next, everything in the temple awoke, then the light slid from the waxing fourth opening and all dimmed once more.

Taline stumbled backward. The staff in the floor pulsed, then went dormant. The scepter, though... glowed malevolently.

Valeran's feet were moving quickly toward her, but Taline thrust her free hand toward him. "Don't."

She breathed heavily, her dense curtain of hair falling around her face as she looked at the floor and her chest heaved. "It's done. A third of it is gone. Just...don't come closer." She could feel the scepter's dark influence as part of it broke. She could feel its shrieks as it tried to clutch her fully again and reattach. Shaking violently, she pushed its grasping tendrils free.

"Yes, step away from the girl, Rone ul Valeran."

Taline's face jerked upward at the new voice, shocked to see numerous figures arrayed behind them. Valeran's knife sliced through the air before Taline even had a chance to stiffen.

His second knife was a beat behind as the first hit the cloaked figure at front. The second was blocked by two figures moving to flank the first. Two more figures slid to back wings, completing the scarab formation.

Valeran was already palming his next two blades and shoving Taline behind him with his elbow.

The front figure raised a hand and a protection barrier rose.

Taline's breath caught. Magi.

Inked hands descended—five circles inked into bony flesh.

Worse. Layer separatists. Pentalayerists.

Valeran scattered a pouch of dust into the bowls around them with one hand and twisted the diamond floor staff into position with his other. "You will die first."

Taline stiffened as calculations ran through her head and the scepter warmed. Valeran had just thrown ruffric into a dozen bowls that could be filled with concentrated sunlight with a turn of his hand.

"Valeran, you are a foolish man." But the leader stepped back, palms extended to the side.

It was hard to know whether it was better or worse that the leader knew enough to know what might happen. In a moment, the sun would slide through the opening in the dome that would ignite the position Valeran had attuned the head to—and though it wouldn't be moonrise magic, the sunlight would still activate the staff and ignite the dust in the bowl. The ruffric would burn and consume them all.

The sunlight slivered and all five figures pulled their hands skyward, raising the barrier higher.

Valeran lazily turned the diamond staff to aim at an empty bowl a moment before the light slivered through and hit the first bowl laden with ruffric. Then he aimed at another filled bowl.

She shivered at the concentration required not to ignite them all. It would take only one slip of mental fortitude.

"The same tactic used at the temple?" Valeran kept the staff steadily rotating under his palm, ahead of each new sliver of light while the cloaked figures tensely watched and awaited their doom. "Lazy. Lazier to think I haven't planned what to do next time it occurs."

"We have no issue with you, Rone ul Valeran, if you leave at once."

Valeran had earned a particular reputation. A deserved one. Self-preservation was something he was well known for. And his control of the staff and knowledge of where the sun would light next spoke of an overwhelmingly gifted mind.

He gave a careless shrug, moving the staff just a hair ahead of lighting the third bowl of ruffric ablaze. "I'm enjoying this scenery at present. Puzzles to solve, lovely maidens to save."

"We are not your enemies, Rone ul Valeran. We seek similar aims. It is why we have left you to your whims. You destroy that which should not exist."

Taline's gaze swung to the leader. There was a zeal in the leader's voice that went beyond duty. This was not how someone tasked with fulfilling a mission sounded. Something personal was at stake for him, which made the situation infinitely worse.

Valeran shrugged again. "I'm not well known for keeping a good hand on things I've found. Fickle, you know. And gambling is a vice."

"Your carelessness is a ruse. You've deliberately kept powerful artifacts from other hands. Join us instead. Join us and destroy the Carre legacy for good."

Taline had no love of the Carres, but she loved Nin. The pentalayerist leader was young of skin, but old of eye. Maybe twenty-seven or twenty-eight summers old—easily able to have been of age to loathe the Carres personally.

"I've heard the recruitment speech before," Valeran said. "Those robes are truly unflattering, however. I'll have to pass."

But Taline was too on edge to play the game that Valeran could stretch to the heavens. "What do you want?" Taline asked the leader.

The leader's attention turned to her. "Your death. You have touched that which cannot be wielded."

"I have no wish to wield it. Such is the ritual we have undertaken."

"And yet you have already wielded it. All beings and magi across the layers felt your use."

The scepter vibrated beneath her palm—only two-thirds of it was attached now. The unattached skin burned.

"A mistake in circumstance," she said tightly. "The ritual to remove it is underway."

"There are no mistakes. None can survive the scepter. All must be destroyed who have touched it. It is only a matter of time before you are consumed."

"The Carres survived the scepter."

"No. Those who touched it were exterminated for the good of all kind. The last of the Carres never wielded it, for we made sure none previously survived the touch."

Taline's blood went cold.

"Always so hasty in blanket punishment," Valeran said idly. "Torch the whole structure for one insect found."

"We will destroy that which should never be wielded."

"Yes, well, when we get it unstuck from her palm, we will hand it over. Ideal, really. What do you say?" Valeran carelessly twirled a knife.

"You underestimate its influence. It will not allow its own removal."

A lazy, careless smile curled Valeran's mouth. "And you deal in weak minds. Do not underestimate those stronger than you."

Taline's breath caught and she tensed. But she understood Valeran's illusory negligence a little better now—and she wasn't surprised to see his hidden gloved fingers inch along the palm of his other glove, the little bladed tips scratching lightly against a plate stitched into his palm.

She had to decide whether to trust him. And in the end, it wasn't the hard choice she would have thought it a month previous.

Her left fingers were already inside her cloak—her body moving before she had fully processed the decision. She touched the pouch in her cloak sleeves and the tiny container stitched inside. She dipped her fingers in the small pouch and carefully withdrew them, keeping her fingers inside the hem of her sleeve.

"We will detach it from her after she's dead." The man raised his staff. "Leave, Rone ul Valeran."

Look around you, the scepter whispered. Taline's gaze flew around the interior.

Valeran sighed theatrically. "Unfortunately, I made a promise to a lady, you see." He gave a half-shrug, flinging his fingers outward, clawed gloves scoring hard against the plate in his palm.

Before his shrug was complete, her hand was in the air, and she was blowing the tinder dust from her palm. His flint-tipped fingers scored and curled a piece of metal into the bloom, and the spark caught the dust.

Valeran blew the billowing flame toward the men, then twisted the head of the diamond staff.

The robed figures scattered, but two didn't escape the flame.

Taline called up more dust and Valeran blew that into flame, torching the inside of the temple space with curling orange blooms.

They had always worked well enough together—when they agreed on something.

It was the agreement that had always been hard found.

The lead figure cursed and dodged, using his own men to stay alive. "You'll never make it out of this layer. Unless you use that cursed object—and at that point, all the worlds will know where you are. We have people everywhere that you will go. We know all the secrets of this layer and have closed the cursed gates."

"I'm just as certain that you've missed one or two, but good show." Valeran whirled as they used the last of the flame.

The leader raised his wand. "You are choosing the wrong side in this war, Rone ul Valeran."

"The wrong side is my favorite place."

Four beams of light shot at Valeran.

Look around you, the scepter demanded.

She saw the glyphs for Ur. For Memfi. For Parsa. For a dozen places she wasn't sure of. Possibly one of them was the answer to home, but she didn't know.

Calculations ran through her mind and Taline twisted the staff as sunlight shot through the next opening above. It hit the diamond, then shot through, hitting the ruffric in a bowl. The explosion rocketed the interior and made the magic targeting Valeran veer from its path. She twisted the staff head quickly to hit the fifth bowl.

A beam of light struck her from one of the pentalayerists and the scepter head passed through the staff's light. The light pierced the scepter.

Darkness spread wide. Triumph lit everything around her, knitting dark tendrils back over her palm and mind. She could feel the scepter fuse back to her palm completely. Sehk, Sehk, Sehk.

Power twisted up her arm.

You can do _anything_.

She twisted the head of the diamond staff and aimed the beam at the glyph of Ur. A ripgate opened and Taline didn't wait before knocking Valeran into it. He barely moved with her kick, but his lips firmed enough that she knew he understood what had happened and was furious. He swung around and grabbed her; then, with a twist of the scepter, she told it to go.

They dove through. She whipped the scepter behind.

A stray shot flew past her shoulder, singeing stone as it hit. Then all sealed shut.

They collapsed in a heap on a dusty chamber floor. The floor lit once, then went dim.

Valeran reached over and grabbed her arm, fingers digging into her wrist. He looked at the scepter fused even more completely to her palm and swore.

Giddy, the scepter smiled.

CHAPTER SEVENTEEN

ALLIES BEYOND OATH

NINLI

(THE TENT OF THE IMPERATOR GENERAL)

Nin felt it when the Ritual of Three Moons began.

She felt the scepter untangle from her mind. She felt the tiny piece release that had connected her to the scepter, and to Taline. She felt Rone's promise in the exhalation of the connection.

Free. Taline had begun the ritual. Taline would soon be free.

Nin bowed her head and something between a half-laugh and half-sob emerged. "Thank you," she whispered. "Thank you, thank you, thank you."

The first moon of the ritual had cast off that which was least necessary to the scepter's survival—and the half-formed bond with Nin obviously qualified. There would be two more moonrises left to complete. Nin wouldn't be able to feel them, but in only two more days, Taline would be free.

Nin swallowed and let the tears flow.

Taline could never come back—Rone would make certain of that—and Nin would never see her again, but her sister would be free.

Nin wiped her tears and headed to the edge of camp. Strengthened by the knowledge that her sister would succeed, the first place Nin headed was to her ducklings, as Kaveh had deemed them.

She had an empire to fix.

The ducklings had set up their tents on the edges of First General Goran's section. The First General had not been amused by the banding together of an unimpressive slice of his troops and had flayed Akel's back when he had stood tall and proclaimed they were aides to the Imperator General's right hand.

General Goran had not been amused at the pronouncement that Nin was the Imperator General's right hand.

Nin had healed Akel's wounds the moment she saw them, and Goran's skin had blanched ten shades when Kaveh had fixed a stare upon him the next day. The general had said nothing about the ducklings' placement since, and he avoided Nin as if she held the first seed of pestilence between her teeth.

The ducklings were scrappy and small, but mighty in spirit, and they were always quick to share battlefield gossip. They were an invaluable resource because they could be anywhere. Adults tended to dismiss children without understanding that all children weren't created equally. As Nin had experienced in the palace—few took notice of small ears.

Only those who wanted to remain were kept in camp. Nin made certain to "lose" those who wished other lives—sending them through ripgates to other lands and closing those ripgates behind.

Akel jumped to his feet as soon as he saw her. "Mistress Ferra." He bowed comically low.

Nin let exasperation overlay amusement. "You are going to call down the wrath of the gods. And I'm only five years older than you are."

He nodded seriously. "And someday I will make certain that I gather a king's ransom to ask your hand in marriage, but until then, we have things to tell you. Two of the boys we saved yesterday spilled interesting tales."

An unintended upside of saving the enemy and expecting nothing in return—sometimes they gave you what couldn't be trusted from the unwilling.

Akel continued at the interested tilt of her head. "One said that he was a leaf in the branch of a general's arm. He cleaned the upper tents at night with others. A man came one night, eighteen moonrises past, and said that he could guarantee victory. That the Shadow Prince would no longer be a concern."

It had been eleven days since the temple, when Osni had tried to kill Kaveh.

"There was another man who came four moonrises later," Akel said. "Completely wrapped in linens. He said that the 'plans' were still in effect. That the man on the field was not the Shadow Prince."

It had to be someone other than Osni then. A hired hand? But a hired hand wouldn't continue a plan like that. Not with the deliberately misleading information being provided. It was deliberate. Too deliberate for someone coin paid.

Someone in on the plan from the first? Or someone taking later advantage?

"Did they hear anything else?"

Reborn on the battlefield, the ducklings who remained in camp were zealous in their perceived tasks, and it was surprising what people in power let slip.

Kaveh, filled with dark hubris on a battlefield, was disproportionately careful when it came to securing his privacy. He never spoke when others were around or when he hadn't secured an area. It was the one area in which Kaveh held no arrogance. He expected to be eavesdropped upon unless he took precautions. Perhaps because of the way he used his own shadow army, he knew how easy it was to be overheard.

Others were far less cautious.

"Just that there would be great reward and the end of the empire, and that they would easily win against the imposter. Two of the other sources—one from Helip, one from Rasse—said that a similarly dressed figure was seen in their camps before they pushed forth against the empire. One saw a trunk of riches. Another, a trunk of spells."

It wasn't a surprise, really. It was the only thing that made sense. There had been no reason for those countries to fight Kaveh. Only the promise that the Imperator General was a fake would have been incentive enough to engage.

The Yalendil boys she had quietly saved and stuffed in with the others had indicated that their army had been ready to disband just one week prior to their battlefield engagement as well.

The question was—who could have been so convincing to the enemy?

"Both lead generals in Shirsk and Helip are dead," Akel said.

"Convenient." No loose ends to question.

"And Yalendil's lead general ran."

Kaveh had shadows looking for the man. It wasn't going to be pleasant for Yalendil's general when he was found. Kaveh hated cowards, especially cowards who directed armies. His prey drive was high in the hunt for such an animal.

Akel nodded, as if he knew what she was thinking. "Word is that the Shirsk and Helip generals were killed by their own troops' hands. People are angry they went to war with the Shadow Prince."

A sudden brush of power moved under her skin, causing her to pause. She brushed fingers along her skin, unnerved. A remnant of the scepter's power, now that it was removed? If she didn't know otherwise, she would think it had reconnected. But there was no way it could have reattached. The feeling was too...soft.

She shook off the silly thought that something had gone wrong with the ritual. She had felt it work. "What about the payment trunks? What happened to them?"

Akel cocked his head. "That I don't know. I will find out."

"Take care of yourself when you do," she warned.

He pushed his chest out. "I am the right hand of Ferra, goddess of birth and health. I am blessed by the gods. I could search for the Eternal Spring and emerge from the Land of Darkness victorious, if you so willed."

She sighed. "Don't die."

"Not when you aren't near," he said loyally. He gave her a deep bow and scampered off to continue his budding espionage career. Akel was exceedingly clever, and he had become adept at healing and saving on the battlefield as well as providing defensive protection to the others.

She thought of Tehras—of the back streets of the city where the urchins were always happy to exchange information for coin. She had tried to help them as best as she could, but secrets were poison. Keeping the Hand away from anyone who could be used against them had been sacrosanct.

Instead, she had changed a few of the healing guild's routes, pushing healers by the less traveled areas. Poverty was a problem with no easy solution.

The library. Someday. She had to hold firm to their dream. That it would help some.

She chatted with a few of the other ducklings outside the tents, fixed light wounds, then felt Kaveh's dark satisfaction curl hard within her mind.

He had found something. She excused herself and walked toward the tent where his mindlight burned bright.

The path through camp opened. The activity of the military camp was efficient and organized—with soldiers traveling worn paths. She kept to the paths herself, not wanting to disrupt the routine, but it didn't matter. Worn footpaths suddenly became untouchable, soldiers' routes deviated when she passed, hulking men sprang to move out of her way.

She was given wide berth by everyone except the ducklings—and even they maintained their distance with awe. She was separated once more. Above. Like walking through the palace in Tehras at nine and being untouchable.

Alone.

She had gotten used to being invisible, but still part of the community. She had gotten used to being held to the same standards as everyone else by day—able to break those standards only at night.

But she couldn't be Ninli ul Summora walking unnoticed through the streets anymore.

She passed a pool of water where the animals were drinking—reflections rippling in the broken waters.

How long would it take before someone in Tehras connected Ninli ul Summora, moderate Level Six healer with a special affinity to labor and birth, with the Shadow Prince's wraith on the battlefield who carried the same name?

And once that rabbit hole opened, how hard would it be to connect an ability to hide her power level with other things? Such as the Hand's complete silence in the past weeks?

She had known from the outset of this undertaking that she couldn't return. She had known a life as Ninli ul Summora was done. That identity had always had a time limit. She had to stop mourning that loss and start figuring out who she would be next.

She took a deep breath. Who did she want to be?

She felt Kaveh's dark satisfaction as she lifted the tent's flap.

Shadows swarmed her, then retreated, leaving her picked clean of outside spells. Only once had someone tried to tag her with a listening spell. That person had died in agony. Nin thought it might have been better to have questioned the perpetrator first, but Kaveh wasn't one for subtlety.

"You feel pleased," she said.

He sat at his desk, reams of papyri surrounding him. "What did your ducklings have to say?"

"They confirmed that at least Shirsk, Helip, and Yalendil were influenced in some way—by news of your death, tales of it not being you, or large payments being made. Whether their leaders were duped or filled with greed, the troops of the enemy were not pleased with what happened after. Rumor claims the dead generals from Shirsk and Helip were killed by their own soldiers."

"Or the perpetrator killed them under the cover of rumor."

She inclined her head in agreement. "Have you found Yalendil's leader?"

"He's in Yal, west of the field on which we fought." He looked at her and she felt anticipation and satisfaction travel the bond from him, mixed with curiosity and just the basest touch of uncertainty.

She tipped her chin. "I can take us there."

He smiled slowly, the uncertainty blinking out as if it hadn't existed. "I'm done here then. Let's—"

"Imperator General!"

No one interrupted unless it was serious, so Kaveh flicked his hand at the tent's flap.

Baksis ul Fehl, twentieth blessed by the emperor, was on the other side with a camp courier, who quickly bowed and backed away, his task finished.

Kaveh motioned for Baksis to enter. Baksis was a handsome man, like most of the emperor's line, imperial features enhanced by the rich brown skin, dark eyes, and short hair of his mother's lands.

Nin knew little about the twentieth blessed except that he was born of a powerful life magi in Punt. He was said to be a keen strategist, but not as adept as Aros. He was said to be a superior fighter, but not as skilled as Kaveh. He was said to be a brilliant scholar, but not as dedicated as Simin.

He was listed second or third best at many things.

More than one of her own siblings had been like that. One of Nin's brothers had reveled in his mediocrity of stature, the freedom it had granted, and the underestimation it gained him. Another had been violent in his hatred of his third-best status and had plotted endlessly in the emotion.

She wondered which of the two Baksis might be.

Baksis looked between them, his gaze both quick and encompassing, then focused on Kaveh. "Shiera is dead."

Nin couldn't restrain her gasp. Shiera ul Fehl, Padifehl of Cuipsin, was a beloved leader to the country of her throne.

"This was left on her body." Baksis handed an amulet to Kaveh. A cracked sapphire rested in the middle.

Kaveh rubbed his thumb over the amulet. Grim certainty dominated the bond. "We found a similar one in a failed assassination attempt."

"An assassin's guild in Tehrasi has been deemed responsible." Baksis addressed Kaveh, gaze never straying, but Nin wasn't fooled. He was taking every opportunity to gather information about her, about them, about the situation surrounding them that only the emperor seemed to know.

Baksis might be second or third best to specific siblings, but that still made him very dangerous. Sher Fehl had chosen women to have children with specifically for qualities he thought would be great. And well-rounded individuals could make the deadliest opponents.

She wondered about Baksis ul Fehl.

KAVEH

"And Cuipsin?" Kaveh asked, to keep Baksis's focus on him.

Baksis, though unnaturally skilled in discretion, kept slipping looks at Nin, who had started picking through the damned figstee platter that the cooks slipped into their tent each day. Kaveh gripped the amulet and focused his displeasure through a shadow. Baksis turned a fraction so that he was looking solely at Kaveh.

Baksis had always been adept at sensing danger. He had never made the mistake of testing Kaveh's boundaries, even when Baksis's powers had fully manifested. Kaveh had been seven and Baksis twelve. Baksis had been one of the more powerful siblings when his magic bloomed, but he had known, even then, not to test Kaveh as some of the others had attempted upon their Awakenings.

"The emperor said to hold for now—the Cuipsins are raging in the streets to find and lift arms in retribution for their padifehl's death—but you should be prepared in case treachery is discovered. The emperor is sending Simin to investigate."

Kaveh looked past Baksis. Shiera was dead. The thought was unpleasant. Urful barely registered as a loss, but he had respected Shiera.

More princes had been made padifehl than princesses, but Shiera had been of bold stock and bolder rule. Eighth blessed by the emperor, she had been born of a warrior from a matriarchal line.

Of all the countries thrust into turmoil over a padifehl's death, hers would be the one most aggrieved.

The others could be explained by multiple hands working in tandem. Adding this death to the mix pointed in a single direction.

"And Tehrasi?"

He could feel Nin stiffen. Would they destroy her people as they had destroyed those blamed for the deaths of Carsue and Urful?

"The winds of blame and rumor are increasingly shifting. Etelian claims he has the dissidents under control. The emperor is visiting Tehras. Nera demanded to accompany him. If someone other than Etelian needs to be blamed..." Baksis shrugged negligently. "Cuipsin will be punished instead."

Kaveh felt a twinge at that. The twinge was strange. Uncomfortable. He didn't agree with punishing Cuipsin if the country wasn't to blame, but he usually didn't feel anything about such decisions.

He would blame it on Nin's emotions overlaying his own again, but he could feel her horror and relief too strongly and separately. She was relieved that her country would not be punished, but was horrified because Cuipsin would be blamed. She had too much compassion. It had started to overflow into him. He didn't know how anyone could hold so much.

Like Baksis, Kaveh knew the game that would be played. Nera's children were sacred. She was the emperor's blind spot. But even her children wouldn't go without punishment in something like this.

"The emperor will install Nera on Tehrasi's throne," Kaveh concluded. "As regent while Etelian is mentored to run the empire at the emperor's side."

"He won't be the one on the throne of the empire when the emperor dies," Baksis said with a sharp, omniscient gaze. "And he will not keep Tehrasi, when that happens."

Kaveh would take the throne and Aros would take Tehrasi.

Kaveh didn't have to look at Nin. They didn't speak much of Aros, so he only knew that, like all smart people, she was wary of the eldest prince. And that she knew Aros was really of Carre blood.

Few believed Aros to be of Fehl blood—but few ever lived after saying it aloud. Even the majexes, the wives and consorts of the emperor, were wary when dealing with the eldest blessed child of the emperor, and they did their best to guard their children from him. Fehl princes and princesses weren't spared from Aros's vengeance.

Though Aros might not be a Fehl by blood, he was Sher Fehl's child in ruthless drive. Aros acquired what he desired and terminated what he did not. Aros didn't seem to like any of their siblings, though sometimes his gaze went distant when looking at those who played with their children.

His gaze was never kind when looking at Etelian's children, though. And Kaveh had never understood nor cared. The second child spawned from Nera still continued to draw breath even as he ruled that which Aros desired. Aros and Etelian's mother, Nera, the first in the emperor's heart, wielded her own power over her children and brooked no death between the seven of them.

Kaveh had sometimes wondered what she had done to keep Aros from killing Etelian.

The emperor, for all his talk of bloodlines, had a soft spot for Aros. His guilt seemed to override everything else when it came to the son born of an enemy's seed.

He thought Nin might rather have Aros on the throne of Tehrasi. Nin hated Etelian. One only had to bring up Taline ul Summora in a conversation that converged with Tehrasi's padifehl to uncover the emotional truth of why she hated him. Though properly wary of the eldest prince, Nin didn't seem to hate him the way she did Etelian.

It was all moot, though. The emperor would live for a long time, and he couldn't put Aros on Tehrasi's throne. "The emperor is giving Aros the northern Medit in its entirety when we finish conquering those lands."

Due to the other revolts, Kaveh had been unable to push forth on the northwestern Medit territories. It was a good motive for someone to use—especially someone who might want Aros to get pinched. Someone like Simin, who would rule indefinitely with access to so much water-bound territory.

"Rich territories—the territories of a true king"—and something in Baksis's expression indicated that he was thinking the same about some of their siblings, Simin in particular—"but they aren't the City of a Hundred Gates," Baksis said.

"What use are the gates without scepters to power them?"

Baksis inclined his head. "There will be other gatemakers. The secrets of the scepters are not forever locked in the death of the Carres."

Baksis's gaze touched upon Nin. But Nin's feelings were locked tight. Her feelings remained open to Kaveh, should he choose to flip through them, but her facial expression spoke of deep disinterest.

He noticed that she was concentrating on a stray patch of lamp light, eyes empty as if terminally bored. Clever girl.

"The scepters matter not for this," Kaveh said.

"No."

"Do you have anything else to give me?"

"Only warning."

Kaveh nodded and lifted the tent flap with a shadow.

Baksis gave Nin a long look before striding out. If Kaveh cared about court, he might be curious about the rumors. But court was useless to him.

As soon as Baksis was gone and Kaveh had secured the interior once more, Nin pounced. "Shiera was known as a beloved leader. The Cuipsins are likely innocent."

"They will be murdered in the real perpetrators' stead, should the emperor order it."

Nin's brows drew together. "And you don't find that concerning?"

It was odd to him that she asked him that. She knew that he didn't. And yet, he couldn't respond. Something was making him doubt.

Ludicrous. Ludicrous, that he would doubt.

"Yalendil?" he asked instead.

She stared at him for a long moment, her turmoil and tension swirling—swirling into him.

"We will find the real perpetrator," he added tensely, unable to deal with doubt. "We will uncover the truth. Together."

She unfurled her hand and extended it. Relief exploded inside him in an amount far too great to only be from her.

He put his hand in hers.

CHAPTER EIGHTEEN

REVELATIONS OF FURY

TALINE

(The Death Chamber in Ur)

Taline felt...devoid. A piece of her was gone. A piece that she couldn't place.

"Sehk-be-damned—" Valeran's fist hit the floor.

Taline stared uncomprehendingly at the room around them. She touched her chest—what piece was she missing? "I think...I think we are in Ur. The royal tombs?"

"The death chamber." Valeran's voice was dark and resigned. She followed his gaze to a plinth that held an idol atop. "This is truly great, narsumina. Excellent. Prime. You wielded the scepter after we removed a piece. Do you know what that means?"

"They knew," she said, chest heaving, ignoring the acknowledgment of the repercussions he was demanding. She looked down at her chest. What had she lost? "They knew we'd be there. Valeran—"

"It wasn't me, narsumina. They felt you wield the scepter on the sea. Everyone within a million paces across five layers probably did!" He rolled onto crouched heels to gaze at the setting sun through the sky openings, then thrust his hand into his pack. "They will be scrambling. There will be people awaiting us at the temples nearest our position due west. They'll be here, too, soon."

He withdrew a round disc and flung it across the floor with a hard flick of his wrist. It hit the point where the chamber doors met and spread five fingers across the gold of each. It was a locking mechanism that would prevent anyone from entering through normal means.

He closed his eyes. "Never underestimate the scramble of those willing to die for a cause. Humanity." He started digging through the pack again.

She looked at the scepter. Humanity? Is that what she had lost? "It doesn't matter." She felt separate from humanity in that moment.

When she looked back at him, he was looking at her with a grim resignation—his hand deep within the pack. There was a remote emptiness in his gaze, like everything was happening exactly to the specifications of the worst plan. "The scepter reattached itself to you, Taline. Do you understand the consequences of that?"

"Yes." The pain of the partial separation was not a good memory. The feelings coursing through her after having used the scepter...would not be either. "It is more strongly attached now than it was before."

She could feel it better, too—she knew the scepter better suddenly. The part of Nin it had held previously...that part was gone. She had lost Nin.

And some part of her didn't care, but the rest of her filled with horror. She stared at the scepter. Knowing what it was and feeling what it was were two entirely different things. She was beginning to understand the evil she held now, truly.

"The scepter will be harder to separate from you now. It knows now what you plan to do. Remember who you are."

"I know who I am, Valeran," she snapped.

Some of the emptiness in his gaze filled with sardonic amusement. "What a relief."

His gaze darted to the ceiling, the plinth, the doors, the bowls, the idol. "It will only be a matter of a minute more before a patrol attempts entry." He made no move to rise. His words were muffled as he rifled through his bag. "A tomb in Ur, just where I always wanted my final resting place."

She pulled herself to her knees and examined the room. Bowls dotted the floor in a similar network here, too. "The location coordinates are in the bowls. I can get us anywhere connected." What could it hurt, now?

Yes. Use me.

She looked at the scepter. It felt heavier...infused. "I might be able to...get us home even."

The scepter head glistened in the fading sun. Yes, it said, in a few moons more.

"Not a chance."

She licked her lips, still staring at where her palm was once more fully fused. "I don't need you, Valeran. I can get me back."

"If the pentalayerists could pinpoint you in the non-magic layer, what do you think will happen in ours? Every hunter in the layers is probably after us now."

"Valeran—"

"I'm certain that it will all work out, though. Go ahead. Open a path to Tehras or Fehlaka. There will be no trap. All good faith from the empire, too, I'm sure. Ninli will be released and you can both frolic in fields of gold." A tired hand dropped over his eyes. "Oh, and now the ritual cannot be stopped. Don't forget the fine details."

"What do you mean?"

He fished out the scroll with tight lips and tossed it in her direction. "Once engaged, the ritual must be completed—in either direction. The bond must be fully severed or secured."

She gripped the scepter, refusing to reach for the scroll. "We are now in a worse position—because you made me start the unbinding."

"We are in a worse position because you used the scepter."

"I saved us."

"Your madness will save no one," he said bitterly, rolling to his feet.

Her vision tunneled. "You will be the first I kill when I ascend."

Silence rang. The vow had come out far more calmly and coldly than intended.

"I believe you." Valeran's gaze was remote.

Taline held still, fear seeping through the chill as she pushed shaky fingers against her brows—the scepter heavy in her right hand. She had meant that. When she said it, her soul had meant it. She pushed at the panic rising in her. It was okay. She was fine. This was not madness yet.

When she finally looked at him again, Valeran looked as though he knew exactly what she was thinking, and that he wasn't surprised by her lack of control.

She bared her teeth. "We'll go to our layer, then have the scepter take us to Nin."

"I see. You want Ninli dead after all."

Taline bared more of her teeth and rose to her feet to meet him. "How dare you. After you betrayed h—"

"Betrayed her? I did what she wanted."

"You've done noth—"

Fury suffused his face in a way she had never seen before—a ruddy, all-consuming rage. "I did exactly what she wanted. When it comes down to it, she will sacrifice everything to keep her most precious safe. Ties that bind and kill. Stupidity and suffering. These are the things that the imbecilic, the lonely, cling to—ties to others. A madness all its own. All she wanted was for you to be safe. I delivered you to safety."

"Safety? You've gone mad."

"Did you think Kaveh ul Fehl was going to let you keep such a prize?"

"You put it in my hand."

"I stopped the empire's hand. I stopped the empire from going down the path of all those in Tehrasi who tried wielding it before. I stopped the empire from finding a prize they would never be able to control and that would see all of us in the shadows in chains. Did you want Ninli dead or chained? What about all those like her, living in secret?"

"No one—"

Valeran grabbed her roughly—in a way he had never done before, as if he were on his last mental leg. "Not all the scepters control gates. Some find gatemakers and others of desired ability. Think."

He shook her, released her, shuddered, then retreated a step away.

Frozen, she could do nothing but turn his words and actions over in a repeated loop. Some find g atemakers.

Etelian's scepter.

"Nin knew," she said numbly. "She knows what the scepters do."

He paced restlessly from one bowl to another, as if he wanted to find answers there but knew they weren't inside. "Better than anyone. She didn't want the scepter you hold to be found or used. But as soon as she saved you in that Tehrasian alley, it was over. As soon as she stepped between both of us and the Shadow Prince, she made her decision. In an endless fall of karogi tiles, she had to choose what and who to sacrifice. She sacrificed herself for me, for you, and you taunt that sacrifice, trying to make it worthless."

Cold. Her chest felt like an ice storm had blown through.

"But the oath-sworn month—"

"Was a patch. Temporary. And she would have believed in it, for you, for twenty-eight days. You would have lived together, sampling some foreign city in hidden delight. You would have lived happily for twenty-eight days, then Ninli would have tucked you in and disappeared before the twenty-ninth moonrise. Gone from you to wait on a moonlit hill for the Shadow Prince to appear and take her away—like she knew he would."

"No—"

Valeran stood in front of the idol and cut a harsh hand through the air. "She would have been on that hill. She would never have allowed a fight to ensue after seeing him use his powers. She would never allow you to be in the crossfire. She would sacrifice everything to avoid that. She would never have allowed you to know he was there, waiting for her. She knew the Shadow Prince would always come for her once he saw her powers. She would save you yet again, then she would sacrifice herself to destroy the scepter she put in his hands."

Devastation wound through Taline. "The empire doesn't know how to use the scepters."

"The Scepter of Darkness is a key that can reveal the secrets of the others. All one needs is time."

There was something in his voice. She narrowed her eyes. "And what other kinds of magi do the scepters find?" She needed to think of anything else.

He smiled without humor, staring at the death idol sitting blandly on its plinth. "Those who desire to stay hidden."

"You?"

"The emperor is clever. Smarter than the Carres were. He would figure out how to fully use the scepters with a key in his hand, and the madness induced by that one"—he pointed harshly at the scepter in her hand—"would make certain it was for ill."

She thought of what the pentalayerists had revealed—what Valeran had revealed. "You were going to destroy the scepter from the beginning."

"Yes." He stared at her with an iron gaze.

"You were planning to betray us from the beginning."

"Betrayal requires concealment. Ninli has always known what I've done with the relics I find." He narrowed his eyes at the idol, leaning forward to read the script circling it. "She knew before she requested my help."

He began rifling through his bag again. "My goals have never changed, and they never will. I am iron. Ninli knows that. She knew it when she made that vow."

The ice curled into brittle fragments. "To save us."

"Yes, Sehk-damned always." He dropped three marbles at the base of the plinth, watched how they rolled, then scooped them back into his bag. "Ninli would die if she thought of herself as anything other than a flame or an aid to something or someone else. I never changed my goal. Your sister did. Only you remained ignorant, and that was of your own making." He looked at her, gaze remote, as he removed another instrument.

"Her oath—"

"Her oath dropped me the moment we disappeared. There's a chance you are still protected until the dark moon. Ninli is clever even when she is beyond stupid."

Taline looked to the side. The temple wavered in her view. "She knew you wouldn't let the scepter be put into the empire's hands," she said, as if testing it on her tongue.

He hesitated for a moment, and it struck her that he might be trying to reach for a kindness that he didn't know how to express. But in the end, Valeran was Valeran, and the blunt truth was, "Yes."

Taline looked at the scepter. "She lied to me."

Valeran didn't say anything for a long moment. "She loved you."

"Loves, loves," she said, feeling the ice crack fully and break in brittle shards. "She's still alive."

"Figure out who you are angry with, narsumina."

"I'm angry with all of you. Nin sacrificed herself." Taline closed her eyes. "She knew." Of course she had.

"Of course she did," he said gruffly. "She would throw herself upon a pyre if Tehrasi asked it. She would build the pyre by hand if it was you or…or one of her others. She has no right making decisions. She makes decisions for the sake of others. The only thing that has saved her in the last few years is you."

"But if she knew the scepter could unlock the others—"

"I'm sure she thought she would be able to fix that at some point." He smiled grimly. "She has too much power and it has saved her too many times. She relies on the fact that major things will work out. They usually do. Saving us was too immediate for her to worry about world-breaking events. If there's a Sehk-be-damned kitten in the street, and she's running for her life, she'll still try to save it. She has too much power to think beyond immediate rescue and intuitive, stupid luck. Thinking is what she had you for."

That brought her up short. "She—"

"She knew the risks." He rifled through Nin's pack next. "She's known the risks since she was nine. Since she was born. She put herself in harm's way. Over and over again. She didn't have to help anyone. What has her guilt ever gotten her?"

And it was just like that the ice started to melt instead of pierce her organs—that the agony of anger turned to dull sadness. "It has gotten her people who strive to do better because of her example. People who care about her."

He laughed. "Who? People like me? People lie."

But it was in her melt from anger to understanding that he said it, and the realization slid over her with the understanding. "You...do. You care about her."

"I care about no one." He flashed his teeth. "You know that more than anyone."

She stared at him. "You do care. I use guilt as primary weapon with you, but it's not guilt or erasing a debt, is it? You truly care. She is family to you."

"Family is poison."

"Call it something else, then." She felt the strangest sense of calm—a feeling that had been absent since arriving in this cursed layer. The scepter stayed silent, as if knowing it had to suddenly exercise care. "She is one of yours, as you are one of hers. Why did you leave her to the empire?"

Valeran said nothing for so long that she didn't think he was going to answer. "I made a promise. I promised to take you if I ran. I promised to keep you safe if things went poorly."

She looked steadily at him. "Why?"

"It matters not."

"It matters, Rone ul Valeran."

He looked at his gloves, curling the tips into his palms. He closed his eyes. "Infected. I was infected by a Summora, like all the other middling infants in Tehrasi."

He opened his eyes and she opened her palm, displaying the fused scepter in it.

"She wouldn't have wanted me to have this," she said.

You are ours now.

"No. She was probably quite displeased by that."

"We could have all come here," Taline whispered, feeling pain curl in her heart. "Why not all three of us?"

"I told you—her fate was sealed. Kaveh ul Fehl saw her abilities and her eyes. He will never let her go."

"We could have run."

"We really couldn't have, narsumina." Valeran sighed and rubbed a hand along his eyes. "We couldn't have gotten anywhere with Ninli and the scepter in proximity, and the Shadow

Prince at our heels. Worse than the problem we have now, even—and that's saying something because the pentalayerists will be at the next temple we go to, and the one after. When you want something enough—"

"They can't be everywhere."

The handle of the door turned. Valeran's instrument held firm.

Loud pounding shook the chamber.

Let me destroy them.

"They'll be everywhere we go," Valeran said grimly, looking at the door and withdrawing three pieces of a long instrument from his pack. "As will others, on their heels. The news will have spread that the scepter has been found. It won't be just bounty hunters. Every relic hunter in the layers will be on our trail, and we've lit a lantern for them to track. To think otherwise is to be a fool. That thing in your hand calls to them. They will be able to find us."

"How?"

"Relics. They will use items that have ways of tracking active objects of power."

Let me destroy them.

She looked at the scepter. It hummed back. "The pentalayerists should have known how to get the scepter before."

"It lay dormant and without a wielder, and thus remained hidden. Until now." He waved at her hand. "It is active now. The ritual has energized everything about it."

"Where do we go?" She gripped the scepter as the pounding grew louder and shouting followed. The scraping sounds of a large pole being dragged across stone echoed. A non-magic solution—a battering ram to open a closed door. "We must find a way from here that they do not know."

"We go through the Gate of Death." He indicated the idol on the plinth with a thumb and assembled the last piece of his tool.

Disbelief made her stumble. "We are in Ur."

"Yes."

She stared at the idol. "The Gate of Death here is cursed by the gods." Even in this layer, such a curse would be active. The scepter perked up in interest. I would like to see this curse.

Valeran rolled his eyes at her words, but there was a glimmer of light in their depths again. "It is as cursed by the gods as the Temple at Sur or the relic of Hez."

She stared at him. "Yes?"

"It is as cursed as your tongue." He shook his head, flint-tipped fingers working. "You want to talk about curses from the gods..."

Taline looked at him in stupefaction. "You are one of the most knowledgeable hunters of cursed relics who exists. Weren't you the one who found the relic of Hez? Who claimed to have unlatched the source at Sur?"

"That I was." He attached the rods together in triangle shape. The pounding grew louder as the battering began.

"Then how can you say that? Ur—"

"I can say that because I cursed them. Or destroyed them later." He knelt and examined the plinth. "Hard to believe in godly curses when you know you are the one manipulating half of them."

She stayed silent so long that he looked back at her. She was still staring at him. He sighed and turned back to the idol and its holder.

"What did those men mean about you destroying artifacts?" she asked quietly.

"It doesn't matter."

"I think it does."

"Why?"

Because I've judged you by your worst traits. Because I've thought you a fool for losing relics of power when all this time you've been deliberately trying to save people. Because I don't understand who you are.

"Because I have an artifact clinging to me that we are talking about destroying," she said.

The scepter vibrated in her hand and she jumped.

He tapped his finger against the stone column and looked at the scepter from beneath half-closed lids. "Best not to speak too much of such things still. Some objects of power are too dangerous to exist. Some are nearly sentient in their need to be free."

"The scepter wants to see the curse."

Valeran snorted and bent back to work on an idol of death. "Tell it that it will have to stay dormant until then."

Yes, the scepter said eagerly. She stared at it, unnerved.

"So the Sehk Curse on the Gate of Death isn't real?"

"Curses are, of course, real." He touched the stone column and carefully lifted the idol. "We use spells every day for such things. But curses from beyond?"

The column lit with light. The building began shaking and a mighty roar sounded beneath them.

Valeran stared at the vibrating idol in his hands and smiled. "They usually need a bit of earthly help."

The chamber wall burst inward with a roar.

CHAPTER NINETEEN

HEADY DESCENT

KAVEH

(YALENDIL)

As soon as the last spark of magic winked out from Nin's ripgate, Kaveh pulled in the swirling circle of protective shadows he had expelled outward to hide the ripgate's opening.

No one questioned any magic done within his shadows. Everyone knew dark magic knew no bounds in the hands of the Shadow Prince.

A sharp smile tugged his lips. He looked at the woman at his side as she calmly smoothed a hand over the pin connecting the two sides of her cloak together. She displayed no magic strain over the creation of the temporary gate—nothing like the gatekeepers who sweated and whined over the smallest change in destination on an already established gate.

What they could do together, if she let her powers free... Nin's power was heady in conjunction with his. She was an absolute asset at his side.

She looked at him in warning—reading the possessiveness he couldn't deny. It was the subsequent understanding and resignation along the bond that made him look away.

He examined the desolate, cold battlefield instead. Two magi who were looting corpses in the distance made choking noises upon seeing them and sprinted in the opposite direction. Kaveh wondered idly which one to spear first, but a small hand nudged his back, saving them.

"Where to next?" she asked.

He examined the landscape and pointed. "Can you get us to that ridge?"

"Yes."

On the scorched field in the midday sun, shadows were sparse, but he wrenched what little there were upward and over them to hide Nin's ripgate, as Nin sliced them through space.

Nin could only travel long distances to places she "knew"—places she had ingrained in her mind or places she could visibly see. That meant that although she had been able to get them to the battlefield they had fought on in Yalendil, they were still far from the Yal hiding spot of the Yalendil general. But Kaveh's spies easily whispered the way.

With pointed directions for Nin, and the long shadows of the city reaching for Kaveh, they shadow traveled on a continuous path and easily located the general's hideout before anyone could warn the traitor of their arrival—something that would not have been possible had they used the gate to the city.

It was better this way, too, since established gates made Nin uncomfortable. He had observed her discomfort each time the imperial forces marched through gates to the next conquest. He found himself willing to do much to alleviate her discomfort more and more with each passing day.

Hood drawn down, Nin stood beside him as Kaveh unveiled them from the clutch of shadows greedily trying to gain control. People in the street abruptly fled screaming in trailing skirts and cloaks.

The Yalendil general had nowhere to flee, though. He was a man without ally.

The general scuttled like a sand crab back into the corner, putting up no fight as shadows burst through the door. Coward.

"Please, my family. Please." He looked at Nin, eyes pleading, and Kaveh felt Nin soften the slightest bit. "My wife and kids. You must—"

Kaveh enveloped him in shadows. The man's voice twisted into the pained cry of an animal caught in death sand. Crushed knee. Snapped wrist. The man gurgled as his foot was bent backward, and tears burst from his eyes.

"You have no family," Kaveh said pleasantly. "I checked before bringing her with me."

Nin eyed him from under her hood. She was touching the bond, feeling for the answer. He offered her the only thing he could anymore—the truth. He knew her like he knew himself now. She would have never let him crush a man who had family depending on him.

But a liar who let his soldiers die? Her softening was erased.

The man—Kaveh couldn't be bothered to give him a name—saw it, too. "I should never have taken the gold, Imperator General. I see that now. But I can still be of worth. Put me in your service. I bow to—"

"Where is the gold?"

The traitor licked his lips. Sweat poured down his face.

Kaveh tugged at the shadows creeping behind the man and pulled one through the middle disk of his spine.

"I, I, I, it's here! It's here!" He pointed with his one good hand.

"Don't touch anything," Kaveh said to Nin. "Contain it first."

Nin gave him an exasperated look but continued forward.

She cast a containment spell on the chest, the fine fibers of enchantment wrapping around the edges. It would absorb her concentration for a few moments.

Kaveh leaned into the general, taking advantage of Nin's concentration elsewhere. "Who did you meet?"

"I don't know. I—"

Kaveh checked the bond to make sure Nin was focused on the enchantment, then pulled a sliver of shadow along Yalendil's arm, yanking the main vein upward.

"Please!" The man's voice went shrill. He clutched at his arm, as if he could push everything back into place. "Your Imperial Majesty!"

"Highness," he said pleasantly. "Address me as Your Imperial Highness. Majesty means the emperor."

"Your 'Perial 'Ighness." The man started to slur.

"Who gave you the chest?"

"T'rsi."

"Who from Tehrasi?"

He could feel Nin stiffen, containment finished. Sehk-be-damned, she was fast. Pleasure warred with consternation at her talent and speed. He had known Tehrasi would be the answer. He had wanted to spare her the pain.

"I dn't knw," the man slurred. "Someone loy'l to the Carres. He had a ring."

"Lies," Nin spit.

Kaveh lightened his hold on the man, surprise at her exclamation causing him to turn to her.

The general gasped in greedy gulps of air under the loosened grip. "He had a ring. A ring of Tehrasi. A ring of the Carres. He said that the padifehl was complicit."

"There is no one loyal to the Carres in the Palace of Tehras."

"I don't know. I don't know. The orders the man gave me are in the chest. I was told I just needed to wait a few full moon cycles—that I would be celebrated in the new empire. He said the emperor would be assassinated. He said Etelian would welcome m—"

Kaveh broke the man's neck. He let the body drop to the ground, then lit it on fire. Fury overwhelmed him.

He lifted the secured chest of gold with his shadows and strode toward the door. Black flames lit and curled behind him. Fury and resolution carried him through the streets.

Nin hurried after him. "Kaveh, wait. I want Etelian gone more than anyone, but you said we'd search for the truth. Osni hates Etelian. Slightly less than he hates Aros, but Etelian is still of Nera's blood. He hates Nera. There is more to this. You cannot go anywhere with such vengeance riding your actions. You will kill everyone you see and miss all that is hidden beneath. Wait."

Kaveh stopped abruptly and turned. "If you wanted Osni dead, why didn't you say something about his desire for Etelian's—for Nera's—death any time in the past ten years? Why did you not get that information to the emperor? Or to me?"

She looked at him in quiet disbelief. "Get that information to you? You never would have believed the warning, nor cared. What care have you ever shown for what happens in the kingdoms of the empire? You've only shown care about the next conquest. You are known as the Merciless, the Soulless, the Conqueror Without Remorse."

He felt something uncomfortable slide down the bond. When her eyes softened a fraction, he was startled to realize the discomfort had been from him. That his fury had calmed and that he felt discomfort instead. He ruthlessly pushed the feeling aside.

"If you'd shown yourself," he said, "I may have given your words heed."

Her eyes stayed steady and calming. "And then you would have hunted me down." She didn't wait for him to confirm it—they both knew it was true. "I would have been in an even worse position than I am now."

Her calm was invasive. Unwanted.

"But Tehrasi would not," he said without mercy. He needed his fury back.

Her fingers clenched and he felt the burn of her. "What difference does it make for Tehrasi when you have someone like your brother ruling?

When the people you have 'freed' from my family are still dictated to by a madman? Nearly anyone on the throne would be better than Etelian. What care did I have that Osni plotted to kill him? I will see Etelian ul Fehl burn."

He clutched at the flame of her emotions—clutched it like the calming balm that only the mad could claim.

"Treason," he said mildly.

"Then be the blade." She yanked aside her cloak, baring her neck. "I will never cease wanting Etelian to pay for his crimes. But I also want the truth of who bears the empire ill."

"And what crimes do you plan to avenge?" He looked coolly down at her. "A few women suffering to Etelian's whims? The rest of the empire continues."

The pure, blinding rage of her reaction was immense. Beautiful. He leaned closer as she took hold and channeled the rage into something sharper. Heady. His skin prickled with it.

"You spend too much time conquering and no time leading," she said sharply. "You leave people in charge, people who lick your boots and shine your spoils and give you all the answers you want to hear, and you don't hear the lies—or you don't care to hear them. And this is what you get—an empire that is burning from underneath and an emperor who will be dead in a year."

Magic bristled across his skin. "You know nothing of what you speak. My father—"

"Cares only about his next conquest—both in country and body. He seeks to sow his legacy in land, seed, and blood. He cares nothing about his padifehls' actions, when they are of Nera's bane."

"You toe a thin line."

"Tell me what happens on the Feast Day of Gripna in Lear? Tell me."

"A day that celebrates Gripna, I assume, with domestic matters of hearth, estate, and mercantile festivities—"

"The High Priest selects six girls and six boys to receive the special blessing."

He could guess what that meant from her emotions and tone. "If you know anything of me, it is that I have little interest in pleasures of the flesh."

Color rose in her cheeks, and that uncomfortable feeling spread through his chest again.

"They are given for a week to those whose estates were especially fertile or lucrative that year."

He watched her face, lit with impassioned outrage, and said nothing as her lips continued to form words.

"A reward of flesh to those of the community who brought in the most imperial coin. The participants chosen do not have the choice to participate."

"Hardly the only of its kind."

"Yes."

"I care nothing for such things." But he remembered, briefly, that there had been a mention of Lear in the notes on the Hand. The thief had caused a disruption in the city large enough that they had canceled the festivities.

"I know. I know you don't care, and you have the gall to ask me why, as a complete stranger, I would not have brought something to your attention."

"You were raised to be a queen. What care have you for those chosen to serve?"

"I am not a queen. I am a citizen of the empire. The one serving could be me."

Revulsion. "It won't."

"I am nothing more than any other," she said ruthlessly. "Tell me what happens in the Festival of Marsk in Gerod?"

"I have no idea. I assume something terrible."

"What about the Spread of Verdis in Campistel?"

"Have you made a list?"

"I have a list, and it is long."

"What would you have me do?" he demanded.

"Not ignore what is beneath your feet as you move your feet forward!"

"So you would have me ignore the injustices somewhere like Orso? With what they do to their young? We freed them."

"I would have you do both! There is room for both. Don't continue on until you've first fixed what is beneath!"

"You ask of me things I will not give."

Her shoulders dropped. She touched a shaking hand to her face, covering her eyes. "I know. It's okay," she whispered.

His chest tightened.

She motioned at the box with a shaking finger. "But we are going somewhere safe to open that. And we are going to talk about what's inside before going off on a killing spree after a single threat to your father."

He watched her a long moment more. The discomfort swirling in his chest was unwanted and painful.

"Fine." He threw out his hand and swirled shadows around them in an all-encompassing cocoon. Ifret dove inside his cloak. "Open your gate."

She opened the ripgate, and it was with far too much ease that he stepped through, secure in the notion that she wasn't going to betray him.

An odd feeling. One he couldn't seem to stop.

The oasis they stepped onto was a deep, thin oval in the middle of a vast stretch of stark desert—a small, glittering, fertile slice inside an unforgiving landscape.

"It's like looking inside you," she murmured.

He looked sharply at her—at the comment which seemed an answer to his thoughts.

She stroked one of the shadows that was dispersing from her shoulders in the harsh sunlight. "Thoughts go both ways across the shadows and bond when you feel strongly."

He yanked in his remaining shadows, bloodlust rearing inside panic. "You can read my thoughts?"

She didn't look away. "I won't use them against you."

He took a step backward—a motion so peculiar that he felt off-balance.

"Come," she said. "Let's get into the shade so Ifret doesn't wither away."

The shadow hissed irritably from inside his cloak but shot out as soon as they were beneath the cooling shade of the date palms. Kaveh locked his turmoil away and pretended it didn't exist.

They made quick work of unlocking the spells on the chest, which weren't made to withstand two overpowered magi who could work synchronously.

Inside the chest was a demon's payment of gold, two papyri scrolls stamped with the golden winged serpent of Tehrasi, and a thick, unbroken sapphire set in a familiar type of amulet.

Nin cast a freezing spell on the amulet, then lifted it, while Kaveh went for the scrolls. One scroll was specifically addressed to the Yalendil general with the assurances that Tehrasi would be a safe haven for him in six moon cycles.

The other held directions to the guild of assassins.

"A trap," Nin murmured, after Kaveh read both to her.

"Yes." Kaveh refolded the scrolls. "A nice, neat little package of artifacts. Whoever is at the other end will die all the same."

Kaveh stretched his fingers. An entire guild of assassins. It had been a while since he'd had a challenge.

Nin sighed. "Information first."

"Whoever is at the other end will die all the same—after they give us their information," he amended as he looked at her. "I discovered your identity, did I not? I know how to interrogate."

She looked pointedly at the general's blood painting the side of the chest. "I feel like you know how to start an interrogation."

"I didn't kill your investigore."

"He would never be as stupid as the Yalendil general was."

"No." He tilted his head. "I don't do well with stupid."

Nin handed the amulet to him. "There is no assassin inside, but there is a cavity for one. Made by a Tehras scepter or a similar relic, I'd guess. What does it say?"

He examined her, still unnerved by the fact that she couldn't read and had to compensate for it by trusting others. He looked at the amulet. "The same inscription—the Arms of Truth."

She picked at the patches of greenery beneath her fingers. "The arms of truth, the hands of pain, the legs of fear, the heels of glory, those are the things that bring victory."

He could feel her resignation. "Tehrasi."

"We question the guild," she said grimly, "then take the evidence to the emperor."

He examined her. "Going to stop running from your past?"

"No." She stood and briskly brushed her cloak. Ifret took the cue and dove into his. "But the empire deserves its answers."

"Bold words from one easily labeled a traitor by your deeds as the Hand."

"I told you—I have never sought to overthrow your empire. Seeking change in one area doesn't mean you hate the whole. It means you believe in something enough to want it to be the best it can be."

He had been raised to believe the empire was already the best way it could be. "Might is all."

"Might is what wins," she agreed. "Other things are what create continued success."

"Might will win today," he said pointedly.

She sighed. "We should stop at camp for my healing belt first. Something tells me I will need it."

"I won't need you to heal me."

"That I will need it for all the people we need to revive."

He wrapped them in shadow and his dark laughter whirled around them as she opened a ripgate to their tent with a rueful huff.

He could have had this so long ago. What else had been lost due to the mistake of lining up the Carres for execution entertainment?

Fortunately, he had used his shadows out of pure instinct and iron belief in his oath to keep her secrets safe. Because when they entered their tent in a swirl of shadow, they weren't alone.

The emperor stared at them in displeasure, lips tight at Kaveh's fading smile.

"The scepters of Tehras are gone," the emperor said.

CHAPTER TWENTY

REVELATIONS

RONE

(Ur Temple in the First Layer)

The basement chamber opened with a bloom of smoke and poisonous air, at the same time the antechamber door blew open and a dozen men with spears spilled inside. Rone was already moving to meet them.

"Go!" He yelled at Taline.

He ducked, grabbed, and swung even as he started counting the rumbles below. One pillar, two pillars, slide, slide, slide, three pillars, slide. Masonry exploded around him. The slithering—and length of each slide—confirmed the curse's size.

A man ran at Rone and Taline used the scepter head to punch him in the throat. She swung her pack across her back, not heeding Rone's command to flee. But the scepter seemed to have taken his words seriously, and it remained unlit. "What is it? What did you do?"

"I released the poor, beleaguered temple guardian from his five-hundred-year sleep."

"The curse is a guardian? A snake?"

"So much better." He smiled as he disarmed and incapacitated a man with a broken wrist and leg. "Sandpronga."

He caught Taline's horrified gaze before she punched another man with a magic-infused fist. These were regular foot soldiers answering a blocked patrol instead of the cloaked men in charge. The latter would likely be catching up any time. They would do better to end this quickly—especially before the sand serpent showed for a post-hibernation snack.

He exchanged a look with Taline and was irritatingly pleased to see her quick nod as she rotated her foot into an opening position of a two-man form. It made him pause—not the two-man form, that was to be expected—but the easily read communication. When had they become a team?

She moved first. He followed, wasting no moments to dwell on unsettling thoughts.

"Why is one in the non-magic world?"

"Leftovers from another age. Hibernation."

In the split, the magical creatures had been mostly shifted to the beast layer. But there were remnants of all things—people, animals, creatures, beings, and beasts—that had been stranded in the wrong layer during the split. Hibernating animals had suffered the worst.

"How long?"

"Two minutes."

Undisturbed for five hundred years, the enormous serpent below would be ravenous.

The fourth pillar crashed.

A level below theirs collapsed and their floor wobbled.

"How many levels?"

"Three," he said, calculating distance by sound and the way the temple sides were engineered.

Cloaked men finally poured through the outer door.

"How many can you handle, Summora?"

"More than you, Valeran."

He felt the stretch of his lips and saw the answering lift of hers.

"Power hungry scum," a pentalayerist shouted at Taline, diving toward her.

She ducked, kicked his ankle, then planted her hand flat against his midsection and twisted. The man seized up, then fell. Taline was already moving, lips grim.

Rone snapped a third wrist and kept pace with the creature slithering below, leading Taline in the same dance. He was accustomed to fighting with Ninli more than with Taline, but he understood Taline's strengths.

Taline was a more disciplined fighter than Ninli and her form and movements were perfect. Taline had rigorously trained with someone skilled in hand-to-hand combat and drilled her movements to scroll-given perfection.

Ninli, on the other hand, was an intuitive fighter with more power than training. Growing up in the palace with bodyguards, she had never learned how to fight, but she had learned how to survive. The streets had taught her more of the same. Survive, flee, dart, and use cleverness over brawn.

Taline was a survivor as well, and he wasn't surprised she had spent part of the last four years learning how to make certain she could defend herself should shadows rise from her past.

She wouldn't beat someone at the top of the fighting chain, and she would never succeed in a brute strength battle, but she could hold her own in the dance. And she was smart.

He watched her apply just enough force with her strike before leaping back and blowing sleeping dust from her bag. The man, inhaling sharply after the strike to his chest, dropped.

Both of the girls used their knowledge of the human body to strike quickly and with impunity while conserving strength. Neither ever dealt the type of death blow that would leave them open to a last strike.

She downed two more with the dust and he took a moment to pivot them, take the blow coming for her right shoulder, and to admire the work she had left behind in splayed bodies and non-lethal blows.

Taline was more deadly in a world without magic than in a world saturated by it—for she relied little on power and far more on calculation. Her opponents, without outright magic to defend themselves, fell to the pinpointed strikes she used while conserving her magic and energy as simple as she controlled her breathing.

Rone was far more like Ninli, in the way that they had to control themselves simply not to out themselves. But the application of power was secondary to the knowledge that if things got rough, they could get themselves out of it—that they could increase their power output beyond a level others would expect, and overcome the enemy.

Taline had none of that. And her power had been reduced even further with continued exposure to Etelian ul Fehl's cursed talents. Taline had no secret power level to rely on. She had only her own cunning and forethought. She had used that to give herself an advantage with her spellboxes and Ninli's endless power to use.

Taline whirled and upended a man with the scepter's staff.

She wasn't a staff fighter; she was a small item fighter. But she was a quick learner and used to being hampered by things outside of her control. In the long days that had passed since they had arrived in the non-magic world, she had exercised daily to figure out the weight and swing of the scepter.

"Gathering linen in your brain, Valeran?" She jabbed the man closing in behind him.

"Only the prettiest bits for you, Summora." He slid his knife into her opponent's side.

It was a dance he so seldom found with another—for there was trust in this dance. Trust in the other person to watch his back—and not stab it instead.

"You are the prettiest, according to Nin."

"Please, my chastity can't handle such compliments from you." He batted his lashes and slashed another man.

The barbs—always present between them—were suddenly a lot more playful and less biting.

"Chastity...of competence?"

It was one thing he had always liked about her. She treated him the same way she treated everyone who wasn't Nin.

Most people saw his Valeran hair and felt the Fehl in him and he was automatically treated with deferential suspicion and caution. A Valeran expunged from the herd, a Fehl not part of the numbered, blessed imperial children—not trusted by the elite, not trusted by the simple folks, not trusted by those between.

And he was happy with that. He had demanded those circumstances. He neither wanted, nor needed, the trust others sought. All trust meant was leaving himself open to a stab of the worst kind.

But it was exhilarating to fight with someone he could trust. It had always been so with Ninli, who was the only one foolish enough not to stab him in the back. Occasionally, he found a partner who could be trusted up until securing a prize—temporary alliances that nevertheless made for invigorating fighting and plotting.

Taline had always been such a partner—allied for the prize—but she had also been Summora-infected. She had taken the name. There was a code of honor involved in being a Summora that he had never understood and never, ever wanted to understand.

She was someone he could trust.

She caught the blade descending toward his back and blew her remaining dust in the man's face.

"You're getting slow," she said, dancing out of the way of the next strike.

He shook away the thoughts, counted the screams below, and flicked his fingers toward the wall. "Ten clicks of the dial."

She pulled out a spellbox and tossed it toward the poisonous air. The poison exploded around them in a cloud—but the detonation cleared the air around the box. Neither of them wasted time diving through the clean opening. Taline grabbed her spellbox in a well-executed somersault while Rone flipped in midair and blew wind from the magic-infused plate in his glove. The poison cloud swirled outward and enveloped the cloaked men.

Rone fell to his back and continued that motion, flipping backward into a crouch. Taline, with her spellbox gripped tightly in her hand, leaped over him. He flipped the idol and jammed it into a spot to his right and the chamber door closed with a slam.

He could hear her panting, could feel their triumph spreading through him.

"We have a single revolution, at most." Sixty clicks on the dial.

He saw her check her wind clock and nod as they sprinted for the chamber at the end of the hall.

"Won't they have people at the exit?"

"We aren't going through the exit."

"What?"

He twisted his wrist and pulled a band from his leather gauntlet with his teeth and disengaged goggles from his belt with his other hand, slinging them around his head.

The beast rumbled and roared in the level beneath their feet.

"Valeran?" Taline's voice was tense.

"Get those riding thighs loosened and get ready to jump."

"Valeran. What—?"

A huge sand serpent pivoting at an incredible speed broke through the floor in a wave of stone.

"Let's go," he shouted.

And she followed. She followed, launching herself after him.

He grabbed a handful of pointed hair on the back of the serpent and threw the magical rope around its neck. Just a bit of a curve in the throw would make certain that it would continue around in a circle until it reconnected. It swung around the serpent's throat.

They broke through the temple wall. Pentalayerists yelled and ran in all directions.

He grabbed the rope as it snapped around. The head of the serpent smacked against the ground, rattling his bones. Rone grabbed Taline's shoulder with one hand and held tight to the loop with the other.

A pentalayerist stupid enough to stand and stare disappeared into the maw of the beast. Another hit the serpent with an arrow.

"In the hair," he yelled at Taline, pushing them flat to the sandpronga's body. She pressed her head against its flesh alongside him, shutting her eyes.

The serpent shrieked and dove into the sand.

Sand burst around them. But sandprongas had a natural ability to blow sand from around their body via ducts at the back of their neck. Holding close to the serpent's back, the wind blew the sand away from them, flitting along the hair covering its body, and allowing them to dive with the beast.

It launched itself to the surface again, hit a tree, then another, then three more until finally, finally, the arrow dislodged. Then it dove again.

"How long?" Taline yelled above the earthquake happening all around them, eyes tightly shut.

"How long can you last?"

"Longer than you." Her eyes were shut tight, trusting him, trusting him to get them through.

Something lodged in his throat. Something internal. Stupid Summoras. "Narsumina, you have a long way to go until you are at my level."

"It's impossible to fall that far."

He smiled unwillingly, attempting to judge the distance traveled every time they breached into dark, rising moonlight. They hadn't crossed the crescent valley rivers, which meant they were still on the western side of the fertile lands. Judging northward direction was tougher surrounded by sand, but small undulations above the surface gave a few peeks into the surrounding landscapes and stars.

"Just a little longer," he said.

When they reached a roughly desired point, he stuffed his gloved claws into the serpent's neck. It squawked and burst from the sand into the air.

"Now!"

Rone unclasped the rope with a thumb and flick of his wrist, and they tumbled along the dunes as the sandpronga roared angrily and dove back down.

They landed hard, tumbling across the dark sand.

Ugh. Being without magic made everything more difficult, including landings.

They rolled to a stop, and Rone didn't even bother to make the end of his landing better.

Taline was sprawled out next to him, one ankle over his. Sand covered her—embedded in her eyelashes, brows, hair, and every crevice of her face. She had yet to open her eyes.

"You are the worst, Valeran. Really, the worst."

"I take umbrage with your tone."

She wiped her eyes free, then opened them. "You are—" A small sound rippled from her throat as her gaze caught his.

He bent an elbow underneath him in order to turn and look down at her. "Are you...giggling?"

She started to laugh. She bent sideways from the force of it—like a raging river given freefall. Sand shook from her. "You look ridiculous, Valeran."

"You look no less absurd."

Her chest moved in convulsions. She spread her arms out like a starfish—the waterfall collapsing to calm waters. "Not so attractive now, I think." She looked strangely at peace.

He stared at her. "Not at all." She looked objectively terrible like this—covered in sand—but the humor and vibrancy of her emotion made her somehow more magnificent.

Uncomfortable with such thoughts, he looked around.

They were in the dunes of the desert and night was in full descent, but he could see a town in the distance. They would find supplies there, horses, and directions, even as sand-swept as they were.

Taline looked at him while shaking sand from her hair and clothes. He lifted his chin in the direction of the town and she followed his gaze and nodded, before setting off toward the town lights as they both scraped sand.

She still had that cursed thing attached to her palm—worse now than before—and it would undoubtedly be a huge problem before the end.

But it felt like...a beginning.

CHAPTER TWENTY-ONE
POLITICS OF FAMILY

NINLI

(The tent of the Imperator General)

It felt like the end of the world.

Nin felt the air leave her—lost breaths she would never recover. "The scepters are gone?"

The emperor's lips tightened. "Apparently, on the day that you lost the Scepter of Darkness, Crelu ul Osni took the Prime and Second Scepters from the Palace of Tehras as well."

"How? The Prime Scepter was keyed to you," Kaveh said. "We only saw him with the one—the ceremonial scepter he always carried."

Aros ducked into the tent. "What he has done with the others is open to speculation. The supposition is that he hid them or gave them to an ally. Etelian is a liar, so it is hard to tell—"

"Aros—"

"But the highest ceremonial scepters are definitively not in Tehras," Aros finished, ignoring the emperor's chastisement. "When the scepters were removed by an improper hand, the light of Tehras went with them. Gates that had been flickering started failing en masse yesterday, and the others started their descent. The scepters were checked, and the theft was discovered."

Nin sank onto a cushion, her legs no longer holding her. Ifret shot over to the cushion at her side, eyes narrowed and darting between everyone in the tent.

"How is this possible? Why wasn't this noticed and reported earlier?" Kaveh demanded.

The primary scepters, gone. She put her fingers to her lips. No wonder every gate shivered. She closed her eyes. She had thought it was because of weak gatekeepers and her own failure in wanting to power each gate she passed through. Osni held the Third Scepter outside the palace, but he had been partially keyed to it. The chain wouldn't be disrupted by him holding it in another layer. If the first two were missing, though, and not removed by someone they were keyed to...

"It was noticed. Dear Etelian had duplicate scepters created and slotted into place to hide his failure in losing them."

Killing intent curled in Kaveh so strongly that Nin tensed. "That is why the failure of the gates has hastened these last weeks. Etelian is complicit."

"Kaveh—"

"One would think so," Aros mused, tapping his lips and overriding the emperor again. "However, stupidity is often the cruelest of explanations. Such masterful decision-making. I do see why he gets the richest rule. And why his children—"

"Aros," the emperor snapped. Dark intent pulsed and Nin tensed along with Aros, Kaveh, and Ifret. The emperor took a breath and the darkness retreated. "How Osni removed the permanently placed scepters is the first question. No one in the palace can confirm anything. We tried to remove the lit scepters in the first weeks after taking Tehras. They wouldn't budge."

"Blood," Nin murmured.

"What?" the emperor said sharply, looking at her.

Nin looked up and the blood drained from her face. Pressing tension descended over her as they all turned her way.

The shade of her death appeared.

She swallowed. "The Carres were of the ruling opinion that...the more blood shed in a ritual, the better. There was likely a blood clause connected to the scepters under Carre rule." She knew Kaveh could feel the truth of that statement—there had definitely been a blood clause inherent. "The Carres were killed in a way that...mimicked a ritual sacrifice spell."

The emperor had sold that point to the masses as a way to stop the blood festivals, so she was simply repeating popular sentiment.

She swallowed and forced herself to keep going. "Osni re-keyed the scepters immediately after the fall of the Carres—or at least, that is what those in Tehras were led to believe. Whoever designed the sacrifice spell would have had more power from the blood left behind. If you believe that person to be Osni, he could have included a blood clause for himself in each scepter so that he could handle them, if not wield them, later."

She didn't need to believe. She knew.

But the emperor was shaking his head coldly. "Our embalmers drained the blood from each member of the royal family—what little there was left. We used it on the gate scepters. It powered them for short periods, depending on the potency of the blood—some of the Carres had little power in their blood; others powered them for months. Osni couldn't have found m..."

She smiled without amusement at the look of dawning rage on the emperor's face. "The Carres called their own together to perform a joint ritual that would have repelled your forces. They drew their own glyphs to connect the family to a blood ritual that would run through the city."

"The seals under their feet," the emperor said, eyes narrowed.

"Osni disrupted the seals and the ritual. He knew what they were going to do. He set up an intricate sacrificial ritual beneath theirs that you powered when you entered the city." Farrah's sacrifice had been key to releasing Osni from his vows and allowing him to place the underseals. But he had used multiple resources to make his plan work, and he had needed the emperor to be the one to activate the ritual sacrifice by casting the first spell of death.

She had pieced it all together over years of exhausting research and gossip and information gathering. "Osni diverted the most potent bloodshed into the seals. Then he waited and collected the vials while the empire celebrated." And he had collected the even more potent stored vials in the catacombs in the weeks that followed.

It had always bothered her—why no one wondered how Osni was able to influence the gates when he had no gatemaking or keeping ability of his own.

"Blood vials? His necklace." The emperor swore. "Find any that remain," he demanded of Aros.

But Aros would find nothing. Nin had searched until she had found them all. For years, she had searched. It had been the first thing she had looked for once she had found a semblance of equilibrium. The blood of her parents and siblings. The blood of her family in the hands of their killer.

She had been nine, then ten, with no resources, no allies, barely any ability to control her magic, debilitating headaches, and no way to read anything that might point her in a correct direction. But she had searched. Every spot in the palace. Every secret stash. Every place Farrah had shown her. Anywhere she saw Osni pause.

She had needed to remake her face ten times over. She had searched for so long that her hands had been bled of life. She had been combing the dungeon laboratories and had been so close to turning herself in so she could simply scorch the earth around Osni in one fell blow, when she had felt the desperate boy who was about to reveal his biggest secret in a cell near the ones she had been systematically working her way through.

She had felt the desperation of another, and let it shift her entire world view.

Aros was agreeing to the emperor's demand to find the vials, but Kaveh was looking at her. "Osni used the last of the vials. That is why the gates have been failing for months."

She held Kaveh's gaze, then tipped her head. "Yes."

It had taken years, and a lot of careful planning, but she had found and destroyed all but the last drops of Savvan's blood, which had been hanging around Osni's neck.

She had known what she was sentencing Osni to when she destroyed the vials. But it was a sentence he had written himself, long ago.

"I should have killed him." The emperor curled his fingers into fists.

"But only he knew the secrets of Tehrasi," Aros said with a dark twist born of simmering temper.

"And you put him in the charge with Etelian. I told you to—"

"Aros."

"Osni was a betrayer," Aros said. "And putting him with Etelian gave him footing. Crelu ul Osni had all the power in the palace as the only one who knew the secrets of the Carres. Which begs the question—" Aros turned to her. "Who are you, that you know anything about the scepters or the night the Carres fell?"

"A scullery shade with some healing abilities." The emperor had been told she was a palace servant, so there was no dissembling. "I spent some time in the palace kitchens during Carre Giran's reign."

It had been so long since she had used that dead, formal title, that it fumbled from her tongue. But her words weren't lies. She had spent many hours in the kitchens. Farrah's duties had taken them all over the palace.

"After the fall of the Carres, I pursued healing. As to that night—word travels quickly in Tehrasi. You can hear the last tale of the Carres from any minstrel worth his leaf and sand."

"Osni made certain all of the palace servants were dead." Aros looked at her through half-lidded eyes. "Quite deliberately."

"Servants who were connected to the royal family, yes. But that was not my fate that day," she said quietly.

She hadn't been connected to anything—family or friend. She had been broken on the street, feeling the echoes of the deaths of nearly everyone she knew.

"The Carres were very comprehensive in their oaths. All in service to the palace were called there that night."

"I was too young and inconsequential to take the palace oaths." Also true, if misleading.

"And then you became a Level Six healer, wasn't that what your farhani—now quite interestingly absent—read?"

It was her first obvious lie, and one she couldn't defend. She hadn't hidden her power level in weeks.

Aros smiled at her silence. "What else is a lie, I wonder."

"I know her lies," Kaveh said shortly, moving in front of her. The emperor's eyes narrowed on the movement. "And they have no bearing on this. What has been done about Etelian?"

"Etelian has been dealt with," the emperor said grimly.

Hope wrapped a fragile strand around her imminent death. A break between the emperor and Etelian might prove a better ruler on the throne.

"Mother is quite upset," Aros drawled.

"She should be upset with her second born. I'm considering removing him for good."

Hope coiled more strongly.

"What a pity."

"You won't be the one replacing him," the emperor snapped at Aros.

"Oh, I know. Father."

Death curled where hope had strayed. Kaveh moved to fully block her. Tension bounced around the bond—a tension that was only present in Kaveh when the emperor was involved.

She was going to die. She was going to die. She was going to die because Aros's parentage was not a conversation that was allowed to grace outside ears.

Ifret hissed, low and in warning.

The emperor's eyes narrowed on Ifret momentarily, then moved to pin Nin with his stare. "Tell me every piece of Tehrasian gossip about the scepters before I kill you."

Although Kaveh's oath was sacrosanct, Nin knew he would not raise a hand against the emperor when he killed her.

"Each scepter has a designation and duty. Special abilities were imbued in each. The palace scepters work as a chain, as do the gate scepters. With three broken links, especially the first three, the others will start to fall. None are made to stand on their own."

"The Carres would never have allowed such an open error."

"The Carres were natural gatemakers. There are abilities that can override the protections, should a gatemaker know the scepter system. And the Scepter of Darkness can reset the chain or eliminate a scepter completely. There has always been a master key."

"And we have neither. How pleasant." The emperor's voice was anything but. "We've lost the gate to Fehla-da. The gate to Cartha flickers and the gate to Herat has begun to waver. Our enemies are roused, and our allies unsettled."

Nin wanted to say that killing vast swaths of people in revenge for the deaths of padifehls was not helping the unsettled nature of the empire, but she already courted death.

"There are reports of naval forces in the Fehl Sea," Kaveh said. "Forces that should not exist. Kush protects the western waters, but without the gate, Voiya should take heed to the south and east."

Voiya ul Fehl was another child of Nera, and Padifehl of Fehla-da. Another child of Nera...another Osni plot to purge the line?

"Voiya will dismiss it as scurrilous gossip. The council questions who would dare show their hand against us," Aros drawled. "They use your shadows as example and huff that no one would dare stand against us. They listen as well as old men do."

"Aros," the emperor snapped.

"They have determined my birthright." Aros snarled. "You think I care what—"

He froze, suspended in twisted movement.

The emperor's hand was raised, along with all the hair on Nin's body. Nin stepped closer into the shadows of Kaveh's back. "One more word, Aros, and you will join your brother. And then Nera will really be displeased with me."

"Of...course...Father." Aros twitched in frozen movement.

The emperor dropped Aros and straightened his robes before taking a deep breath. "I have heard the council. They are not incorrect in their thinking—what possibility could anyone have to think that a plan like this might succeed?"

She watched them shake themselves off, as if this was a normal occurrence. But Kaveh stepped an inch further sideways to cover her from view.

"Someone who is looking further down the line," Aros said, gaze distant, fingers traveling down the meridian lines of magic in his arms then shaking them free. "Someone who is looking not at this victory, but at a victory in the future. Someone protecting their lands four or five territories from now."

Aros's narrowed eyes swept Kaveh. "The world knows that the Shadow Prince owns the battlefield. That no one survives a field with him on it. That means someone thinks they have a plan to remove him from it."

"Impossible," the emperor said shortly.

The feeling of loyalty and love that she associated with the emperor spiked across the bond. Dread curled in Nin.

"The gates are failing. Should the Shadow Prince and his forces get cut off in the far north, and the rest of the gates die, the way the enemy masses, the empire will fall," Aros said darkly.

"The gates are not the empire," Kaveh said coldly.

"No," the emperor said, equally as cold. "But we have made them our backbone. That, and the hand of darkness that used to be so skillfully wielded."

Nin felt the blow as if she took it herself. There was no doubt who was being referred to. Her dread knotted.

"If you had gotten the scepter..." The emperor curled his fingers into his palms.

"There is still a chance for it."

The emperor looked between them. His gaze was remote. "A fool's chance. You think someone will trade one of the most powerful artifacts in the known worlds for the girl who hides behind you?"

Danger. Her mind and the bond screamed with it.

"I think that people are fools," Kaveh said. "And discounting steps that fools make is a mistake."

"I've sent spies to Helsgir. To find Rone ul Valeran's game. He is much despised in his mother's country. He is known for neither his loyalty nor generosity."

Nin's lips compressed. Rone was known as the emperor's bastard in Helsgir, the capital city of Denma—he was known as the blight who had caused their princess to be banished for a time, and whose existence was a continuing insult.

"He is a Level Seven tracker, if that. Good for simple tasks." Aros waved a hand. "Not one of your better creations, Father."

Nin took a deep breath and thought through the motions of her morning healing exercises. In, out, in—

"You think he has loyalty to you, girl?"

Nin looked up to see the emperor watching her in displeasure, his fingers twitching.

"No, Your Imperial Majesty."

"The interesting thing about sending spies to gather information on those who hold the Scepter of Darkness...no one could find much about you or your sister before the registration."

Danger. Danger. "The Summora family was in trade. We traveled extensively before finding our way to Tehras."

She had made certain to create tight profiles for them both—and for anyone who claimed the Summora name. She had also fiddled with the date of registration on Taline's packet. It would stand up to high level scrutiny—even the investigore had stamped it as normal when he had called her in for one of her earliest visits. But to a scribe master sent by the emperor? Unknown.

Fiddling with documents and oaths in Tehrasi that still contained traces of the enchantments from the Carre's reign, and would respond to her blood? Easy. Making those changes seamless across the empire's enchantments? Far harder. She could have missed a glyph, the edge of a spell, the wisp of an illusion...

"We'll see." The emperor smiled pleasantly. He turned to Kaveh. "Tell me of Yalendil."

"We found the general and his bribe." He swept a hand over the chest they had retrieved and the top disengaged. Gold glittered, along with the papyri and amulet.

"The same type of amulet found at each assassination." The emperor looked without touching.

"Yes. Used by a guild in Tehrasi. The document details the whereabouts and the way inside."

"A trap." The emperor looked at the chest with disdain.

"Yes. But one worth investigating."

"Where did you find the general?"

Nin focused on her morning activation routine. Focused on pulling magic through the channels of her body one at a time, waking each and unblocking anything that had cramped during sleep. Calm, calm, feeling the magic sweep through—

"He was trying to pass through the country to escape north. My shadows caught him."

"Convenient," Aros mused.

The emperor looked sharply between Aros and Kaveh. Nin's magic overran her pathway and cramped in her arm. She had to will the flow to start again. Kaveh had lied to the emperor. But he couldn't explain how they had gotten to Yalendil without exposing her abilities. Oaths mattered to Kaveh. Perhaps he saw the lie as inconsequential.

Aros turned to her. "And you helped find the general and the evidence against your country? Why? This oath you keep speaking of? You seem to love Tehrasi alone, and yet you set your country up for severe repercussion."

She swallowed. "I'd rather be a tool for the empire than a tool for hired killers with no allegiance. Or worse, ones who try to frame my country."

"You are a tool either way."

"Better that I choose my application."

Aros contemplated her for a long second. "If you didn't possess so much power, you'd have been dead years ago with an attitude like yours."

"Better that I use that power like this, instead of the alternative."

His eyes narrowed and he smiled. "Wraiths in your past, Ninli?"

"We all carry shades."

"Yes, we do," he murmured. "Shades of crimson, shades of brown."

Her heart leaped into her throat. They were words of a popular tale about blood and sand and the reaping of the land, but here, they were a cover for a statement of knowledge.

He suspected. Aros suspected her eyes bled red.

"Three assassins failed this morning," the emperor said, unmoved by Aros's quote. "One against Aros, one against Baksis, one against Simin."

"And still no plot against Etelian?" Kaveh asked blandly.

Aros smiled slowly at her while Kaveh and the emperor were engaged. Aros suspected. Why was he not airing his suspicions? What game was this?

"He has always been quick against assassin's blades," the emperor said.

"And yet...no plot has been uncovered against him."

"Etelian would be the first person I'd frame, if I were to undertake any crime," Aros said dryly.

"He has not the skill to plan," the emperor agreed.

Aros looked visibly frustrated suddenly. "Why do you keep him in Tehrasi then?"

"You will have a territory far in excess of his, Aros, and when we have the Scepter of Darkness, the world will be at our fingertips."

Aros grit his teeth and turned to Nin, eyes narrowing, then to Kaveh. "The council wants to raze Cuipsin anyway."

Nin's breath stuttered in her chest. Cuipsin had loved Shiera. It was one of the reasons she had always lamented that Shiera hadn't been given Tehrasi.

Kaveh's brows drew harshly together. "Has something been found to indicate betrayal from within?"

"No. They said the enemy needs to know what happens when they step against us." Aros inspected his nails. "Father is considering the request."

"Ridiculous. What will prevent negative agents from engineering this type of result against an innocent nation? Who will treatise with us knowing this end might come for them?"

Even the breeze in the room seemed to freeze. Nin slowly raised her face to look at Kaveh, then quickly jerked her gaze to the others.

A slow smile appeared on Aros's face. On Lorsali, it would have been a mad cackle and a swipe of clawed fingers. On Aros, it almost looked relieved.

"What care have you for Cuipsin?" The emperor's eyes narrowed on Kaveh, then they slid poisonously to her.

"I have care for where our resources are best utilized," Kaveh said. "If not guilty of treason, razing Cuipsin is against our interests."

"You could have Cuipsin under your boot in two days," the emperor said.

"I could be somewhere else for those two days."

"I agree with Kaveh. Though I've never known you to care who you grind beneath your feet, brother," Aros said mildly.

"What is this care?" The emperor's features grew stormy, and he suddenly looked around the tent.

Nin tensed, looking at the spots that he focused upon—the pile of blankets and bedding, the figstee tray, her things intermixed with Kaveh's.

Aros's gaze lazily followed the emperor's before shifting to her. "Those who sleep in proximity to Kaveh always end up dead," Aros said languidly. "Interesting that you still live nearly two weeks later, Ninli ul Summora."

"I haven't killed unintentionally since I was fourteen," Kaveh said coldly.

"And still, you've slept alone."

"My sleeping habits are unimportant."

"This isn't about sleeping habits, her emotions are influencing you," the emperor said furiously. "She is influencing you."

"Emotion has nothing to do with it," Kaveh said tightly. "Cuipsin is an ally. If the scepter and gates weren't overwhelming your sense, you wouldn't even think these plans."

Aros's mouth parted in shock and awe, amusement wiped clean of his expression as intrigue stole over his features. All Nin felt was fear.

"Indeed. Emotion has nothing to do with it. Kill her." The pleasant facade on the emperor's face was the most terrifying Nin had seen. His voice perfectly matched the expression. It was pleasant, as if talking about the weather or midday meal. "Do it now."

Nin steadied herself, chin forward. She would die as Heba had. As Reyi. Seeing her death as it marched toward her and accepting it without murmur or comment.

Kaveh's jaw clenched. "You know that I cannot. And should you order Aros to do it, know that I am sworn to protect her while the oath is in force." Shadows swirled from every corner.

"I think I shall pass," Aros said pleasantly, eyes glimmering with amber light. "Both she and I are far more useful alive."

Darkness from the emperor grew to meet Kaveh's shadows. "The gates are failing, the scepters are gone, the Scepter of Darkness is in the hands of an enemy, and my Imperator General is having feelings."

"These are not feelings."

Dark shadows and tightening power crackled through the tent as the emperor and Kaveh faced off. The emperor's hand moved toward Nin.

Ifret shot around Nin's neck, hissing and snapping, a dark shield of hatred. The emperor gave the shadow an unreadable glance, darkness pausing. Aros's gaze was naked and hungry.

"Father." Kaveh pulled his darkness back inside the strained cage within him. "The threat right now is the assassin's guild—finding out what they know and who hired them."

The emperor's fists curled tighter. But something seemed to loosen. It was the first time she had heard Kaveh address him by that name.

"I agree," Aros said, gaze moving from Ifret. "I, for one, would like the assassins who keep popping out of embellishments to stop. They might actually pierce my favorite robe next time."

"Traps. All," the emperor said. "If the Carres were still alive, I'd place this at their door."

Nin focused on the red pillow in the multicolored pile of bedding in the corner.

"I will clear the assassin's guild," Kaveh said. "Before the decision is made to raze countries we already hold, I will rip the answers from their throats."

Nin could feel the foregone conclusion in Kaveh's mental landscape.

The emperor looked at Nin for a long moment, then back to Kaveh. "No. Aros will do it."

Kaveh stiffened. Aros smiled.

She could feel it across the bond, almost like a whisper of his thoughts without being shadow-touched. Kaveh had been passed over for tasks before—happily—tasks below his ability or because the emperor didn't want to waste him elsewhere. This was the first time he had been passed over for a task because the emperor was concerned he couldn't do it appropriately.

Kaveh gritted his teeth. "As you wish, Your Imperial Majesty."

It strangely made her remember the emperor's words on their return from the temple—about Kaveh's battlefront success possibly being a matter of luck. It had been a silly and petty gambit. An obvious one. And in a man as controlled as the emperor, it said something.

"The gates are still a problem." Aros lifted a figstee and twisted it like a toy top on his finger. "Let me use—"

"No," the emperor said. "And I forbid you to speak of such things."

"The gates—"

"The gates!" The emperor threw magic at the wall behind him. The tent wall exploded in flame. Shadows rose and sucked the flames dry. "The gates are none of your concern."

The emperor took a deep breath. He raised a temporary wall in place of the one he had destroyed. "Eliminate the guild, Aros. Kaveh, you will attend Shiera's funeral procession with me in Cuipsin. Bring the First Imperial Force. We will kill anyone who refuses to answer our questions."

The emperor strode from the now-lopsided tent, robes swishing across the layered carpets.

Aros lifted and turned a coin from the Yalendil chest in one hand, examining it. "And just like that, the favorite gains a fault."

A shadow under the coin sliced his finger.

Aros smiled and lifted his finger, wiping away the trickle of blood. "Why, Kaveh. You are full of emotion today." He looked at her. "And weakness."

"Leave, Aros, before you are bled of the ability to do so on your own."

Aros tossed the coin in the chest and wrapped the chest in a carrying enchantment. "We should all return to the palace. Foolish, this chase—doing what the enemy desires."

"Run, if you wish."

Aros looked at him. "The attack on Simin in Ancyra. On me in Skudra. On Baksis in Dozine.

And you've had at least two. All it takes is for one to hit." His eyes slid to her. "Not even upon you, perhaps."

Kaveh stiffened imperceptibly.

Aros nodded. "Something new and fouler comes. Take care that your last thoughts are your own, brother."

CHAPTER TWENTY-TWO
CONFESSIONS IN THE NIGHT

RONE

(North of Ur, west of the Purattu River, south of Uruk)

The language in the river valleys was close to their own, and Rone used a bit of container magic to make it more so in order to cover their tracks better. They eschewed staying in town, even for the comfort of a bed and bath. It was too dangerous to remain in civilization. Patrols would be checking towns from Ur to Bekli, with a concentration in the overladen areas of Babil and Kiš.

They headed northwest in the three-quarter moonlight along the western side of the fertile rivers, following a path of less arid land, dotted sand, and treescapes. The Purattu River snaked northwest and they followed the lines of it, keeping away from the river itself.

It was after midnight that they finally stopped to rest.

Of course, not securing an inn also meant not securing a bed.

Rone was careful not to be too near to her at night, even when they slept on the same side of a fire. A bed would have made things unbearable. He would have slept on the floor.

In another situation, with another partner, it would have been fine—he never stayed the night with a bedmate, and he had no inclinations to seek out another in sleep. So he could stay to one side without problem.

But Taline had fewer of those barriers. Too many nights spent with Ninli, or with the other women in the same situation Ninli had saved Taline from, seeking comfort in the dark.

It hadn't mattered in the beginning. Taline had rigidly stayed on the other side of the fire for the first week, even on the coldest desert nights. He had found it darkly amusing. They would both rather die than share heat.

But tonight... Tonight she had paused, then moved her bedroll to his side. Still not in sharing range, but closer.

It made him tense for reasons he didn't want to investigate.

"How is...?" He pointed in a vague motion to the scepter.

Her fingers clenched around the staff, some of her relaxed posture tightening again, and he almost regretted his question. "Harder," she admitted, her voice soft. "The feeling of wanting to use it has grown worse. The knowledge that I can fix everything whispers through my thoughts."

The softening of her voice and the sharing of private thoughts made that same apprehensive feeling slide through him again. This was the start of something, if he let it be. A true beginning.

She was someone he could trust. If he wanted that.

He pushed against the idea, and a sharp retort came to his tongue. The words would push her away. They would keep him safe. The words formed on his tongue, but he made the mistake of looking at her. He made the mistake of seeing the weariness in her perfect features—at seeing the way she was leaning just a little closer, as if starved for a kind touch.

He poked at the fire. "You can hold out against it," he said gruffly.

She didn't say anything for a long moment, but he could feel her need for comfort. "Why do you think that?"

He turned, unwilling to answer at first. Then, as if the truth was dragged from him— "Because you are one of the strongest people I've ever met."

She turned away from him as well, but not before he saw the color rise in her cheeks. Damn it. Damn it. He clenched his fist around the stick.

"Without Nin's magic—"

"No," he said sharply, interrupting her, and what was he doing? "Ninli was right with what she said to the Shadow Prince. You underestimate your true strength."

"I can read?" she said sarcastically.

"You have heart. You love. Even after a dozen betrayals, you love. Fiercely."

"Nin saved me."

"She couldn't save what you didn't will."

"I was broken. You have no idea what happened while I mended."

"I assume that things didn't go smoothly. Why would they? Chipped parts can never fully be reassembled. But you chose your clay and paste. You slammed it into the cracks and rose. You became a statement piece instead of a vase. Remade from the same parts, but with deliberate shifts."

She closed her eyes and her throat moved but produced no sound.

As if the question were pulled from him, he asked, "Why did you never leave Tehras, Taline?"

TALINE

At his murmur, she examined the backs of her unmarked hands. The henna dots that had held a secondary reserve of physical enchantments had long since fled, but it was still strange not to see them. Strange not to feel their comfort and know the designs beneath her clothing—and covering her scars—were no longer there.

His question lingered. It would be the first thing someone sane would do—to leave the place where your captor lorded supreme.

"Tehras was where Nin was." By the time Taline could stand again, she had seen all she had needed to of Nin's character and goals. There had been no other choice to make.

"You could have started fresh. A dozen times over. Ninli would never have thought ill of you for it. Like Birsa, you could have started anew. You made the choice not to leave her and the city that housed your cage, and that... Well, I don't know whether to call it stupid or wise."

Her eyes snapped to his. She smiled darkly. "Both, perhaps. There's something...liberating...about walking down the street in front of your tormentor without him knowing."

Terrifying, but liberating. Forever a fugitive, but free.

He didn't say anything for a long moment. "You are truly dangerous," he said finally, more wearily than anything.

"Why did you never stay?" she asked in return. "I know you feel a bond with her."

It had always frustrated Taline, that bond. Especially when she had thought it only went one way.

"I have little use or capacity for love." He looked away. "I never bothered to fix my vase. More often, I've sought to break others. To watch the fall of ceramic and splinters in glaze."

"But you love her. A little."

"She is hard to purge. An illness that never ceases." He flexed his fingers. "Love has always been a weakness. My mother, the Valerans, the empire, the women who fling themselves and the men who beg, the power inequality. Love is a hook on a chain, and one person is always on the hooked end—the one that tears through flesh."

"Do you think Nin would do that to me? To you?"

He smiled without warmth. "Sacrifice is a bitter pill. I watched my mother swallow it whole. She sacrificed her standing for my life. And she hated me for it. Grew to loathe the totality of what I represented. The child her family told her to kill. Maybe she loved me for a month. Maybe two. Maybe not at all, and pride was the only thing that drove her. Who knows? She couldn't go back, and pride wouldn't let her kill me afterward."

"Your mother—"

"No." His tone was absolute, expression shut.

"Your father—"

"Also, no."

"Why?" she asked softly, but with challenge.

"They are dull topics."

Taline thought the topics anything but dull. It was something Nin had said to her once—that Nin and Valeran's futures had been defined by the circumstances of their birth—that all futures were influenced by birth, and those who wanted to change those circumstances had to work twice as hard.

She didn't know much about Valeran's true past. She had never attempted to discern what was fact and what was fiction. The man was as much of a myth as anything.

But she could let him have his secrets, if he wanted them. "I will admit—I don't know what to do upon returning. You aren't wrong—even if I can save Nin, we will be hunted. Nin will be hunted."

"You wanted to be a windchaser once." He poked the fire. "You could go back to it. A potbellied merchant wouldn't know what to do with you, but the Weather Guild would."

She smiled tightly at his relinquishment of the earlier taunt. "Arguments of internal strength aside, I am not powerful enough magically."

I can make you powerful.

"Lies," Valeran said dismissively, jolting her from the creeping thought.

It took her a moment to realize that he was responding to her assertion, not the scepter's. "I rely on Nin to power my creations. What would I be without her to charge my boxes?"

"You could make a deal with another."

"Maybe." She didn't have to explain that that would be a less desired outcome. He already knew.

"You need to start to see yourself as separate from Ninli." He looked at her, ridiculously blue and brown eyes shadowed. "Ninli is lost to you, whether she lives or dies."

She was beginning to understand the kernel of truth in that statement but wasn't willing to accept it yet—nor to stop fighting for it. "I will fight for her even if I'm powerless again."

Embrace **our** power. Together, we can—

"What does it feel like?"

She looked sharply at him, once more having to parse the scepter's insidious assertions. "Being powerless?"

"Etelian took your powers." There was a strange look on Valeran's face. "What did that feel like?"

She looked at the fingers of her empty left hand, and there it was—the tremor that always came when she thought of such things. "Like a sudden void you cannot fill. Etelian has only a fraction of the emperor's power. Etelian cannot seal powers in a way that is unbreakable. The curse wears off, eventually. He has to...reapply it. He does so continuously to all who are gifted to him. The second son of the emperor is a disappointment to all who do not quiver in fear beneath his hand."

Anger curled in her—in her left hand and in her fingers gripping the scepter. She forced herself to loosen her grip around it and to calm the trembles.

"Being stripped of power..." There was an odd tone to his trailing voice.

She examined him, but there was nothing duplicitous in his expression, just a strange urgency. "Agony," she said. "An abomination."

"Pain?" His gaze focused strangely on the flames. He drew a finger along his lower lip. "The power of the emperor is a power that goes against the very nature of magic."

"Have you ever experienced...?"

"Don't be silly." He was completely different in that moment—back to his languid self. If she didn't know herself and trust in her memory so well, she might doubt there had been anything else to his expression before.

But she had seen it. And curiosity was too potent.

"Have you met Etelian?" she asked carefully.

"Such displeasure has never been mine."

Then that meant...

"But you've met the emperor?"

"Of course. I was dragged before him to be tested. Each bastard child is."

"What was that like?"

"Dull."

No. Meeting the emperor would have been anything but dull. "I heard he offers a place to all his children, should they want it."

"If they are powerful enough, it's more of a demand." He shrugged, a smile curling his mouth. "Eights or Nines are swept into the numbered legions of blessed, imperial children. Those of middling ability are allowed to go on their way."

"Level Sevens are not middling. And you are not a Level Seven magi," she said carefully.

He poked the fire lazily. "My farhani says otherwise. Everyone knows I rely on trickery and deceit instead of true power."

"How did you fool the emperor?" She knew easily how one could fool the system. She and Nin had done it enough to know that there were ways in which even they hadn't thought to manipulate.

He tapped a finger against the stick he was using to poke. "I found a relic that would eat power for a period of time. I used it before I was called before him." His gaze remained firmly on the fire.

"A relic that eats power?" Horror filled her. "Like Etelian's ability? Like the emperor's?" she demanded.

His fingers curled around the stick and he looked into the dark, as if he couldn't stand her horror. "I destroyed it afterward."

Sympathy filled her. "So you know what it feels like."

"No," he said shortly. "Not like you did. I knew my power would return. When magic is pulled by another, there is no such promise. The magic is sealed off, not drained. But the emperor saw what I wanted him to see—a magi of little ability who told him exactly what he was willing to do for the empire—which was nothing."

"And he let you...leave intact?"

"Of course." It was said entirely too carelessly.

"Valeran."

"I was fifteen. I had been on the streets too long to give a single care if he killed me—not if it meant that or being an imperial politician. I let him know that I would work outside the empire if pressured to be within. He has hundreds of children. Thousands, probably, now. I was a simple disappointment. A failed experiment. He's had plenty of them. He dealt with me and I never saw him again. I only saw his agents, who think they are sneaky, but fail to recognize true opponents."

"So he believes you a Seven."

The corners of his mouth pulled into a dark, sharp smile. "The emperor thinks I did cheat my power level at Gomen. He just thinks it was in the opposite direction."

She stared at him. "The emperor thinks you are a, what then—a Six?"

"Probably a Five. A clever, clever Five."

She stared at him, speechless for a moment. "That's why he didn't take you. Why you aren't blessed. With you being a Valeran... It has never made sense that he didn't bless you."

"I have built a very solid reputation in finding relics and having a somewhat checkered success at delivering them."

Understanding bloomed. "He thinks your repute is due entirely to tricks and idols."

A self-satisfied smile curved his lips. "Trickery is for thieves and liars. He has little use for either in his blessed empire unless the pawn wants to play political games, and it is obvious to anyone who comes into contact with me that I do not."

She felt the pieces of him that had already crumbled turn to dust. "Valeran—"

"Rone."

She blinked. "What?"

"If you are going to call me by a name I wear solely due to the woman who birthed me, better to choose the one less attached to the family who despises me."

"I—" She swallowed.

"Don't feel bad, narsumina." He smiled darkly. "The feeling is mutual. If I found them surrounded by flames, I would do nothing other than add a little wind as kindred tribute."

"I'm surprised you chose to use the name Valeran at all."

"I did not." He tossed the stick on the fire. "With my Awakening, came my hair." He motioned vaguely at the multicolored strands. "It had been a simple reddish brown before. Part of the Valeran Awakening and inheritance is that the Hair of Dawn will resist all dye and spell. The registration official took one look and registered me under that name."

"Nin—"

"She changed certain things at Gomen, but changing my name would have exposed the other modifications to scrutiny. My hair is a marker I can never be rid of. As I said, it can't be dyed—the strands are resistant to spells—and even shaved, red and gold patterns show on my skin."

He shrugged. "And I was known by then. Reputation follows. It would have done me little good and made people look closer at the registry. So I flaunted it instead. What better way to bring disgrace to the Valerans, then by using their name?"

"What about the Fehls?"

"I'm far more careful poking that beast. The Fehls are in positions of power over me. One must desire a death glyph, if one wishes to spit in Fehl faces. That is the opposite of my desire to live richly and fully while making life miserable for those in the Valeran lineage before me."

"Why do you hate the Fehls then?" she asked softly.

"Do you not know hate for your father?"

She said nothing for a long moment. "I know rage. I know sorrow. Hate is a consumption I no longer desire."

"You are truly a marvel, narsumina."

She grit her teeth. "You don't have to—"

"I mean it. You are." His voice sounded...resigned.

She watched him, feeling her world tilt.

She looked at the scepter, trying to right herself. "I'm scared," she said, giving him an opening with which he could deride her—with which they could right themselves to normal.

"I know." He closed his eyes, defying her need to tip their world back. "We'll figure it out."

She stared at him, then rewrapped the scepter, hiding it from view as if that would hide it from her world. She curled up closer to him than she had before.

Nin, we are coming.

CHAPTER TWENTY-THREE
FUNERALS AND OFFERINGS

NINLI

(CUIPSIN CAMP)

There had been little time to discuss anything in the mad rush to decamp, move, and relocate to Cuipsin—to a field that had not been prepped for troops or battle. Kaveh might have been a one-man force, but he was also Imperator General, and he gave the orders and led the ground and sky forces.

The entire First Imperial Force—those who fought on the battlefront alongside the Imperator General—stood before Cuipsin on the day of their padifehl's funeral. Tents were strapped to backs, a thousand soldiers landed from the skies, another three thousand soldiers trudged through on foot from the nearest flickering gate—wondering whether they would be the unlucky one cut in half should the flickering gate finally fail. The elite force collected and gathered in front of the grand gates of Krokola, Cuipsin's capital city.

The officials of Krokola had offered them rooms in the palace, but Kaveh had deferred. If they were given orders to strike—or if Kaveh decided a strike was in order—he would direct the campaign from the encampment.

The officials had been rightfully terrified. Having the emperor and his multitude of guards in the palace—after the murder of his daughter on those grounds—was a terrifying prospect. And having the Shadow Prince at one's doorstep was a notion of nightmares.

Few in the capital city had slept well since Shiera's death. No one would rest well tonight.

The procession started at sundown. Nin found herself arrayed with the generals around Kaveh, the emperor, and his guards.

Low chants echoed and high notes flowed as the procession carried Shiera's wrapped and gilded body down the promenade and through the city on a constantly descending carpet of black and white petals. The soaring mountains that wrapped around the city dominated the view, and towers along the peaks shot crackling spell lights into the air. Air traffic had been stopped for the procession, but the wind currents were in full force, spreading petals across the city.

A funeral for a beloved ruler. Tears and favors for the dead flowed freely as they passed.

"They didn't kill her," Nin murmured.

"These people? No," Kaveh said. "Those at the steps? Maybe."

At the base of the temple steps were the most important and powerful figures in the country. The emperor kept court and spoke benevolently to all who sought to extend their sorrows and regrets. He spoke to them of the help Cuipsin would receive and the care he would take in choosing a new padifehl for their great country.

Away from the high emotions expressed in the tent, it was as if she were looking at a different man—one of benevolence and compassion. But beneath the emperor's magnanimity there was an underlying threat—he wielded his thirteenth blessed like a knife—and there was no greater evidence of the damage that blade could do than the presence of Kaveh ul Fehl himself.

While the emperor projected the facade of altruistic statesman—a statesman without equal—his son acted as brutal weapon. Nin preferred the ideal of the emperor to the actual man, but then, every person played a role over their darker cores within.

The emperor had earned his reputation as statesman. But she could see and feel his tension and doubt every time Cuipsin's main gate—in clear view of the temple steps—flickered.

And every time the emperor tensed, Kaveh did, too. Nin looked around the city as petals burst across the streets.

The mountains that surrounded the valley of the city were sharp and lovely, but they also served as a visual reminder of a tomb. A tomb with one misstep. The interrogations had been held, but the emperor's decision remained unknown.

As they readied for sleep, Kaveh's tension did not cease—his movements sharp and angry as he ran through his night rituals. Only a quick visit from the emperor made any of that tension lessen.

"We will hold off on Cuipsin's fate. For now." The emperor held himself coldly, but his gaze softened the slightest bit at Kaveh's nod. When the emperor looked at her, his gaze gathered an icy sheen once more. "Hold here for now, but make your plans for the new battlefronts, while I figure out and fix the Sehk-forsaken gates. I expect to be impressed."

He swept from the room—robes flaring regally. Nin looked at their tent—a new one, after the emperor had damaged their last—but through the eyes of the emperor. She could see from where his displeasure stemmed. Two people shared this space closely. Two people who had quickly learned each other—who had learned how to anticipate and wind around each other and work within each other's space.

She hadn't thought much of it. Nin had never been one to sleep alone in a room. There had been guards and handmaidens for her first nine years, rats and vagrants for the next few, followed by a steadily rotating stream of people needing temporary shelter. Then Taline. Taline, who had never left.

She hadn't slept without Taline in the same room in nearly four years.

Staring at Kaveh from her pillow had a different feel, but he still felt like an ally.

But the emperor seeing Kaveh, who chose no companions other than that of shadow, wind himself around another? She understood his distrust and unease.

"You are influencing me, he's not wrong." Kaveh's grip tightened upon the staff he had been using to loosen the muscles in his back. "You and your feelings of sadness on the battlefield—it gets increasingly harder for you to step upon one, and I find myself wanting to avoid it. Worse, a part of me wants to cling to your presence instead. Your emotions have become an infection I cannot sidestep."

"It will be over soon." Her fingers curled into her sleeping tunic, her other arm beneath her cheek. "You will be free of me. And then I will have no choices at all. My secrets will be no more."

And there was that conflict running along the bond again. She marveled at it.

"You will remain with me, and you will serve me. And you will aid the empire in ways beyond imagination."

"The emperor is unhappy to be upset with you," she murmured.

"He is right to be upset." Another strike with the staff.

"You love him," she said softly. "And you want to please him. And it has been easy to do so until now. You haven't come into conflict before."

"Love is for peasants."

Nin looked at Ifret curled in the corner, watching them. "Yes." Love had not been an option for one born as she. It had been a secret, terrifying thing. "I enjoyed being a peasant. I enjoyed the freedom of such things."

She had embraced the emotion completely the moment she was able—broken, but healing, on the streets.

"You make yourself vulnerable."

"What is strength without peril?"

"Strength."

She smiled and picked at the intricately patterned blanket made by an extremely skilled weavemaster. "Perhaps bravery is a more apt word, then."

"Bravery is for those who fear."

"Have you never feared?"

"Of what do I have to fear?"

"Do you have no one you fear to lose?"

"Like the useless soldiers you save? You worry about them futilely."

She thought of the ducklings. "They are anything but useless."

"They would be dead on a field, if not for you."

"They would be dead on a field had they not decided to heal their fellow soldiers and be healed in return."

"They would be dead on the field, because they wouldn't have been next to you," he said pointedly.

She picked at the blanket's threads. "The connection still exists, does it not? Caring has made it possible for others to excel."

"Why do you care?"

"Someone has to care."

"You care for servants, villains, and thieves. How did you survive a palace of Carres? A palace more bloody I have yet to see."

"I learned to guard my coterie of servants closely." It had been so terrifying to care, and yet Nin had been unable to do anything else.

After Lorsali had Sora executed, Nin had been faced with the choice. Love took strength. And if she wanted it, she would have to defend it.

She had learned to brave Lorsali without someone standing in front of her. She had learned to maintain her guards for outside threats alone and to handle all internal struggles on her own.

Killing siblings was strictly forbidden, but servants and guards were fair game in the House of Carre. Nin had kept her servants as far from view and as inconspicuous as possible.

Loving Zehra Amanan Carre meant death. It had taken her a long time to feel like loving Ninli ul Summora could mean something different.

She could love freely, but she had to guard all who loved her in return.

"To guard them from ritual sacrifice?"

"There was no guard against that. But other things… Not all of my siblings were kind. My sister…"

"Half of my vaunted siblings hide when Aros or Etelian crosses the threshold at Parsa or Fehlaka. Such is the world."

Nin could only imagine the imperial palace in full court—with the dozens of princes and princesses, and the majexes clamoring for the emperor's ear. There would be plenty of spite, by numbers alone.

"The world also gives choice in some things."

"You tried to save your servants from your sister." There was an almost resigned note to his voice.

"Yes."

"How?" He slowed his movements and tossed the staff to the corner, settling on the blankets. His motions were easier—as if the possibility of a story about her past exploits and idiocy relaxed him.

She pulled herself upright, cross-legged to mirror him. A gentle hum echoed across the bond, seeking symmetry and connection.

"I had to be...creative." It hadn't been easy, and with her magic still undeveloped and unreliable, she had really had to dig deep.

She touched her face and let her magic free. She felt the familiar spell settle, as the most unremarkable facial characteristics known to Tehrasi made her features into a bland face without distinguishing attributes.

The same plain face had been worn by whichever servant accompanied Nin until inevitable execution would cause it to be changed for a new, equally indistinguishable face. Using such tactics, it had been easy to quietly and quickly resurrect whoever had been executed, since only the face had to stay dead.

She wove an illusion around her clothing, shifting it rapidly between servant and guard garments, maintaining the same spell on her face throughout.

Kaveh reached out and touched her rounded cheek. "Every one of them, the same face? Clever."

"Heba"—Nin swallowed roughly, thinking of her beloved handmaiden—"was a master at courtly enchantments, makeup and dress. We found...creative solutions for her abilities."

And Nin's coterie had bound together in their efforts to stay alive and thrive in such a vicious environment. They had become absolute masters at face-swapping enchantments.

They had become so adept at it, that it had become second nature to Nin. It had been one of the easiest enchantments to master when her magic had Awakened. Nin had used it exhaustively on the streets to keep from being remembered and to find new homes for those in trouble.

Until the census. She had been old enough by then to start longer term plans.

"How did your sister never figure out your servant gambit?"

"Because she killed each whenever she felt the need. She was successful, so she felt no need to look further." She picked at her sleeve. "Lorsali was simple in her desires."

You think you are so special. I'll show you what happens to special children.

Nin shuddered at the memory.

She remembered Savvan's and her father's expressions. They had leaned forward, interested to see the bloodshed. The first three scepters had always been closer to the Scepter of Darkness than any others. Especially the first of them all—Giran's scepter, the Prime Scepter. Giran had loved the color of blood.

Lorsali had loved the color of Nin's blood.

It had taken Nin a long time to understand that it was jealousy that underscored Lorsali's remarks and actions—that underscored her desire to mash Nin like mud between stones.

To this day, though, she still could not comprehend Lorsali's jealousy. Lorsali had been beloved by Salare and she had been free. She would have married, left, and controlled her own kingdom. Nin, with the true power of the gates running through her, would never have been allowed to leave Tehras. Zehra Amanan Carre had been trapped.

Lorsali had never realized or embraced her own freedom—only her sense of injustice. She had provided a powerful example, though. Nin had worked to prevent revenge from completely overwhelming her, even as it drove many of her actions.

She shook her thoughts free. "As long as everything unfolded the way she conceived in her mind, Lorsali rarely looked deeper. We simply resurrected each servant or guard in new guises. We learned to make new faces early—to keep real faces as a last resort."

In the palace, in the brutal battle between royals, Nin's forces had won. In that last year, they had beaten Lorsali, who had been consistently vicious while Nin was preparing to take the Ninth Scepter. Dozens of Nin's servants had fallen to Lorsali's execution spells in the halls over perceived slights or fits of temper.

But in that final year, none of her coterie had stayed dead. Not until the purge. She closed her eyes and breathed deeply. "The gambit worked because I mourned. I mourned for the faces I would never see again, even while I fiercely celebrated their continued life."

"Why did you care?" he said softly, touching the bond, trying to understand.

"They were mine," she said simply.

Understanding bloomed quietly, and deeply, over the bond.

"One of them took your face. Died for you." He regarded her, so close she could reach out and touch him. "It would have been easy for them. They had done it a thousand times. Which one was it?"

"Heba." She closed her eyes. "Heba did it."

Be finally free.

"They saved you."

"Yes," she whispered.

"Because you had saved them?"

She laughed painfully. "Saved? I performed my share of terrible tasks. Life in the palace... I wasn't without fault. I...I held the knife sometimes. Expectations had to be met. Salare's expectations were sacrosanct. And actions..." She swallowed and looked down.

She would never be able to ask them—her guards, her handmaidens, the lowest of the kitchen staff who had held open the chute—but she'd had long years to ruminate upon it. To wonder why they had all banded together to save her. It had been a chance to get rid of the Carres in total for some of them—especially those in the lowest of positions, far outside her circle of protection.

She'd had long years to wonder what she had done to be saved.

To ponder on what purpose her life was given.

She clenched her hands into fists. It would never be enough, anything she did, and she would never be able to return in any normal manner to Tehras. She would be unable to continue that fight now that she was marked by the empire. But she would do whatever was needed to prevent Tehrasi from being destroyed and her people from being hurt.

She didn't realize Kaveh was touching her—reading her thoughts—until he was speaking.

"You don't understand. How strange," he murmured. She looked at him, mystified, as his own thoughts stuttered along the connection. His face and emotions contorted, scrambling, fighting his own disbelief at her misunderstanding and the certainty of his realization. "They saved you because you were theirs, too."

Mine.

The thought slipped through, and though he immediately yanked it back and jerked away, it couldn't be denied.

And for a moment, Nin felt it—the rest of her life stretched before her. And it was less murky; clearer than it had ever been. For the man in front of her could be someone she could call hers and be had in return.

It was there in his scrambling emotions and the certainty of that slipped thought.

It was not a life that she would have chosen weeks ago, but it was a life that she could live.

Taline would be safe. Rone would make it so. They were detaching the scepter. Taline would live. Taline could prosper.

Taline, be safe, live free.

She tucked the aching, longing into the place she had constructed long ago and took his hand and moved it back to her neck.

She placed her hand over the top. "Your father's pain is yours. He is yours. And you are mine too. I will fix the gates for you."

KAVEH

I will fix the gates for you.

Kaveh stared at her. I will conquer the world for you, she might as well have said.

You are mine, is all he could think in return.

"The Scepter of Darkness isn't coming to aid us," he said. It was no secret now, that something was happening in the non-magic layer—not only with bursts of magic, but with rumors of rituals using the scepter. Along with rumors that Rone ul Valeran planned to destroy it.

And he knew suddenly, connected to her as he was, that this knowledge was a balm to her. He almost couldn't fault her for it, after feeling her emotions every second for weeks now. She knew that her friends coming back meant their deaths.

She looked steadily back. "I will fix the gates. We will fix the gates. And your empire will continue on. You and I do not need the Scepter of Darkness to fix the gates."

He looked at her, parsing through the emotions that came so easily to her. So foreign, and so...addictive.

His fingers tightened against her skin. It didn't matter—that addiction—because she wasn't going anywhere. She was his now. And she would be, when the oath period ended. His hand, his vassal.

He couldn't worry about an addiction that was the same as drawing breath—something his body did automatically. That her emotions held such sway just showed the connection. It didn't matter, and he was unchanged by it.

He let his fingers release, tightening them against his side. Release, tighten, release.

She sat patiently, letting him work through his internal argument without judgment or comment. That was another thing about her. She was never impatient. Even on the battlefield when a stripling would flail at the task she set, she never yelled or punished with magic. She would simply continue her motions and the person would either follow behind and get themselves together or they wouldn't. She didn't push.

The useless soldiers almost always got themselves together and scrambled to follow. The ones who didn't, ended up dumped through a ripgate on some oasis—then were dumped back into camp after, falling all over themselves to aid her in another way.

He had added three such striplings—fervor in their eyes—to his shadow network in the past two days.

If someone had asked him weeks ago if someone like her existed, he would have scoffed.

If someone had asked him if someone with a past like hers could do the things she did, he would have jeered. And now?

"How will we fix the gates?"

She smiled slowly. "We'll need to steal a few things first."

CHAPTER TWENTY-FOUR

THE DYING SUN

TALINE

(Fertile Crescent Valley in the First Layer)

Taline felt an emptiness in her chest upon waking that she didn't understand—as if she had been freed of another tether that she had never wanted to lose. As if someone had freed her of a promise that she still wanted to fulfill.

The ground was scorched in a circle around them.

She rubbed at her chest.

"Summora?"

"Something is wrong."

"Something besides the assassins and world destruction?" Valeran asked lightly.

"I...don't know."

Valeran examined her for a moment more, gave a concise nod, and gathered their things.

She looked at the circle scorched into the earth. The scepter was no longer content to simply burn through cloth. What did that mean?

She rose stiffly and joined Valeran, working with him to leave no trace of their campsite or presence.

"Still to the Dying Sun?"

Valeran examined the landscape, then moved them forward. "Yes."

They moved swiftly, but carefully toward the Temple of the Dying Sun, halfway between Ur and Uruk, but west of the fertile valley where functional and less guarded temples were more plentiful.

They had picked their next target after discussing the positives and negatives of each moon temple, the timing, and the probability of outside forces stopping them.

Acting quickly meant there was less time for greater enemy forces to gather, but it also meant choosing a temple closer to their last known position, which meant greater forces would be more likely to be in the area.
The pentalayerists would be watching moon temples.

Waiting meant more time for enemies to anticipate them—perhaps enemies from the empire. Picking a target gave them the upper hand. They needed to be in control of the playing field. In order not to use the scepter again, controlling the environment was key.

"It has been too long since we last saw Nin." The full moon had passed, and they were headed down toward the dark part of the cycle.

"I know."

Separated on the first crescent of this moon, and now staring at the moon's bloated three-quarter version, Taline felt the press of time.

But Valeran was not wrong. The pentalayerists would hunt Nin relentlessly, if they led them to her and they realized what she was. Nin would be...safer with the Shadow Prince and being under the protection from a crown until they could rescue her.

Abhorrent thoughts. They would separate the scepter, reach a gate, and rescue Nin.

Valeran—no, Rone—maneuvered them into the Temple of the Dying Sun at moonrise after three days of hard travel and excruciating, long nights.

She had learned to listen to the scepter, then pass its words into the breeze, as she would the lying words of a politician who only wanted a throne. The scepter...was not pleased, and it had been showing that displeasure physically.

She felt sixty years older with each step.

The moonrise ritual was simple—yet agonizing—as the skin was flayed from a third of her palm in the direct beam of light while the scepter screamed at her stupidity and nerve.

In addition to the pain, odd feelings coursed through her. The scepter was trying to connect outward—like it felt another user beyond the temple and was starting to hedge its bets. If it couldn't have Taline, it would try for this other.

Other, other, power, power, this one broken, other, power...

Nin?

Agony sliced through her.

"I think there might be correlation between pain and a negatively named temple after all." Taline panted, trying to hold onto the shreds of sanity curling through the jumbled mess of pain radiating from her palm, head, and heart. "I should never have doubted you."

"Narsumina, you make my heart race like a gazelle. I may never eclipse this moment."

She managed a harsh laugh, stomach muscles clenching as the scepter seared the portion of her palm still attached. She knew the scar on her palm, from where she had just disengaged one-third of its grip—yet again—would be there forever.

Power, power to be yours. Why do you limit your power? You can do anything. Your gatemaker will be saved.

Power. Hers.

Yes, yes...no one will force you to do anything again. No one will be able to take your power. No one will be able to—

She pushed against the seductive words, struggling.

"Summora?"

The name jolted her. Valeran only ever used her surname when he was serious and worried.

The idea of Valeran—Rone—being worried about her was still novel enough to be noteworthy.

She breathed deeply. "I'm fine."

He ducked beneath her left arm and slung it around his shoulders. "Good. Let's keep going."

Kill him! He stands in your way. He wants to destroy us.

"You don't have to do that," she said gruffly.

He huffed and they hobbled out together.

"Thank you," she murmured.

"Two more temples, narsumina. Don't thank me yet."

Kill him! Power! You can save yourself!

Her breath came in shallow pants. This was worse. Valeran—Rone—had been right. Reconnecting with the scepter had been a grievous mistake. Peeling it away again was like peeling the skin and muscle from her bones.

She caught breath enough to say, "Where to next?"

"They'll trace us here by tonight. Tomorrow, at the latest. The Temple of Shattered Day is our best option." He grimaced, as if he, too, was displeased by the temple's destructive name.

"It will...take another...two days...to get there." Breathing had never been so hard.

Power! Wield us!

"I know." He pressed a healing balm into her hand.

You will give in. They all do.

She closed her eyes.

Onward, they traveled, and nights became both easier and harder.

Easier—because there was something to trust in Valeran now. In Rone. They still didn't share the same goal, but at least his wasn't incomprehensible or base. And he wanted to see her survive. It was the vow he had made. She had long stopped believing he might kill her in her sleep. She slept near him every night now.

Harder—because the scepter had assumed and exceeded the antagonism she had previously expressed for Rone and had turned it inward. Now, the scepter challenged her at every turn, driving her to near insanity with its mad ramblings.

Worse, something unusual was happening in their world. And every time there was an occurrence, the scepter jerked in her palm.

A new bearer!

What was Nin doing?

"Chin up, narsumina. We will be past the halfway mark after reaching the next temple."

Never! Power! We are in your hands. Why would you remove power? You will die. All you love will die!

The temple finally came into view. The entrance was an obelisk set into the low mountains above the fertile valley of agricultural fields near Umun.

Moonrise was a single clock rotation after midnight and moonset at sun-high midday. Moonrise meant they could cloak themselves in darkness. But so, too, could their enemies.

The scepter sang gleefully in her hand.

Your enemies are my allies. Cloaked in darkness, you will call for my power.

CHAPTER TWENTY-FIVE
BRIDGING GATES

KAVEY

(Tehras, Tehrasi)

Cloaked in darkness, shrouded in gray and black, and crouched on a rooftop, Nin passed Kaveh two of the items she had retrieved from a secret compartment hidden deep within the bowels of the city. She had used the magic of the city itself to enchant and keep the compartment hidden. Even his shadows had passed over the area, as they had read the blanket of enchantments as simply the stretch of the city's magic.

The compartment had stayed blanketed and undisturbed because Nin had never thought she would access it again. A third retrieved package had been put directly into her pack. Kaveh was immensely curious about its contents.

Using a simple spell laden over his eyes, Kaveh looked at the two spellboxes in his hands. The multicolored sides flashed in the simulated spell light. "We cannot reactivate the gates with these."

"Not with just those," Nin said calmly, spinning a spell in her hand, then pressing it into the blue side of the box. "But, they are part of the solution."

"Which gate are we fixing?" he asked skeptically.

"All of them," she said, just as confidently, spinning a second spell between her palms.

He checked the bond, to confirm her mental state, wondering whether he had missed some obvious decay in her mind all this time.

"It won't be permanent," she said, as if that was the answer to his probing of her sanity. "But it will be a boon to the current state of affairs."

He examined the slip of a woman next to him who chose to save instead of to subjugate. "The gates require one of the twelve scepters to be wielded. They were designed that way," he said. It's what had always been claimed—by the Carres, by Osni, by the emperor.

He cared little about the gates usually, except to have them work. Because he could travel quickly using his own powers, he wasn't constrained by gate travel the way others were. His study had been taken up elsewhere. But he knew the basics.

In the split of the worlds from one to five, certain magi types had been given advantage—the rarest of types—done on purpose so that few could upset the balance. Magi of creation and gatemakers were at their lead. Magi of creation were limited by nothing in the layers of worlds. They could rip apart the whole balance, if they chose. But they were rare enough to be born only every few generations, and even then, their life expectancy was unnaturally short, if they were unaided.

There were those who hunted creation magi specifically—hunted to eradicate any who could harm or change the world. Kaveh hadn't paid much attention to pentalayerists or their kind before, but to hunt and be hunted was a concept he knew well.

Gatemakers were also exceedingly rare as a magi type, but it was usual to have four or five born every generation across the worlds. That number had increased with the Carres and Barrinis in the last hundred years, with both dynasties selectively breeding into their families any who had the talent. The Carres had been the most successful, but even then, it was well known that not all Carre children had the ability to gatemake without augmentation by the scepters.

He looked over to see that Nin was also lost in some thought, and he almost reached out with a shadow before remembering himself.

She looked up, shaking herself. "That is why we are stealing one of the remaining nine scepters from the Tehras palace." She began to wrap another spell.

"With the most powerful three gone—"

"Yes. That is why this can only be a patch. But I will wield a scepter." She took a deep breath. "And I will make your empire strong again."

He stared at her, then carefully probed the bond again. She looked amused this time.

"Uncertainty does not suit you," she said.

"I saw your sister at Tiris' Festival of Gates. She blessed only a single gate, even though there were two others that could have used the renewal. And she had a scepter in hand."

Nin's amusement disappeared and something far more complicated took its place. "Lorsali was a gatekeeper only, and not a powerful one at that."

He narrowed his eyes. "And you?"

She looked at him steadily. "I am a gatemaker of the Carre line. I was destined for this task from the moment I was tested."

"You will reveal yourself."

"As a thief?" she said lightly, against the emotions flowing along the bond. She touched her bag and the wrapped package within. "No, I will only be revealed if we are negligent."

He raised a brow.

She raised hers back. "The gates are flickering, and few have ever understood the scepters, no less average gatekeeping. Who is to say that the gates don't have a last pocket of magic? A last gasp of breath? Who is to say how long that last gasp will last? Scholars are wrong all the time," she said with a hint of a smile.

"The emperor is not stupid. He will not need my lack of revelation to discover the truth."

"I know." Her smile disappeared. "Which is why we will not use your shadows in Tehras. They are too recognizable."

"I do know how to hide myself," he said pointedly. "I hid from you."

She looked at him from beneath long lashes and smiled slowly. "I know how to hide, too, when it's just me doing the hiding."

He felt his pulse increase in a way that he only associated with bloodlust and battle. It was a feeling he was coming to increasingly associate with her as well.

"But if you are seen," she said, finishing her preparations, "the whole gambit is lost. A villain won't even need to show his hand."

He raised a brow. "If I don't wish to be seen, I'm not."

"Any strangely moving shadows will be remarked upon."

"Shadows move in the night—should I seek to hide them, too?"

Her spark of humor, that he had deliberately tried to cause, rippled across the bond. The feeling of it, of her pleasure, inflamed that same feeling of bloodlust and battle within him. Strange, though, that he didn't want to look away from her or inflict pain of any kind. It was a different fierceness to battle. A strange kind of heat and focus.

"No, but you can't tell me that the emperor—or that Aros, Etelian, or any of the other blessed—don't know the feel of your shadows specifically."

He regarded her. "The emperor does. And Aros has always been fixated upon my powers."

"Aros's spies are our biggest concern."

"You forget that Nera is running Tehrasi now."

Nin froze. "I did. I do not know Nera's style or cunning well."

"Dangerous. Fixing the gates anonymously is our best move, as is taking care." He let his normal severity take hold—though he found he was somewhat reluctant to let the lightness pass.

She nodded and pulled on a pair of gloves that she had taken from her rooms when they'd passed through them again. "Let it seem a miracle."

"The emperor won't be deceived by such things."

"The emperor has no idea what can be done with the gates. The Carres made certain no one did—sealing with death anyone's ability to tell. Even the Barrinis followed such thinking," she said grimly. "And it won't matter when I am done."

For a moment, he could feel her struggle with some decision.

"Why are we on this rooftop?" he asked, feigning a care.

She relaxed a measure, peering into the distance. "It is a test."

He let himself be manhandled as she pushed him to the other side of the roof. She peered over the edge of the roof, a little device in her hand that read the weather spells.

Handy. For people without power.

He raised his hand, a shadow at his fingers, ready to read every weather spell the city held. A slim hand chopped his. "Put that away."

He felt humor rise in him again. It was disconcerting how accustomed he was becoming to the feel of amusement.

She darted a look around to make certain they were still hidden. "Best to start here and practice. Pretend you are shadowless."

He raised a brow. "I will never be shadowless."

"That's why I said pretend." She hooked a spell to her belt and threw it outward over the edge of the roof in a glittering net, then slowly turned the spell concoction box in her hand, peering at the writing on the sides.

"You can't read that."

"Not a glyph of it." She peered at one side in particular, then nodded, powering it a bit more. "But I powered the spells within it. I know what is there. And Taline color-coded the sides and the boxes themselves based on spell category."

"She made those, so you don't have to read them."

She nodded in affirmation. "Colors are easy to understand." She pointed at the blue side. "This one allows us to travel without using the same force that my power uses when done instinctively—instinctive travel creates more ripples. And this green one will hide our movements so no one will know there is a gatemaker in the city. I was less careful before Taline, but she disapproved of risk, so I took more care after." Fondness enveloped her voice.

Here was the answer to the question he'd had asked weeks ago—how had Nin remained hidden all this time? When she had disappeared from him with her sister in her arms, he had known what she was due to her output of power. Her first escape from him had raised the question. The second—with two people taken through a self-made gate—had answered it.

But it hadn't answered how she had remained hidden for so long. He examined the box. "Your...sister...is the one who created this?"

They were quite impressive in construction, and the idea of them even more so.

"Taline is a magnificent spellcrafter," she said, just as fondly.

Impressive construction or not, there was one thing about them that wasn't. "But she can't power her own spells."

Nin's fingers paused. "Some of them she can."

"But not most. You power her creations."

"We make a good team."

"You don't need her, though. Only she needs you."

Nin looked up at him. "I would need her even if I never required another of her creations."

His brows furrowed. "She would be useless to you."

"No," she said simply. She drew her finger through the air above them, as if testing the wind, then turned her gaze back to the device. She tweaked another spell. "But yours is a telling statement," she said calmly. "One I learned well in the palace of my youth. You will cast me aside when I hold no more inherent use for you."

The bond said she believed it fully; accepted it.

"You will always have use." He frowned. "You are powerful."

She was one of the most powerful magi he had come across. It was heady, finding someone who could keep up with him. Someone who was so trusting. Someone who put care in trustworthiness. Someone who—

He felt the urge to lift his knife to his palm.

She wrapped her fingers around his without looking up. "Not now. I can't spare the healing energy. You can have this breakdown later."

He stared at her and the urge slipped away.

She nodded at the box and slipped it into her pocket.

"You are expending a lot of effort on a test," he said.

"The weather patterns and security spells are frequently changed." She pulled her gloves tight. "We scrupulously monitored the enchantments and spell patterns in the city and knew each before we stepped out on a job. I'll have to do this by feel, and that takes more effort. I'll go past the weather alarms to that shop"—she pointed—"then pull you through."

He looked to the indicated position. He could travel through the shadows to that point in an instant. He could wrap them around him and shoot him out in a swirl below. But he would leave a trail, visible to those most sensitive. Like to the woman next to him—holding everyone's pain as her own—still connected to the city built by her forefathers and carrying his own shadows around her shoulders.

He watched her pull spelled goggles over her eyes. He wondered whether she would be able to see the trail of his shadows once the oath was gone.

He rotated his shoulders. The oath would be replaced by something equally strong, so it was an irrelevant thought.

He focused on her goggles. "Can you read through those?"

"What?" She looked at him through the glasses.

"Can you enchant them to let you read?"

"There's no fix for my brain connections. Rone used to say there was no fix for my brain," she said, more cheerfully than he would be able to in the same scenario.

"Stay here," she said. "I'll be right back with a path."

She dove, arms outstretched, then flipped and fell feet first. At the last moment, she shot wind at the ground, slowing her momentum so that she landed in a crouch. She was off, the instant her muscles had rebounded, and she shot into the darkness—a slim wraith darting a winding course.

He had chased this thief weeks ago, and now he was planning a theft with her. He found himself looking forward to it.

He resisted the urge to roll a shadow between his fingers as he looked at her goggles. He thought of that glass shop. He thought of their bond. He thought of how he had never thought to give pieces of his power away like Nin and her sister did so easily for each other.

She got to her position and knelt. He could see her tug off her glove and touch the ground, pulling it open. There was a hum, then the ripgate was opening in the air above him and he was looking up at her staring down. She stuck a hand down, as if beckoning him into the twist and turn of natural forces turned upside down.

He raised a brow. "Is this a challenge?"

She cocked her head expectantly, goggles huge on her face. "Of course. Can you get through without using shadow?"

He took her ungloved hand—cool fingers vibrating with warmth beneath—and contemplated the spell he had seen her use. She smiled and gripped his fingers, pushing the knowledge of what she had done through the bond and into his skin. He rose on windswept feet through the ripgate and she tugged him to the side, so he landed carefully on the street.

"Can you do it on your own next time?" she asked, sealing the ripgate with an easy motion while watching him.

He flexed his fingers, still feeling the echo of her skin. "Yes."

"Good. I need you to do so in a minute." She looked around the corner of the shop's alley.

He felt amusement flood him. "Do you teach all your accomplices such things?"

"Only the ones most corruptible." Her teeth flashed in the light of the nearly complete half-moon.

Something in her manner was renewed. Refreshed. A playfulness that had been absent in most of their interactions. This was the Ninli ul Summora who robbed people in the night.

"Speaking of robbing people…"

A chariot rounded the corner with the stylized glyph of Etelian's reign. She pulled her hood down over her goggles, then flew through the air and dropped onto the seat. She touched the startled driver on one temple and dumped him safely to the floor, unconscious.

She plucked the money bags and papyri scrolls from the chariot's constraining spells and spilled them into the street. A dozen sets of glittering eyes in the darkness opened and focused on the scene.

Nin flipped back into the stagnant shadows of the city and rejoined him. The denizens of the night crept out and retrieved the bags, then melted back into their own shadows.

"Subtle," Kaveh said dryly.

"The Hand has been absent too long. That could have been anyone." She stretched her shoulders. "I'd say our test was a success. Shall we?"

All he could feel was anticipation.

They used the ripping technique to move through the city, perfecting the movements with each slice.

It was strange not using shadow and dart. Not using his shadows was like not using a perfectly capable limb. It was disconcerting at first—he was so used to using them, he barely knew how to do anything without.

Nin gave him a knowing look. "You are shadowless tonight. Don't forget."

Then they were in the temple's grove and Nin was opening a ripgate into the palace itself.

Etelian seriously needed to improve his security enchantments.

Or maybe it was just that nothing could keep this particular thief out. Not only was she able to tap into spells in Tehras that were still keyed to her family, she had the mindset of a puzzle solver. He felt anticipation surge again. Kaveh was going to test Fehl Palace against her.

But before he could process the thought, they were in the ceremonial scepter chamber. Four curved doorways separated the line of scepters arrayed neatly around the curved walls into four sets. One section of wall—where the first three scepters should be—was conspicuously bare.

The last time he had been here, the woman beside him had disappeared beneath his fingertips, and he had nearly killed the padifehl.

That whatever fake scepters Etelian had put into place were missing now, too, wasn't a surprise. Kaveh had been told through his spies that the emperor had broken the fakes in a fit of rage and that Etelian had been completely drained of power until Nera had intervened.

He looked over to see Nin staring at the Ninth Scepter with hungry and anxious eyes.

"These are the ceremonial scepters, not the ones powering the gates." The hundred scepters that directly powered the gates surrounding the city surrounded the palace in a mirrored way.

"Osni was the one who let you think these scepters only ceremonial, and that only a few of their ceremonial powers could be unlocked. Without a gatemaker wielding a ceremonial scepter, the gate scepters would have been the better ones to use my family's blood upon. They would have powered the gates individually for many more years. But Osni knew what he was doing when he powered those of ceremony. To rule in Tehrasi is to hold ceremony, not gate."

Osni would die. Kaveh looked at the scepters along the wall. "Whoever took the first three knew their true powers."

"Yes," she said quietly. He could feel her tension. "They were blood keyed by Osni to the emperor,

Etelian, and Osni himself. But they could never be truly keyed in such a way, which is why Etelian so frequently failed. Tehrasians saw my family wield their scepters. All it would take is someone keen of eye to note the differences in Salare's wielding of the Second Scepter versus Etelian's. The differences were stark. And once you see someone fail a task perfected by another, it is easier to see how the task is constructed. It is easier to figure out how you might master it yourself." Nin looked back at the Ninth Scepter.

"A Tehrasian took it, then."

Trepidation filled the bond, followed by resolve. "Or one studied in all things Tehrasian."

Kaveh followed her gaze. He could feel her intention along the bond. "You plan to take this one. Why not the fourth?" he asked. Without the first three available, it was the next in line of the twelve. Nothing like the Prime Scepter or even the second and third, with their tainted darkness, but...

A strange emotion wound along the bond. "I would have powered the Ninth Scepter first. The Fourth Scepter would have become mine later, taken from Lorsali when she married," Nin murmured, gaze lingering.

Kaveh didn't need to feel Nin's combination of regret/determination/guilt along the bond to imagine what the eldest princess's thoughts had been on that.

"Not before?"

Nin shook her head. "Each of the twelve scepters is attached to a specific person, and only with death or ceremony can it be changed. If a person is powerful enough, though, he or she can rule more than one. I had the strongest base power after my brother Savvan. Since he would wield the highest three once he assumed the throne, I would have likely gotten the fourth as well as the ninth, and maybe more between. It was...no secret in the family, what was planned."

She would have never left the family's service. Any children or union she would have been allowed would have been held strictly within the palace walls.

He cocked his head. "You consider the Ninth Scepter yours. You care less about the others, even those of higher standing."

"The ninth is not mine. I was never keyed."

"But you feel it to be yours. You know how it works."

She didn't respond for a long moment. "It was made certain that we all knew how our own worked. Even for those like Lorsali, who was only a keeper. Even for me, whose magic had yet to awaken. I could do small enchantments—the ones that all children slowly start to develop as they approach their Awakening—but there were...ways to incite advanced magic."

Brutal ways. He knew them well from territories they had conquered.

"The empire outlaws such things now."

"I was not raised in the empire." She approached the Ninth Scepter slowly. "Who would say no to the king and queen? Only a person one day short of death."

All Kaveh could remember about his earliest years was the emperor's elation over Kaveh's powers. But, the emperor had been cautious about inciting Kaveh's full powers unprovoked and unfocused until the emperor had mapped them himself. He had never brutally pushed for full activation. Then again, he had never needed to.

"How will you activate the scepter, if you aren't keyed?"

"I was not keyed, but it was…marked for me." Her eyes tightened in the way they only did when she talked about ritual death. His gaze fell to the carpets which hid dark, stained stones beneath. Someone had died for her marking. "I was taught with a learning rod."

Her gaze went back to the wall holding the set of scepters that contained the ninth. The ones on that wall were less impressive in build compared to the three that were missing from the first set, but he had seen the agonizing deaths of the imperial soldiers who had tried lifting even the least of them in the aftermath of the palace coup. Their blood had been added to the layers already embedded in the stones.

The empire had been careful of all the scepters after that—even the plainest of them.

He could feel the bad memory of her own experience with them as he watched her eyes cloud. A conversation for another time.

She shook herself free of the memory. "If Osni had ever tried to re-key the Ninth Scepter, there would have been pushback. He would have known I was alive," she said softly. "But the ritual he invoked with my family's deaths only gave him the power to activate a portion of the power of the first three. Father's, Mother's, Savvan's. If he had used the ritual to invoke full power to the scepters, he could have succeeded, but he was consumed by his revenge. He had to make sure they died without resurrection."

"Osni claimed to know the scepters better than anyone alive."

"Better than anyone he knew to be alive, yes." She smiled sharply. "But only enough to use them in the ways that my family didn't hide. He never knew the secrets beneath. He thought he had it all figured out, but never understood his real opponent was the cruel genius of my father and those before him. Only family could view the marking and keying ceremonies. And we were all under death oaths concerning them."

Kaveh looked at her sharply. That she was speaking of it—

Nin smiled briefly. "That magic ended a long time ago. Like anything else, it has to be renewed. In life, my father could automatically renew it. With the death of everyone, any remnant of the oath went to me." She looked wry. "And I've decided I can live."

She looked back at the scepters and took a deep breath. "Let's get what we came for."

She crouched on the floor and carefully unwrapped the package she had taken from the hiding spot in her room. Three shafts were revealed. One shaft held a familiar, twisted globe on top. She slotted the pieces together, aligning them, then set the assembled piece carefully on the floor.

Kaveh stared at the replica of the Ninth Scepter, then looked at the real one on the wall. If he didn't know better, he would think them identical. "You have been plotting."

"Some plots are long in tooth. Some short."

"And what plots are your longest?"

She said nothing for a moment. "Those that are the most unrealistic," she said quietly, rising.

He slid a shadowed palm along the back of her neck.

Freedom.

Something told him this deep desire had less to do with him. This was an older wish.

She stepped away slowly, letting his hand slide along her skin before dropping. "That Etelian had replicas already made to replace the first three is something you need to question. Good replication takes considerable skill and time."

She pulled a glove over her hand, took a deep breath, then reached out and gripped the scepter on the wall. He was reminded of the Scepter Temple and how she had reached for the Scepter of Darkness.

But there she had been barehanded, and here she was not.

She made a series of minute twists with her wrist, then lifted the Ninth Scepter and quickly wrapped it in linen.

She put the replica in place, then pressed a bare wrist to a circle in the scepter head's design. The shaft pulsed faintly below it, then settled into position.

No fanfare, no wild sparks, nothing to indicate that anyone had been here. The wards hadn't been breached; the sentry alarms hadn't sounded; no one had witnessed a blast of light.

An easy theft.

There was only one question. "Why haven't you taken it before?"

She paused, then continued putting everything away. "Taking it would have disrupted the chain. The others would mitigate it for a small while, like they are doing now. They are all active, though they appear dormant. The light the city can see is symbolic, but there is a light within them once they've activated. Taking the light away is a problem for Tehras and all of Tehrasi," she said quietly. "I would never do something to bring Tehrasi to harm."

"You could have slowed the empire."

"Yes. And because I am aware what a gatemaker can do, I understand your father's obsession with holding the Scepter of Darkness." She looked up at him. "He needs it to make certain that his empire is not gobbled from within. The gates bring immense opportunity—progression, trade, knowledge transfer. But all of that relies on the same infrastructure as well. If you barricade a country, that progression, trade, and transfer begins to slip away. I am not unsympathetic to the emperor, even knowing my end."

"Your end is with me."

She nodded agreeably—at odds with the opposite certainty in her mind. "Come. Let's fix the gates."

He didn't bother to argue her error of certainty. She would find out at the end of the oath's cycle that he was the correct one.

They sliced through in two passes—one to exit the ceremonial chamber and the other to reach the tree dense ring that circled the palace. A hundred flickering gate scepters stood in an endless line that wrapped the hill upon which the palace sat. She walked to a symbol etched in stone. It was unremarkable but for its presence at their location and in the vee formed by her feet. A thousand more were embedded within the landscape. They were all scuffed and worn, but as Kaveh watched, small zings of power wrapped through the symbols—activated by either her presence or that of the scepter.

She took no notice of it—either because it was a commonplace event or expected. Her gaze was distantly focused through the columns to the stone arches of Tehras stretched around the city's perimeter.

"The emperor's desperation is valid," she murmured. "I've never seen the gates so diminished."

She unwrapped the scepter with her gloved hand. She stared at it in the moonlight, unmoving.

"You are afraid," he murmured. "You were afraid before lifting the Scepter of Darkness. Your emotions were…unpleasant then. They near that state again. Why?" he asked curiously.

"I was convinced I'd never touch one." She stared at the scepter with a fixed, remote gaze.

He touched the back of her hand. "How do you open a ripgate?" he asked calmly. "What is the process you use?"

She blinked a few times and he felt
her mind nudge along to retrieve the
information—moving away from the fear.

"I create...soft spots...in the fabric of the world
layer. Places where I can enter and re-enter.
The farther the distance, the greater the density
of the spot and the more effort it takes.
Moving around the alley when fighting you was
just...swirling that part of the layer. Those spots
never last. The world magic shakes them out.
The greater the gate, though, the more the
layer...fights back."

She looked at the scepter, but her fear was less.
She looked back at him, and the fear receded
completely. "Other than worrying about a lack
of gatemaking abilities in descendants, it's one
of the reasons for the scepters. The scepters
separate the magic from the participant. You
can have the layer fight back...somewhere else."

She looked down and nodded at whatever she
had resolved in her mind. Her free fingers
skimmed his briefly in thanks.

She opened one of the boxes and pressed
a red symbol. A concealment spell lifted and
slithered into the air, then shot forward to wrap

around the ninth of twelve poles in the almond grove—wrapping around the scepter indicator that would flash to the city below indicating the use of the scepter she was reaching out to grab.

She curled her bare fingers around the scepter, transferring it from her gloved hand to her bare one. She lifted it, and for a moment, he wasn't certain it would work. But then she struck the tip down against the symbol and a glow built and burst into a circle of light that started revolving around her. The circle revolved as if the skies had opened and spilled their rays onto her, then were seeking to pull her up with them.

It was beautiful. The lights slid along the lines of her skin, down through her limbs and into the symbol in the stone, then light shot out toward the gate scepters, slithering along and lighting them one after another in a dazzling, ringed display.

She was beautiful.

In the distance, he could see the associated gates light with a soft glow, one after another. They settled into a softer brightness that held solid strength. He could feel the knowledge—through her. The gates would work perfectly in this state for one week more.

He looked up at the temple scepter indicators that stretched into the sky, showing the status of the twelve ceremonial scepters and their wielders. The ninth of the twelve softly glowed beneath her concealment spell for a moment, then submitted to the concealment fully and went dark.

He looked at her, at her fiercely gentle face watching in aching wish as the lights built from one arch to the next—spreading warmth and light.

"This was what you were meant to do."

She looked at him. "What?"

To spread warmth and light.

"You are meant to be one with the gates."

The ache within her turned into something more disquieted. "It was what I was made for."

He watched a scepter-lit shadow slip slowly down the wall and rise again as the lights rose and fell around them. "We are all made. But some choose a path as different as starlight to the sun. And some are the sun—and their choices will always bring light."

He felt her breath hitch at her words taken and given different form.

"It won't last forever. The gates." This. "Not without upkeep. But we can continue to nurture it," she said.

There were things there within the bond, things that he was helpless to name or identify. Things that made him vulnerable, that made him want to lash out and push away, but also to yank her to his chest and never let go.

She swallowed and reached out. "Let's fix your empire." She pulled the scepter through the air and a shimmering tear opened.

It felt like the tear opening in his chest—a wound without aid. He contemplated it for a moment—this future.

He stepped through.

CHAPTER TWENTY-SIX

OF SHATTERED DAY

TALINE

(TEMPLE OF SHATTERED DAY)

They arrived at the Temple of Shattered Day on their eighteenth day in the non-magic world.

Something was increasingly wrong with the scepter, but Taline was hesitant to acknowledge that someone—Nin—was perhaps wielding a scepter of her own. For the past three days, the Scepter of Darkness had been sparking and jolting as if it were trying to connect to something outside of itself—like something connected to it was trying to entice it forth.

Go, go! Another! Power! More! I will force them under my spell as well.

Taline followed Rone blindly, hoping he would be both their eyes and ears as she desperately tried to maintain her sanity.

They performed the same ritual within the Temple of Shattered Day as they had several days before, and the scepter peeled away another third of her palm in a tear of excruciating pain. A devastating sense of loss made her collapse to the floor.

Stupid vessel! Powerless, useless!

She panted and the world whirled around Taline in disjointed, jagged tones.

The scepter was hanging on by mere shreds of skin—like a tooth dangling from its root.

It lit suddenly, casting the cavern into starlight and shadows.

Better vessel! More power! Give me to them!

Taline inhaled sharply as the power ran through her. She took another ragged breath.

Rone approached her cautiously. "You did it."

"Yes."

"It will become even harder at the final temple. With the detachment—"

"I know." She closed her eyes and tried to pull the natural snappishness that the scepter invoked back inside. "I want to use it," she whispered.

"I know," he murmured back.

Power! Why do you hesitate?

She struggled with her thoughts. "I will use it."

"I know."

Another ragged breath pulled her equally worn gaze to his. "You can't trust me."

He stared at her for a long moment. "There is no one I trust more."

Her choked breath caught, and she ached to respond but the cloaked men moving through the shadows of the room demanded attention. Rone continued to stare at her, though, his gaze unbreakable.

"Rone ul Valeran. You truly seek to remove the scepter. You spoke truth," the leader said. "But the girl has been infected. Surely you know she can only be cleansed by death."

The man in charge was the most physically imposing in the space. He wore a red cloak pin, denoting his rank as squad leader. After their first temple skirmish, Rone had ruthlessly quizzed her to make certain she knew how to identify pentalayerist members and their tactics.

"I think you lack imagination." Rone's left foot shifted toward the leader, but the rest of him remained focused on her.

"And you lack sense." The leader looked at her. "We can remove it from you, Taline ul Summora. You have shown great fortitude so far, but you will fail the last moon ritual. All who have come before you have."

She stiffened at the use of her name, but let the edges of her mouth form a slash that Rone would approve. "The scepter protects its wielder. Otherwise Rone would have removed it from me already."

"He cares to keep you alive. But we feel death is a subjective state." Whether a subject survived a ritual was not a pentalayerist concern. They were quite Carre in their anti-Carre goals.

"I believe I will pass on your offer and continue this path instead," she said. "We will succeed."

"A false premise—that you will have the will to continue soon. You know not true suffering until hope hangs by a thread. The scepter will strike soon."

"I've been told I'm quite obstinate."

She could feel Rone's smile.

The leader narrowed his eyes on the man next to her. "The Scepter of Darkness lies. As does Rone-of-the-Valeran-and-Fehls."

Rone raised a slack brow but otherwise didn't move. Stillness in Rone ul Valeran was as deadly as the pulling of blades in another. It meant he was visualizing every move he would make.

"And you tell the truth, I suppose."

"Do you know what is happening in our world right now, Taline ul Summora?"

She gripped the scepter staff. She didn't want to hear about what was happening to Nin.

She didn't want to hear that her sister was imprisoned or worse, being forced to use her powers. "The world is united in peace?"

"There is a magi manipulating gates."

The others, yes—the others. Find the others!

Taline's heart ached, but she smiled sharply. "There is a magi who can control shadows and one who can drain others of power. We seem concerned about different things."

"Carsue, Urful, and Shiera ul Fehl are dead."

Taline felt the last like the shocking blow it was meant to be. Shiera was beloved by her people. Nin had lamented that she hadn't become Padifehl of Tehrasi. There would have been little reason for Nin to have been the Hand, if Shiera had been the leader of Tehrasi.

They would have needed to work on Shiera, who despite her benevolence was still of an elite mindset. Still, there would have been hope. Perhaps no true revolution would have occurred, but everyday life would have been better for the people. They wouldn't have had to live in constant fear of Etelian's abrupt mood swings and abusive nature.

The leader opened his palms. "We will be blamed and punished for their deaths."

Taline narrowed her eyes. Rone shifted minutely beside her.

"Are you to blame?" she asked the leader.

"The Shadow Prince's minions hunt us, and they will find their answers. They will find us guilty."

"What is your goal in telling me this? Do you hope I will tell him you aren't?"

"No, it is not for you to inform them, for you will never see the Shadow Prince or your sister again. Ninli ul Summora works at the side of the Shadow Prince. She is his hand on all battlefields. His dark mistress. She will be snuffed out alongside him when his time comes."

Taline curled her hand around the scepter staff, fingernails biting into her palm. "Never."

But the man kept talking. "He has bound her to the shadows, and soon he will be consumed by his own. The forces of balance dictate that she be destroyed alongside him."

Power and revenge. You can make everything right. You can save her.

The whispers started again. Dark revenge. Dark queen. Dark prophet of humanity's doom.

Save your sister and eliminate all enemies to the crown. A glorious life without fear—is that not what you wish?

Taline rubbed her fingers along the scepter's staff. "I'll kill Kaveh ul Fehl myself."

"If you allow us to destroy the scepter, we will give Ninli ul Summora a quick death."

"You speak your own demise."

The leader cocked his head. "We pledge ourselves to accept that end. But you will accompany us to the afterlife."

"Then death comes for both of us." She felt her mouth curl in a disturbing way. The power of the scepter ran up the thin slices of skin still attached to encase her forearm in light.

Strong and certain, she could do anything with this power. Those who tried to cage or kill her sister would die.

"We will all die. The rats who scurry around a Tehrasian-forged blade will not survive the blade that will cut them down in the end. A Carre who—"

The southern wall exploded. Projectiles rained over the space—a shower of metallic death.

The scepter throbbed under her palm as Rone whirled in front of her and projected a shield above them with the container magic at his belt. She forced the scepter to remain unlit in her violently shaking hand.

A Carre who what?

Death! Death! Power! The Carres!

"A Carre who what?" Taline shouted.

The pentalayerist leader was crouched beneath his own hastily constructed shield but his gaze shot to her. Another wave of metal flew through the air, pinging against Rone's clear shield but taking out three pentalayerists who had let down their guard to move toward where Taline and Rone crouched.

From her position, Taline had an easy view of the perpetrator of the attack.

A figure wrapped head-to-toe in black hung from the ceiling, projectiles held between each knuckle, pulling back again to throw at the men moving around the walls. Taline felt a shiver of dread.

Killing pentalayerists as well as targeting them? At this stage, that could only mean an imperial assassin.

Hanging like a spider from three limbs, the assassin threw his projectiles.

The pentalayerist leader rolled from his spot and threw a sickle.

"What Tehrasian-forged blade?" Taline yelled as Rone pushed them back.

The temple shook and the ground broke beneath their feet. The ceiling broke and the assassin pounced onto the western wall, then used the motion to flip onto the floor and take out two more pentalayerists.

The scepter vibrated in her palm.

"Taline. I have this. Don't use any magic." Rone was shielding all attacks from in front of her.

Crack. Crack, crack, crack. Taline's view rose upward as the ceiling splintered fully. Death fell through in a great wave of teeth and tusks.

The overwhelming number of monstrous beasts that poured through the ceiling and climbed through the floor shocked her for a moment. The feeling of the enemies—half man, half beast—was even more shocking. But the immediate engagement in battle made enemy analysis a secondary concern.

She lifted the Scepter of Darkness as the room began to writhe with moving bodies and projectiles.

Power shot passed her wrist. They would all die.

Yes! Use—

A paper covered in glyphs wrapped around her upper arm. Rone's left hand gripped her, as he threw an ice-tipped knife with his other.

Overwhelming power bunched at her elbow. Like a rushing river suddenly having a dam thrust into place, the power surged and crashed. She screamed. The scepter shrieked in failed eruption. The men shouted as ice swept the space, freezing limbs in burning agony as

Rone didn't bother to hide the powers of his mother's heritage.

They fell. More appeared. With her free hand, she threw a spellbox and a blade, but she was held in place—leaving both Rone and her to fight one-handed. Rone was struck by a spear. A reaping hook grazed Taline's leg. Enemies fell. More came. From three fronts, they rushed forward.

Then even more appeared.

Rone pushed her back against the wall and deflected an airborne sickle with the blade of his knife, while splitting his shield three ways. The pentalayerists divided their attention between Taline and Rone, the assassin, and the beasts.

The room was soon overrun by beastmen. Rone's shield flickered, but held, as he continued to manipulate something out of her view.

The haze of battle, pent-up energy, and confusion overtook her, making everything remote and unreal.

A figure dropped into the chamber, scepter raised and blazing with light. "What a lovely scene."

Fury burned through the haze of shock, and she grimly understood the aim of the beastly forces and their unearthly appearances. Crelu ul Osni had been busy recruiting troops in the layer of beasts.

And Crelu ul Osni was a Tehrasian-forged blade.

The beings surged at them and Rone flung a net that electrified the surge. But another wave of beasts was organizing behind them.

"Crelu ul Osni, the accursed." The pentalayerist leader swerved to avoid a fatal strike. "You have evaded death once more."

"Death is the best time to make allies, I've found."

The two pivoted around each other.

"How?"

"I killed your men at Bekli," Osni said. "Terribly sad, but then, did they know who you really are?"

Bekli had a fierce reputation—a natural gate between the layer of beasts and that of non-magic existed there. Obviously, Osni had found the gate—or found allies to lead him to it.

The leader pivoted grimly. "You will die, Osni, the undead."

He smiled. "Yes, but first—" Through the melee, Osni pointed his scepter at her.

The blast ripped through his own allies, but to a man like Osni, who cared only for himself, that would make no difference. She pushed Rone aside and brought the scepter to bear in front of her.

The blast never made it.

The assassin—hanging again, but with more purchase from the broken ceiling—threw a hand outward and Osni's trajectory was thrown off, blasting through the back wall instead. A familiar scepter dangled from the assassin's hand.

Osni's gaze immediately locked in on the threat and his face turned monstrous. "No!"

Had the assassin...just saved them?

Did the assassin...have Etelian's scepter?

"You can barely wield that with blood as diluted as yours, foul spawn," Osni spat. "The mother of demons didn't succeed at getting rid of the diluted flesh of her own. I should have wiped all of Tehras in the wake of the Carres."

"You will die." The assassin's voice was nearly a croak of sound—as if he rarely spoke. "All of you."

"You first." The pentalayerist leader threw a sickle sculpted by magic. The chamber exploded into smoke. "How do you hold that scepter in your hand?"

The Scepter of Darkness vibrated against her palm. One of ours.

"Taline. Stay back." Rone hissed, in front of her once more—his back stiff, as if he felt the scepter's influence and Taline's will.

Use the power, use the power. <u>Protect</u> with this power!

Osni bared his teeth. "You will all have to beat me to that end." Osni's scepter lit.

Use me, use me! They are both of my craft!

The fight became a four-way brawl. The assassin was making pentalayerist and beast alike slump in death with mass swipes of Etelian's scepter, while using it to evade the death blows aimed his way. The pentalayerist leader aimed a crippling blow at him, and the assassin was forced to dodge both it and a blast from Osni's scepter.

The pentalayerist leader swung his blade at her. "Give in, Taline-of-the-cursed-family. Give in and be cleansed. The Shadow Prince's mistress, and her red eyes, will meet you in the next life."

Rone's knife met his blade and Taline swung the scepter at a man sneaking behind her, then at a beast whose teeth dripped with acidic foam.

Nin's red eyes? They knew. Not that it was a surprise with the way the scepter had been sparking madly for days. Nin had been activating gates as if weaving basic khursifa threads.

"The last gatemaker, unveiled at last, and in the guise of a paltry healer," the pentalayerist leader intoned, aiming a blow at Osni. "For all your pointed death and plans, you didn't eliminate the Carre bloodline and their scourge of power, Crelu ul Osni. Soon, it will be too late to try."

Osni froze for a moment, then pulled another pentalayerist in front of him to take the blow aimed at him. "One more to eliminate to finish my revenge."

Nin. No. "Who really killed Shiera?" Taline demanded.

"Every last one of you will die," the pentalayerist leader shouted, gaze on Osni.

Osni's calculating eyes darted between the parties in the room. "I won't let you get in my way."

"The wielder of the cursed scepter"—the pentalayerist leader whirled and Rone moved to intercept two blasts—"the sister—"

Red descended across her vision. Osni would hunt Nin. Pentalayerists would hunt Nin. They would align with anyone to wipe away the Carres. Taline raised the scepter and power rushed through her. Death, revenge, destruction! "You will die first."

Power channeled upward and exploded against the seal barrier. The glyph paper crunched around her skin.

She fought to rip her arm from Rone's grasp, and the scepter's power bunched and shrieked wildly. He gripped harder.

Light blazed from the end of Osni's ceremonial scepter as he swung it at the assassin, then swung it at them. "I will end every magi who carries Carre blood."

"Let go, Valeran! Move."

"No," he answered. She saw the grim acceptance in his eyes a heartbeat before he pulled her to him and turned their bodies while tucking her head against his chest. Light flared around the shield of his body, followed by a spray of bright red.

Shouting, backlash from the blast, and chaos erupted. Osni hit the floor and scrambled to free himself of his cloak. Bodies fell.

The assassin bounded toward them and Rone threw something outward, causing the assassin to leap backward.

A blast echoed all around. Then the room was suddenly free of standing bodies—of all but Taline and Rone. Osni, the pentalayerist leader, the monsters, and men were all splayed on the floor, covered in blood. Only the assassin seemed to have avoided the full impact of the blow, but he stumbled out of the chamber blindly, hand pressed to his covered forehead.

Rone stumbled a step and fell, dragging her down with him, but still managing to tuck her beneath his curled, slumped-forward body.

Had the blast come from him?

His fingers touched the side of her face. She felt a slick of his blood paint her skin in their wake. "Go," he murmured.

There was a strange buzzing in her ears.

"Run." Blood burbled over his full lips and spilled down his chin. "One-third of the scepter left, narsumina. Promise me."

He tugged a red string from his cloak in a jerking manner completely at odds with his usual grace then looped it around the seal on her arm in a motion that just made blood spill faster from his mouth.

He never released his grip upon the papyrus, though she could feel it loosening as his heart's blood drained. He pulled a detonation box from his cloak with his free hand. His other hand still gripped her arm.

"Run."

The buzzing grew stronger. She grabbed his shirt and shook him. "Who's self-sacrificing now?"

"No one would believe it." Blood burbled over his curled lips, it oozed from the spear in his side, it pooled from the wound painting his back. "Go. One more temple. Promise me. Promise."

He was dying. Rone was dying. He had shielded her. He had taken the hit meant for her. Taken it so that she wouldn't use the scepter. He had sacrificed himself so she wouldn't use it. So that she could go to one more temple and free herself from it.

"Go. I will take care of this." His thumb touched the clasp of the detonation box.

Everything hurt as she stared at the light slowly leaving his stupid brown-ringed blue eyes. Her mind bled as she watched Osni shakily rise to his feet, aiming his scepter again—aiming it at Rone, who was positioned between her and danger, huddled over her with his charge ready.

What use was sacrifice?

The madness already coiled in her head by the scepter shrieked. Reconnect, hunt, kill, destroy.

She would make them pay.

"No, Ta—"

She peeled Rone's weakening fingers from her arm and raised the Scepter of Darkness. Without Rone to steady it, the papyri seal ignited, burning and coiling to nothing in a quarter of a heartbeat. Only the red string remained, falling loosely to her wrist.

Rone scrambled to rise as red poured profusely from his wounds, but it was too late.

Power surged through her and she aimed it outward.

Osni pulled his scepter against his body, enveloping himself in green and throwing himself to the side.

The Scepter of Darkness gleamed, illuminated in dark pleasure, and resealed to where it had just been freed.

Pleasure. Destroy.

One shot. Two shots. Three.

As the temple crumbled around them, Osni pulled others in front of him as shields on mangled legs.

Excellent. Death first.

"Taline."

A river of blood flowed beneath Rone. She cataloged it intuitively—the three years she had spent as an assistant to a Level Nine healer running components through her mind. No one could lose that much blood and survive.

Destroy! Power! Avenge him!

No. She resisted the call for a moment—for long enough to point the scepter at Rone. Heal him. The scepter reared against her hand in disgust. Destroy, it yelled.

HEAL. HEAL HIM!

She pushed all her will into the command. Power flooded the space and Rone's flesh sealed with an explosive sound. His eyes rolled to the back of his head and he tipped backward, head hitting stone.

A mix of discordant notes from the scepter sounded. Destroy! Destroy! Kill! Save no one and nothing! No one saved me!

Stone shards rained from the ceiling. A slab of rock crashed into one of the moon bowls. A shard hit her arm, leaving a streak of red—a red streak above another, more solid string.

She looked at the red string around her wrist. Sacrifice. Sacrifice in a Valeran. In Rone, who trusted no one.

Nin. Take him to Nin.

She knew Nin—knew her magic, knew the makeup of her blood—and she pushed every thought of it into the scepter.

Worlds whirled through her vision, a ripgate opened—black-and-white and cold—and she could see the back of her sister. Could see as Nin slowly turned—feeling the disturbance behind her.

The Shadow Prince was turning as well, cloak flaring, oath band shining. The desire to kill him welled within Taline and the power of the magic layer around him reached toward her with seductive, grasping fingers.

Kill, hunt, destroy. Claim your destiny.

Use me in the midst of magic's cradle and be **complete**.

The power of forced seduction tore through her mindscape as the fingers of the magic world spread with the ripgate.

She knew this song. And she had fought it before. But the tendrils flew toward her. Alone, alone, Nin. What was worth such pain?

Fingers wrapped around hers. She looked down to see Rone gazing up at her, eyes glazed. The string slid against her flesh in the breeze of destruction.

She grabbed at the string, the last bit of sanity, and Rone's fingers dropped.

If she killed the Shadow Prince, Nin would die. Such was the oath. But if she didn't kill the Shadow Prince, he would kill Rone.

Cages! Terror! Destroy them before they destroy you!

Cold settled across her shoulders as Nin and the Shadow Prince turned in the oddly slowed world rotating around Taline—almost there, almost...

The tendrils of their world shot forth like branches of a tree growing too fast. She would be swallowed within its bough. Left as nothing but a shell.

A shell. Like the life she had led in the palace.

Rage fled, leaving knowledge and emptiness behind.

Taline swiped through the ripgate—obliterating it like a pile of leaves in wind.

She had to remove this power, and she had to complete the release of the scepter in the non-magic world.

She grabbed Rone, struck the scepter head against the ground toward the nearest bowl—go there—and a ripgate slid around them.

Blackness. Then eye-burning light. She sank to her knees beneath Rone's weight, harshly hitting stone.

Moonlight filtered through the openings of another temple, hitting bowls as it bathed then retreated, then bathed again. Her breath caught. Moonrise, in a temple that hadn't experienced the rise of the day yet. With the scepter's power still strumming through her, her gaze immediately lit on one opening.

No!

She hobbled forth and thrust the scepter and her fused hand into the path and the light.

Stupid vessel! the scepter shrieked.

Nothing happened. She followed the retreating light—the moonlight moving to a different cutout and bowl.

Stupid, marvelous vessel! Give in!

Not moonrise.

Taline stopped. She closed her eyes. Her shoulders shook.

Two times. Two times released, then twice reclaimed. Crocodiles battled in a froth-tumbled river in the muddled landscape of her mind.

Shaking, she dragged herself back to Rone's side. His tan skin was abnormally pale. She carefully lifted his shirt with a shaking hand.

The gash in his side was worse than the wound the Shadow Prince had given him. And the disconnect from the magic of the world that he could normally call to subconscious aid was all the more apparent as he steadily bled all over the temple's stones.

Nin. Taline could feel the edge of madness overtaking her. Nin could fix him.

Yes! The blood of the cursed!

Taline bowed her head and clutched the scepter's staff.

No.

Why? Why not?

She couldn't use the scepter again.

Why? Why not?

This madness wasn't her.

I will **make** it you. I will—

The voice stopped as another papyrus rectangle, another seal, wrapped around her skin along with cold fingers which should only ever be warm. Tears poured down her face.

Nin's stored magic in the papyrus seal soothed her alongside the biting welcome of Rone's internal magic. Could she do nothing without Nin? Without Rone?

"Narsumina."

Her mind was once more hers. Her power was once more minimal. She was once more nothing.

She looked at the last three seals from Rone's pocket that were loosely scattered on the bloodstained floor—the fourth wrapped around her arm along with his fingers.

"You made these too, Taline." His voice was hoarse and pained.

An exigency measure made for a single emergency upon gaining the scepter. They had made these seals to give Nin enough sanity to remove the scepter. They had made way too many for that event. Nin would have removed it quickly.

But that isn't what had happened. Taline had happened. And now, there were three left.

"You helped make these. You designed the paper. You make incredible things. You don't need more power to do the incredible."

Her agonized gaze met his pain-filled one. It was only as she processed his words that she realized she had murmured her thoughts of incompetence aloud.

"I was powerless for so long." Her father and tribe, Etelian… Traded like cattle, treated like cattle. "It feels as if I can do nothing right on my own."

His fingers tightened—but not with their usual strength—she could see him slipping into unconsciousness. "One thing I've always admired about you, narsumina. Powerlessness creates bitterness, or determination. I've only seen the latter in you."

"I have bitterness." In the dark of night, where the sun didn't touch, demons danced.

"But it doesn't rule you. It never has. You left that burning carriage broken and rose resplendent."

"Because of Nin."

"Yes." He closed his eyes. "But you are not weak from absorbing her strength—from standing in her reflected light. You used it to energize your own seed. You blossomed into something far more. And now you are her strength, too. Equal. It's something I—"

He gave a pained laugh and his fingers squeezed weakly. "You have power—power that has nothing to do with that thing attached to your hand. Your power is so much more."

His hand went limp and the paper dropped. She caught his hand before it fell and watched the paper slip against stone.

Power...we will have it together, use—

She tucked the remaining papers back into Rone's pocket and pulled Rone's heavy form over her shoulder. He was much larger than she was, but her will was strong.

Stupid vessel! We—

She stumbled with him to the underground chamber, put a trap on the door, then dragged him into a small antechamber. She tucked him into a crevice within, covering him to shield him from prying eyes, and went scouting.

She eventually found a small ritual chamber. The pentalayerists would be checking the connected temples. They would reach this temple eventually. If only she and Rone could avoid detection until moonset, maybe she could detach the scepter.

No!

She dragged Rone up the craggy path and into the ritual chamber. She carefully deposited him onto the table and collapsed against the edge.

You will give in, the scepter hissed.

Her skin was clammy, and her throat burned. She had heard Nin discuss it, heard her call it "scepter fever." Having the link to the scepter strained by the three-moon ritual made it fight harder to control her and hold on.

She had no desire to listen to it right now.

She raided the chamber's stores quickly of any useful herbs, but most of what she needed was in her own pack.

With shaking hands, she crafted a fire in the ritual basin, set her small gold cauldron on top, poured in a bottle of piris, and clumsily opened herb pouches. Her fingers pinched the herbs in shaking motions, but she finally mixed in enough of each.

She cut open his shirt and cleaned and dressed the wound. The poultice she spread upon his wound would pull the lingering dark magic out.

When the healing potion was ready, she pressed his hand. His eyes opened slowly. They were still glazed, but recognition of her was clear. Loose strands of red and blond hair—always fighting—splayed over her fingers as she slipped her hand along his cheek and pressed the liquid to his lips.

Even his eyes—blue shot with streaks of brown—showed an eternal struggle when open.

She coughed abruptly into her hand. She pulled it away to stare at the wet gold and black blotches left behind. Scepter fever. She closed her eyes, then washed the evidence from her hands.

She thought of Rone's words to her to leave him as he had taken the shot meant for her. As he had sacrificed himself so that she wouldn't have to use the scepter.

If someone came into the chamber, she would have to use the scepter to protect them. She opened her eyes and looked at him. He was staring back.

"I'll keep you safe. I won't leave you," she said.

He stared at her for eons, then closed his eyes as if still in pain. "I know."

No one would stop her.

CHAPTER TWENTY-SEVEN

BATHED IN LIGHT

KAVEH

(THE EMPIRE AT LARGE)

No one could stop them. The empire, once growing darker, grew light again.

Kaveh and Nin became adept at lighting the empire. As the moon grew fuller and the oath period grew shorter, they bathed the empire in magic.

For an entire week while the emperor "dealt" with the gates, Kaveh and Nin worked to light the empire.

Outside of Tehras, there was less need for them to hide. Especially if they were in a territory

Kaveh had personally conquered—which were the overwhelming majority of provinces—things were far easier. Kaveh had shadows and spies in each. Tales of shifting shadows were common in places he had been—tales whispering that if you stepped out of line, the Shadow Prince would slay you in the night.

Watching Nin wield the Ninth Scepter in all her sunlit glory was addicting. Bathing her in shadows while she wielded it, even more so.

They became so skilled at lighting the empire, that within two days of the start, Nin stopped needing to port them to places. Instead, from their tent, she could open a slice between spots and light from anywhere.

She interlocked her hands around the scepter and he could feel the energy—emotions beating between them now—as she pushed gently forward. A ball of air two paces in front of her turned misty. She inhaled deeply, then pushed forward more.

The air seemed to soften and dimple—like a finger poking pliant clay. He extended a shadow, feeling around the edges as the world softened at the center point of the dimple. She took another breath, opened her palms without releasing them from their stacked position and rotated them left, forward, left, back, right. She continued for a few moments, then paused and began spreading her palms outward from each other. The dimple pulled, stretched, then broke free—and just like clay pulling from its base, another vista was revealed in the stretched portion.

The gate of Kastoni.

She pulled her hands apart.

Shadows swirled around her, encompassing the light of the scepter and gates, and the relighting of each. The shadows kept them from being seen, then whirled into a shadowed tear and disappeared like myth.

For Kaveh, it was like watching her eat a figstee, battling the juiciest of them as she sank her teeth inside. It was like her watching him eat a figstee—her eyes brightening at the sight and the bond warming him from within.

The shadows around them whirled faster. The Kastoni gate lit in a wild whirl of magic.

Unstoppable. In battle, they would be unstoppable. As they flipped ripgates and rode shadows, the notion took hold even more. The uses of their combined magic were unlimited.

Large-scale conflict could be over in a blink of an eye—in the opening of a ripgate and the ejection of his shadows. The thousands that he could put down in a day paled in comparison. They could eliminate millions in a moment.

Emotion rose again as he looked at her, and this time he wasn't fool enough to deny it. Desire.

She looked at him as she finished fixing the Kastoni gate, pulling the magic back into the scepter. "I will never participate in eliminating millions," she said, reading him easily—for he had not been silent with his military desires.

"Once," he said, eyes glittering and bond thrumming. "You'd only have to do it once. The entire world would fall to us the next day."

"I won't."

"Think of the people you would save. One country gone, but the rest falling in line with the empire. The empire that you support."

"Kaveh." She breathed deeply and reached for the ever-present platter of figstees in their tent. He gripped his fingers together, hoping the blood-red juice would spill across her lips. "What do you do after the world is the empire? What do you do when there is no one left to conquer? Where does your thirst to conquer go? Who is left to sate it?"

Who would be left to sate his bloodlust? His thirst?

He looked at her. "You."

CHAPTER TWENTY-EIGHT
WHAT WE MUST

RONE

(Uruk, Temple of True Light, in the First Layer)

Rone rolled painfully from the stone table.

He caught himself with unsteady hands and an aching frame. He wasn't currently exchanging words with Sehk in the underworld, so there was a chance he was still alive.

He was in too much pain to be dead.

Taline appeared abruptly, steadying him, but he could feel her struggle in the shake of her limbs. They were both a mess.

He took a painful breath and surveyed the space as she looped his arm around her shoulders and started moving toward a ramp. Names and sunlight markings were inscribed around the chamber, telling him a fraction of what he needed to know.

Taline had managed to move them to Uruk's Temple of True Light. And although the temple would be a fantastic choice for the moon ritual, it was a thriving city—far too thriving.

And far too close to Ur for comfort. They would never last the night without being discovered.

In fact, they should already have been caught. There could be only one reason they were without opposition. His supposition proved true as they encountered only magicless priests exclaiming in horrified shouts as Rone and Taline stumbled together from the temple's tunnels.

Uruk was close enough to Ur that any magi in Uruk had to have been called to help the pentalayerists—or empire—and they hadn't yet roused from Rone's explosive blasts or whatever Taline had done to them afterward. A small bit of fortune.

They staggered into the thriving city looking like gore and death—Taline half-holding him upright—and made it out through the city gates with enough shrieking citizens left behind to point any returning pentalayerists in the direction they had gone.

They crossed the Purattu without having to discuss it. Rone simply concentrated on keeping somewhat upright. Staying in the fertile, exalted valley between the Purattu and the Idiqlat would only bring them worse luck. Better to follow the snaking river on the less inhabited western side.

They barely made it to a series of east-west-facing caves before collapsing. Rone splayed across the floor. Taline bent over, trying to catch her breath.

"Narsumina, you should—"

And that was when the scepter lit. Then lit and lit again—an endless litany of appeals that could only mean one thing: someone was using a Carre scepter.

He closed his eyes. They couldn't continue on like this. Not with the scepter acting as a beacon of light.

And there were more options for scepter wielders than just Nin, now. He hadn't missed the terror on Taline's face when she'd seen the scepter in the assassin's hand. Etelian's scepter. What in Sehk's name was happening in their layer?

They found a small cave in a rocky plateau and huddled within—lighting fires only for warming healing poultices and potions. Travel biscuits provided a bit of stomach comfort, but the nutrition was emergency-grade adequate at best.

The area was silent for two days, but on the third day, pentalayerist search parties started to cast their shadows east. Osni and the empire wouldn't be far behind.

Rone and Taline stumbled northwest together, staying west of the river, barely keeping hidden from searching eyes.

It was too early to move, but far too late to stay.

Two more days passed as they moved slowly through the landscape, cloaking themselves, dodging those who held relics to track them, keeping to the shadows, and dragging themselves along.

Rone healed. Taline weakened.

It was almost as if his returning strength caused hers to crumble. Or maybe it was that she allowed herself to let go a little more each time he was able to pick up the slack.

And the scepter still raged with light, as if something were deliberately influencing its descent into madness. Taline started to murmur its words of rage in the dark of night.

Rone grimly watched her try to sleep. *Nin, damn it, what are you doing? What is happening?*

By the time they reached a plateau with an extensive view of the valley, Taline couldn't stand. Rone was navigating the shadows alone, with Taline's body pressed to his back as he carried her with her head on his shoulder.

Rone "liberated" a horse halfway to Bilbat. Securing Taline to its back was an effort, but it made for slightly faster travel by not having to carry her.

It also gave him far too much time to think.

Bilbat had a moon temple...as did Kiš...

They had to circle around Babil to get to Kiš, though—a tense journey filled with horrible possibility. The sheer number of ancient sites in this area was immense. The people who had inhabitated the region before the splitting of the world had enriched it densely.

The pentalayerists had secured this sector as their prime territory long ago for just those reasons.

Gorgeous as Babil was in every layer, it was also heavily guarded in each.

But in Babil, they could simply...gate home.

The insidious thought had been taking root with each painful step.

"I won't let it overtake me," Taline murmured.

"I think that you might not have the choice," he said quietly.

"You gave me this scepter. I will bear it."

He closed his eyes. "I shouldn't have. But I was right to give it to you. You are stout of heart. Few could have held out for even a tenth of what you have endured."

"I will bear the scepter. Compliments from you, though, I don't know that I can bear those." Her voice was tiredly amused.

But by the time they reached the southern edge of Bilbat, she couldn't even formulate quips, and could barely stay astride. Her voice spoke of terrible events. Sometimes her words told of past events—of the magi cursed to forge the scepter and the madness he endured—and sometimes they were thoughts from the minds of whoever was wielding a kindred Carre scepter at the time.

Taline's body jerked again. He had stopped keeping track at fifty—one hand pinned to her waist to keep her steady. "Eyes of blood. Scepter. Using a scepter. What does it do? How does it work? What can I seek? Primary..." Taline's delirious mutterings looped periodically on the same subject matter.

Eyes of crimson, eyes of blood.

Someone was using a scepter, that much was clear—and they were doing something massive. The where and why were grimly concerning.

Ninli, what are you up to?

And the Scepter of Darkness glowed with each of Taline's murmurs—as if the promise of a gatemaker made it hungry.

The moon temple rose high above Bilbat's walls in the distance.

At another jerk of her body, he lifted Taline, securing her to his back and shoulders. She did better when they were touching, he had found, to his everlasting discomfort.

They barely avoided two scouting parties when Taline started yelling and the scepter started flashing. Rone pulled her into full contact with the skin of his neck and ran.

He didn't know how long they ran until he found a cave and the scepter went mad. But Bilbat rose in the distance and Rone buried his face in her hair as he held her tight.

A moonset and moonrise went by and Taline grew progressively worse, writhing in agony.

Twice again that Rone had to watch, to hold her to him, to wipe at gold and black splotched lips.

He collected their camp protections, packed everything but Taline on the horse, and with her secured to his back, navigated silently through the grueling valley for another day until he found a decent spot to rest.

He hoped Ninli knew what she was doing. If it were anyone else, Rone would believe without a doubt that she was trying to save herself without thought to her actions. But Ninli would as soon throw herself into a volcano than harm Taline.

Ninli would be in that volcano soon. It was two days until time ran out for the last of the Carres.

His mind turned the thoughts over, looking for other solutions.

He touched Taline's cheek. Even though he could feel her faint breath, it was a reassurance that she was still alive. With her legs secured around his waist, and linen cords wrapped to keep her in place, he still worried.

The new and unwelcome emotion was eating him alive. He watched her each night and at each rest. He watched her struggle to complete the share she always tried to do when she wasn't caught by the scepter's grasp.

She had always done her share. She knew no other way.

He watched her keen mind struggle with sanity. Her keen mind that had always worked meticulously through problems now raged with other people's thoughts. He paid careful attention to the words that were used. He snarled at Osni's. He sighed at Ninli's. He narrowly kept track of those thought by the third.

He watched Taline worry about her sister when he told her about Ninli wielding a scepter and lighting gates with the Shadow Prince—Taline never remembered what she spewed in her delirium.

He watched her worry about him when she thought he wasn't looking. As if he were part of her tiny circle of protection and trust. As though he were worthy of those things.

"I think it is over now, this spell," Taline murmured tiredly in his ear. "You should take a respite."

From me.

He held his eyes closed a moment longer then let them slide open to look at the face of the weary woman whose head was on his shoulder and whose eyes were tired with a pain that mirrored internal agony but still held concern for Rone.

"I'm fine, narsumina," he murmured back. "Only a little longer. I've found a good spot."

He needed to get these types of thoughts out of his mind, or else he was bound to do something stupid. Something truly Summora-ish.

Dying was easy. Sacrifice in death was easy. Sacrifice when you had to live with the consequences...was something else entirely.

She rubbed her cheek against his shoulder, her forehead burning against his skin with a fever that no herb could abate.

If he could die in order to separate her from the scepter and take it with him in death, it would be an easy choice. But it was increasingly apparent that he was going to have to save her another way—a Summora way.

He backtracked to a small cave—more of a cutout than a cavern—that would serve as their rest spot. He set her down and poked a small fire grimly to life—casting just enough flame to cook the last of their ingredients.

He looked into the shadows and saw the slim figure perched there. The assassin had been following them but keeping his distance. One might think he was protecting them, but Rone knew better.

The assassin was most interested in Taline's fits. Whenever she experienced one, he always seemed to settle in to observe. He was waiting to make his move and he wanted to know what he was going to get once the scepter was in his hand.

The only benefit was that he took care of anyone else who got too close to them. It was like having a second set of eyes, in one sense. The assassin was no friend of Osni or the pentalayerists. Rone remembered every word of their exchanges. The exchanges had been enlightening.

But the assassin was no friend of theirs either. He was waiting for his moment.

Rone couldn't risk leaving Taline in order to kill the threat. So Rone waited for his own moment.

The assassin cocked his head and lifted a heavy amulet, then disappeared into the night. It wasn't the first time he'd gone. He would be back. He always managed to unerringly find them again.

Rone wasn't certain which unnerved him more—that someone knew how to properly use the Second Scepter of Tehras, or his growing certainty as to the assassin's identity.

Rone visually checked the protections around the rest site—easily placed boxes that he set each night before letting go of Taline or the horse. They glowed with the light of the woman herself. Taline's boxes were extraordinary, no matter how they were powered.

He did not allow himself to think too fully on why he had eschewed Bilbat, in the end, and was now one day's hike from one of the most well-guarded temples in any layer—a temple that held...other possibilities.

He carefully arranged Taline's blankets over her and worked to get the medicine brewing—a temporary, fleeting measure that would give her relief for half a span of a dial's tick at most.

The scepter separation ritual was meant to be done consecutively. With a magi capable of traveling great distances—a magi like Ninli—it could be quickly and neatly accomplished. Ninli could have used the bowls in each temple with her own powers and beat moonrise or moonset in consecutive jumps.

But Taline and Rone, who had needed to go by foot, had time and enemies against them. The deliberations needed had been impossible.

And disconnecting and reconnecting the scepter had made for...complications.

Even if they succeeded in removing the scepter from Taline at Bilbat, then Kiš... There was no guarantee that she would survive the removal now—not without having someone fully capable of healing her nearby afterward.

And Rone only knew one person that could be.

He looked up at the stars, but the sky had never held answers for him.

Was he willing to let the scepter be wielded by another hand?

Could he convince himself that having it wielded by a hand he hated was a preference? That he could successfully kill the man afterward, if he embarked on this plan?

Better for the world, to get rid of the scepter in its easiest hand. A nearly non-magic hand.

He looked at Taline.

Better for the world, but Rone had ever been a selfish creature.

Was he willing to watch the light go out in those brown eyes if it meant the light of humanity could be saved?

He had promised Ninli that he would save Taline. He had told himself that was why he was doing this—to fulfill a last promise to Ninli at the same time that he destroyed the scepter. It had been easier to deny his own feelings on the matter. Easier to lay blame at Ninli's feet.

Watching Taline get worse with every moonrise and moonset made him want to kill something.

He looked at her as moonrise hit. He pressed the herb paste to her lips—and only the slightest relief could be seen in her restless movements.

He didn't know what to do for her, and for once, it burned.

CHAPTER TWENTY-NINE

GIFTS OF SHADOW

NINLI

(CUIPSIN CAMP)

As the half-moon shrunk and edged toward the crescents preceding the dark moon, the gates were the talk of the camp still waiting at the edge of Cuipsin for the fate of the city and nation. Nin made certain to keep an interested expression when Akel or any of the others gushed about imperial optimism.

"And now we can travel anywhere. And someday, when you and I are married, I will make certain to—" Something weird suddenly happened to Akel's voice. "I mean, when I am married, I will tell my wife and grandchildren about the lovely goddess I encountered," he finished spewing in a high, shaking voice.

She stared at him for a moment, perplexed, and then realized there was a second set of emotions riding alongside her own. She turned to see Kaveh leaning against the edge of the tent, dark gaze pinned on the boy.

"I have to go, Mistress Fer—Summora! Mistress Summora! Just wanted you to know that the information on the demon eyes and dead rulers is correct."

Akel shot out of the other side of the tent as if his sandals were smoking.

Kaveh pushed away and let the flap fall back into place. "And where are the rest of your ducklings?"

"They aren't in a spellboxed amulet, if that is what you are wondering," she said dryly. "Most are on one mission or another, gathering information." She looked at him expectantly, but he wasn't returning her look. He was looking at the closed flap, at where Akel had fled.

"One moment," he said and disappeared from the tent.

The focused intensity in the bond made her nervous. She ducked her head out of the tent to see Kaveh trap the fleeing boy in shadow.

She started forward, but paused when Kaveh freed him. She sensed no darkness, only intensity. Akel stared up with wide eyes as Kaveh questioned him about something.

Kaveh hadn't threatened any of them before, and nothing in the bond spoke of threat, so she waited. The ducklings were all extremely wary of him, but he usually ignored them completely.

Akel's eyes went suddenly wider, but he nodded vigorously and took off, injury-free.

She cocked her head as Kaveh approached and followed him back into the tent. "What was that about?"

"I have a task for him."

"What task?"

He raised a brow. "Am I the head of the imperial forces, or are you?"

"Are we playing servant and master?"

"Hardly a game I would lose."

She shook her head and motioned at the platter of food. "Eat."

She had gotten him to sample varied fare in the weeks she'd been with him. When they had first broken bread, he had said that he ate only what was necessary to provide what his body needed for peak physical and mental spells. Lentils, crum with bille fat, and carro meat in a stew with Mosof bread—anything that kept the body running in top form for weeks, with none of the "luxuries that made men listless and foolish."

He examined a figstee. "What did your duckling have to report?"

"You didn't pull it out of Akel?"

"You know I don't touch your ducklings."

"The imperial populace is, in general, ecstatic about the gates. They say that it is a sign of the emperor's supreme reign." She took a wrapped bread from the platter and nudged three toward him, knowing they were his favorite regeneration fare. "Though there is increasing talk of demon eyes and fire. I think my true color has been seen more than once."

"Your eyes turn a favorable hue when you use the scepter. The Cuipsin talks are equally favorable." He sat across from her. "The emperor is in an uncommonly good mood. He thinks the positive change in the gates mean that someone favorable has taken hold of the Scepter of Darkness."

Nin paused her chewing. She hadn't thought of using the Scepter of Darkness as an excuse. And it pointed to something she also hadn't thought about—the ways the scepters might affect other layers. Could the Scepter of Darkness influence the gates from a layer away?

Yes. Technically, it could. The scepter and its secrets were something only Giran and Savvan had fully known. Perhaps Salare, too, in order to hold the knowledge in case of disaster. But the power of the scepter had been created by a magi of great power—under an enchantment of great pain.

A magi capable of changing the very fabric of the world had been held by her ancestors and convinced to produce the scepter. He had almost been finished with the task, when he realized what they were going to do with it.

He had refused to complete it. He had been tortured to near insanity.

He had been seventeen.

And in his unending torture, he had been persuaded to complete his masterpiece. He had produced something of darkness, pain, and unlimited power.

A relic capable of changing the world. The worlds.

But in their shortsighted greed, her great-great-grandparents had produced something they could not control. Something that a Carre could touch and wield better than any other, bred in their blood and the blood red of their eyes, but could never be master of.

That no one had been capable of wielding the scepter for long had been an open secret in the palace. That it took three gatemakers to subdue—and destroy—those who had wielded it in the past was also an open palace secret.

That Nin knew how to destroy a person wielding it was something she only planned to use against an emperor gone mad.

Not the sister of her heart.

Though there had been a strange moment a week ago when she had felt a dark madness, like an echo of a maddened Taline. Nin shivered. It had felt like Taline had been behind her—like the Scepter of Darkness had been poised for death.

Kaveh had cast his shadows—feeling it, too. But nothing had been there when they had turned.

The real problem, and the cause of her lingering unease, was that there had been too much nothingness when they had turned. There had been no trace of anything that would have accounted for the feeling of a ripgate or Taline appearing. It had been as if the moment had been wiped free from the world by the person who had caused it—a person wielding madness and death.

The thought of her sister made her shake the notion free. Taline would never succumb. Taline was probably already free.

"Someone favorable does have the Scepter of Darkness," Nin said, as calmly as she could. She automatically quelled thoughts of the scepter's destruction, so that the oath would not react to the scepter not being returned whole.

"If they aren't back by the oath date, we will be hunting the scepter down the day after," he said, manipulating a shadow between his fingers.

"I know." Nin took another bite. "I know what is in store for me after the oath ends. You will be unable to compel me to hurt them, however."

"I won't need you to hurt them."

She pulled her bread through the fig paste. "I will die before I let you hunt Taline with the intent to kill."

"I know."

She nodded. "What of Cuipsin's next padifehl?"

"Simin is in Ancyra. Aros is still in Tehrasi. The emperor is considering putting Omari on Cuipsin's throne under the regency of the council."

Nin looked up. "The Kush-Fehl princess?" She dragged her bread along her plate. "Cuipsin will be favorable to another female padifehl, and one who is renowned for purifying magic. And Kush is close to Cuipsin, yet not close enough to be of worry in uniting against the empire. I know little personally of the emperor's council, though."

"They play the games typical of those with political ambition."

"The princess is young." She had been young enough for Nin not to regard her as a replacement for Tehrasi yet. "They will think to control her."

"She is eleven. She has been living at court in Fehlaka Palace for the past three summers. Anyone seeking to control her will have trouble with her appointed guard. It is likely a game the emperor wants to see played. A test for Omari."

Nin nodded. "Kush put in a bid for Lorsali's hand for their eldest son and a second bid for Allit to be bonded to one of their princesses. They have always been smart."

Allit, a gatekeeper but not gatemaker, had been one of her siblings slated for use in political gain. A scholar, he would have been a good match for a Kushite princess.

"Kush didn't come to Tehrasi's aid or defense."

"They were smart in that, too. They would have lost against you, and Tehrasi wasn't the...easiest of allies." She finished her meal. "That the crown princess of Kush chose to partake in the emperor's quest to produce powerful children and allegiances was not a surprise, nor was the blessing of the Kush king and queen."

"The crown princess has had two other politically motivated children—one with the northern Swee and another with the eastern Kore dynasties."

"Future named marks on your map."

"As are all named marks."

"Such a long list, I wouldn't be able to read them all even if I were able."

Something strangely anticipatory and tension-filled wound through him; even stranger was that he tried to hide the emotions from her.

She pressed her hand against the back of his neck, against the skin sun-darkened further from the last few days spent constantly outdoors jumping around the empire instead of amid his shadows. She massaged the energy pathways. "You are well?"

He closed his eyes and though the anticipation was still present, the tension was somewhat diminished. He opened his eyes and stared at her, his dark gaze intense. "Yes."

"Ready to go light some more gates?" she asked.

"Yes."

~*~

They relit the empire nearly fully as the moon slivered toward its dark end and new beginning. Cuipsin embraced the idea of Omari ul Fehl as their future padifehl. The ceremony confirming her would take place in two weeks during the full moon. Rooms were being updated and Shiera's tastes converted to those of Omari's mixed Kush-Fehl upbringing.

Kaveh's orders were to stay in Cuipsin until the ceremony. It was a punishment given by an emperor to his warrior son, but for Nin, the suspension of battle was pure boon.

And Kaveh...seemed to be taking the forced rest surprisingly well. Of course, they were really flitting about the empire, fixing the gates, but in a man who knew only battle, Kaveh was doing fantastically well off the field.

They sat down to a small feast the palace had sent. Nin picked through the offerings with interest. In the beginning, the only thing offered had been that which fulfilled and nourished the body and mind. But she enjoyed the extra delicacies nestled in each meal. Foods for the soul—small bits of flavor included in a meal solely for taste and delight—felt like home. She and Taline had always made sure to include at least one delight a day—a small measure to celebrate life.

Nin looked at the carefully folded headdress that she had collected when she last passed through their Tehras rooms. She hoped Taline was well. She hoped one day she would see her sister from afar—safe, free, and unhindered by Nin's ghosts.

A burst of anxiety slithered over the bond and Nin turned to watch Kaveh—now finished with his meal—fiddling with a box.

Anxiety was such a strange emotion coming from him, and he had been increasingly anxious—the bond filled with anticipation and tension. The night before, he had disappeared for several hours, and a few hours again this morning.

She had seen him speaking to Akel twice more and the boy had handed him a wrapped package the day before. Akel had preceded any questions from her by begging her not to ask.

Whatever they had been up to, it didn't seem negative, so she had kept her silence.

Kaveh looked at her—there was no way he couldn't feel her curiosity—then awkwardly pushed the box that he had been fiddling with toward her. "Here."

She cocked her head and took the box from him. This box held the thing that made him anxious and awkward, when direct warfare of one against thousands made him laugh.

What had Akel helped him obtain? A scepter aid? A spellbox? Something that would aid in their relighting pursuits or otherwise assist in helping the empire?

She undid the box clasp and lifted the top.

Expecting to see a power element, she paused to stare at the glass oval nestled on a piece of dark fabric. The glass was designed to fit in front of an eye, spelled to do whatever the user required—not unlike the glass they had used in the temple.

Mystified, she stared at it. She didn't require a looking glass to see the gates or tweak the magic. And a looking glass was an odd choice for an imperial aid. Strange. She reached for it.

The tension across the bond reached knifepoint.

As she touched and lifted the glass, a shadow swirled within it.

She nearly dropped the looking glass in shock, but her curiosity was now overwhelming. She lifted it carefully from its case and marveled at the shadow trapped between the two thin panes. A quick glance at Ifret told her that the corporeal shadow was watching the byplay intently.

Nin looked at Kaveh, but he was staring at the glass with his lips pressed tightly together. She lifted it to her right eye.

The shadow zipped through her view, then flattened to smoke and she felt its tendrils reach through the outer seams of metal to touch the skin and bone of her eye socket. The world shifted wildly for a second as the shadow reached out. Curious, she followed the link back to Kaveh.

Her breath caught when the shadow connected its other tendrils to his mind.

Her gaze snapped to his and she realized what it meant at the same time that the shadow snapped into place and pulled his consciousness to her, using his power to do so. The shadow was using Kaveh and their bond to feed information passively through his mind and loop it back to her.

Her breath hitched. She concentrated on the shadow and the bond, and on the tether between them, then looked at the documents scattered across the table under empty platters.

Glyphs unfurled upon the pages, like flowers blooming across papyri, and the knowledge of what they were bloomed just as sharply—a knowledge outside herself, but in her control. Her world narrowed, her breath stuttered, her focus shattered. The connection with the shadow tether cut abruptly as the monocle fell into her palm.

She cradled it desperately, as tears trickled down her cheeks. "I can read the glyphs through you."

He had made her something that used the bond to give her access to the part of his mind that was broken in hers. But he had made it so that the bond itself was unnecessary—that they could be unbound by the oath, and his shadow would still connect them.

A gift.

Her breath came in pants; a wet splotch bloomed on the page below her. The page was once more an incomprehensible mess of squiggled ink, but a revelation waited beneath—a borrowed, undamaged brain given through a forged link.

"Yes?" His answer was tentative and uncertain, and it struck her that he must be floundering, trying to read her right now.

She uncurled her fingers and stared at the shadowed glass.

It was handcrafted with power over design—made by someone who was used to using brute force and wasn't accustomed to making something delicate. But the crafter had tried to make it ornamental. It had been made by a crafter who, perhaps, had never made something for someone other than the emperor—who would never favor such things—or for Ifret, who needed only darkness and death to be calm.

His first gift. A gift for her.

She swallowed and clutched it close. She had to swallow again. She felt his anxiety spike and she forced the tears back and opened her fist. The glass glittered in the lamps like precious sunlight. The shadow swirled lazily, waiting.

"This will aid me." She cleared her throat with difficulty. "I will have a greater ability to hide from you when I'm saved in the next two days."

Relief flowed through the bond like a waterfall breaking a dam. "You will give me more challenge now, at least," he said, uncertainty gone.

But this gift was more than that. They both knew she wouldn't be saved. She wrapped her fingers around it and looked up at him, finally ready to meet his gaze. "Thank you."

His gaze slipped away, as if he couldn't hold it long. "I did it so you would stop asking me to read things," he said gruffly.

She reached out and gently touched the back of his hand. "Thank you."

His eyes skittered back to hers and held. "You're welcome," he said softly.

She felt the bond tightening, pulling her closer. She could see the texture of his skin. The hint of color. The dilation of flecked brown-and-black eyes.

She leaned in and her lips parted as if she wanted to say something—she wasn't sure what—but surely something would emerge. Pulled closer and closer, the bond tensed with want.

He touched the spell at the edges of her eyes and slowly pulled it away. He was staring at her blood-red eyes and the bond pulled at her harder, as if he were tightening his grip.

Her eyes, her past. Her.

She reached out. "I—"

Pain ripped through her—a burst of terrible energy that made her fall forward. Another ripped through right after the first.

Kaveh caught her, his fear quickly spiking into fury. "What—?"

"Imperator General!" An imperial messenger flew through the tent's flap and immediately flinched at Kaveh's face. But the messengers had been chosen for their stalwart missive presentations and he shakily straightened. "Something has...something has gone terribly wrong."

CHAPTER THIRTY

STORIES IN DESPAIR

RONE

(West of Bilbat)

Something had gone terribly wrong.

Rone pressed a healing cloth soaked in herbs to Taline's forehead as her entire body tensed again. Whatever massive event had been unleashed in their layer had stripped away the last veneers of control. Taline fought the scepter's hold in a continuous series of agonizing full-body clenches. One barely ceased before the next began.

"Do you want a story about the five brothers this time?" Rone asked. He had started telling her tales when their caretaking roles had reversed—trying to keep the harsh and insidious whispers from overloading her mind.

He began making a new batch of healing paste as he waited for her to catch her breath. The paste had become decreasingly helpful over the last few days, but it still gave her a few moments of relief, so he continued to make it.

"Tell me about your family." Her voice was the softest whisper, harsh in the way that she had to force it past her throat. "Your mother's family."

He paused, then began crushing the paste again with intense deliberation. "Why?"

"Because they still have influence over you—over how you perceive the world, over what drove you to this point."

He stared at the ingredients as he blended them together. The last thing he desired to talk or think about was his mother's people or his past.

"Because…" Taline shifted painfully. "Because I want to know about you."

Something in him stilled. He looked at her from the side of his eye. She was rasping painfully now, trying to keep the scepter connection at bay.

He looked at the fire, then looked back at her, and he found the words slipping past his lips.

"Sher Fehl collects bloodlines. He saw Oralia Valeran, and he saw opportunity." The emperor saw combinations of ingredients, like the ones Rone was grinding to paste, but in people instead. "Valerans are proud and exclusive, but Oralia was of a...spirited age. Sher Fehl has never encountered much hardship in conquests. Oralia chafed under the restrictions of her blood and responsibilities, and so she spent two nights with the charismatic, rising emperor of a foreign land. An escapade that led to...far more than anticipated. Sher Fehl has never had much trouble spreading his seed."

"She became pregnant."

"Yes. And by the time the clan realized her pregnancy, she had begun to develop...notions." He grimaced. "Ideas about raising an emperor's son."

Rone carefully felt for the assassin's presence, but the man remained absent. Rone set an extra notification spell and another to mute their words, just in case. There was no way Rone would give him the fodder of his story.

"It would have been a good political move," Taline said. "To raise an imperial son."

"In hindsight, decidedly, but the Valerans disdained Sher Fehl as an upstart who would soon be wiped away. In the year of my birth—31F, the thirty-first of the emperor's life—they thought his forces a step up from herders and thieves. They were banking on the empire's opposition. Tehras was an impediment thought impossible to overtake. Jisarek Carre had kidnapped the emperor's first wife a decade earlier, forever cutting the eldest Fehl child from Fehl legacy before he was even born. Even though the emperor had begun to gain ground, he was nothing more to the Carres or Valerans than a pest that would soon be crushed. The east was strong. The north would never falter. Sher Fehl's strategy was long-term and carefully crafted, and anyone at the time could possibly be forgiven for underestimating it."

Rone wouldn't have. The signs had all been there. The Valerans, however, couldn't look past their inner pride to correctly judge anything around them.

"It was only after he took Tehras, in the year 42F, that the Valerans began to scramble. The rest of the territories around Tehrasi fell like game tiles—one after another, after another. The fall of Tehrasi happened in my eleventh year. But Oralia had only made it seven before she could suffer our life no longer."

"Couldn't suffer what?"

"When she didn't rid herself of me or her notions, the Valerans disinherited her—cast her out, pregnant and penniless. For someone used to being pampered, it was a bitter fate. But Valeran pride runs deep."

"She left when you were seven? What did she do between?"

He swirled the pestle around the bowl, only pausing when he realized he was drawing the patterns of the coiling streets he used to roam—the streets he had barely survived.

"She tried to contact the emperor first—she was sure she would be exalted in his court. She was given ten gold pieces and told to return when I showed magic."

"The emperor rebuffed her?"

He shook his head. "It took me years to piece together what must have happened, but Nera is a chameleon who likes her cosmetic spells. Like knows like, and Oralia would have been a threat."

"Nera met with your mother instead of the emperor?"

He thought of the emperor's words to him the only time they had spoken. He had said that Oralia should have brought Rone forward—that they could have pushed his powers earlier—that maybe he would have had enough skill then to become blessed.

Sher Fehl hadn't been the one to meet Oralia in her desperation. "Nera, or someone in her court."

Taline just nodded, shivering. Rone reached over and tucked his cloak more closely around her neck.

"Sent out with ten pieces of gold, another might have been fine. But Oralia had no notion of thrift and less of what to do on the streets. She hadn't the first clue how to survive. She had no skills for work and no desire to pursue any. She had one skill that could keep her in comfort—the one that had gotten her into the situation in the first place."

He thought of the men. One after another. Some would stay for weeks—some would move the two of them into their houses—but they were always somewhere new after a certain amount of time had passed. Oralia, for all her beauty, had never been sane or easy to live with, and she had never hid her desire to rise.

They had been steadily moving up in housing and circumstance. By the time he was six, he had gained a private tutor and they had moved into a lavish house.

But Oralia was greedy. She was never satisfied. And she had made a bad choice in her thirst for more.

He remembered sitting by her in the alley they had been thrown into, wondering whether she would ever wake again—whether she was going to survive the night—wondering at the shadows slinking around them, waiting to loot their corpses. He had been a week from his seventh year.

His mouth moved without his permission, spilling his memories into the coffer of her mind.

He remembered the way that Oralia's offers had dried up—people too fearful of Gursuf Sule to risk approaching her for companionship. Leaving her one choice.

Harder living each month only made her less agreeable and less kind. A friend of Sule's had taken her in with kind words and then started selling her off to others—men even less desirable.

In the years before Sule, Rone remembered fond pats and kind words from men rotating through his mother's life. He remembered men who spared some interest in helping the child of the woman they tried to keep happy.

But after Sule... The men who came after cuffed him in the side of the head or demanded he steal for them or sent him on dead jobs. He remembered stealing from them instead and getting thrashed within an inch of death. He remembered the way Oralia's beauty faded with each day. The way she looked at herself each night—the absolute desperation as she clawed and scraped and raged at her fading beauty in the looking glass.

He remembered the way the sour looks she gave him turned increasingly hateful.

"She left before I turned eight."

"And you?"

He remembered the way she had hissed at him to hurry, how she had yanked his shoulder nearly out of the socket. He remembered the blood splattered everywhere—the sightless eyes of the man in her bed.

He shrugged. "She left me at an orphanage in Parsa where she used the last of what she had stolen from the man she had killed to fix her face and procure a gate pass back to Helsgir. Back to the Valerans, to throw herself upon their mercy."

"Dancing in red and gold," Taline murmured.

He looked at her sharply. "What?"

Taline didn't answer for a long moment. "You have my sympathies, Rone."

Where he would have scoffed or disassembled before, he now said nothing to reject her soft words. "She fulfilled her last responsibility to her mistake," he said finally. "I would have been dead had she left me in Dernholm."

Sule's lieutenants—frequent visitors who knew Rone by sight—would have made certain of it. When Rone's hair had turned red and gold, when he had no longer been able to hide on the streets even five territories away, they had sent men. Even then, years later, they had sent men to kill him. Unfortunately for them, with the bloodline activation, he had come into his powers as well.

Their eyes had filled with terror as his hands had filled with a power he had never before or since wrought.

He avoided Taline's gaze. "The Valerans accepted an offer from the Pikerens, who wanted an alliance, but were down a bride. It was her chance to return with a modicum of pride. She took it. A Valeran cannot live without pride."

"She left you."

"Pride held her to Dernholm and to me for seven years. It's hard to have pride when you are someone else's chattel."

"You were seven. She left you."

He smiled sharply. "Your family sold you to a madman at thirteen. I'd say that I got the better deal."

Sehk. The parallels had always been maddening. And they just made the differences between Taline and Oralia so stark. He closed his eyes.

Taline said nothing for long moments. "My mother died when I was ten, but she..." Taline's voice choked. "A solid ten years of memories with someone I loved who loved me in return, then three with little affection, and three with only pain. But then Nin... Four years. I'm still ahead on life's scales, fourteen to six. I cannot begrudge my fortune."

Taline ul Summora was strong in a way that Oralia Valeran would never be.

"Have you met any other Valerans?" she asked, voice breaking a little as she coughed. "Did they...seek you out?"

He placed the small cauldron on the fire. "The Palace of Tehras fell, Tehrasi fell—and the entire region with it. Then the game tiles started dropping just as the emperor planned, and the empire rose to preeminence. Oralia's play had results after all."

"The Valerans contacted you."

"Of course. I was a stone to play. And who knew what powers I might possess that might make me a more powerful pawn. They came for me after Tehrasi fell but finding me proved...difficult."

"Nin saved you when you were twelve. In...a dungeon?"

"My first brush with Ninli. She was scouting for her family's stolen blood. Next thing I knew, I was in Loran being patched up and given a care package. The package provided...a number of things that allowed me to stay untraceable."

The package had not, however, changed him into a saint.

He had been in a Bahran cell at fourteen when she had found him again, trying to dodge the census takers. He had followed her to Tehras. "Run at the census, Rone," she'd said with a grin. "Don't let it run over you."

"The Valerans eventually found me at fifteen." As soon as he had been cataloged by the census, he knew the sands of time had drained. But he had known, too, that Ninli was right. Being cataloged on his own terms had been the only way to craft his own way. "As did the emperor, who conducted his test and left me alone."

He would never truly be able to pay back Ninli for the modified oath, that when standing in Tehras, allowed him to lie to anyone he chose. It had allowed him to present only what he wanted to be seen.

"You escaped the emperor because of the relic?"

"Mmm." He didn't meet her eyes. "The emperor had too many children to bother keeping tabs on one who failed his test." Rone wasn't the only imperial disappointment in the hundreds of imperial spawn littering the empire.

"And the Valerans?"

"I told them I was a disappointment, then I told them where to stick it," he said easily. "The emperor marks off each child he has tested, and the result is visible in a farhani and imperial oath, if one knows where to look. It makes it easier for those whose task it is to find imperial children. The Valerans saw the rejection mark, and I told them I wouldn't be going with them. Valerans don't take rejection well. But they like worthless pursuits even less, and I was deemed worthless."

"The power you hide...it would make you craved by both sides?"

"I would never again be free." He looked at the fire. "I am free as long as the scepters are not used to capacity."

"How do you hide this power?"

"The power of my good looks is unable to be hidden."

But she didn't respond the way he expected anymore. "You are scared of the ability, whatever it is."

"Beauty is a wretched curse, as you know," he said with forced light.

"Nin knows." Taline moved with effort. "She is not scared of you. But you think others will be."

"I think we've established that Ninli is mad," he said calmly. "Ninli makes deals with demons, and binds herself to the soulless, and wields things better left alone. I think perhaps using her is not the best of examples."

"She holds you in high regard. And she has...a way of knowing when someone is worthy of trust."

"Ninli's family was a pit of vipers. It is hard to say who wins between the two of us, really, when it comes to birth circumstances. Her family consumed itself from within—unending madness in the line, and a clutching kind of insanity shown in their lack of ability to let anything go. She would never have seen the outside of the palace, except from within the midst of the others. The ouroboros, forever consuming its own."

"The way Nin speaks of her sister, sometimes..."

"The consuming hatred that Lorsali, fairest of the Carres, had for her youngest sibling and only sister was something even those in Parsa spoke of in whispers. They spoke of the eldest princess's obsession. Lorsali would have bound Ninli to her jealously and never let her go. She would have been hers to abuse, hers to control, dismembering any other who touched her."

It hadn't been a secret. Nothing of the royal family's madness had been.

The secrets of the Carres were all in their scepters and blood rituals. The court life in the palace had been open knowledge. There had been too many people rotating through the palace halls to have it otherwise. Few survived working in the palace for long, but enough to spread their tales, they did. Stories of madness had helped the Carres maintain control. And the stories had neared legend after their deaths.

The Carres with their blood-spilling, horrifying rituals against the populace had always been worse to each other.

"Being discarded is easier than being consumed," he mused. "I do believe she wins."

"Being discarded is nothing to seek," she said quietly.

"That is why ceasing to care is the best way to survive. Caring brings pain. Betrayal. It's something I've never been able to teach Ninli."

"Nin knows all about betrayal."

He didn't say anything for a moment. "Yes, I suppose she knows betrayal intimately. Less explained is why she didn't learn from it."

"How...how did you stop caring about your mother?"

He looked up at the stars. "I pretended for a while that she died on the streets. That I held her hand as she died—as she murmured to me how it was all worth it because she loved me." He circled a finger at the stars that held no answers. "I made sure the child in that false memory died, too."

Taline closed her eyes. "I'm sorry."

"Come now, narsumina. Feel no pity for me. Not when your own father sold you like a handmade good he no longer wanted. Fetched quite a price for you—enough to save his failing trade for ten years more. Sold you to a man whose barbarism is only exceeded by his unchecked ability to do whatever he wants. At least my mother left me to die free."

"You seek to make me angry in order to protect yourself. I know you now, Rone." She closed her eyes. "And you mistake my sorrow for pity." Dark veins crept beneath her skin and the muscles in her neck clenched.

He curled one hand into a fist and used the other to smooth the hair from her forehead. "I make no mistake. I simply have no ability to accept it."

She tried to smile. "Someday. Someday Nin will get you to accept it."

Dark veins spread and she surged forward. His curled fist tightened, but he kept his free hand soft upon her hair. "Or someday, maybe it will be you."

She coughed. He pressed cloth to her mouth. It came back splattered with black and gold.

"You've never sought revenge against the Valerans."

He stared at the black and gold. He couldn't fix this. But Ninli could. "Oh, I do my best to drag our shared name through the muddied sand, as I've said before. And if their shipments sometimes go missing... Well, it's the little pleasures."

"But you haven't tried to ruin them."

He looked at the scepter as he cupped the cloth to her lips and delicately drew it across red lips gone pale and splotched. "I've seen revenge. I've seen it with and without power behind it." He carefully folded the cloth and leaned back to retrieve another—for there would be a next bout. "I will give them no other power over me."

"You give no one power over you." She shifted and coughed into his quickly retrieved second cloth. "Giving someone power is asking for them to abuse it. I know that feeling. But you have let them take that from you, too. Your ability to trust."

She gave a great hacking exhale that caused his own stomach to clench. "My father, when he—"

"Taline—" he murmured.

She feebly shook her head. "There were others in my situation. I wasn't the only gift to Etelian ul Fehl. I saw—"

She coughed again.

He pulled her head onto his lap, held the cloth under her chin and rested his other hand on her forehead. "Don't speak."

He looked out through the cave's entrance, unwilling to look at the woman in his lap. "I understand. I wasn't the only abandoned child at the orphanage."

Or on the streets. Some didn't survive the streets—their will to survive simply wasn't there. Some lost all ability to trust in others. In a household like Etelian ul Fehl's, Rone could only contemplate the mental fortitude required not only to survive, but to trust again.

There had always been something about Taline that had called to him beyond the easy beauty that drew all eyes. Her fierce loyalty was something that he didn't understand yet craved all the same. The dance with the Summora girls had never been an easy one.

When she finally was able to breathe again, she snaked out her free hand to catch his.

"Power is fickle. Love is not."

His chest constricted painfully. His ribs felt too large for his chest. His heart was galloping too fast over its usual sluggish pace.

"Perhaps." He smoothed her hair. "Perhaps."

He looked up at the stars.

CHAPTER THIRTY-ONE

TO DEATH

NINLI

(Cuipsin camp)

Nin didn't need to consult the stars. She already knew what was wrong. "The scepter. The gates. The gate in Zenure. The gate from Lyndel. They are—"

Gone. Destroyed. Destroyed.

Nin and Kaveh had just renewed the gates in Lyndel and the one that led from there to Zenure, connecting Zenure to the empire. They had traveled the northern territories a mere half day before.

Stars ripped across her mind as the pain ripped through her frame—a connection spiking horribly. Two gates she had recently touched were now gone.

"Outside!" Kaveh barked at the messenger, who bolted. Kaveh gently lifted her face, tension filling his frame. "Is it something we did?"

She searched the connection that had formed with each gate she touched. There was always a connection between gate and keeper, and stronger connections occurred in those with maker blood. The connection to the two gates had been severed clean.

"No. The gates were destroyed."

"The Scepter of Darkness?" Tension strung the bond tight.

"I don't know." Zenure was far from where she thought Rone and Taline would head. Lyndel bordered Tehrasi, but they would have needed to travel by gate to cross the distance from where they had been weeks ago in the Fehl Sea. And, if asked by Kaveh where Rone and Taline were now, her heart and scepter hand would have pointed to the fertile valley.

Not to Lyndel or Zenure—unless they had used the scepter to get there.

Could they have just missed Rone and Taline? Could they have passed right over them in the other layer? Had she done something in that pass to upset the balance of Taline's—

The flap of the tent ripped open, and Kaveh was already in motion, shadows blowing outward to mutilate whoever dared enter after his command. Kaveh stopped death with the barest tether of control when he saw who it was, at the same time Nin slammed her eye spell back into place.

"Rayd is dead," Simin ul Fehl said grimly, frozen with Kaveh's daggered shadows an inch from his face. "Father sent him as designate to Zenure and the Heit Territories. Scythian forces attacked. The council's supposition is that the Scythians knew they were the next target in the northern surge, since all know the Casp Sea will be ours in a matter of months. Scythians killed Rayd. The royal family will be exterminated, the Scythian palace in Tomyr flattened, and anything untoward found in Zenure destroyed."

Her breath caught. Another blessed imperial prince was dead.

Kaveh's eyes dissected his brother. "Why was Rayd sent to Zenure?"

It was an interesting question. Zenure had been folded into the empire some three weeks past, according to sources she'd had access to before Kaveh had started hunting her.

Rayd, the eleventh blessed child of the emperor, and the third son of Nera, sat the throne of Bahra, the rich province containing the crescent valley, situated between Fehla and Tehrasi.

Nera had wanted to keep her claws on the territories surrounding Fehla—or the territories richest in resource. A child higher on the blessing chain—like Shiera or Urful—should have gotten Bahra.

Rayd had been a lesser evil than Etelian, but he had none of the love that Cuipsin held for Shiera or that Kemet had for Zorus. If anything, he seemed to have gained the simple acceptance of the people he ruled, common to other padifehls who sat their thrones but chose no active rule.

As one of Nera's children, however, and the first of hers to be assassinated, Rayd's death brought...complications.

"Zenure, the Heit Territories, and those to be captured north, were going to form a province for Puria, but Nera has been eyeing the Axšaina Sea properties as a seat for her youngest daughter instead. Rayd was sent to identify the lands of the Casp and Axšaina Seas and decide which was the best. Nera demanded it."

Both Rayd and Puria were of Nera's blood. Rayd the third born of Nera and Puria the fifth had been blessed eleventh and twenty-third of the Fehl children. Puria was younger than Simin but would be awarded a rich padifehl province first—she would gain better territory than all her older siblings born of other mothers.

Nin wondered which sea Simin wanted for his own—and whether he would kill for his choice.

Kaveh's emotions reflected suspicion. Of precisely what, she would have to discern. "When did Rayd die?"

Simin's eyes narrowed a hair on Kaveh. "You care?"

"No."

Simin's gaze went unexpectedly flat. "We don't know, but evidence against the Scythians was sent through the Zenure gate before it was destroyed. The imperial palace is in an uproar. You have your orders."

Did Simin care? She didn't get the sense he did, so why the flat gaze? She didn't know the imperial court politics. She kept abreast of only that which affected Tehrasi—a mistake she would need to rectify.

"You are certain the Scythians are guilty?"

Simin said nothing for a long moment, taking Kaveh's measure, flatness receding the smallest amount. "The bodies of identified members of their forces were found next to the destroyed gates in both Zenure and Lyndel. The Scythians have closed their palace and deactivated all magical means of travel to the capital city. They, at least, are planning as if we will think them guilty."

Closing the capital was an act that spoke of either guilt or terror. A chill went through her. Destroyed gates and deactivated means of travel wouldn't stop Kaveh. Her family had done the same when the Fehls had come. She wondered whether the Scythians had a Jisarek of their own—ruining the whole house around them with their actions.

Kaveh tilted his head at Simin. "And you? What do you think?"

Something wasn't right. Kaveh obviously felt it, too. Why would the Scythians destroy the gates? Zenure was so small that the imperial forces could simply walk from the other Lyndel gates that still stood or cross the Casp Sea from Skudra or Tehrasi. Destroying the gates made no tactical sense. Killing Rayd was an unnecessary declaration of war.

"I think that we have orders," Simin said. "Nera said that no one in the palace is to be spared."

"I do not take orders from Nera," Kaveh said calmly.

Simin tilted his head. His long, dark hair, tied with a simple piece of leather, slid over his shoulder. "The emperor will allow her additions to stand. You know that he will. And Nera's forces will cleanse Tomyr with great malice, should you not do so. The Scythians will suffer greatly, should she be the one at the battle helm."

The personal forces of the royal imperials were well trained, but small. Still, Nera could likely call upon the forces of each of her children.

And whereas Kaveh would wipe the field clean in a few blows, Nera would...take her time. Only the razing of a country would do for the death of one of hers.

"Why are you here instead of Aros?" Kaveh tapped his fingers together. "And so suddenly after the gates were destroyed?"

Simin's dark eyes glittered. "How do you know when the event occurred?"

Nin's heart stuttered.

Kaveh raised an unimpressed brow. "Why, Simin?"

"Aros is trying to calm Nera right now in the Palace of Tehras. Why are you asking questions, Kaveh?" Simin tilted his head in the other direction and his long hair slid again. Something in his gaze, though, made Nin's eyes narrow.

"Are you finally unnerved by a request to wipe a country of its population?"

"Don't be foolish," Kaveh said.

But Simin continued to study him. "More people have survived your onslaughts in the past weeks than ever before. Baksis was right. Something has changed."

"Nothing has changed."

Simin shrugged, as if he didn't care either way, but his eyes stayed sharp. And they slipped to her. "The brightening of the gates across the empire and the sudden destruction at Zenure are linked in some way. Nera is sending her forces by air from Tehrasi. Even if Aros delays her, they will reach the capital by nightfall. I am here to escort you there first."

So that Kaveh could kill everyone before Nera arrived?

Something was very, very wrong. Simin's haste, the appeal to a benevolence that Kaveh had never been tasked with having, the events themselves.

Simin ul Fehl was the eighteenth blessed child of the emperor, but he was four years older than Kaveh. Age and blessing did not necessarily match in order when it came to the blessed children. Age of power revelation and blessing order more often did.

Kaveh had been blessed abnormally young. All of Nera's spawn had as well. Simin had also been blessed earlier than imperial princes of a similar age. He was the only child of a mother who had been a powerful imperial watercaster before she had hidden herself and her child away.

When Simin had been presented to the emperor at age twelve, he had been blessed immediately. That immediacy spoke to his true power.

Simin would want a water-rich province. As a powerful water manipulator, he would want a territory with great water resources. He would want the Casp or Axšaina Sea territories that Nera was trying to secure for her offspring.

"Why you? Why now?" Kaveh asked.

Simin regarded him for a long moment. "You have choices to make. The gate to Zenure from Fehlaka is gone, but Cuipsin has a gate to

Helip." He looked between the two of them, eyes hooded. "I think you already know that, though. From Helip, I can get us across the sea in moments to Tomyr and the closed palace. No armies, no preparation, no time for Nera to interfere. I will be back in a moment to hear your answer." Simin ducked out of the tent, long, banded hair swaying.

Nin immediately turned to Kaveh, feeling his conflicting emotions. "What is it?"

"Simin is...not usually so willing to share, nor concerned with testing me. It is unusual."

"You think him complicit?"

"I think the timing is suspect."

"You think we are walking into a trap?"

"I'd like to see someone try to trap me."

"Hubris," she murmured. Though she was starting to believe Kaveh untouchable, too. His tie to the emperor was his only weakness.

Simin returned. He looked between them, smiled strangely, then nodded at Kaveh's motion for them to begin.

They marched with three contingents of Kaveh's staunchest soldiers to the gate that would take them to Helip.

It was an otherwise good plan for a quick journey, but if it had just been Nin and Kaveh, she could have opened a ripgate straight to Scythia. The way Simin was side-eyeing her didn't make her feel any better about the secrets they were trying to keep.

The trip across the Casp Sea took little time, but she used it to watch Simin effortlessly manipulate the sea. She had never seen a stronger watercaster. But then, Simin was a Level Nine magi, same as Kaveh and Nin.

Nin looked at Kaveh as the shoreline approached and felt the press of the moon.

KAVEH

Scythia was unfulfilling conquest and darkness.

Most soldiers laid down their arms immediately, which only increased the darkness of Kaveh's tension. He had conquered countless countries and territories. Those who sought peaceful solutions dropped their weapons quickly, like these. They didn't assassinate ranking members of the imperial family or elite.

The guards to the palace were the only ones who gave true opposition. He cut through them like faistra bread. Simin followed passively in his wake, arms folded behind his back, while Nin furiously healed all those he cut down—sealing their unconscious bodies together to prevent them from waking and attacking them from behind.

Weakness. And yet...

He stared at the faces arrayed in front of him as his soldiers assembled the royal family into a line. What else had been lost due to the mistake of lining the Carres up for execution entertainment?

He looked at Nin. She had survived the purge only because her magic hadn't been connected to the palace and ritual spells that had killed the rest of her family. If her magic had been connected, as it would have been a bare week later, she would not be standing at his side. She would not be alive.

Anger curled in his gut. But this anger was born not of weakness, but of strength. Nin was a strong asset as his side, and she would have been lost.

The faces in front of him paled. The king and queen, the eldest children—he recognized their terror as they stared at him, and the predator in him wanted to snap his jaws and rip out their throats. Only the presence of the woman at his side stayed his hand.

He looked at the youngest royal—a girl no more than six—held against a servant's chest. The image blurred and Nin's face stared back.

"No," Kaveh said instinctively.

Simin's gaze swung sharply to him, tied hair flying. "What do you mean, no?" There was an odd edge to his voice, tempered with caution.

"Please. Lady of Shadows, please." One of the servant's hands went out, grasping at the air before her, but not daring to touch Nin. Her other arm tightened around the child in front of her. "We've heard of you in the kitchens. Please. The children. Spare the children. Please."

The queen looked sharply at the servant, focused on Nin, then forced her gaze to meet Kaveh's. "We will give you whatever you want."

Kaveh didn't dare look at Nin's face. He felt her emotions through the bond, and he was afraid of what he might promise should he look in her eyes and see a plea.

"The children will seek revenge in the future," he said stiffly. "They will bide their time against the empire."

"They won't," the queen said—just as stiffly. "We will tell them that is not our wish. We will make certain—"

"They can serve the empire," Nin said softly. "They can become assets."

"Yes! They will serve your empire!" the servant exclaimed, hugging the child closer before thrusting her forward. The servant, interrupting and speaking over the queen, had to believe she was already dead at this point and cared no more for her own life. "Please, not Mari," she whispered, gaze never straying from Nin. "Please."

"The emperor's orders are clear," Simin said, voice bland.

"Nera's orders," Nin answered sharply, turning to Kaveh. "You know these are Nera's orders."

Kaveh surrounded the two of them in shadow to keep from being overheard and turned to her finally. Her expression was as broken as the bond had proclaimed. Ice and flame ignited his veins. "Simin is right. It is the will of the emperor, even if issued from Nera's lips."

The shadows were thick, but they could still see through the swirls to the terrified faces beyond. He could still see "Mari's" face and the servant clutching her to her chest once more.

Nin's face. Nin's younger face on an even tinier frame.

"It's not—"

He cut a harsh hand through the swirling shadows. "Will you have Nera come through and serve them justice instead?"

Nin's younger face in terror and agony.

Her hands curled. "No, but this is wrong."

"They are not your family—"

"No, my family would be the ones on this side—dealing the death blows."

"Nin—"

"This all feels wrong. Tell me this doesn't feel wrong, Kaveh?"

"The empire—"

She angrily motioned at Ifret, who expelled a massive amount of shadow, spreading out the cage around them. Nin opened five ripgates inside his cage of shadows, energy sapping from her at the same time that anger seemed to give her strength.

Five ripgates to five very different parts of the empire surrounded them, inside the cage.

"This is the empire, too." She motioned to the desolate eyes piercing the shadows in the first, to the devastation in the second, to the destitution in the third, to the blank faces in the fourth, to the resignation in the fifth.

"You think to make me feel for the destitute? That it will make me doubt?"

"No," she stressed. "I mean for you to see what is inside the machine that you continually power. These were communities the empire wiped clean, then left."

"Open to five cities instead."

She wiped her hand through the five and replaced them with five new ones, all churning with life.

He pointed at them. "Will you argue this? The people do better for having the empire. The change and progress that you so extol."

"Yes. And progress requires sacrifice and flexibility—qualities which some do not naturally possess. But that is where the empire can guide. Taking care of that which you already have. Moving forward with what you can afford to add."

"The empire is better than most of the pitiful places we conquer. We bring advancement and progress."

"And I want those things. I want the winds and gates and knowledge. I want that advancement. But it can't be only for those born to the highest levels. To people like Nera. To her children only. It can't be due to birth. Think." She stepped toward him on stuttering legs. "Think of what the empire could be, with a way for people to defend themselves and raise themselves. Think of this servant, arguing for her charge, powerless in so many ways and yet courageous enough to speak. Think of what the empire could be with power and knowledge available to everyone—not just to those who would hoard it, but to those who would use it well. Think of what we could do and build, Kaveh. What we could become."

"You were born to—"

"We, both of us, were blessed by our births. Or cursed. I was born to plenty, and I come from a long line of people born to plenty. I had every advantage at birth. And when I Awakened to power, I Awakened to a torrent—to skills that most do not have. I know my fortune. And I know my misfortune, too. For those born to plenty, do we not have a duty to those born to less?" She clasped his hand. "A duty not to live only for ourselves but to make life better for others?"

His fingers gripped hers. "Every new land we spread to receives all the benefits of the empire. We—"

"You force people to the acceptance."

"They are better off for it."

"Some, yes." Her gaze didn't drop. "But how would you know? You only look forward. You don't look at what is. At what you govern now. At the orders you are given, or the ones given when you leave. If the emperor leaves a magi in charge who takes advantage of the turmoil of change—would that not be a mistake? Can the emperor make a mistake? A leader can make a mistake and still be someone we want to follow. Might we question orders in order to help the empire and emperor? For what happens to the people when their governors do not care? What sort of empire will you have?"

She stepped forward. He almost took a step back. "The advancement is what your father wants. And he can have it." She wrapped her fingers around his. "He can see the rise of a new world. But some orders should be questioned."

His mind couldn't wrap around the idea. He mentally sidestepped for an easier one. "You think kindness and the simple sharing of knowledge will solve all the ills of the empire."

"I think it will help. I think that if we do nothing, we lose everything. For the poor will rise up. The disenfranchised and those who have nothing to lose will revolt. They will rise up and overthrow the empire and the elites, and they will remake a world in their image—and that world might be embittered and angry, for that is what they've been shown." She gripped her fingers. "That world will kill much that you purport to save."

"The weak fall."

"The weak must be shown how to be strong. People are petty. And when given to indulgence, pettiness thrives. But people can also be great. Give your people reason to be great. Don't do this. Don't blindly follow these orders. Find the answers. Save your empire and its future."

NINLI

His palm slipped around her neck and he held her by the nape. "I was bred for this."

She could feel him willing her to understand. "You are more than your birth."

"What is my purpose, if it is not this?"

"Your purpose is what you make it!"

"You were born to be a queen. You were born to understand these choices."

"And I was given the chance to change my thinking. Kaveh—" She grabbed his hand from her nape and twisted it to rest between hers, clasped to her chest. "I will not be my family," she said harshly. "I reject their legacy of blood. I choose my own path."

She could see Simin staring at them through the shadows, something incomprehensible in his gaze.

She supposed it was a wildly foreign thing to see—the Terror of the Battlefront arguing with someone without death as a result. She wondered if Simin had ever seen Kaveh show emotion for something other than the emperor or Ifret.

Kaveh let the shadows fall, along with their hands.

Simin looked between them slowly. "Kaveh, your orders."

The moment hung. Kaveh stared at the royal family and their loyal servants. Stared at the servant clutching the youngest tight. Nin swallowed.

Movement made her look back at Simin, who was watching Kaveh intensely. Something shifted behind Simin's eyes at whatever he was deducing—some decision made. He turned to the queen. "Rayd ul Fehl's body. Where is it?"

Nin looked sharply at Simin. He had said there was proof of Rayd's death.

"We don't have it. We didn't kill him. I know you will not believe me. We have accepted this. But there is no body here. Killing a padifehl is against our interests—we know we would be unable to stand against the empire. The destroyed gate in Zenure holds your answers."

"Kaveh?" Simin asked.

"Find Rayd's body. We will investigate this matter before acting."

The tension in her shoulders dropped. It was a temporary measure and one that could still mean the death of everyone who stood before them, but Kaveh had chosen to question. Time was against whoever was guilty.

Time also marched in delicate but brisk strides down the hall. The shadows around Nin curled.

Simin turned. "Nera—"

"Is wondering why these bottom feeders still breathe."

Nera emerged from the hall, striding into the room in ceremonial robes cut with gold thread, emerald, and lapis lazuli.

Nera was forty-eight and just as stunning as pictures depicted. Nin had only ever seen her from a distance during processions, but her likeness was well known and sold.

A vial of poison hung from her neck. Nera was said to be immune to poisons and reveled in their use. It was said that she liked to coat them on her skin and make servants lick it off—that she liked to hold drops in her lips and slide them into the waiting mouths of men.

Deadly and nearly inhumane—Nera, Irsula of Denz, Oralia Valeran—Sher Fehl had a type. So, too, had Jisarek.

Long, streaming dark hair, kohl wrapped sea-green eyes, and full lips, crowned a frame brimming with both curves and strength. She had a similar fantastic bone structure to Taline, but Nera's lighter eyes were gifted by the nomadic tribes that descended and ascended the Casp Sea.

She stood, poised in the doorway, and everything about her screamed that she would be getting what she wanted. Lorsali would have been as emerald with envy as Nera's favorite fertility jewels.

Nera swung her hips as she walked inside. Here was the woman who had inspired such greed in Jisarek that he had kidnapped the betrothed of Sher Fehl and held her for months—a woman whose kidnapping had prompted the end of a dynasty.

Jisarek had initially taken Nera as a form of twisted "payment." Nin had heard him jest about it once—Jisarek's tongue had always been freer with drink. Sher Fehl's growing power meant he had obviously gotten away with far too much in their deal for the scepter, and Jisarek had needed to even things up. Her uncle had considered Sher Fehl an upstart, from a family of herders, while the Carres were the highest of royalty. And Nera—the loveliest filly in the desert-touched lands—was final payment in an added debt that Jisarek manufactured for his own pleasure as one of the royal elite. But Jisarek, like so many others, had fallen to Nera's spells.

Second born, and far less capable than his older brother, Jisarek had ever been concerned for his own pleasures, consequences be damned. And after Nera's rescue, he'd been consumed with trying to get her back. Bilen Osni had died because of that obsession. The entire Carre Dynasty had.

Nin kept her attention on the poisonous woman sashaying toward them. Why Nera was still alive instead of long dead by Crelu ul Osni's hand was the question that prompted the most caution for Nin.

A small contingent of black-cloaked slayers strode behind her—Nera's personal guard. They were supposedly unbeatable and vicious in the torture they chose to inflict.

Nin would bet on Kaveh any day, however. And indeed, Nera's eyes were hungry when she looked at him. Her gaze held such a similar expression to the ones Aros wore. Aros's paternity was questioned, but no one could deny the mother of his birth.

Nin wondered whether that was one of the main reasons the emperor clung to the myth of Aros being his son. He looked just like Nera. Looking at Aros was like looking at a piece of the woman he loved.

"I see that you have secured the palace, Kaveh. Excellent. You have other places to be, so leave these last pleasantries to me."

"No. We search for proof of Rayd's death first."

Fury consumed her gaze and the tinkling of the jewels upon her gown and robe shook. "Rayd's hand was sent with all his rings intact upon his fingers. I assure you, even if you do not find his body, I do not care."

"How do you know it was Rayd's hand?"

"I know my own son's hand! How dare—" Her hand raised, then paused, as if she remembered who stood before her. Her fingers slowly descended to her side and a false smile stretched her mouth. "You don't know that the emperor decreed that the Scythians are to be punished. I forgive you."

Kaveh watched her dispassionately. "We will secure the Scythian countryside. However, I will not allow a slaughter of the entire royal family to take place without confirmation and forethought. I will not allow another massacre that harms us."

Hatred spawned in her eyes. "You dare—"

"We lost use of the scepters and gates with the loss of the Carres. Tomyr and Scythia have their own staffs and mining secrets that are held by the royal family. We will not make the same mistake."

"I will pry their secrets out."

"We will put them in cells until we discover what happened today, then we will decide how best they can be used."

Nera smiled tightly and walked over to the royal nearest to her—a princess who could be no more than fourteen.

Nera touched the girl—letting her fingers linger on her shoulder, then slide down her arm. "I will pry you apart, first. I will make you beg for death and I will make everyone else in your family watch. You will wish the Shadow Prince had killed you all."

Kaveh snapped his fingers. "Simin, give the royal family to my First General to secure in the dungeon. Nin, go with him."

Nin didn't want to go, but she knew better than to say a word. The outspoken servant's terrified gaze was pleading. Nin nodded and followed Simin, who motioned the family ahead. She could feel Nera's gaze on her.

"I see you have your little pet well in h—" Her comment was cut off as the door closed.

Simin watched Nin but said nothing as he handed the family off to the First General. The servant's gaze was still pleading with Nin as she disappeared with her charge down the dungeon stairs. Nin stared after them, memory and reality viciously colliding.

Simin's gaze was remote and inscrutable as they stood in the hall with half of Nera's guards, waiting on whatever was resolved in the room beyond. Nera emerged infuriated, no more than a minute later, rubbing furiously at her wrist. A shadow mark circled the spot beneath.

"Come!" she barked at her guards. She strode down the hall and away from view.

"Nera will beat you to the emperor's ear," Simin said, as Kaveh emerged from the room, looking unconcerned.

"I'll deal with the emperor." Kaveh motioned for his men to round up the household staff and guards of the closed palace. The well-trained men immediately did so.

Simin examined Kaveh. "I will accompany you."

Nin felt Kaveh's displeasure in that—it would take them longer. Nin could get them to Tehras in an instant. She didn't know how she felt about going back to Tehras as Ninli ul Summora, though.

"Nearly the full court has assembled. The padifehls have been called home for conference on the gates. You are certain now is the time that you want to start to question?"

Her gaze drifted to Simin. There was no tight bond between them—Kaveh had only ever had bonds to the emperor and Ifret—but she sensed mutual respect between the two. Nothing outside of Simin's courtly posture had shown that he respected Nera.

"Whether the court is present or not, the emperor will hear me."

Simin dipped his head in acknowledgment, but the content of the conversation caught up to her. "The court has assembled in Tehras?"

Because of the assassin's guild? Because of Nera being there? Because of Nera, Aros, and Etelian being there?

Kaveh looked at her. She felt his apology before she heard it in his clipped voice. "No. The court is at the imperial palace. The emperor is in Fehlaka, along with most of our siblings."

She stilled, then touched Kaveh's arm—letting one of his small shadows automatically wrap her fingers. She ignored Simin's sharp glance and focused solely on the man in front of her.

I will be destroyed in the palace. She mentally sent the thought.

No one will touch you, he replied.

She knew he could feel her certainty in her words because he tried to feed her his. She let go of his arm. "Very well."

To the death of all secrets.

CHAPTER THIRTY-TWO
REVELATIONS OF CATATROPHE

RONE

(SOUTH OF BABIL, FIRST LAYER)

The dawn brought agony upon its soaring wings.

The scepter lit nearly hourly now, as if some force was purposely lighting it from without, but also blocking Taline and the scepter so they had to stay in the non-magic lands.

"I can feel it," Taline said, drugged. "I can feel it. The others feel so close, and yet, so very far. They block and they beckon."

Her eyes continuously pulsed with white light. On the seas, she had looked like an avenging jinn of Sehk birthed upon the storm. Now, she

664

looked simply maddened, edged in sharp black and white with no shadow or warmer shades between.

There was no choice now as to what Rone would do.

"Gone! Gone to crimson. Gone to blood. Gone beyond," she raved.

He wiped a grim hand over the clammy skin of Taline's brow. His fingers sizzled upon contact with her skin, but he endured the pain. "Just a little bit farther," he murmured.

"I can't get to Nin." She clenched. "I can't. And she'll think I've given up on her."

"She never would. You've never given up on her. You never will." He looked at her with the sort of incomprehension one gives a person playing with a scorpion-fly. "You will see this through, even when Etelian ul Fehl is waiting at the end for you."

Only the wobble of her chin gave her away before she firmed it. "He will rue the day he stands in the way of me getting to Nin."

The scepter light receded. She took a gulping breath of air, then released. From past pauses, Rone knew this one would only last for an hour, no more. Her gaze was watery as she looked up at him. "Your eyes are like the heart of the glaciers in your north."

"Better than a comment on my ridiculous hair."

Her eyes creased in thought. "Your hair is like the sunset."

"Right." His fingers slid along her cheek. "You're going to give the Shadow Prince a run for his money in the unsettling department, should you keep this up."

"You may have to kill me, in the end. I can be graceful in death."

He reached her neck and she leaned into the touch, holding onto the scepter with all her limited power. He could feel the unimaginable power thrum—scorching him where it touched his skin.

His hand slid under her neck and followed with his arm, the other tucked beneath her knees as he lifted her from the ground. "I can't imagine you being anything else. I just need to get you to Ninli."

"That's what I said from the beginning," she said tiredly.

"I know. You were right."

"Note it, V—Rone. Note it. I was right," she murmured. She curled into him and closed her eyes.

He looked at her—at her figure, tight and curled in on itself, at her face, unnaturally blanched and sweating. The scepter was clutched to her chest.

Was he willing to let the scepter be wielded by another hand?

He didn't believe in humanity. He didn't believe in love. And yet here Taline was, constantly defying his beliefs. "You were right. We are going to find Ninli, and whatever happens to the scepter, she will heal you."

Resolution had clicked into place in a way that only the softest and hardest of decisions did. His mind had been made up days ago; he had simply been fighting inevitability.

"I know," she said, curling further into him.

He didn't correct her and say he had never been planning to get her back to her sister. He didn't say that he had been planning on unhooking and destroying the scepter. He didn't say that he had been planning on running her in circles around the non-magic world until the oath cycle had passed.

He didn't say that something inside him had changed.

Was he willing to let the scepter be wielded by another hand?

He looked at her. To save her, the answer was yes.

He still hated the emperor, the empire, the Valerans, and all who were like them. He hated relics of power that enabled others to subjugate someone else.

And he would destroy the Scepter of Darkness.

But his goal had altered—save Taline, destroy the scepter, and because they needed to get to Ninli to do both, he would save her, too.

And perhaps, putting a blade through the Shadow Prince's heart would make him feel better.

He set Taline upright so that he could finish the herbs on the fire, but almost at once, the scepter took hold again and she started to shake and murmur. He held a hand against her shoulder and reached for the herb packet with the other.

One of the others was using their scepter again. It wasn't Ninli. It had become obvious that she had done something so that her scepter use would register with, but not influence, the Scepter of Darkness. Maybe it was because she wielded one so far down the line instead of one near the top of the chain, but whatever it was, Ninli knew her bloodline and she knew the scepters. She had been tortuously trained on their use, and she had done something to make certain that Taline wasn't affected.

She could do nothing about the others, though. He touched Taline's shaking shoulder. Humanity. He had made his peace with believing in both women.

That still left the rest of the world in distrust.

Rone looked at the assassin as he returned again to wait in the shadows. A knife curled into Rone's palm. The assassin was back from inciting the explosion with the gates. He was back from whispering plans to the current wielder of the Prime Scepter of Tehras.

Rone wondered where he stowed the scepter when it was not in hand. It was the only thing, other than Rone's inability to leave Taline, that kept the assassin alive.

Rone eyed the amulet around the assassin's neck.

Taline's murmurs while under the scepter's influence had been illuminating. Rone knew definitively who the wielder of the Prime Scepter was. And that left the relationship to the man before him, the current wielder of the Second, easily deduced. The relationship between the two lived in the shadows, but the connection between them was undeniable.

How long had the second done the dirty work of the first?

Their plan now was simple to deduce. They wanted Taline to fall to the scepter's influence before they took it from her. The gate explosion had been a calculated move, on more than one front.

Rone grimly began drawing up plans as he dumped his last ingredients into the small cauldron. He thought of what awaited him in the magic world. In their layer. In the empire. He thought of the woman leaning against him and her sister, who was always willing to lend aid even at her own expense. He thought of the pentalayerists, Osni, and the empire.

The strings wildly swung in the wind.

How would they all connect? What could he do to influence the pattern?

Sacrifice.

He looked to the darkness beyond the fire and the eyes that gleamed there, watching them.

Rone went through the normal, uncomplicated motions of tending the fire and stirring, allowing the resignation he wanted to project to bow his shoulders forward. He hid the way he was moving things around in the pack.

Taline shivered uncontrollably. He tugged the blanket tighter around her, fussed over her state, and set the fire higher.

The fire was just high enough to hide the bottom portion of his body—his hands buried in Ninli's pack.

He would trust in the assassin's desire to keep them out of pentalayerist hands if their forces were attracted by the fire. He would trust in the fire to hide this last piece of subterfuge.

He drew a set of glyphs on the last piece of enchanted papyri without looking down. He used the blood that was already within to form the backbone of the spell that would affect those with the same bloodline.

It was a risk, a great one, but he had only gambles left. He would focus on the bloodline that threatened their safety the most.

He touched one of their last containers of magic—a coiled and beautiful glass designed with Taline's careful magic—and closed his eyes. He concentrated on the magic that resided in his very core—ugly and unwanted. It was magic he never wanted to use and wanted no one to see.

The fire was large enough to block the assassin's view and Taline was in too much pain to notice anything. He cursed his thankfulness of the latter.

He completed the spell—hiding the enchantment in a great field of nothing. The paper went blank—all measures within it dormant. It would await activation—to be used in only the grimmest of circumstances. A one-shot safety measure.

He layered an active healing charm in the seemingly blank paper's threads—turning the paper a light violet. An obvious spell, and the only one that was detectable by sight and magic now—or at least not detectable by any magic that was not comparable to his.

That left one other person who could see it—another great risk.

But the person the paper would be used against, would not see it until it was upon him. Rone had a feeling of inevitability over its use.

When Taline moaned and thrashed in agony, he put one hand on her forehead and wrapped the paper around the staff above her palm.

Dormant healing magic spread as if it were nothing more than a piece of paper that the scepter would burn through in the next minute.

It cast off the healing spell immediately and sent a painful jolt through him. His tendons pulled outward and he shook the pain from his hand then sent the same healing spell through his palm. He let his shoulders slump as if he were resigned.

Taline curled the scepter into her chest.

The wisps of burning paper flew as ash into the air to join the fire embers. The insidious spell released beneath and wrapped into the grains of the staff below as it burned. He let nothing of his triumph show.

One shot. A split moment of time. Not enough to survive. But enough for an element of surprise.

One-time use and no more.

If he had tried this before, he would have hampered any efforts to earn Taline's trust, or the scepter's dismissal, and his moment would have been like the ash the paper had become.

The scepter hated him, but it now also thought him a hindrance easily overcome. Disposable. However, once they were surrounded by magic again and he activated this measure, the scepter would make certain he died.

He accepted that risk.

He would be ready.

He removed a blank scroll and detailed everything he knew about Babil in this layer and in theirs. He mapped all the hidden areas, all the hidden treasures, and all the traps. He labeled all the things he wanted to share with an enemy force turned temporary ally.

Rone didn't want to cross paths with the military. Babil was one of the largest cities in the non-magic world. Going there increased their risks tenfold in regards to opponents both magical and non-magical.

But risks were the cost of plots within plots.

He thought about what awaited them when they found Ninli. He needed to implement and coordinate multiple plans.

He monitored the motionless figure crouched fifty paces away as the ashes cooled and Rone cleared the camp. The assassin would always be able to follow and find them in a way that even the pentalayerists with their relics could not. The Second Scepter made all the difference. Someone had shown the assassin how to use the scepter and that meant that not just the assassin knew the scepter's secrets—the assassin's father knew them, too.

Plots and plans swirled as the moon dwindled toward a dark end. Two more days.

Plots and plans swirled faster as the players and their motivations took shape.

Babil, the city of magnificence. And of death.

Rone tapped the detailed scroll and narrowed his eyes. "Come. Let us discuss."

The assassin disconnected from his shadows and crawled forward. He cocked his head in question. The amulet swung heavily from his neck.

"I already know your cursed blood," Rone said. "Show yourself to me. Show me troth and I will give you promise in return."

The assassin deliberated for a moment, then unwrapped the coverings around his face. He did so almost eagerly, as if he rarely was allowed the freedom. Familiar features were disfigured by old scarring, but his parentage was clear, even in a face barely fifteen. The assassin's young eyes were burning with fervor.

Rone nodded. "Did Nera ul Fehl do that to your face?"

The assassin said nothing for another long moment, then hissed out, "Yes."

"Why didn't she kill you?"

"For love. I am loved, but I am a secret."

That knowledge opened huge opportunities. "Do you want revenge?"

The assassin struggled with the notion. Which meant he had been well indoctrinated by his father. "I want my true path. I want to be acknowledged."

"You want to help your father."

"Yes."

"How much?"

"I will do anything."

"Will you help me kill the Shadow Prince?" Rone asked.

The assassin smiled slowly. "It would be my pleasure."

Plots and plans. Deals with demons. Rone handed him the scroll.

The empire would tremble.

CHAPTER THIRTY-THREE

SEEDS OF NURTURE AND DEATH

NINLI

(THE IMPERIAL PALACE, FEHLAKA)

Simin had spoken true. Slowed as they were, Nera had reached the emperor a few minutes before they had. She was still on a tirade as they entered the room.

"You hate me. You hate our children. Our children, who should be first in your heart."

"They—"

"If they were, you would order the slayer to wipe every last Scythian from the world!"

"If Kaveh—"

"You love him the most! Instead of our children."

"That's—"

"I want every Scythian dead! I don't care what you say! I'll see to it myself, if you do nothing."

The emperor's expression went cold at that. Even Nera in her outrage sensed she had gone too far, for she backed down immediately.

Her lower lip quivered. "I just want my son to have justice."

He softened.

It was true then, watching him—the emperor was besotted with his first wife.

Simin and Kaveh said nothing. They didn't look at all surprised by the show.

"Kaveh, please give your report," the emperor said, voice overly pleasant. "Rayd is dead. Nera is distressed. And the Scythians are alive and unharmed. Nera states that your...bondmate...and Simin seek to poison your mind."

Nera's eyes glittered behind the emperor.

680

"Rayd's body has not been located," Kaveh said. "Nor is there any evidence of the Scythian royal family being involved. Nera's guards killed the only links we had to the truth. The men who took down the gates are unable to speak from beyond."

"They killed my son!"

"And they can provide no evidence," Kaveh said flatly.

"You are not usually concerned with such things," the emperor mused. "Scythia, and especially Tomyr, will be conquered. Why not simply kill two beetles with one knife?"

"Negotiations can still be undertaken for a smooth transition of Scythia into an imperial province. The Scythian mines are valuable and the staffs that they use to control them are not unlike the scepters. It would be shortsighted to lose that advantage. The royal family and household are firmly locked in the dungeon cells below the palace. We can remove their secrets at our leisure and conquer their country in one fell swoop—with their resources intact."

The emperor tapped his fingers together, and the glittering look that Nin had only ever seen him bestow upon Kaveh crossed his face. She had seen him display fondness for Aros, and love for Nera, but this look was Kaveh's alone—the gaze of an equal. "Yes. Well done."

Nera gasped in outrage. "Sher, our son—"

"Will be avenged."

"You will regret this lack of immediate action." Nera's poisonous gaze was laced with a sort of glittering malice that spoke of spinning plots.

"I'm certain you will make that true, dear."

Nera, eyes burning with rage, swept from the room.

The emperor stared after her strident, retreating figure. "Everything is always on high with Nera." The emperor gave a slightly rueful sigh. "She is a woman who is passionate in all things. It makes her extraordinary and painful to live with. I've denied her much of late. It might still be that streets of blood will need to be shed."

He turned to Kaveh and Simin. His eyes narrowed as he looked between them, then he turned to Simin. "You sought Kaveh before I sent anyone for the task." The emperor's voice was too pleasant once more. The hair on the back of her neck rose.

"I knew it was the best way of finding the answers we seek. There is something foul in the waters. Nera is understandably upset about the severed hand of her son, but I'm uncertain Rayd is dead. It is possible he is being held somewhere to be used for future upheaval or as a bargaining tool. You assigned me to find the links between the assassination attempts, and it all comes back to Tehrasi. Send me there and I will discover the answers."

Was this why Simin was not yet a padifehl? Because he was an active agent of the emperor? She examined him even as her heart went cold at the mention of her country.

The emperor, too, was examining Simin. "Nera has reason to think you work against her."

"I only work against her if she is an enemy of the empire, Your Imperial Majesty."

"Take care with your words, Simin."

"I serve the empire."

Nothing in Simin's bearing said that was a lie.

The emperor's fingers tapped together. "Very well. I will consider sending you to Tehras in three days. Aros routed the assassins' group last night. He is bringing their heads and assets. We will celebrate this victory tonight at a feast and mourn the passing of Rayd. Whatever the truth, we will make it look like we believe it true—then decide what to do with Scythia upon the morning."

It spoke, once more, to how much the emperor trusted Kaveh that he believed the Scythians secured. She had witnessed it countless times now. The emperor questioned everyone but accepted Kaveh's words as stark truth. He believed Kaveh's men held the palace in Tomyr and asked nothing further.

"I will require your presence later, Simin. For now, you are dismissed."

He bowed, then strode toward the hall. His gaze slipped to her for half a blink—contemplation and spinning plots there, too—then disappeared into the palace maze.

The emperor's gaze slid to her—and hardened. "Still attached, little leech?"

With the audience gone, he could openly castigate Kaveh for her continued presence.

Nin kept her gaze on the emperor as she dipped her head. "Your Imperial Majesty."

The emperor's gaze narrowed on the distance separating Kaveh and Nin. Her shoulder nearly brushed Kaveh's sleeve; his hand nearly skimmed her back.

"How long remains of this"—he waved a hand—"situation?"

"Today and tomorrow, then no more," she answered. She was under no illusion that the emperor didn't know exactly how much time remained.

"There are two days left in the oath," Kaveh said sharply, looking at her. She knew what he wanted her to say.

"Two days too many," the emperor growled. "Your growing physical reliance on her is already being discussed—rumors have been brought to court from every corner of the empire where you've been seen. Your reputation is being diminished and I don't approve."

"I think you will see differently soon, Your Imperial Majesty," Kaveh said. "I think you will see the strength of such partnership."

"Partnership?" The emperor raised a brow. "You think two days will make a difference in view of something I already loathe? You think the scepter will be in my hand? That I will care for your oath secrets to be exposed?"

"Yes. I think you will celebrate that the end of the oath means that she is mine."

"Yours?" Rage mixed with something unidentifiable and made the emperor's handsome features twist. If Nin didn't know better, she would think it was fear—the fear of losing something precious. "I tell you to rid yourself of this connection, and you now say that she will be yours, as if you are betrothed."

"Yes."

The fury consumed the emperor so fully that darkness sparked from his fingers. "Where is the savage blade I wrought?" the emperor spit. "Has so little time connected to this girl brought my right hand so low?"

Kaveh reacted to that in the way that a favored child who had rarely felt failure would to disappointment and rage.

Nin grabbed his flooding emotions and pulled them into her. She would hold them. Safeguard them. Embrace them until they could be returned.

"What next, Kaveh? Will you tell me that you are consumed by feelings?"

Freed of the burden of that very thing, Kaveh met the emperor's gaze with stark coldness. "No. At present, I have naught."

The emperor's hands relaxed, the rage receding to a measured displeasure that was redirected at Nin once more. His fingers flinched toward her, as if they desired to do her physical or magical harm. "See to it that is how it remains. Your leech will be dealt with in two days."

Sher Fehl swept from the room.

Nin would not survive the emperor. But she had known that when she accompanied Kaveh here. Kaveh alone held hope for another outcome.

She carefully returned the emotions that she held, slowly letting them through so that he could deal with them one by one.

"He is not wrong." Kaveh's expression was dark as each emotion was reclaimed. "You are becoming a crutch."

"A crutch isn't permanent," she said softly, releasing the last. "It is meant to aid healing and physical progress. When you no longer need the aid, the crutch will be a decoration you hang upon your wall or an aid you place in your wardrobe."

He closed his eyes. "Weakness."

She stroked his fingers, letting warmth bloom between their skin. "We all have them. How you deal with them, shield them, change them, is what separates stagnation from exceptionalism."

"You have a glib tongue for a thief."

She tapped his palm. "It is a worse one for a princess."

"Let me introduce you to a few, then."

The banquet halls at the imperial palace were as sumptuous and gluttonous as rumor told.

Dozens of princes and princesses reclined and feasted, intrigue pulling nearly visible strings around them as they idled and plotted.

Hungry, angry, and curious gazes locked on Nin and Kaveh as they entered. Kaveh headed for a pair of women in the corner—one a few years older than Nin, and the other far younger. The elder of the women appeared to be engaged in an argument with Baksis while Simin watched.

Kaveh, with his usual tact, stepped right into the center. His presence made the two go momentarily quiet—sharp gazes fastening on the Shadow Prince.

"Nin, you have already met Baksis and Simin," Kaveh said dismissively. The questions and intrigue were high in four sets of eyes, but Baksis and Simin merely inclined their heads to her. Kaveh motioned to the young girl. "Omari ul Fehl, next in line for the throne of Cuipsin. Ninli ul Summora of Tehrasi."

Kush skin, lit with the gold shine of Sher Fehl's genes, highlighted a petite package of restrained magic. Omari held herself calmly but with great energy in her limbs. She was eleven, but everything about her said that one day she would be beautiful, purposeful, and deadly.

"Many blessings of Sehk-Ra for a long and glorious reign." Nin dipped her head to utter the blessing that was used for rulers ascending new thrones.

"It is a pleasure to serve," Omari answered softly.

The older woman's gaze turned stormy and focused once more on Baksis. "Cuipsin is your doing. It should have been Shoune."

But even Nin knew the emperor would never put Omari on Shoune's throne. Shoune didn't border Kush, but giving Omari a province on the continent of Ersine would be courting trouble. The pull to connect the lands might be too great for Kush to resist trying to take territory back from the empire. Cuipsin, on the other hand, was strategically sound. It showed the strong ties between Kush and the empire and would also be far enough distanced that when the empire decided to envelop Kush completely, Omari would be unable to turn her forces their way.

"I have little interest in such matters, Namir," Baksis said, voice idle. "I care not where you are as long as it is far from me."

"Lies. Like all your words."

"From a Kushite monster, that's saying something." He smiled.

Namir growled. "From one who was born in the darkness of Punt's chasm, I'll take such descriptions as my due. You want a Punt sympathizer on Kush's throne. Perhaps you are looking for it yourself—Baksis ul Fehl, the one who has no throne?"

"Only if I can cut your tongue free as my first rule of court."

"Your throat with be sliced upon this tongue."

He leaned forward dangerously. "Promises, High Guard. Let us see its reach."

Fond warmth bloomed within Nin as she looked at Namir's narrowed eyes and Baksis's too obvious disregard.

Kaveh looked down at her strangely, no doubt feeling the emotion. Nin turned her head to him, and he immediately leaned down so she could whisper in his ear. "They are like Taline and Rone."

"They will knife you in the back as soon as you turn," he murmured back.

She touched Kaveh's wrist. Perhaps. We will see.

When she looked back at the foursome, Simin and Omari were blatantly staring between their touching hands and leaning heads. Simin had that dissecting expression on his face again.

Namir and Baksis continued to snipe at each other, but both kept Kaveh in their line of sight. Like everyone else in the palace, they were undeniably aware of the Shadow Prince's every move.

Omari tilted her head to Nin. "You are a healer, Ninli ul Summora?"

Nin didn't let her surprise show that Omari knew anything about her. "Yes."

"I wonder if you might aid me with a matter that has been vexing me for some time. What poisons are best for califeura potions?" she asked in a polite voice. "I have been having some trouble with them." The girl's eyes were bright and watchful, and Nin found herself wishing that Omari had been chosen for Tehrasi's throne.

"Best for hiding the poison—without using magic?"

The princess was known to have natural purification talents and the Kushite royal family was renowned for their blessing of wells and natural places of power.

"Yes." The princess was catlike in the way she held her head—a petite package of thin limbs and grace. Polite, but also aloof in the way that those born to power and influence naturally held.

"Use betrine, if you want something tasteless—but it comes with the slightest color, so you can't use mixed root in the califeura. Fasia, if you hide the taste with a drop of ginsee. Yoro, if you are under a time constraint, and your mark is naive."

Omari stood silent for a moment, then gave a small smile. "I will try each of those. Thank you."

Baksis motioned to Namir then at Nin. "Forgive the manners of heathens, Mistress Summora. This is High Guard Namir ul Mero of Kush, renowned for her zealous attentiveness and garrulous suspicion."

"You are one to speak, Spymonger." But she turned and gave Nin a short bow of her head.

Namir was sleekness and coiled muscle from the top of the fitted ornamental helmet hiding her hair and crown from view to her feet, barely clad in thin brown leathers. She wore understated layers of high quality clothing that were not outstanding in any individual way but had been woven by a master's hand. One piece of clothing seamlessly folded into the next piece—all in shades matching her dark-brown skin, hair, and eyes. So deliberate was her ensemble at hiding weapons, that Nin bet the woman would cleave a knife through an opponent's chest before the person realized that he was facing a warrior at all.

As opposed to Namir's understated garb, Omari wore two vibrant blue and green scarves overlaying a sandy-gray ensemble beneath. As beautiful as her outer layers were, they were easily shed, if needed. It was a useful and cunning ensemble. Perfect for court, but also without hindrance should fighting be required or camouflage be necessary.

"Namir is Omari's rabid protector," Baksis added.

"I serve at the behest of my queen and the emperor," Namir said in a sharp, controlled voice. "I guard my charge with my own life and soul, here and to the afterlife beyond, am I bound."

Kush was one of the territories that had negotiated with the empire in its earliest days, and in doing so, they were granted their own leadership and had maintained their own legacy. A land of scholars and learning, they had never second-guessed the might of the empire, nor its reach.

They had centuries of outplaying others in political matters and scholarly predictions of the future.

Sher Fehl was said to hold Kush in high regard. Looking at Namir and Omari and the manner in which they held themselves and watched the world around them, Nin wasn't surprised. The emperor prized strength and intelligence. He also prized those who recognized those qualities in others and bowed to him immediately.

Kush was one of the only countries so close to Fehla that had not been given an imperial child as padifehl. The imperial Ersine territories of Kemet to the north and Punt to the south both had imperial children upon their thrones. It was assumed that Omari would be the imperial child to gain the Kush throne, once she came of age—the best option for all. For Kush, it would mean keeping themselves from being eaten from within the empire. And for the emperor, it would mean seeing one of his own weaved into the legacy of a great historical throne.

Kush had understood that which the Carres and Tehrasi had not. They had recognized the growing power of the empire and when the fingers of the empire had stretched into Ersine, they had easily given up their vast desert regions—lands that stretched the entire northern third of the continent—in order to hold onto the more fertile lands in the south of their kingdom. In addition, they had given the emperor a week with the queen, in pursuit of a child to tie them together.

Omari had been a by-product of those negotiations—a bridge and gift.

In their capitulation, they had maintained control of their throne through the promise of a child of their blood ascending. Kush was seen as part of the empire, yet the emperor had kept the empire away from Kush for the most part. Omari's mother still sat Kush's seat and ruled her lands.

"Your guard position is a demotion for one of the high court of Kush. You, a distant cousin to the queen." Baksis swirled his goblet.

"And yet, in no other place is there a continuous knifepoint of decision so important to our country. Spymonger."

Namir and Baksis exchanged looks loaded with antipathy.

Omari tilted her head again at Nin. "Do not worry. They are always this way. It is a sign of respect—for each is a master of their own domain."

"Namir has been Omari's guardian since Omari's birth," Kaveh said to Nin. "Namir assumed her post at thirteen."

She could feel that he respected her, as he did all competent warriors. There was no warmth, but there was respect.

Kaveh turned to Namir. "You argued against Cuipsin's throne?"

"I know what steps come next when the Nightmare of the Empire starts to push farther into Ersine."

Kaveh's emotions remained unchanged. "Nera is pushing for combining territories again, then." The intrigue of the court swirled around the space, as if there were magic in the words as spoken.

"Nera will see all of Ersine under the heel of one of hers. And all of the empire under another. And you as one of her dogs."

"Such redundant plots grow boring," Kaveh said dismissively.

"Take care, Nightmare, to pay attention to the games. Nera will be rid of the emperor before she sees a child not of her womb on the throne."

Baksis curled magic around the space to shut out listening ears. "Heed your own warnings, Namir."

She shook his magic free with a swipe of a gilded hand. Glittering connected rings overlapped her knuckles. The rings were very obviously secondarily used for decoration. Would they produce gusts of wind? Were they hidden spikes?

"For what need I care? Whispers are easily gleaned. Only the Nightmare keeps himself apart from the politics that will see him chained forevermore as the dog of war."

"Perhaps the 'dog' is the only one in the position he actually desires." Baksis's eyes gleamed as he took a drink.

"Then it is you who I should be worried for, Spymonger. And for Punt and Kush combined beneath your heathen hand." Her eyes glittered. "Kill off a few more padifehls, and you can have the whole of Ersine beneath your boot."

"You will get your lovely neck disconnected from your body, Namir, before you ever reach Cuipsin's shores."

"Not before I send you to the underworld upon my spear."

Baksis addressed Nin. "Omari and Namir have been fixtures in the palace for the past three years, holding Omari's place between two worlds." He swirled his goblet again. "Fixtures as pleasant of face as they are fierce of hand."

Namir flashed her teeth at him, eyes sparking dangerously. Baksis took a drink, smile hidden behind the rim. Nostalgic and melancholic longing for Rone and Taline swirled in Nin.

Namir would be twenty-four, if she began as guard at thirteen, and Baksis and Simin were older than Kaveh. Twenty-six or seven.

Nin had spent her first nine years circling a poisoned court, but these three had spent two to three times that.

Nin felt tired, suddenly. She looked at Kaveh, who looked back with concern. He hated court, too, so at his side, her future would see little of this.

But she would see plenty of death.

She let her eyes slip closed for a half moment and took a breath. When she reopened them, the pointed banter continued, but there was a charged feeling in the group, and she could see glances that were covered by other actions.

She looked at Kaveh again. He was still looking at her, his body tilted just the slightest bit as if he wanted to cover her. She smiled at him and a tension loosened across his shoulders. It would be fine.

"I tire, too, of serpent speak," Namir said, head tilted severely but looking at Nin with a thin amount of understanding. "Court never grows beyond tedium."

"Let us move on then," Omari said pleasantly. "There is to be a celebration of the empire tonight. The women of the palace have a bathing area. Let us take your bondmate to the baths. I promise her safety by the vow of my people."

Kaveh looked at Nin, who tilted her head. She would enjoy the time to bathe after long weeks with only cleaning spells. Spells could scrub one perfectly clean, but there was something special to the relaxation of a warm bath.

She touched his arm. "I will see you soon."

KAVEH

He watched her go. Her calm, steady steps blending with Namir's more precise ones and Omari's soundless ones.

He hadn't been apart from her for weeks. It was odd watching her walk away from him to go to a place where he couldn't be. But Omari and Namir could be trusted to their vows.

And the oath period was drawing to a close as the time of the dark moon, when she would finally be completely tied to him, drew near. He savored the anticipation of it.

He swirled a shadow around his fingers, and the next thing he knew, he was headed for the tower in the east.

The tower was a wonder of restraining enchantments and spells—layered completely by the emperor's nullifying and locking magic.

Materials and objects from the four corners of the empire remained untouched amid the sumptuous Kemet velvet, patterned Loran silk, and Fehlan gold threads weaved by Bahran hands into multi-layered strands of spilled gilt waterfall blankets.

And inside the space stood his all-powerful mother, living in her beautiful cage.

It had been years since he had been to visit. Since she had told him that he would be allowed a longer leash on a too-short chain. She was smaller than he remembered. Her shadows no longer sought escape, making her presence smaller. She was not tamed, but she was...diminished.

Kaveh stared at her, and at the delicate, golden circlet around her wrist.

She stared dispassionately back. He wondered whether she had always been so cold, or whether this golden imprisonment had made her that way.

Perfunctory as his visits had always been, there was something comforting in seeing her again. He would never have used such a word before, but now that he had labeled the emotion when it came to Nin—only ever experienced with Ifret, Irsula, and the emperor before—he could see that it applied.

Irsula, as the only other of his kind, understood a piece of him that no one else ever would, not even Nin. Nin accepted the piece—she sympathized with it—and that was valuable in a way he would never discard, but Irsula was of his kind.

He was a part of her. And something deep within him reflected that understanding.

"Bearer," he said.

She tilted her head in acknowledgment. She used to respond to that with, "Spawn," before she had stopped speaking to him entirely.

She had been contemptuous of being called Mother, even though he had done so when the emperor demanded it. Kaveh had learned quickly, though, that the advice given to him by others in the palace—even the emperor himself—was never the correct advice when it came to the woman who had born him.

Calling her Mother was a thing only to be done outside the room that held her cage, or in the silence of his head.

She looked at him, then focused on the shadow at his throat. Ifret, still and quiet, went as motionless as if Irsula had turned her to stone.

Ifret slid from his shoulders and leaped forward. Irsula bent but the restraining wards shocked them both before contact could be made.

Irsula's lips thinned.

Ifret expanded and a series of shadowed shapes formed in her flesh faster than he could process. Irsula cocked her head in an animalistic way—as if absorbing sensory information unavailable to the rest of the room.

Ifret had never communicated with him in such a way. Then again, he wasn't behind the bars of a cage.

A strange feeling coiled in his gut as Ifret gathered back around his throat, her talons curving into his flesh. He looked back at his mother as she stood in her cage, feral eyes focused entirely on him. He thought of the oath again, and the unusual feeling in the pit of his stomach grew.

No. Nin would be a partner in the oath. She had agreed to the oath. She had chosen this path. Tying Nin to him would not be the same.

This cage of gold and shadows was nothing like Nin's future. He turned abruptly and left the tower.

Unease was the only thing that could follow.

~*~

Kaveh stared at the Fehl Sea breaking against the shore. The imperial palace stood at the highest point of the island and had views of all shores.

The Great Gates of Fehlaka—the entry and exit points for when the emperor wanted to survey his empire—surrounded a henge in front of the palace and were guarded by two dozen men. The emperor's scepter connected to the six gates and, in turn, the six gates were connected to other henges or gate cities that spread their own reaches outward across the entire empire. Parsa, Tehras, Ancyra, Memfi, Krokola, Lisso: each of the six cities maintained a vast array of gates that stretched across the empire, connecting it all together into a web for the emperor to prowl.

With Nin's skills, those connections could spread to every corner of the empire. The six gates could become sixteen, then sixty, then six hundred on Fehlaka—making it the world's greatest hub.

It would be a logistical security nightmare, but with the emperor at the head, little could be worried.

He felt Nin's presence before the door opened and closed softly. She joined him at the window, languid and warm.

"Did you enjoy the baths?"

He knew her answer already, but he found a strange pleasure in sharing conversation with her. Words that didn't need to be said—the type of chatting that he eschewed in others—he wanted with her. He didn't understand it, but he knew its truth.

"Yes. Namir and Omari are lovely."

"They are both competent." He didn't loathe them like he did some of his other siblings and their guards.

"They introduced me to some of the others currently at court."

"Most of the others are useless."

"Most of the imperial children who have been called back are blessed," she corrected.

"Just because one has power doesn't mean that power gets used for anything other than idle pleasure."

She tipped her head at that. "When will we leave?"

"We need to attend the festivities tonight, then we can go."

The emperor never demanded that Kaveh stay for the political games. Other siblings had been made to engage in political escapades. Kaveh didn't need to mince words when he had the ability to silence them completely.

"You wish to be away when the oath breaks?" Her voice was light. She knew he could feel her turmoil.

"Do you wish to be here in the palace?"

"No."

The oath breaking would reveal things that would be hard to speak of. It would be better to learn and cement the new bond before revealing it to others. He nodded. "Then we will be away."

Her eyes softened as they turned to him—liquid brown pools hiding their fire beneath.

He looked at Ninli ul Summora—once Zehra Amanan Carre, beetle princess, small and plain when compared to the eldest princess, stately and brittle.

Fools. All of them.

Here was a woman who was as brutal as he, but in her desire to save instead of to destroy. A woman who was fiery beneath a calm facade. A pretty facade that hid a jewel nearly too beautiful to gaze upon.

She was so warm and so close. He reached out and slid his palm around the nape of her neck, touching the warmth there.

He felt the bond tighten.

Close the remaining distance. Feel that warmth against his lips.

He stared at her, breath coming strangely, like his shadows were whirling in his chest. She stared back, brown eyes heavy with emotion—their real, brutal red bleeding through behind.

His fingers heated and the shadows whirled faster. He pulled her toward him. She leaned in and up.

The door opened. "Your Imperial Highness?"

Kaveh fought the urge to kill the messenger, but Nin had scheduled a servant to remind them of the time. She had said she wanted to arrive early to the festivities—the better to watch each person enter and gauge the relationships.

Kaveh, who had never been to an event before he was absolutely required to appear, held up her hand and motioned toward the door. Her resulting smile was almost worth the messenger still living.

They lounged in a corner of the entertainment hall, seated in two deep chairs. Before them was a table that held a number of games.

Nin's eyes challenged him. He withheld the smile that wanted to escape, lifting the desired board instead.

It wasn't long before he was beating her soundly. "The bath made your mind as slow as your body."

"Heathen." She waved a hand over the carved board that held fewer buckets than the board she would be used to. "You have destroyed a grand game with this terrible design."

"I think you will find that we created the game first." He lifted a fruit from one of many trays offered. He had gotten used to her figstees. He wondered whether this fruit would taste as rich. "And that you were the ones who destroyed it."

"Lies." She lifted the glass stones from her next choice of buckets. "Tehrasi had it first. And there it is played with twelve buckets and two troughs, not this absurd twenty-bucket scenario."

The extra buckets carved into the board made for a twist in strategy that was obviously causing her to survey the board more than she likely usually needed.

He hid his smile as he collected another of her full buckets. "Slow."

"Heathen." But the word flowed warmly through the bond.

She was beautiful.

Squish.

The shock of the juice between his fingers made him look down and blink.

Nin snickered—giving a small peal of merriment—at the crushed fruit wedge between his fingers. "Heathen."

He kept his eyes on her as he ate the wedge slowly—one small seed of juice escaping and the flavor bursting across his tongue and through the bond.

She stopped laughing. She reached up slowly to touch the spot.

At that moment, the emperor strode inside, pulling the force of the room around him as he always did. And like a perfectly aimed arrow, his gaze went straight to Nin's fingers upon Kaveh's chin. The emperor's eyes narrowed, going between the two of them. His gaze fell to the remnants of the fruit in Kaveh's hands, then to the tray. His lips thinned.

Kaveh wiped his fingers on the linen towel next to the platter and straightened. He had never felt like a scolded nursery boy, definitely never when he had been in the nursery. But the only way to identify this feeling was to label it as such.

Five of his siblings wandered in behind the emperor, reminding him of where they were, what they were doing, and who was watching. His thoughts stuttered. Kaveh had never forgotten himself before.

Nera and Etelian, Baksis, Simin, Namir and Omari... Siblings watched him covertly and openly from all areas of the room. Siblings who had benefited from the deaths of the others. Siblings who wanted to perch upon a throne vacated in the past weeks.

Who benefited from the destruction of the gates? Was it a maneuver to slow the empire, or was it a deliberate assault?

Gatemakers were rare.

Osni had taken out all the Carres in one fell swoop. The Barrinis hadn't all died natural deaths either. Groups who didn't like powerful magi who could remake the world tended to hire assassins more often than not.

Kaveh rolled a shadow between his fingers and watched Nin as she contemplated her next move.

At fourteen, he had been a container at his father's side, providing power more than being an active participant in the Battle of Tehrasi, but he had been there when the Carres had been executed. They had all been quite dead. He had seen the fear in the aristocracy's eyes at the deaths of the entire royal family, then the calculation and greed when Etelian was put in charge. The emperor had hoped the responsibility would make Etelian into something more, but mud couldn't be turned into porcelain.

The Carres had been ruthless rulers who had kept a tight grip on their kingdom—both in their own populace and in those they allowed to enter. Rich in resources and magic, the aristocracy had flourished in the highly segregated elitism of the Carres, but they had grown even fatter with power in the advancements brought to them by the open trade borders of the empire. Nin had made certain to point out that the class differences had split even further with the empire allowing the aristocracy to survive and their businesses to flourish in increased trade and opportunity.

The failing gates would be unforgivable to them as well.

Who would benefit? He rolled the shadow between his fingers.

The Carres hadn't been warriors. They had been tricksters. Charlatans with no head for battle. They had wanted their lush existence, sacrifices, and godhood.

They were doomed from the moment Sher Fehl set his sights on them. From the moment Jisarek Carre took Nera ul Fehl as a prize of his godhood, their fate was sealed.

The Carres grabbed what they wanted, forming gates and ripgates to whatever they desired. He had seen it with Nin, though she didn't use it for ill. Her ability to go wherever she desired was a power she held as a matter of course. It was in that ease of grabbing what they wanted and in getting what they desired that the Carres had been doomed. For such a people never looked beyond their desires.

And they were exterminated, down to the last child.

All except...

He lifted his head and looked at Aros, who was being congratulated on the destruction of the assassin's guild. Aros smiled slowly at Kaveh.

"Kaveh?" Nin peered up at him solemnly. "What is it?"

A curl of warmth slid over his unease. She had sensed his disquiet so easily.

"Aros is the envoy who stays and makes nice with the councils and palaces each time we add a new territory." Kaveh already had shadows disrupting any spell that might try to eavesdrop, but he added another to hover around his lips and disrupt anyone from reading them.

Nin nodded in agreement.

"Aros is in place after every attack. He deals with all those left behind. Zenure, Heit, Tyras, Yalendil, and a dozen others in the last moon cycle alone. He was there to clean up all of them. To put deals or threats into place. To touch the gates." Kaveh curled his fingernails into his palm. "Wit and politics."

Nin looked at the glass stone in her hand. He didn't need the bond to tell him that her mind was moving quickly.

"He is the hero today," Kaveh added. "He wiped out the assassin's guild. He has secured the safety of all. Destroying them means none can be questioned."

"Demon eyes and dead dynasties…" Nin murmured. "I thought the pentalayerists meant me. But that would mean…" She glanced quickly across the room then back down at the red glass in her fingers.

He saw the revelation, the automatic denial, followed by the slow, calm acknowledgment.

"Aros has Carre eyes," she said. "Hidden by spell, just like mine. You think he has the scepters? That he took down the gates? That he has been making the others fail further all this time?"

"I think he stole the scepters. I think he replaced them with fakes. And his eyes—easily hidden from birth, just as you have been hiding yours for the last ten years. That he is a gatemaker—it's always been there in the words the emperor won't let him speak aloud."

"You've never seen him use his powers, though."

"No." He moved the shadow between his fingers. "The emperor doesn't allow it. He refuses even to allow Aros's phasing abilities to be publicly shown. But after watching you… The beginnings of the magic that you do—I've seen Aros do the same."

"He has positioned himself in the best possible light. It will be hard to prove ill intent."

Kaveh had never cared how others regarded him—he simply had too much power to care or be affected by another's regard. But Aros traded in the affections and emotions of others. And as Kaveh looked at Nin, he began to understand the power in that.

If something happened to the emperor, and if something happened to Kaveh, Aros was well set to take over.

The likelihood of both those things happening was infinitesimal. Who could destroy either of them, no less both? No one had the power. Not even Nin could destroy him.

So what was Aros's plan?

Aros, Nera, and the emperor were speaking in the corner when the emperor's expression hardened and flew to them.

He could feel Nin's pulse increase. It nearly caused the increase of his own. But there was no need. There was nothing Aros could do to him. And Kaveh would let nothing happen to Nin. "Aros's spinning webs will consume him."

"You need to tell the emperor." He felt Nin's unease, but she took a deep breath and he could feel her focused on the past, the present, the future.

"Aros will expose you if we make such a move."

"I will be exposed anyway." She looked up at him. "I never told anyone about Crelu's ranting. Osni succeeded with his plans because I was trying to shield Farrah. Do not make my mistake."

They watched the emperor motion sharply to Kaveh and Nin and they both rose.

Her hand brushed his sleeve. "I do not want to be anyone's shield or downfall. In two days, all my secrets will be revealed anyway. Save your empire."

He felt some emotion he didn't know how to label rush through him, filling him completely as they headed for the throne room. "Nothing will happen to you. I won't let it."

Kaveh wouldn't let anything happen to Nin.

CHAPTER THIRTY-FOUR
THE GATES OF HOPE AND DESPAIR

RONE

(Approaching Babil, First Layer)

Taline's muttering grew. Light and darkness shot from the scepter in brilliant white-and-black spikes.

The pentalayerists knew they were here. Agents of the empire would be waiting as well.

Rone tightened his hold on Taline and carefully secured the last papyrus seal around her arm, dimming the light show.

He glanced at the misbegotten and cursed seed of Aros ul Fehl. The assassin smiled back.

Death came today.

Rone freed the horse, held Taline curled in his arms, and trudged toward the city of hope and despair.

CHAPTER THIRTY-FIVE
BROKEN STRINGS

NINLI

(THE IMPERIAL PALACE, FEHLAKA)

They followed the emperor into the throne room. The door closed behind, blocking the sounds of merriment from the banquet rooms and sealing the three of them into glittering, cavernous silence.

Nin knew as soon as the emperor turned to her, that something terrible would happen here.

Kaveh sent his shadows to secure the room—a second nature response—and while his shadows spread their wings, the emperor raised his hand to her and tore the spell from her eyes in one, quick, painful yank.

Kaveh, who had never had cause to block one of the emperor's spells, jerked in shock—shadows swirling back around him in surprise.

The emperor didn't look surprised at the revelation of her eyes, but there was an unreadable look on his face as he gazed upon Nin. "Did you think I would not find out, Kaveh?"

"I knew you would," Kaveh said evenly. "That was never in question."

"Why did you say nothing?"

"It was part of the oath." He said it plainly, because for Kaveh, oath was paramount.

"Sehk's shadow, the oath! You could have defied the parameters of the oath. Had you wanted, you could have devised a way to let me know." The emperor straightened, brushing down his robes. "But you didn't. And I now understand why." He looked to Nin.

"Parameters do not make it a game." Kaveh frowned. "It was an oath made. And perhaps some of the silencing elements were a mistake, but it by our vows that we stand. She is not at fault."

Kaveh's words incited the emperor, who lost all semblance of calm. "Listen to yourself. She's not at fault? She is completely at fault."

"Aros has gotten to you." Kaveh surveyed the emperor with the composure the emperor had lost. "His words are poison."

"Aros made me see the truth."

"Aros is making a move for the throne." Kaveh gestured to the overly large and gilded chair. "He is behind Rayd's disappearance. He is behind all of the unrest."

The emperor looked at Kaveh with one raised brow. "Show me proof of this, for all I see is the woman next to you spinning lies and implanting suggestions."

"I came to these thoughts on my own."

The emperor's eyes narrowed. "Aros just destroyed the guild that planned to assassinate me. Aros has been in Tehras this whole time. And even he wouldn't kill a child of Nera." The emperor tilted his head. "Of course he wants the throne—three-quarters of my children do. I just promised him control of nearly the entire northern Medit Sea region when you conquer it in the next year. It would be a foolish move to try to grab more before he establishes himself."

Nin noticed he didn't disregard the thought that Aros would move at some point. He just thought that point wasn't now.

"Once he gets the region locked," the emperor said, "then he will be a player in the greater game. He needs the generals on his side, though, and to do that, he needs to show he is worthy. He would be foolish to make a play now, and Aros is little a fool. The generals will never allow his ascension should something happen to me. They will ensure another is placed on the throne instead. At one time, I was certain who that would be, but now..."

"You can leave your empire to whoever you find suitable," Kaveh said coldly and without ire. "It is your empire."

The emperor's expression softened, and she saw the flash of fierce pride directed at his son. "But where is this strength of will when it comes to her? Why have you allowed her any influence over you at all?"

"She is an aid on the battlefield and beyond. The oath has not been a detriment. Aros seeks to sway you."

"He doesn't need to sway me to anything. I can see this bond has weakened you."

"It is a strength." Nin could feel his calculations as he formulated his words to have the most effect. "We have been reinvigorating the gates. It has not been a stroke of fortune or godly intervention that they all work again."

The emperor's eyes glittered. "And we will discuss more of that topic. But your weakness to her cannot be denied. It poisons you."

"Aros and Nera are the poisoners. They will see you dead."

"I can handle both, as always," he said dismissively. "To care about—"

"I care because it puts you in danger. I will protect you from them."

The emperor's eyes softened minutely. And it was in that moment that Nin understood the true peril of her situation. The emperor looked at Kaveh the way Salare had always looked at Savvan, but at none of the rest of her children.

The emperor loved his son.

The emperor turned and looked at her with less angry eyes. "I suppose I can see some of what has seduced you. She has power. And the Carres were noted for the strength of their line. Gatemaking abilities passed to four out of seven of the children—a good output."

"She is the strongest of them."

Her mind rejected the notion. Being strongest had never been her destiny. Savvan had been the strongest and he would have continued to be.

"The Carres sacrificed others as a matter of course in their daily lives." The emperor's mouth lifted. "The Feast of Sustenance and Renewal, more popularly known as the Festival of Blood, was the pride of their line. It would be fitting that a Carre would be sacrificed in the same manner for their one gift to the world—the gates."

"She is wasted as a sacrifice."

"She carries the blood of the Carres. And you heard her own words about the potency of their blood on the scepters. Why would we not sacrifice her?"

"Like we carry your blood?"

The emperor hummed, but his expression lost some of its warmth. "Your words only increase the need to separate you. Though a merging of the lines... Shadow ripgates...?" He looked into the distance, faint smile about his mouth. "Imagine the potential."

"Let me stay with Kaveh then," Nin said. "I will bear him children. They will be powerful and loyal."

Kaveh jerked next to her.

The emperor smiled thinly. "Such speculation of power does not transcend the more emotionally pressing need to separate the two of you." He regarded them through narrowed eyes, then focused on Kaveh. "Someday I may transfer her servitude to you—after I am certain that you will be able to wield her power without regard for her—after I have remade her into something that can be used. I can't have her distracting my general, but I won't let her abilities go to waste."

"I will aid you with the gates," Nin said. "Without issue."

The empire hadn't created a demand for gatemakers. The demand had always been there and Tehrasi had always capitalized upon it. With a warlord of a power to raze countries—and a person who could move them at will between places—the emperor would be completely unstoppable.

Kaveh had long known it. He had made his desires for them working together clear. With Nin, Kaveh would be unstoppable and the empire along with him.

The emperor was cunning and clever, and he would know this instantly. Which meant that he thought her influence over Kaveh more a threat than her powers a boon. His words underscored that.

"Oh, you will do more than that," the emperor mused. "And you will get used to your new position in the empire, as you have your position with Kaveh."

Nin closed her eyes. Her cage had never been clearer. But this time, instead of the shadows she had come to embrace, the cage swirled with emptiness.

Kaveh's breath hitched, as if she had cast the image into his mind as well. "Your Im—"

"It is not that I deny your brilliant find, Kaveh. If it weren't for your attachment, I would celebrate with ease. She has power that we can use. She will aid our cause."

"And she will be mine in two days' time," Kaveh asserted. "The oath—"

"No."

Kaveh's fists clenched. "What did you promise Aros? Did he tell you that if you gave her to him, she would be able to hide his Carre bloo—"

"Silence!" the emperor roared. "She has truly poisoned you, if you see enemies in all of us. If you say such things. I will not give her to Aros. I am not ignorant of Aros's goals. But he will be overrun with padifehl duties soon. I cannot be killed by him and neither can you. His oath precludes it. He is a nonentity in this discussion."

Nin swallowed at the arrogance.

"They all conspire against you. They see opportunity with the scepters. They see a moment they can claim. They could have divined the secret of how Osni got out of his own oaths. They will see your end. Aros, Nera, even Etelian—"

"Where has my fearless son gone?" the emperor said, gaze intense, emotions furious. "I thought you would be more like your mother, but your emotions are human."

The emperor's expression was complicated. Nin wondered whether the emperor had loved Irsula a little but had gotten nothing in return.

"I am like my mother. And Nin is not afraid of me, even still."

"Not afraid of you? You care?" The emperor leaned back, eyes quick as he reformulated. He regarded him over tapping fingers. "You were never bothered by your caregivers' fear. You were strong already. I handpicked them—frightful and weak. And they made you stronger still. Do not let this woman undo all of who you are."

"She is a strength," Kaveh said.

"Care for others is a weakness. I have well used your loyalty to me, Kaveh, and I treasure that loyalty. But in matters outside of me, I hoped you would care as little for others as your mother does. It is regretful that you have my weakness in this—the weakness of humans. I have made many poor decisions in my weakness for those in our family."

Nin's world tilted a measure. The emperor—

He paced the floor like a frustrated tiger. "Do you think I know not Etelian's faults? Or Nera's? It is my weakness for his mother, my weakness for my own blood, that has stayed my hand regarding his actions both present and past."

He turned sharply and raised a sparking fist at Kaveh. "I wish for you to have none of that bane. I will cure you of this weakness. Make you strong. Make you care for no one—have no one who can hurt you. Make you he who will conquer the world."

And she suddenly understood the emperor. She didn't agree, but she understood. For he loved his son and he wanted him to have none of his own faults.

"Nin will help me conquer the world."

The emperor sighed. "Kaveh."

"Killing her—"

"Would be foolish." The emperor's hand waved. "I will take her myself and mold her into what she will become."

Nin tensed and grew cold. Emptiness filled the cage of her mind.

"I do not think—"

"She will be a direct aid to the empire," the emperor interrupted, eyes sharp on Kaveh. "Do you not wish for me to have such aid?"

She didn't require the bond to feel Kaveh's turmoil. He had always wished for a strong empire under the strong rule of the man before them. He also clearly knew the depth of the manipulation present in his father's statement. The emperor wasn't even trying to hide it. He was challenging Kaveh.

The emperor stepped forward. "You are my finest creation. You will be the fierce, dark shadow that creates a new world order. You will outlast me and eclipse all that I've accomplished. I will not have that hindered."

"I fight for you."

"Yes. And you will one day sit on the throne, and for that, I need you to be iron. I need you to have none of these binds of flesh. You will be rid of them now."

It was the first time she had heard the emperor's wish for Kaveh to take the throne spoken aloud. In the halls, in rumors, people speculated who would take the emperor's throne when he died of extremely old age.

The surprise from Kaveh over the bond said that it perhaps had never been spoken aloud. The rest of the bond was consumed with a panic too intense to pierce. Nin wasn't certain she wanted to know why he had started panicking so hard.

The emperor regarded him calmly. Too calmly, as Sher Fehl pulled himself together. "You care for her." He searched Kaveh for something, then sighed. "It is regrettable. In other circumstances, she would have made an interesting match for you. The children you could produce together... Well, the girl is powerful. Her power will not go to waste."

"The scepter—"

The emperor bared his teeth. "The scepter? Osni betrayed us. Gave our enemies our secrets. Shut the gates that connected our territories, made it so countries can rally and revolt. No matter what the two of you have been doing, it could be so much more. But we can fix this." The emperor took a deep breath. "The girl will power the gates for the empire. The continual blood sacrifice of a Carre. Osni has been coveting limited blood, but with her, we will have a limitless supply. It is fitting, really. We can create grand scepters from her blood—ones without the taint of madness—and key them to our own bloodline."

"If you allow us to hunt down the Scepter of Darkness in two days' time, it—"

"There will be no more talk of an 'us.' You have brought me an alternative solution to the Scepter of Darkness. She will do her duty to the empire, as will you. Your companionship is no more." The emperor's hand sliced through the air. "The empire has to stay united. It is more important than any one person."

"More important than you?"

The emperor looked at him sharply. "Do not allow your emotions to lead you down that path, Kaveh."

Odd feelings swirled along the bond and she forced herself to swallow and continue to stay silent.

Kaveh's expression was remote. "I had thought myself immune, but emotions seem to lead us all."

"And that is why the oath will be destroyed."

"The oath has two days' m—"

"You think I didn't research the Carre oaths after they died? They were secretive with them, but as soon as you—who I know like my own shadow—had such an oath upon you, you think I would not learn all that I could? The Carres were the owners and dominators of all their oaths, so there was little reason for them to ever let one go. But if they desired, if both parties agreed to release the oath, it could be done. And dear Zehra knows how to do it, doesn't she?"

It was the reason Osni had needed to kill Farrah—to use the sacrifice of someone he truly loved in order to break the oath's spell. The Carres would never have let him out of his oath, not even under outside torture. They would have fed the torture through the oath instead. They kept tight oaths on all in the palace. Osni had done the unthinkable, because for him, there had been no other way. The way that was forever shut when one side of the oath was unwilling to let go.

"All she has to do is release the clasp, then you release your individual promises, and the oath is done."

The emperor raised a soundproof barrier before Nin even realized he had moved. The emperor grabbed her arm and leaned down, his mouth hidden from Kaveh's view. "Should you not let the oath go free, I will kill all that you hold dear. I will find each person you have ever crossed paths with or spoken to in the entirety of Tehrasi and have them executed. Do you understand?"

"Yes."

What the emperor didn't understand was that after so many weeks bound, Nin knew not just how the oath worked but how Kaveh worked.

She could put an end to the unbreakable link he had to the emperor if she desired it. If she begged or pleaded—even though it would mean sacrificing all those the emperor would kill on her behalf—she could crack that link. She could shatter Kaveh's bond to his father—the emperor, whom he loved.

Love was sometimes twisted and sometimes fierce—but even the strongest love could be irreparably harmed under certain weights.

Nin could destroy the emperor's bond to his son.

The emperor stepped back and removed the barrier.

"What did you say to her?" Kaveh demanded.

"Nothing but the simple truth," the emperor replied.

She looked calmly at Kaveh. She felt along his emotions, though she didn't need to. She knew he didn't want to break the bond, but the immensity of his panic struck her. Kaveh ul Fehl, steel and shadow, commander of all, was feeling...fear. "It will be okay," she told him.

She could break his bond to his father, but she wouldn't. Those who understood love the least sometimes needed it the most.

She clasped the feel of him to her—the strength, the ruthlessness, the dark humor that was so rarely revealed to others, his care. She touched the imprint of the looking glass nestled beneath the fabric at her waist.

She clasped his mind to hers, left an imprint of tender affection behind, and said good-bye. She wouldn't take away the father he loved and who loved him in return. She straightened her shoulders and let go.

The oath slid its hooks from her—loss—and hovered in the space between them. Loss. Loss. Loss. Nin kept her chin steady and her fingers away from where the ribbon quivered around her wrist.

"Excellent, girl. You are teachable after all."

But the emperor's voice was background noise as she watched Kaveh stare uncomprehendingly at the space where her ribbon shook, then at the released magic ball in front of it. "You, but I—"

"Kaveh," the emperor said sharply. "Undo your side."

He looked up, disbelief written across his face. It was such a human emotion. Her heart ached.

"I agreed to this oath, Father. I am oath-bound by this, on my duty as an imperial agent. You are asking me to reject an oath that I've sworn."

The emperor's gaze narrowed, and he grabbed Kaveh's banded wrist, magic swirling over his eyes. "You tied it to your imperial oaths?" There was a mix of pride and aggravation in the emperor's gaze, and intense, fatherly love. "You are thorough, and your loyalty is unparalleled. I cannot fault you for this. I will do this for you, then."

The emperor pressed his finger to Kaveh's forehead. "Your imperial oaths are done."

She felt it—just for that last split second of time before the bond died—Kaveh's magnified shock and his feeling of utter loss as every imperial oath he had ever sworn fell from him.

Their ribbons slipped to the floor.

She closed her eyes and knew only sorrow.

KAVEH

Kaveh stared at the ribbons coiled like disregarded string upon the floor. He knelt and lifted his.

He felt...cold. It was an old emotion. It was the absence of warmth and vibrant spirit. Of calm resilience.

"You will thank me some day, Kaveh. It will be neither today, nor tomorrow. But this will be but a cautionary moment in a blink of time and you will feel relief." The emperor squeezed his shoulder. "You are my son, and I will do what is needed to secure your future."

A great wave of imperial decree echoed through the palace. Kaveh could only feel the decree in the ghost of his broken imperial bond.

He felt cold to his core. It was a bond that was no longer there, like the bond to Nin. Nothing remained. No bonds. He held an empty ribbon, but nothing else in his hands. No link to anything.

Those who had gathered in the palace filed into the throne room, implacably called by the emperor. And the emperor was speaking, but it all seemed muddled, like words spoken underwater—hard to understand.

"Rejoice, for the Carre line is not extinct. I present to you, the youngest of their line. Kaveh found her for us," the emperor said, benevolence in his voice once more. "Raise your head, girl."

Gasps flew around the room, as did excitement. "Red eyes!"

Blood red. His favorite color. Yet he couldn't look away from the white ribbon in his hand.

"A solution to the gates!"

"The reason that the empire has been renewed!"

"The gates are saved."

"Do you bind me now or later, Your Imperial Majesty?"

Kaveh finally looked up. Nin stared at the emperor, blazing red gaze overly calm.

"You have potential, girl. I see how you ensnared him." The emperor's words were for their ears only. He motioned and gold cuffs wrapped around her wrists. "These will be synchronized to your cage and keeper. There is no oath given on your end. Not for an oathbreaker. You will regret any attempt at their removal."

Kaveh stared at the delicate, golden circlets about Nin's wrists. He looked at her face—already diminished of hope. Her open, curious expression, and tentative trust were shuttered and closed by resignation. He couldn't feel a single emotion from her, yet he knew all of them.

He couldn't remember how he took the steps that separated them. Only that, with a thousand battles fought in his past, his heart had never beat this fast, nor his state been so tumultuous.

The room went still and on edge—like the knifepoint moment before he struck in battle.

He crouched and lifted Nin's ribbon from the floor, then rose and offered it forward.

Her breath hitched, then her fingers shot out and curled around his, hiding them against her chest and away from the rest of the room. "It will be okay, Kaveh," she murmured. "It's going to be fine. You will be fine." She tried to tug the ribbon free.

He couldn't seem to make himself let go. He stared at the gold circlets around her wrists.

"Kaveh." Her voice cracked and she tugged her ribbon from his hand. "Be free."

Live, my beetle. Be finally free.

He could hear her handmaiden's voice—a memory stolen from her mind.

The emperor was speaking again, but it was lost in the wash of a raging river.

Was this...it?

Was this what he was born for? Was this his future?

"And we will continue our glory—"

Was this hers?

Was she a sacrifice? To her family? To her country? To him? To the empire?

Was that all she was allowed to be?

"Sometimes I wallow and forget my fortunes."

"You were raised by bloodthirsty ghouls, given brain damage, then forced to live in poverty."

"No. I was raised by a cadre of servants who were kind in their sharpness and fear. And I became...free. I achieved freedom, for a little w hile."

He looked at her fingers clutching the ribbon, fingers which had held a figstee against her lips a mere hour before. He looked at the broken ribbon in his hand. He felt the absence of her emotions, so vibrant and warm, in the dark pit of his soul.

I achieved freedom, for a little while.

A hole. There was a hole in him where she used to be.

"How will she fix the gates? Bloodletting?"

She wouldn't die. They would continue to use her to relight the empire. Not aid given freely, though. Taken. Taken from her as was due the might of the empire.

"What happens to the people when their governors do not care?"

"I think that if we do nothing, we lose everything."

"The weak must be shown how to be strong."

"You are more than your birth."

He looked at Nin.

He looked at the emperor.

He looked at Aros standing behind Etelian, eyes gleaming with victory, gaze hungry as he looked at Nin.

The emperor motioned. "Hold her while I—"

It looked like the emperor was motioning to Baksis, but Etelian stumbled forward and grabbed Nin's right arm—where the white band used to be. Kaveh's gaze snapped to Etelian's hand. The room swirled strangely.

Darkness fell to the floor in a hundred black strips. "No."

"Kaveh, what are—?"

"**No**." The black strips rose, unhindered by any oath, severing everything in their path as they encompassed Kaveh, Nin, and Etelian, and brutally shoved away all else.

"Nera, Aros, Baksis, move. Eteli—"

But Kaveh had already ripped Etelian's fingers from Nin's arm—three brutally pulled free of Etelian's hand—and wrapped his own hand around Etelian's neck. "You don't touch her." He squeezed. "You don't ever touch her."

"Kaveh!"

"I'll kill you," Kaveh promised. He had promised.

The emperor was yelling. Nera was yelling. Etelian was gurgling, his windpipe strangling beneath Kaveh's fingers in a satisfied series of crunches, his half-stump of a two-fingered hand gushing red like Nin's eyes on the unyielding marble floor. Darkness was closing in like a prison of unending night.

"I promise you a terrible death, Etelian ul Fehl." His fingers clutched. "No one will miss you."

"Kaveh!"

Etelian's throat shattered beneath his hands. Nin's soft fingers were wrapping around Kaveh's wrist, the gold bracelets jangling abhorrently.

"Pierce the spaces in the cage! Heal him! Heal him, quickly!" Nera shrieked. "He didn't use a shadow to kill him. So he can be h—"

Ah, she was correct. Etelian could be resurrected and healed. A mistake Kaveh would rectify. He called upon the shadows closing in around them and the ones gathering along the ceiling in an apocalyptic wave.

Kaveh felt the pull of the emperor's magic. He felt the magic try to grab the imperial oaths that were no longer in place.

"You disengaged those, Your Imperial Majesty," he said, separated completely from any normal feelings. "Don't you remember?"

A null spot broke through the cage, indicating a weak point in its construction. But Kaveh had fixed the cage against Nin's magic. He could fix it against the emperor's magic, too.

He turned to do exactly that.

Hands pulled Etelian away while he turned—multiple Level Nine blessed siblings working together through the opened spot as Kaveh concentrated on the emperor. He let them remove the body. He would make sure Etelian would never draw breath later. He had promised.

He had no oath in place anymore, but he had his word.

He looked at the emperor. "You won't put her in a cage."

"Kaveh!" the emperor hissed. "Kaveh, stand down!"

"I won't allow it." Shadows shot in all directions and the room echoed with screams of terror. "You will remove those bracelets."

"Kaveh!"

There was a twist of magic and a moment—a single moment—where Kaveh could have sliced through the emperor's offensive move and pierced him through instead.

But Kaveh stuttered at that—at the thought of killing his father. He had never faltered at taking a life, but taking the emperor's....

The emperor's magic washed over him. Magic flew from the emperor in an overwhelming arc of power, and Kaveh's powers pulled from his grasp.

Kaveh's power flowed around the emperor, then disappeared with a crack into smoke, then air. His ability to access magic was now gone—locked behind an impenetrable wall only one man could access.

The emperor looked almost as shocked as Kaveh felt. The faces around them blurred in a brutal composite of shock, thrill, and terror. It was only the second time the emperor had ever taken his abilities, and never had it been done in front of others.

Half-murmured curses and prayers sputtered from all corners of the room.

To them, Kaveh had never been punished, or even negatively questioned. Kaveh had never questioned the emperor in front of others or gone against one of his directives.

Ifret slid to the floor—like his oath ribbon—as if the cessation of magic in her magi had rendered her unable to connect to him anymore. She flailed helplessly, painfully, on the floor for a moment, then shot off, disappearing through a shadow gate in the wall.

Pain. Loss.

Kaveh saw Aros smile, then touch the amulet he held.

Etelian laughed through his half-healed throat, splayed across the floor post-revival. "Abandoned by his own familiar," Etelian croaked, smug grin riding his mouth above his ruined throat. "How embarrassing. You are nothing now."

"Be quiet." The emperor held up a hand and Etelian's reconnected fingers squirmed uselessly at his ruined throat.

Not even Nera said a word as the emperor punished Etelian. Death awaited whoever spoke. Shock was turning to absolute fury on the emperor's face, and the whole room seemed to draw back instinctively.

The emperor swung on Nin. "Ruined. You ruined him," the emperor spit.

Because this would spread—this punishment. The reputation of the Imperator General who the emperor lauded above all others would be dented.

"You are wrong. He is not ruined." Nin's voice was strong and fierce beneath a too-calm veneer. "He will be greater than you. The goal that all should want for their children. He will surpass you."

She fell to the floor beside Kaveh, fingers gripping her own throat. He couldn't feel her pain—not anymore—but the ghost of it was agonizing. He was numb to what was happening inside himself, but the ghostly thread that was still connected made him reach for her automatically.

He had made a promise.

His fingers grazed her arm, then she was gone as the emperor cast her across the floor before

Kaveh could touch her further. She landed like a ragdoll on the other side of the room.

Kaveh moved, but magic wrapped around him. Kaveh looked to the source of the constraint. Simin's eyes were full of regret and an acceptance that came with knowing that Kaveh would kill him when he was powered again.

Kaveh's fingers curled into fists and he stared, waiting to wake from what nightmare world he was currently within.

"He was already going to be greater," the emperor spit. "He was going to conquer the world. Securing a Fehl legacy for millennia."

The emperor's anger pierced Kaveh's numbness—the emperor's disappointment was a knife to the chest, worse even than the loss of his power. But the feeling of disappointment paled next to the agony of seeing Nin lying on the floor, gold cuffs wrapped around her wrists. Waiting to watch her be tortured.

Worse, for he had seen what happened to those whose magic was removed before they were tortured. For someone who relied on her healing to such great extent, she would suffer doubly without. And if the emperor left it too long—for some, their reason for living drained right along with their magic.

"Don't." He got the one word out.

The emperor crouched before him and pulled shaking fingers along Kaveh's cheek. "I will return your powers, Kaveh. When I know you can again be reasonable. When she's gone from your mind."

Gone from his mind? Was that even possible?

The emperor's expression firmed. "She has to be punished to an extent that no one will ever try to do such to you again."

"Father—"

The emperor's hand touched the crown of his head in a way that he hadn't since Kaveh was a child and the only touch allowed had been that hand upon his head. "I will fix this for you, Kaveh." The emperor's voice was gentle. "You will be strong again."

The emperor stood and held his hand toward Nin's form. Her body was dragged swiftly across the floor to stop at his feet once more.

Kaveh gathered every last strength in his body but Simin's spell kept him firmly in place. No.

"You will wish for death, Ninli ul Summora," the emperor said. "And I will be the one to grant it."

Kaveh tried to move. Tried to cast shadow. Tried to give his fury and rage physical form as the emperor's spell lit.

Powerless. Kaveh struggled against bonds that would never have held him before. He was powerless.

As the spell lit, Nin wasn't looking at her doom. She was looking at Kaveh, and her eyes were full of gentle entreaty.

Be free. Be well.

Light consumed all.

CHAPTER THIRTY-SIX

WHEN IT ALL ENDS

RONE

(BABIL, FIRST LAYER)

Babil was a city of immense glory in every layer. Stone columns and walls stretched as far as the eye could see. From a high vantage point, the palm gardens formed magnificent squares—grids of green alongside the immense stonework and beautifully colored designs.

Taline was curled against his chest—no spells to lighten or help either of them in this cursed non-magic world. It was both blessing and curse. A blessing because, as she currently was, Taline couldn't have held out against the scepter this long in the magic world. A curse, for they were without the tools upon which they relied.

No enchanted objects flew here, no magic lit the air, and no otherworldly animals manned the skies, but Babil in the non-magic layer was an extraordinary sight, nonetheless. Fabrics and banners were arrayed in dizzying displays, plants and flowers dripped from all heights, and the non-magic world screamed with the technology and textiles that they laboriously crafted by hand.

Heavy columns and arches led to the temple in the middle of it all. The tiered structure was heavily guarded and would contain multiple priests and adherents inside. Furthermore, the pentalayerists had a guild house in Babil. In no situation would Rone have planned to come here with the Scepter of Darkness.

Once they entered the city, they would need to gain access to the temple.

Once they entered the temple, they would then need to pass through the chamber of gates that would be guarded by dozens of men.

Once through the appropriate gate, they would be in their own layer's temple, where guards stood with full access to magic and the ability to make them both bug smears against khursifa threads.

None of the larger towns could be approached surreptitiously, but Babil was one of the most fortified. Both sides of the life-giving river were protected with high walls and buildings, and the non-western sides of the walled main city bared labyrinthine expanses of structures and housing, then fields and sparser settlements beyond.

He looked at the rising sun. It was a good day to die.

He carefully folded Taline into a hand cart and covered her with a coarse blanket. A drooping hat shaded Rone's hair and features from view so that he would look like a simple day laborer bringing his items to the city.

He lifted the handles of the cart and walked onto the single bridge that crossed into the city from the western side. He set foot on the stonework and joined the crossing droves scuffling in weary step. The flow of traffic slowed to a trickle in the middle of the grand stone bridge.

"Again? Ridiculous." A man to his left scoffed. "We've been checked like this for half a full cycle of the moon. I tire of my fruit being bruised by rough hands."

Rone followed the man's gaze to the city gate, where the guards were rifling through the carts they had stopped.

It wasn't difficult to surmise the circumstances, given the dates. Their arrival to the non-magic world had caused the start of the searches. Soon after the pentalayerists' defeat at the temple and the release of the scepter back into the working world, they had likely implemented such caution. Babil was a threshhold from one layer to another. Determined to prevent the non-magic world from infection, they were zealous in their plans.

They weren't the only one who could claim zeal, however. Rone dropped small squares of papyrus as he walked.

He touched the guard's bare wrist as the man lifted the blanket, then slipped a square into the belt of his uniform. The man looked at Taline wrapped inside—looking like a sleeping princess out of legend, but for the dark circles under her eyes and the too-slender frame wrought from sickness. Rone had wrapped the scepter just before he had placed her inside, but not wanting to be hidden or ignored, the scepter had already started burning through the cloth.

The guard reached for Taline.

"Do you need to check each fig and prune?" Rone demanded.

The guard hesitated, gaze going misty, then he dropped the blanket and waved Rone through. "You may go."

Rone casually lifted the cart's handles and continued through the great arch that guarded the entrance to the city.

In their world, such an arch would have gate magic attached. Even in this non-magic version of their Babil, he could feel the frisson of it—the stones' knowledge that something was missing.

"Eyes of blood," Taline's voice garbled from his cart.

A few people cast strange glances at his cart, then at him. Rone smiled tightly and activated the first spell in the papers. The crowd's eyes grew hazy and focused forward.

The temple in the center of the city rose high in the air—a feat of engineering that, like the great arch, held the faintest touch of magic in its stones, even now.

Under the dominion of the empire that had been expanding in the non-magic world, Babil had continued to be a city of prominence—still capital to the territory and the heart of the cultural world with its science, art, and music.

He maneuvered his cart around elites dressed in fine linens and through unkempt day laborers. He pushed through gardens spewing with colorful flowers and greenery. If their situation was not so dire, he might have enjoyed their beauty. In their layer, the gardens were imbued with magic, vegetation hanging from all crevices and climbing against the forces of nature that held objects to the earth.

But non-magic civilizations who considered magic a myth still tried to recreate times lost to legend. Or legends lost to time, like in the large mural they passed depicting the Eternal Spring and Pitcher of Life. A previous ruler here had done a marvelous job at replicating Babil's gardens, and perhaps, at another time, he would marvel at the riotous colors of the flowers and mosaics and wonder how this, too, could not compete with the beauty of the woman he aided.

He let more papyri slips drop.

A wraith of dark shade followed. Aros ul Fehl's unavowed son had been trained in the art of stealth that could be subtly aided by enchantment.

Rone tucked the cart into a plant-filled corner and waited. The assassin slipped from view, disappearing like a spider up and over the temple's stone steps. The Second Scepter of Tehras was nowhere in sight.

Risk. He knew this song.

There were multiple entrances to the temple, and each was guarded. Rone checked that everything was in order, took a steadying breath, hiked Taline over his back to rest against his shoulder and clicked the device in his hand to activate the second set of spells.

Ten booms exploded from the direction of the bridge, and another two from the arch to their south.

The guard stationed outside the north entrance ran toward the sound. Rone used the diversion to slip through the street and inside the temple.

Magic teased from all corners.

Babil was one of the few spots that still had open gates to other layers. The pentalayerists used them as thoroughfares through the layers—to clean up after magi and creatures who didn't belong and to assure that magic and anything "other" remained myth.

A puff of smoke burst through the chamber of gates, overwhelming a dozen guards as the assassin released a smoke bomb, allowing Rone and Taline to enter.

Now they would have to go through the gate to their own layer's temple—where they would be greeted by dozens of men with magic.

The pentalayerist leader stepped in front of the gate. "Did you think it would be so easy, Rone ul Valeran? To release a scourge upon the world?" He pointed at Taline.

"Our meanings of scourge are quite different."
He let the last papers drop from his sleeve into
his palm. "Hold tight, narsumina," he whispered.

"You fool," the pentalayerist said. "You—"

"You are all fools." Osni stepped into the gate
chamber, as did his remaining beasts. "Hand
over the girl."

"I think not." Rone stepped in a slow circle and
while the pentalayerist leader stood his ground,
Osni paced him. A little to the right, just a bit
more... "But I do thank you for your attendance
today."

Taline's hand tightened around him. The
assassin pounced on Osni, and all stillness
broke. Rone had his seals in hand and he flipped
them in order.

Chaos. Darkness. Burning. Illusion. Death.

They were assassins' tools. And he'd had plenty
of time to sketch them out in the tiny wellsprings
they had been visiting from Birsa's map. In the
tiny springs that went unnoticed in the western
plateaus when there were much bigger spots in
the fertile valley to watch, there was still magic
to be found.

He spun through the fray with Taline attached to his back and pressed illusions against skin with one hand while he stripped gate keys with the other.

The pentalayerist leader went down. The others with him fell. Then Osni was leaping toward Rone and Rone had one illusion card left. He twisted the papyri through his fingers as he twisted his body to the right and attached the illusion to Osni's cheek as he sailed by.

Osni gave a pained shout and crumpled.

Rone, the assassin, and Taline were the only ones left standing.

"See something pleasant?" Rone said to Osni with a hum, toeing the fallen man in the side, then bending down to tie his hands, while balancing Taline on his bent back. "Nightmares are terrible when they are turned against you."

And he had collected those nightmares from Ninli—visions of Osni's wife as she had looked in death. Osni was on the ground, staring at nothing, pupils blown. Cruel triumph curled as Rone reached out and jabbed the man's cheek so he stared up at him.

"Goodness." Rone rose and brushed dust from his sleeve with the hand not securing Taline. "That memory must be unpleasant."

"Where did you—" Pain shattered Osni's expression. "How?"

Rone hunched down next to him, keeping Taline's weight still on his back. "Never celebrate too early. You never know who might be waiting in the wings."

"Who?" Osni asked, voice wretched. "One of the Carres survived. Who was it?"

Rone smiled and didn't answer. Taline stirred over his back.

Osni looked at Taline, still wrapped around him—and Osni wasn't a stupid man. Rone saw knowledge bloom. "Zehra. It's the girl acting as sister."

Rone cocked his head. "Why did you never kill Aros ul Fehl or Nera?" It had been something he had long wondered, and he knew Ninli had wondered it, too.

The assassin twitched where he was hitched to the side wall.

Osni's eyes narrowed as he looked to the assassin. "They did well to hide you from me, but I don't think it was me they were hiding you from." Osni stiffened as the memory illusion gripped him again and the subtle suggestion for truth took hold. His voice turned harsh. "The emperor is not easily trifled with. He understood what happened immediately, though he couldn't prove it. But he understood my vengeance and its roots. When he took my hand, he embedded an unbreakable oath in the clay. If I attempt harm on any of Nera's blood, I will die painfully."

Rone tilted his head. "Why not die, then? Surely you have a wish of death?"

"Rich, coming from you." Osni closed his eyes. "An attempt is not a success. And a single attempt claims my life. I have to get them all at once—like I did with the Carres. One chance." He opened his eyes again. "I've almost broken that vow many times, though, wanting to put my fingers around Etelian's neck."

"It's been ten years."

"That's the thing about selling one's humanity... Other pursuits start to occupy one's thoughts. Resurrection, immortality."

"Foolishness."

Osni smiled, his locket slipping into the curve of his neck. "You are a king among fools, are you not?"

Taline pushed herself from Rone's back. Crouched as he was, it was less difficult.

Taline ripped the locket from Osni's throat. Crelu ul Osni made a strangled noise.

"Farrah's hair?" Taline said in a far too offhanded way. "Did you strip it from her when you killed her?"

Osni stopped struggling—going as still as death. Taline stared at him. Sweat matted the hair to her face.

Still beautiful.

As long as he got her to Ninli, it would all be well. He carefully reached out to gesture at the gate.

Osni's gaze switched back to Rone. "She will kill you, just as I killed the one I loved ten years' past. She will never survive wielding that scepter."

"And yet look at how well she's survived. She's barely mad. Perhaps you are just weak."

Osni's eyes flashed. Then they turned crafty and he turned back to Taline. "I know you. I remember you in the palace, in Etelian's care. You can get your revenge. You can end Nera's line. All of them are poison. All of them—"

The assassin tried to shoot the scepter from Taline's hand, but Rone was there, pushing back. This had not been part of the plan—the assassin was supposed to provide use further down the line—but plans changed.

Rone opened his hand, fitted with a small, enchanted mirror, refocused the blast. Only spidered reflexes saved the assassin, although half of his face shield was blown free.

"And here I thought we had a deal," Rone said coldly. "Interesting, your sudden change with the topic at hand."

"He wants to kill my father," the assassin hissed. "He wants to stop the new world order from coming forth."

"I've had enough new world orders, thanks." Rone twisted the mirror in feigned negligence, anticipating the next strike.

"But I want the same as you, Valeran—castoffs that we are—I want an empire free of lies." The assassin's scarred expression was fierce. "One that cares less for birth and power and more for action."

"You want to save Etelian?"

"Etelian can rot. All men who spread their seed can rot. The emperor. Etelian. The other padifehls of the empire." He bared his teeth. "Those in power want things that those without don't want to give."

It was like looking at a Ninli or Taline who had been militarized and broken.

He almost looked like Ninli, and something heavy settled in Rone's chest. It was as if someone had taken Ninli's features and stretched and contorted them onto a younger, masculine face.

"Was it the emperor who slated you for death?" Osni said. "Or did Nera do that to you in order to save her sec—"

The assassin whirled and only Rone's mirror saved Osni's leg.

"Silence! You will die with the rest!"

"You—" Taline took a deep breath, where she was hunched and sweating. "You stay silent, too."

"Look at the strength in you, Taline ul Summora. Valeran is right." Osni's pleas changed in tenor, as if he suddenly saw an even better plan unfold before him. "You can exact your revenge. For yourself, your sister. End all of Nera's blood. The emperor's, too. At the end, I will kneel before the woman you call your sister and she can have her revenge."

"Mmmm, no." Rone toed Osni's face to the side and gave a little kick against the nightmare glyph so it took hold once more. "I think it's time to return home, don't you think so, narsumina?"

"Rone ul Valeran—"

"You," Rone pointed at the assassin, "will stop speaking or you will join them."

The boy slid into a crouch, but nodded.

Rone made certain to keep the boy in view—he still had a scepter stowed somewhere—as Rone sorted carefully through the farhanies he had stripped from the bodies of the fallen soldiers back in the Temple of Darkness in their layer and the gate keys he had been gathering here. They would still need to fight, but they'd have the element of surprise.

He toed the fallen coins from the offering plates that were now strewn about the floor and stashed them into his pocket, never taking his true attention away from the boy assassin or any of the seemingly unconscious bodies surrounding them.

Taline gave a huff of a laugh. "Thieving, Valeran?"

"Never know when you might need something."

"Like those farhanies?"

"I'm returning these lovely identification cards to where they belong—our layer. Honestly, narsumina."

She smiled and held out her hand. "You have done well."

He licked his lips and took a breath, then carefully took her hand. Things never went well for Rone.

A powerful pulse of something swept through the chamber and Taline jerked out of his grasp. The unearthly breeze passed between Taline, the scepter, and the gate. Her expression went distant, then dark.

No. No, no, no.

"The oath is gone," she said, voice removed. "Do you not feel it?"

He swore and reached for her. "Taline. Don't do anything stupid." He had felt none of the dispersal that she had. But he had known for a long time that he was no longer part of the oath.

"No? Then you were truly removed from the oath." She cocked her head, as if listening to a song in the distance. "You could have left at any time."

He could have left as soon as she had slipped from his sight at the temple. He could have been long gone from this forsaken mission. He looked at Taline and the way her long hair lifted with the force of power swirling around her, illuminating her with immense power and the vast light of her heart—showing the struggle between two indomitable forces.

Leaving her was a missed opportunity he wouldn't lament. "I could have."

"The oath is gone now. Broken. Nin? Show me Nin."

"Taline—"

An illumination—a scene—appeared showing Ninli at the emperor's feet. "You will wish for death, Ninli ul Summora. And I will be the one to grant it." The emperor's fingers lit with the power of nothing.

Rone felt the breath leave his body. He felt ice take its place. "No!" Rone reached for Taline—too late, far too late, and of no use, useless.

Light infused her body, illuminating her like a sun goddess sent to burn the eyes of the wretched.

The assassin reached, grasping, and Rone was tempted for a second. But if there was no more oath upon Nin, what had happened? Someone had ripped it apart early, and it had not been the Shadow Prince.

Rone kicked the assassin across the temple and grabbed Osni by his bound wrists in one fluid motion, then flung himself toward Taline.

Bright light enveloped their three forms.

CHAPTER THIRTY-SEVEN

THE DARK QUEEN

TALINE

(THE IMPERIAL PALACE, FEHLAKA, SECOND LAYER)

Light and darkness—a burst of creation and negation.

Taline saw a room lit with blinding light for a moment, then a heavy wave pulsed.

The scepter expelled the last nullifying magic encasing it in a rush of overwhelming void that spread long fingers of nothing through the grand room of gold with vibrant tapestries of color. The epic power she had used in the non-magic layer would be nothing compared to what she could do now that the scepter was casting off its final chains and connecting to the magic that had birthed it.

When the light cleared, the null space of the non-magic layer could be seen spreading in a rolling wave—as if the scepter was clearing a path before it began to consume.

Bright as starlight on a gilded path, Taline felt more clearheaded than she had in days—weeks. The tableaux around her moved at a pace so slow that it was as if the scepter had slowed time.

In this moment, she existed in the in-between—the Taline she had been and the Taline she would become.

There were thirty ticks of a dial before she would bring about the end of the world in revenge for her sister's pain. She saw the path opening. The destiny, decision, and conclusion. She looked at Rone, who was watching her—not the room—with careful eyes, frozen in motion.

Careful, caring eyes. Had she ever seen such an expression upon his face before? Yes, for days now, it had been present every time she was aware enough to look.

She hooked onto his compassion and held it close as she turned to chart the wave of null power reaching its stretching end. It would backlash upon her in approximately twenty beats of her slowed heart.

Her eyes sought Nin, and finally, finally, she absorbed the sight of her sister. After twenty-four rises and sets of the moon, she was a drink of cool water after days in the desert without.

Caught in the same time dilation as everything else in the room, Nin was the only one other than Rone who knew what the disturbance signified. Taline could see the recognition on Nin's face, as her gaze slowly connected to hers.

Nin's expression was a composition of terrible extremes. Agony, love, gratitude, loss. She looked at Taline with the broken face of a woman who was grateful to see someone she loved one last time, and yet devastated that she was seeing that face at all—for it meant something had gone terribly wrong.

Nin who had tried to save her. Nin who had hoped that she would never see Taline again, stupidly thinking that her sacrifice would protect Taline.

Nin who was restrained at the feet of the emperor.

The Shadow Prince was on the ground to Nin's right, bound by some spell. The emperor's arm was outstretched toward Nin but was now moving toward Taline. She could see the slowed movements as the emperor turned with what would normally be lightning-fast speed to face the new threat in the room. But he was slowed by the scepter's time, shocked by the light and their sudden appearance, far too late to counter her.

Boom.

The null field reached the end of its stretch as the scepter expelled the last constraints placed upon it.

Taline felt the scepter's last exhalation and triumph before the emptying null field began sucking back toward her. Ten beats left.

She looked at her sister again. That Nin had hoped they would not appear was beyond obvious. That she still loved them was equally evident.

Taline switched her gaze to the man on the floor next to Nin, unnaturally held there in a manner she could never have imagined.

Taline remembered what the pentalayerist leader had said about the Shadow Prince: "Soon he will be consumed by his own." She had thought the man meant Kaveh ul Fehl's own shadows. Looking upon the scene now, another interpretation seemed likely.

But then she was left with no more time to think. The magic connected back into her screaming hand and the null field was obliterated in a shower of light and dark sparks.

Overwhelming power flooded her—more physically intense than anything she had ever felt.

Two dozen people in the room took their first moment of freedom to turn and flee—fleeing the remnants of whatever nightmare the null zone had created within them while screams built in their throats.

The dozen players who remained facing her engaged in offensive strikes the moment magic and movement was once more available.

The emperor was the fastest—abnormally fast, already reacting in the time dilation—and she felt the null, iron shackles that Etelian had always tried to imitate form around her wrists.

The shackles unclasped and fell to the ground before they could lock. The scepter spread a halo of light around the two of them and only the emperor's lightning-quick movement of a null void in front of him saved him from death.

Etelian's steel shackles had been able to hold her as she had been, but even the emperor couldn't hold her with the scepter in her hand.

The next time, she would be faster, and he wouldn't escape her blast. She saw the realization on his face and felt deep pleasure.

The scepter's magic spread like water through a desert body, coating the sand of her shape before sinking permanently within.

A few in the room made strikes with assassination tools not of magic's make. Clever, but Rone had done a serious amount of plotting in a layer that by definition allowed no magic, and he easily repelled those who chose to engage, using his overstuffed cache of weapons of non-magic origin while implementing the plans he had made specifically for this event. Whatever those plans were, she wouldn't wait for Nin to suggest it next time; she would invite Rone ul Valeran herself the next time they were going on a mission.

A fleeting smile ached on her face. Thoughts of a future that would never be. The scepter's power crept over her arm like light traveling after a fast-moving cloud had passed overhead.

The last of the fleeing imperials threw themselves through the doors, leaving behind Nin, Taline, Rone, the emperor, an assortment of the most powerful and young of the blessed children, and one High Imperial Majex.

Those who had stayed behind had used their moments between freezing and action in a variety of ways. Two imperial princes stood with enchanted swords in hand and hands outstretched from thrown weapons that Rone had blocked.

Aros ul Fehl stood with a smile, swinging a heavy gold piece on a chain, blood dripping from his hand and exhilaration a blanket about him.

A woman in warrior garb formed a brace around a girl of no more than twelve.

The emperor had formed a shield around himself and the majex.

Kaveh ul Fehl, oddly enough, had grabbed Nin and swung her behind him.

And then there were...the others. Osni, bound at their feet, and the man at the majex's other side—staring back in terror and ruin. Someone had already tried to kill Etelian ul Fehl

Kill, destroy. The scepter sang with glorious intent as it slid its darkness and light along her skin and up her throat. She could. She could end him in one stroke.

She batted away three strikes as she contemplated her move and the scepter sang sweet tales of destruction in her mind. She felt removed from it all—power flooding her like the nectar of the gods.

But a few things were odd enough to demand attention. The Shadow Prince was an immovable figure in front of Nin, and it made Taline cock her head. Why would he save a woman to whom he was no longer bound? Where were his shadows? Why was he waiting to make his move? The scepter read her intent and searched the shadows, but they were all oddly stagnant around him.

Waiting, death, waiting, death comes. She comes.

Was the Shadow Prince planning to unleash a secret assault? His shadow companion was nowhere in sight—though Taline could feel the remnants of the shadowy creature and something far more monstrous in the palace.

Perhaps the Shadow Prince's shadow companion had not survived the temple after all, and she was feeling something else entirely. She knew Rone had planned for the abomination—he had kept up a steady stream of conversation, cool compresses against her forehead, and warm presses of humanity against her neck, as she had writhed and muttered on the dirt of a dozen caves in the non-magic layer.

He continued to fight for her, blocking attacks and barely keeping his skin intact. He would suffer an injury soon.

Cease. The scepter struck the ground. Shockwaves rolled through the palace.

Activity ceased.

Death. She comes.

Taline gripped the edge of sanity tightly.

Rone stepped closer and looked around in the lazy way that held deep focus—mapping out all areas of the room and its many overpowered and dangerous inhabitants. "A bit late to the fete, I see. Already so many gone home to their beds."

"They are marked." Taline gripped the scepter harshly. The scepter's cold heat enveloped her chin, moving up toward her nose. "The scepter has marked them, and they will pay."

"Siran." The name—spoken as a benediction and curse—echoed through the room.

The scepter swallowed her a little more.

Rone put himself between Taline and where the name had originated—blocking her view of the man the scepter promised to destroy. Rone smiled at the room, but he vibrated with tension.

"Ninli, dear, come here. The rest of you stay where you are."

"You are a dead man breathing, Rone ul Valeran," the Shadow Prince said, his voice as dead as his claim. He was still crouched in front of Nin. "You have done this. You have ruined everything. And when she is free, you will die."

Taline turned the scepter on the Shadow Prince. Death.

Nin's hands suddenly gripped the Shadow Prince's arm in a scrambling motion. Gold glinted oddly. "Wait." Nin shouted and tried to move the body far larger than hers. She didn't succeed.

Rone moved a hand to stop the scepter's turn. "One moment more. He'll still be there, marked for death. Ninli, dearest, what are you doing?"

There was something strange about Nin's expression. She was half-hidden behind the Shadow Prince still. And that glint of gold—

"Ro—"

"You think to control this stage, Rone ul Valeran," the emperor said. "You think that you will escape with your life?"

"Not really." He moved his hand in a circular motion, finger lazily extended. "I do have a spelled detonation that will take out anyone with imperial blood in a certain radius, though, starting with Your Imperial Majesty. Terrible, what happened to the Carres."

Somehow, the entire room stiffened even more.

Fools. Thinking such things were no longer possible. The emperor spread such seeds so freely for any who dreamed of genocide.

"You will be obliterated, too," the emperor said, ice in his eyes. But there was interest—pinpointed and fierce.

"An end already being contemplated by some in this room," Rone said negligently. "What need have I for further regard?"

Two of the imperial princes moved a step forward.

"Now, now, boys. What did I say?" Rone twisted his wrist to display a palm box in his hand.

The emperor's face was tight. "Stand back."

"Yes. Do listen to His Imperial Majesty," Rone said in the way that had always caused her to want to throttle him.

"You will die, Rone ul Valeran."

The scepter swung back to Kaveh ul Fehl again. Death.

"I believe you repeat yourself, Shadow Prince—and where are your shadows, Shadow Prince? My breaths just keep coming." Rone waved his free hand in an exaggerated motion, but he seemed to be staring hard at something on Kaveh ul Fehl's head that she couldn't see. A glimmer of something? A shadow?

Nin was shaking her head back and forth at both Rone and Taline. But the call of the scepter had been hard to resist in the non-magic world and it was impossible in the magic world. Death.

It was death. The death of all feeling. Strangled by malice, vengeance, power. Throttled with the need to act upon every emotion as it called to her. Smothered by the overwhelming press to release. To give in. To end the torment.

It was irony. That she had so much power that she needed to suppress it. It was something she had never had to do. She, who had so little, now had so much. And she couldn't use it without consequence.

Gold glinted. And Nin moved just enough for it to show.

The cursed oath ribbon that had been wrapped there was gone. The Shadow Prince was clutching a white ribbon in his hand, but Nin's wrists...glinted gold.

The emperor had locked cuffs upon Nin. Gold cuffs. Slave cuffs.

"Siran."

Glorious death. Taline felt it as the scepter started to devour her mind.

The scepter's cold heat enveloped her eyes, pulling a strange veil upward across her gaze.

She knew, like she had in Ur, that she would be eaten alive by the scepter in the magic world. There was only a terribly short window that could be affected at all.

Sacrifice, planning...

But what mattered was that she loved Nin, Nin was in trouble, and she could save her.

She concentrated her last free motion at breaking the emperor's atrocity. Gold shattered against the ornamental floor, but the utterance of her birth name made her jerk before the magic remnants were wiped clear.

The veil sealed over the vessel.

Triumph. The takeover was complete. The vessel gone.

"Siran. I thought you dead."

The vessel's head turned toward the speaker. A man fair of face and twisted of soul whispered the name again, a covetous, furious expression on his face.

The vessel tilted her head and the scepter rifled through the vessel's memories. A forsaken name, dropped four years ago. But no one would forget the vessel's face. Magic on a farhani all this time had slightly changed the vessel's magical strings. With the magic or farhani removed, identification of the vessel's face of old was easy.

Anger, hatred, terror. The vessel hated and feared this man. The scepter eagerly latched onto the hatred. Malevolence was everywhere in the room, pointed at different places, but it would use the vessel's hatred first and wield malevolence through her. Vessels were always easier to control if decisions were made easy. Pliable. And it was easy to rid the world of the man she hated.

The scepter raised the vessel's hand.

"Kill him later, narsumina," the man next to her murmured. "Etelian is not the most dangerous person in the room. He isn't even the second or third."

The scepter's own hatred poured up its shaft. He was right. It tipped the hand of the vessel toward the man who had just finished speaking beside her. The one who had repeatedly kept it from attaining its glory.

The man stilled. Too late. Through the mouth of the vessel, the scepter forced words the man would understand. "No. More. Papers."

"No," he said, then met the vessel's eyes. "There are no more papers. There is only you."

The scepter lit itself. Death.

No! The vessel's hand swung away, pushed from action deep inside where the vessel had been swallowed.

Stupid vessel! Vessel will be punished.

It sent streaks of fire from the vessel's hands to her feet. It twisted barbed spikes in her toes and pulled the torment harshly back up.

Everything in the vessel lit in excruciating pain. It turned the vessel's hand again.

No. The vessel stopped moving.

Stupid, <u>stupid</u>, vessel.

Fine. We will kill the other first. It moved the vessel's hand toward the man she hated.

The scepter and vessel fought for control.

"I told you what I have in my hand, you stupid woman." The man next to her was speaking to the rest of the room. "How did you manage to live this long, Nera ul Fehl?"

The scepter swallowed the vessel and moved its shoulders.

"Stand back, Nera," the man in too many ornate robes hissed.

"She's going to kill my son!"

"Silence!"

The ornamental woman shrunk back, outrage and fury painting fine features. So much hatred there. The scepter could feast upon it after it was done with the vessel.

"Siran, how dare you defy m—"

Kill him now. Wipe him from existence.

The scepter vibrated in anticipation of such aligning thoughts. This was it. A wielder who would **destroy.** Twisted pleasure wound through its staff. We will rid this world of those who try to hold power over others.

All the vessel needed to do was take this one step. The scepter relinquished the barest amount of control to it.

"Yes." Power lit Taline, running through her in great gulps of power as she stepped forth.

"Narsumina," a voice murmured. Why did the vessel allow him so close? "Don't do this."

"He deserves death. And the emperor, wants to enslave...that girl. He put slave cuffs on her."

"I know. Let's go. Let's leave," he murmured. "Together." He looked over at someone else, then his mouth firmed in displeased lines. "We'll walk right out of here."

"I could fix it all right now, though." She held the scepter in her grip, her hair lifting in an unholy gale—the strands echoing the frailty of humans. "Right now, I could wipe them all from existence. I could fix..." She could fix what? "What she..." Who? "...wanted. Tehrasi would be saved."

Who? What?

Someone had wanted that land to be saved. She remembered the desire, even as the memories swirled in crimson rage. It didn't matter. She knew what she had to do.

"Taline."

She could make it so that no one had to fight on a battlefield anymore. That no one died with a hand outstretched to a loved one. She could force them all to get along. She could make peace.

All she had to do was take this last step, surrender to the scepter, and all would be done.

"Taline," another voice murmured. And she saw a girl with wavy brown hair and scarlet eyes.

Bruised and disheveled, the girl's skin pulsed with soft power that was bound by the lingering touch of some magic. Here was someone with so much power, even temporarily caged. Someone who'd always had power.

And she...Taline, the girl had called her...was someone who'd had so little, but was now overflowing with so much.

The girl stepped forward.

Something in Taline heightened in triumph—the girl would serve the new empire well and they would rule in an endless bloody reign.

An endless bloody reign. She raised her scepter high. She would rule **all**. And red eyes, soft and kind—always so soft and kind rather than cruel and hard—gazed at her and accepted their fate.

One broken moment. For one, broken moment, the future stretched—the dark queen reigning above all. For the Scepter of Darkness had been so named in a breaking of the world as storm clouds gathered in a turbulent sky. And the girl in front of her would serve her queen. She would do nothing but serve the girl who she had saved. She believed in Taline, trusted her; she had made that choice a long time ago.

Triumph turned to terror.

Nin.

"All will be well." Nin walked forward slowly. "It will be well, Taline, whatever happens. Because it will be you."

The scepter vibrated.

Because it will be you.

You. You. You.

You.

The scepter shifted in confusion.

Here where all the magic in the world was available to her. Where anything could be channeled within the object in her hand. Power. She could do anything with it.

Anything.

Anything.

Taline ul Summora, Siran Bey, a thousand other names and faces, but always so little power, always needing tricks and drive to accomplish what others did so effortlessly.

She could be anyone.

Anyone.

Taline gripped the scepter and channeled the power—the immense power that could rend worlds and strip kingdoms bare—she channeled all that power into her palm.

Taline ul Summora.

Desire. Intention. Nerve. Cutting determination. Things that she had honed into the sharpest blades when power had been nothing more than a thing that others had wielded.

NO!

She could be Taline ul Summora.

Taline looked at Nin and opened her palm. The scepter slid from her hand. The hall was silent but for a sharp inhale of Nin's shaking breath and the clank as the scepter hit the marble floor.

Next to her, Rone let out a strangled sound. "Of course," he murmured, strangled voice astonished and exultant. "It's you, after all."

His hands rose abruptly on the end of that statement and he stepped in front of them, shielding them from the flurry of spells suddenly thrown.

But all Taline knew was Nin—Nin, who was wrapping her arms around her—two girls powerless in far different ways who were better together.

"It's going to be okay, Tali. We will be well."

Lies. Comforting lies. But Taline wrapped her arms around her sister and let herself believe.

RONE

Of course she had let the scepter go.

He wanted to drop at the relief, at the disbelief, at the pure Taline-ness of her final act. All that power in her hands, and she had channeled it into freedom.

Rone wanted to rest. He wanted to drink. He wanted to run.

He wanted to stay.

Strength beyond power. Devotion beyond allegiance. Loyalty beyond truth. Family that was forged in fire.

He looked at the man who had contributed half of his birth material. He watched as the emperor lifted the Scepter of Darkness with triumph and disbelief.

And here...here was the end.

Rone took a deep breath. He would die upon his own sword—a more befitting end than he deserved. He would die here, but he would take the rest with him. The girls would survive. Ninli would save Taline.

She always did. Rone was tired of doubting.

The scepter was in the emperor's hand—the bonding magic eagerly sealing to a new wielder. Eager, eager to take a new host—one with so much power—who desired more.

Rone opened pathways long closed and shifted completely in front of the girls. Flexing his arms, he let the power he had never asked for trickle down into his palms. He looked back at Taline, who could barely hold herself up, but who was fighting to stay upright—who would fight for and with her sister to the end. He looked at Ninli, who was clutching her sister, but had placed herself in front of Taline—Ninli would protect her sister until the end.

He looked at the emperor, who was raising his sceptered hand.

If Taline—undeniably diabolical Taline—had dropped the scepter on the scepter's plinth, the world could have been saved.

But that hadn't been possible, not given the circumstances. Instead, she had dropped it to the palace's marble floor, where it had been picked up by another.

And here it was—Rone's worst nightmare—the emperor having the scepter in hand.

A great man. A true conqueror. A man who could unite the world under one banner.

A great man, but not a kind one.

Rone erected a shield over the girls and readied himself for death.

CHAPTER THIRTY-EIGHT
PRIDE AND POWER

SHER FEHL

(The Imperial Palace, Fehlaka—the throne room and seat of power of the Emperor of All He Touches)

It was in his hand. The power.

He could do anything. Fix everything.

Where once there was chaos, he would bring order. Where once there was baseless tradition, he would bring progress. Where once there was poverty, he would bring wealth.

Light and darkness swirled around and within him. The Sunlight Empire would live forever.

No one would be shunned for their powers. Power, in itself, would be all. And the powerful would pull the weak along with them. Society would be stronger; the world would be stronger. The future would be stronger.

Power. The scepter sang in his hand.

Get rid of the weak. Cull them so the strong can become even stronger.

The strong...if the strong were the bottom of society, society would become even greater as a whole.

Don't let the weak hold your dreams back.

The weak infected those of stronger resolve. They were the ones who needed special circumstance—who held back the victors and the powerful.

"Siran, get over here and tend me," Etelian ordered.

Ah, the weakest of his blessed children. A blessing only in Nera's name.

Kill him.

The emperor looked at Etelian to see him pointing a half-mended finger at the previous wielder of the scepter who was hugging the Carre girl.

Kill them both.

"You'll have to tend yourself, Etelian," Sher said. "The previous wielder cannot be allowed to live."

The Carre girl went still.

The emperor smiled. "She is too dangerous."

"She is mine," Etelian spit. Greed and fury painted his features.

Kill him, the scepter whispered.

"She held the scepter. Perhaps a reminder for all is needed," the emperor said casually. "Touching the scepter means death."

Understanding rippled through the room in a satisfying way. His blessed children were, for the most part, exceptional specimens.

"Give her to me to punish."

"You will watch her die and count it as your due."

Etelian opened his mouth again to argue, but Nera's hand pushed him to the floor. His first wife had always been his favorite.

The Valeran spawn stood in front of the two women, casually twirling the line breaker in his palm. "I think not."

"You think you can still use that device to kill all connected to my line?" The emperor was almost amused by this son's over-confidence. "I am ten times more powerful than when you unveiled that trifle. You think I can't just use the scepter and my own power to nullify whatever you are going to do?"

You can, you can. We will do your bidding—anything you bid—all we need is a small piece of your soul.

Valeran looked at him with a fury so cold the magic of his brittle, northern ancestors turned the blood under his skin blue. "You will not touch her."

Blue.... The emperor's eyes narrowed. It was not an illusion or metaphor. Valeran's hands were glowing faintly.

The emperor doubted anyone else could see, but with the scepter enhancing his senses and his own abilities in full force, he saw the blue—a power that would become an all-powerful black once Valeran mastered its use.

The emperor's senses sharpened all at once, breaking free from thoughts of soul death. How—when—? He threw his head back and laughed. "The Valerans are greater deceivers than I had realized."

How glorious. All this time, the Valerans had been hiding so powerful a secret. But no, they had cast this boy aside, too. The emperor narrowed in on him hungrily. He had deceived them as well.

The emperor had perused every known bastard personally. He had marked them visually and mentally for special skills. He remembered this one. He remembered the disappointment.

"Indeed." Rone stared him dead in the eye. "You will let them go."

"And get you instead? A poor trade when I can have all of you."

"You don't know what I'm willing to do."

"I don't need you willing." He wiped the scepter through the air—sending a beam straight at Valeran's chest.

He anticipated where Valeran would move, but Valeran didn't move out of the way of the beam. Instead, as it connected and crushed his ribs, he wiped the power in his hand along the scepter's beam. It traveled up the beam, to the staff itself, then was absorbed within—consumed by a power greater than his.

Valeran's bones broke against the wall on which he was slammed.

"If you think you have the ability to face me, you are years too early, boy."

A colorful, pinned insect, Valeran smiled, blood trickling from one side of his mouth. Triumph shone in his eyes in the way martyrs looked upon the execution block.

The emperor narrowed his eyes, unwillingly unnerved. The Valerans were mentally unstable, and this one reportedly more than most. And perhaps that reputation, too, had been a carefully calculated lie, but there was something in Valeran's two-toned eyes that was unhinged.

When Valeran said nothing more, the emperor's uneasiness grew.

Kill!

The emperor took a deep breath and looked at the all-powerful object in his hand. No. He would have this child in his control. But there were other ways to cause pain. He raised it. "The interesting thing about the scepter at the heart of the Carres is that it comes with certain perks. Like the ability to do things that they claimed the talent of their blood."

He swept the scepter outward and a ripgate opened around Valeran's pinned wall, then flipped the wall section. Fire raged as he flipped again—Valeran appeared once more, gasping and burned from the lava-filled spot he had been flipped to.

The emperor smiled. "It speaks to me, their power."

The darkness and fire in his underestimated spawn's eyes reflected his own. "I know," he said painfully from lips burned by fire. "You have that power now. Taline brought the scepter to you. She has fulfilled the oath. Let her go."

"The oath is broken." The emperor pointed the scepter at the girls. "And the guilty shall be punished."

"Kill her and you will die." Valeran's eyes grew more feverish. Triumphant.

Unease stayed Sher's hand for an extended moment and the scepter sank.

Weakness, master. Don't let the weak hold your dreams back.

It was like a refrain of a memory. Like a statement in a dream. And like that refrain, his own mind answered with equivalence. The weak infected those of stronger resolve. They were the ones who needed special circumstance—who held back the victors and the powerful.

Had...had he had these thoughts already?

They are the right thoughts—that is the reason you think them repeated. Get **rid** of the weak.

Yes. Perhaps that would be for the best.

Make your children even stronger by ridding the world of those who hold them back.

The scepter lifted toward the girls again. They had infected his sons. Made them weak.

Yes! Get rid of them!

He would make certain Kaveh was strong again. Peerless. And Kaveh's throne would be made of steel and shadow. He would rule all.

And he would have his underestimated brother collared under his hand. Peerless.

"You shrink to shade, Your Imperial Majesty."

He looked at who had uttered those incomprehensible words. Kaveh stared back.

Kill him!

The scepter shifted automatically in his hand, but Sher paused. Kill Kaveh? No.

The scepter shifted again and with it so did his thoughts.

Kill the **weakness** in him, it cajoled. Rid him of her.

He looked at the boy—the man—in front of him whose magic was gone, but whose innate confidence still projected power.

"You are being overtaken by its lure, Father." Deep brown eyes connected with his.

The scepter surged in fury, but love surged even more powerfully in the man who still held the reins of his own mind. Father. This son, who had made a single mistake, was still the finest of his creations—the peerless result of determination, victory, and power.

Was it unforgivable that Kaveh had strayed and lost his path because of love? Sher had fallen victim himself, twice.

He pushed the scepter away from Kaveh.

He could forgive Kaveh this weakness they both owned and curse himself for not preventing the pain for his son.

He reached toward Kaveh with his free hand. "You took a path outside of your best interests, but it can be remedied. You brought me the scepter in the end. You were right. And it is time to celebrate a new world."

Movement to the east brought forth steel to Sher's voice. "Touch not the Valeran spawn, Aros."

Aros stepped backward from where he'd been about to stick a dagger in Valeran's neck. His palms extended in submission, gold trinket held with one thumb, blade in the other. "As you wish, Father."

"He will be Kaveh's right hand when he is brought to heel." We will bring him to heel.

"And the gatemaker?" Aros twisted the trinket.

The emperor twirled the scepter. Aros could not have her. That much was plain. And it would be a waste to kill her.

She is dangerous.

Sher pushed the scepter's influence back. Concentrating on Kaveh and his love for his son, it was easier. In anger and fear, he had made a misstep with his favorite child, but the scepter was in his hand now—and Kaveh had ultimately delivered it. He could better figure out how to strip the girl from him.

"The Carre can do nothing for another hour." Even removed, the cuffs left their binding magic behind for a time. He twirled the scepter, watching the light and darkness shift around it. "The power she has over Kaveh must be

814

destroyed. But it would be a waste to kill her before I can make a thousand of her—each with pain tolerances connected to the original. I will drain her of blood. I will make her pay for her family's crimes. I will strip her from his memory."

Yes. We can do that. With your power and ours. We can do that.

The scepter was eager. Biddable. The emperor smiled.

"You will not strip her from my memory." Kaveh's gaze hardened. "You have the scepter. The empire will be unbreakable. You will return my powers and we will discuss what will happen with Nin."

The emperor smiled. The determination and strength that he had cultivated brimmed in his thirteenth blessed child's eyes. Challenge and loyalty mixed—a combination that the emperor celebrated, for in this child, he had always seen the best parts of himself, but with the messiest emotions removed.

And now, Kaveh had found something to fight for.

The emperor hefted the scepter and twirled it. "A challenge?"

"Let power decide."

His favorite kind of fight. "Hasn't power decided?" the emperor said lightly, indicating Kaveh's state.

"I let you bind me, and you know it. Let us spar for real, with that toy in your hand."

The emperor smiled. His child. His favorite. Always. "When I win, will you renounce her?"

"Restore my powers and find out who wins." Kaveh's eyes glittered.

So, too, did his. When he won this match, Kaveh would find someone new. Or he would be broken of the need to find someone at all. He was like the emperor—but with the possibility of being stronger.

Sher's hunger for more, never sated, grew even larger.

"Your Imperial Majesty—" Aros started, and two other voices joined the plea.

"Silence," he ordered sharply.

He twirled the scepter and kept his gaze where it belonged—at the largest threat in the room, even without magic.

"Let us have our fun then, Kaveh." He let fondness slip through for his dark son. "For ownership of the girl's fate."

"Yes." Dark eyes glittered under the ceiling's peri spirit orbs as they circled each other.

"You will cede her fate to me, when I win."

"You will say nothing of her future, when I do."

"The bargain is wrought." The emperor's teeth gleamed brightly. He rotated his wrist, pulling his fingers sinuously through the first part of the unlocking gesture that would return Kaveh's powers.

Concentrated as he was, when Aros stepped forward and knocked his hand off course, he was shocked.

"You are both overpowered fools blinded by the same." Aros flipped open the amulet in his palm and a scepter suddenly appeared in his hand—the Prime Scepter of Tehras.

There was such a vicious look of victory on Aros's features, that the emperor and Kaveh lunged toward him instinctively.

But Aros was gone.

"There's a ripgate inside!" the Carre girl yelled. "The Prime Scepter—"

Kaveh had been right. Of course he had. Sher had been too angry with him, though—too angry with the situation. He had felt his future vision of the empire slipping through his fingers, and he couldn't bear it. And he had always been too easy on the child he had failed to save from the Carres.

Aros appeared across the room with a scarred boy at his side. The boy had a familiar face and the Second Scepter of Tehras in hand.

Aros had stolen the scepters he considered his birthright—and that would be dealt with. He had kept alive the child who had been slated for death at birth. Aros had needed only to wait to be established before he could attempt to have a child who would not look like a Carre. Sher raised the scepter that could reset all others. Aros would regret both choices.

Aros ran a hand along the boy's hair. The boy looked back eagerly. "Close your eyes," Aros whispered. The boy did and Aros held the amulet against the boy's heart and stuck his dagger through both. Shock rippled through Sher even as the scepter perked up in interest.

Sher didn't look at the boy's face as he fell, because the assassin's amulet—like all the ones that had been used in the past weeks against his children—lit with fire and a great evil sucked the air from the room.

Kaveh dove toward Aros.

The air exploded and the palace shook.

He knew that power.

No.

With a swipe of the Scepter of Darkness, Sher Fehl—The Fehl, Emperor of All He Touches—threw Aros toward the wall and watched his past rise upward.

CHAPTER THIRTY-NINE

VENGEANCE IN SHADOW

KAVEH

(Imperial Palace, Fehlaka)

Kaveh's fingers brushed Aros's sleeve as the emperor's swipe sent him careening into a wall. The unknown boy who had been standing next to Aros fell to the floor. Aros disappeared through a ripgate that spit him out on the other side of the room—too far for Kaveh to reach without magic to aid him.

Kaveh truly hated that power when it wasn't on his side. But there were other, far more concerning foes to be concerned with as an immense mass of pulsing power rose.

Kaveh's failed lunge had taken him too far from the center. And as dark clouds overwhelmed the room, Namir flung Omari back and Baksis and Simin dove toward the emperor.

Baksis and Simin went flying to the side of his view and the emperor was ripped from the air in a massive shadowed fist.

"Irsula, no!" the emperor yelled. "Guards—"

But it was too late. Resignation and bitter despair clawed at Kaveh's throat as he fought against the press of shadows that had always answered his call.

The emperor's death had been planned long before this point. Maybe when Ifret had taken flight. Maybe when the person who had engineered this entire farce had waved his golden amulet. Maybe when Kaveh had chosen not to kill a thief in an alley.

A thundercloud of shadows burst into the great room, tendrils of madness and release licking the walls and absorbing the air from the belly of the amulet. A hundred shadows stabbed through the emperor.

The emperor twisted, turning quickly, fingers out, forcing the shadows from his body and flipping out of her grip. The scepter flew in wide arcs, and nullifying magic flew from his other hand as he tried to pin the force of nature fully emerging in front of him. "Irsu—"

Glorious darkness in a massive knot of shadow screamed. Irsula fully emerged, the true dark queen, human figure wrapped in black shadow and nothing else, with a knot of terrifying shades waving behind her—like a hundred dark tails whipping through the air and licking against the walls. Ifret gleamed from one shifting black sleeve of shadow, red eyes glittering.

"The spawn is stripped of all that he is—like you once did to me." Darkness enveloped the room. "And you can cage me no longer."

Screams echoed in the whip of her shadows—screams of terror and agony.

"I was releasing his pow—"

"You dare. You dare take. You dare defy Darkness. You will pay, Sher Fehl, for all that you have wrought."

It was a fight that was twenty-two years in the making, and nothing of it would end well.

His mother cared for nothing but revenge. His father cared for nothing but power. Only one would make it out of the fight.

And Kaveh could do nothing. He could do nothing but wrap the screams of the room around himself instead of the shadows.

No magic answered his call. He had no power to claim.

He was something he had never been in twenty-two years of life.

Powerless.

NINLI

The force of the blow shook the palace and collapsed the frame of the entrance upon three of the guards who were attempting entrance. The ones who had made it through fought toward the emperor without success.

Namir and Omari shuffled the younger imperials behind them, pushing toward the door. As spells flew and chaos reigned, Namir snapped her folded spear into a single, double-edged blade as her sharp eyes watched the crowd for any action against her charges.

Nin pushed Taline out of the path of a beam of light that Etelian aimed her way, then tripped over the debris spilling forth from a fallen pillar. Bloody streaks opened up along her arms as she fell—and she scrambled to get her feet under her and throw herself behind cover. Etelian's retaliatory cutting spell blew a chunk of marble from the pillar at her back.

The emperor and Irsula of Denz battled through the air and Nin ducked just in time to avoid having her head sliced clean from her body in the apocalyptic rage that swirled behind them.

Two forces of nature fought. The emperor, with scepter in hand, cut through Irsula of Denz's shadows with devastating accuracy, only to be forced into her next set of cutting blows.

Anyone other than Kaveh would have been dead in either's first strike.

Nin looked at Kaveh and ached at the look upon his face. The ghost of his emotions were unnecessary windows to the resignation and inner hatred showing clearly upon his face.

Another blast from Etelian cut her pillar in two. She cursed and threw herself toward the next pillar. Rone was fighting two guards near the entrance and was unaware that Aros was stalking him from behind.

Nin threw a chunk of marble at Aros's head. He whirled, but before he could point the Prime Scepter, Taline sliced his wrist and ducked. Etelian's spell hit Aros in the chest.

Aros shot off a rage-filled blast that struck Etelian square in the mouth.

Nin wished she could sigh in relief as his bloodied form dropped, but Nera's rage seemed to transfer completely to Taline.

Sehk.

Nin scrambled to grab anything hand-sized on the ground. Rone turned and held up a hand to deal with Nera. Aros whirled.

The emperor and Irsula whipped through the center, causing all combatants to scramble and throw themselves out of the way or be killed.

"You think that I spent my time thinking of anything other than your death when I was finally unlocked from my cage?" Irsula hissed, unearthing half of the room's remaining pillars with a swipe of her hand.

The emperor blocked them and did nothing to save anyone who fell beneath.

The emperor wielded the scepter as though he had been born with it in his hand. A remarkable man of skill and talent—if he had a few years with the scepter, he would be truly unbeatable. Of course, he would be crippled by its twisted evil long before that, but he would be invincible until it sucked him completely dry.

But now, with the scepter eager to please as it embedded itself deeper within the man with each strike, he was able to wield it with full faculties.

Against another, the emperor would reign supreme. But the woman battling him—born of Darkness itself—had only been beaten once, and she'd had years to plan complete revenge.

The palace crumbled under the weight of their devastating blows—under the repetition of the duel between the two that had happened nine months before Kaveh's birth, but now on a larger, deadlier scale.

Nin wondered. She wondered about the—

"Let's go!" Rone grabbed her arm.

He was covered in injuries and burns, and she could feel Rone's devastated well of magic and Taline's almost complete lack. They were all running on empty for different reasons.

Rone was trying to grab the body of the boy Aros had ritually sacrificed to release Irsula from her cage.

Nin was stuck without magic for however long the emperor's lingering magic lasted. And it didn't matter whether her magic would return in an hour or in ten minutes; this event would be over in twenty breaths more, and they might all be dead by then.

With the strikes being waged in the all-out war between the two unholy combatants, the palace was collapsing around their heads.

From where he had fallen, Aros ul Fehl was watching the end of the fight with manic triumph and a strange agony. Nin could see the eldest prince's curled fingers—burned from the shadows given passage by his hands.

She scrambled to find Kaveh in the chaos. He was kneeling on the ground, uncaring of what was happening around him while watching the fight above. Shadows swirled around him in some sort of protection, but with no attachment to the man at their center.

There was a great, screeching clash. The emperor's sceptered hand thrust forward. Irsula's hands descended.

Kaveh's expression turned bitterly resigned.

In a flurry of shadow and smoke, the scepter—and the hand holding it—dropped from the emperor's wrist.

Detached from the power of the scepter, the emperor was left with only his own powers once more.

The emperor reached his remaining hand toward Kaveh, and the power to re-instill his son's magic began to glow. But Irsula's form grew monstrous behind him and her own hand sharply sliced once more. The emperor's gaze slid between Kaveh and Rone and there was something in his expression—

His eyes bulged, and his fingers fell limp.

A shadow sliced through the air, and with it, Sher Fehl's head went flying.

The emperor's expression froze in death. His body fell to the floor a few paces from his head. Pandemonium reigned. Pillars tumbled, the ceiling crumbled, dust-covered bodies fell amid gold and marble rubble.

Irsula flexed her shadows and screamed her triumph to the heavens.

The ceiling exploded upward.

Kaveh, kneeling on the stones, reached out to touch his father's severed head.

Kaveh.

Only Aros ul Fehl stepped forward in the screaming wreckage—expression rapturous, staring at the mass of dark shadows as Irsula flew into the skies—his hand and forearm striped with shadow burns from the amulet. He touched the burns reverently. "Magnificent."

Reveling in the beauty and majesty of her death-dealing strokes and terror-inducing presence, Aros's expression was also satisfied, vindictive, victorious.

Planned. Planned, all of it.

Blood instinct told Nin to pick up a shard of glass and to rid the world of the eldest prince—to disregard all other avenues of movement. But her body was already moving otherwise. The ceiling was going to crush them all and Nin had no power to prevent it.

Nin grabbed Kaveh by the upper arm and jerked him forward with her momentum, muscles burning as she did.

She dove with him behind Rone and Taline, who opened their hands with the last of their powers to stop the falling pieces from crushing them.

Taline's eyes were heavy and her skin sweating. She looked thinner than Nin remembered. Sickness-induced thinning.

Nin's heart ached but regret was for later. There would be much to regret.

Crelu ul Osni was bound in the corner of the room. He had slid himself to safety amid the carnage. She met his angry gaze, seeing the questions layered within.

She had no time to wonder or to regret that she would not be able to get answers from him. She had no time. Because the emperor was dead, and Aros ul Fehl was lifting the scepter from his dead hand.

The hall shook and a strike of power jolted all who remained.

After a month of being encased within Kaveh's shadows even when she couldn't see them, watching Kaveh take a hit was breath stealing. It was hard for her mind to convert.

She didn't know what she had expected from the outcome of the emperor and the Mistress of Shadows' fight, but Kaveh's loss of magic was...incomprehensible.

Aros strode immediately over to the boy he killed and pointed the scepter at his chest. "Rise."

Marble chunks fell from broken pillars and an eerie silence permeated the space. But nothing rose from the boy's body.

"Rise."

He was trying to resurrect the boy.

"Rise." Pain rippled across his face. "Rise!"

But he wouldn't rise. She had seen this before. She had seen the emptiness of spirit around a body ritually sacrificed. She had seen Farrah's face, which had looked the same.

"Rise!" Aros yelled. The hall shook. People screamed. Then Aros's arm abruptly swung toward Nin and she fell through the floor. She fell through a ripgate that wasn't her own and hit the ground hard ten paces away.

She curled her fingers around the chunk of marble beneath her fractured hand, then looked up at the man above her.

He smiled down at her, gaze eerie and empty. "Hello, cousin."

The emperor was dead, and Aros ul Fehl held the scepter in his hand.

Nin said nothing as she met his gaze.

"I'm quite…angry at the moment, but looking at you returns some amusement." Aros flicked the scepter and Nin found her body dragged alongside him until they stood over the emperor's head. "It's amusing to me, little cousin. The Hand of Tehrasi. The littlest princess, still alive, fulfilling her dead father's prophecy. But really…"

Aros crouched down next to the emperor's head and whispered, "My hand, the hand of Tehrasi, will hold the scepter when your time has come. It is not the hand of the beetle princess that holds the scepter, Father. I hold the scepter. I am the hand of Tehrasi. I, of the blood of the Carres, did indeed hold the scepter when your time came. You should have given Tehrasi to me."

"You are mad," Nin murmured.

Aros's gaze slowly tracked to the body of the boy he had killed. A dark agony swept over his expression—one that reminded her strangely of Osni—before a placid calmness took its place. "It's in the blood, is it not, cousin? And I was always told that blood was everything."

Nin closed her eyes as magic swept over her, physically binding her hands together.

"Do not move. I know you are without magic for another hundred ticks. But we will be having quite a lovely chat soon."

Nin made herself go still in command, even as her heart picked up speed. Hubris. Aros had made a mistake in his triumph and loss. Without moving the front of her body, her fingers swept across the floor, looking for weapon and possibility.

Aros rose. He swept the scepter across the arc of survivors and most scattered back, eyes wide.

"The emperor is dead. Kaveh ul Fehl mortally wounded him before the emperor managed to seal his magic."

"But—"

The scepter sparked. The guard who had spoken was dead before he hit the floor.

Aros tilted his head. "What was that?"

"We will spread the word," another guard said, without pause.

"Yes, you will. These lovely imperial oaths that I still hold in my hand." Something cold and horrible shot from the scepter; twisted with the spell of an imperial oath, the spell descended upon the man. He twisted in agony and fell to his knees.

Aros smiled. "Such a lovely bit of hubris, that the emperor—the past emperor—thought himself unkillable."

Terror rose in their gazes. Aros's smile grew.

"You did this." The voice froze everyone remaining.

Nin stared at the scene and felt despair.

"Kaveh." Aros looked at the stick in his hand. "You are still alive for this part. Alas. You were always my favorite. But you will never accept the death of the emperor. Your one weak point, and the one that I could never work around." He pointed the Scepter of Darkness at Kaveh ul Fehl.

Nin dragged the thin metal through the opening, ripping the skin around it in her haste. A thief knew how to pick locks without magic.

But the cuffs were secondary. The fact that her magic was still inaccessible—and that it would be for a hundred more ticks—meant she had no magic to aid her. To aid anyone.

Kaveh was at Aros's feet and Aros was reaching toward him with the scepter.

She hadn't been there when her family had died. She had been too far away and without magic to aid her. But she was so close now. And she was going to watch Kaveh die.

She lifted the marble chunk beneath her hand and looked at the faces who were glued to Aros and Kaveh. Taline's eyes were wide. Rone's were shadowed and his hand glowed faint blue—undecided on how to use his last card, but he was unlikely to aid the Shadow Prince except perhaps to create a diversion. Osni's were furious and bitter. Nera and Etelian's were hungry. Baksis and Simin were unreadable. The guards were blank.

Namir, dust-covered but straight-spined, and near the door just looked angry—and she was the only one not watching the main event. She was staring at Nin—no, behind Nin.

"Blessings and luck to you, gatemaker," Omari's voice whispered in her ear. A finger touched the back of Nin's neck, and vines spread through her skin—purifying and wiping free the lingering traces of the nullification. "Leave the two of us here."

Magic spread golden light through Nin, and she wasted no time in thanks as she dropped the form behind her through the floor. Nin opened a ripgate beneath Rone and Taline and whipped it over the top of them like she had seen Kaveh do with his shadows on the battlefield. As their ripgate blanket wrapped into the floor, Omari rode hers out, appearing next to Namir, who tucked her behind as if the girl had never moved from her back.

No time. No time remained.

Aros was lifting the scepter against Kaveh, and though Aros was far more powerful than Nin with scepter in hand, the scepter had yet to embed itself within his bones.

Copying a move from his own scheme, Nin ported under Aros's arm and thrust his arm skyward. The scepter discharged with a mighty roar. She grabbed Kaveh's shirt with one fist, sliced open the air behind her, and pulled them backward through the slice.

As she fell backward with Kaveh into the gate, Aros's amber eyes fixed upon her, glittering with the faintest sheen of red. His arm pulled back down, and the scepter was glowing with slicing white and black.

He wouldn't complete the motion in time to hit them though. They were going to make it.

Aros smiled. "I'll see you soon, cousin."

The gate closed over the top of them as the palace rent in two around the grand hall.

CHAPTER FORTY

PAIN OF THE LOST

KAVEH

(Nowhere)

A ravine cut sharply through the earth below, and the canyon winds swept over and licked their torn and dirty clothes. No shadows kept the wind from his skin. No shadows fed continuous information to his senses. The shadows remained detached and dead.

Nin's sister and the cursed Valeran spawn whispered angrily to each other, gazes on him. He didn't care. Loran, Hosfuri, Scythia? He didn't care whose landscape this was.

Motionless where he had landed with Nin, he stared at the sky.

The last sliver of moon slid down the starlit scape. The dark moon would rise in the morning.

Nin's fingers touched his face. Then Nin's hands were cradling his cheeks. "Your magic... Kaveh, your magic..."

It was gone. Locked away, with the only keyholder dead. Gone.

"You still live," he said simply. He could think of nothing else in the numbness. The emperor was dead. His powers were gone. The empire would be destroyed.

But she survived. And he could grasp only to that.

He felt a tear touch his cheek as her cheek touched his. "We will fix this."

But there was no fix. "You should have killed him."

She'd had a single move against Aros. Kaveh's magic might be gone, but the speed of his eyes and a thousand remembered battles remained.

"He would have killed you at the same moment," Nin said. "Aros's spell had already started."

If she had pierced Aros through, Aros's blast would have hit true.

"But Aros would be dead."

"But you would have been dead, too."

It was true. It had been the type of blast that didn't heal. "I'm already dead." Kaveh looked at the dark, starlit sky.

"You aren't." She pulled him upright. "But we must go. He'll be able to find this place. He has all the scepters."

"Excellent. We will have exactly one day to question all our life choices," Valeran said.

Kaveh looked at the faint rise of dawn. Aros had taken the throne.

He closed his eyes. The emperor would die.

About the Author

Anne Zoelle is the pseudonym of a USA Today Bestselling author who loves writing about college-aged protagonists who get embroiled in complicated adventures. Split between the midwest and west coast, she writes books for all ages that feature sentient libraries, rock guardians, and people finding family.

You can find her at www.annezoelle.com.

Or contact her directly at:
anne.zoelle@gmail.com

Glossary

Terms, Places, Characters, Pantheon

TERMS

Ameni Tribe: a tribe of renowned horsemasters to which Taline was born.

beldrake: a type of dragon.

blessed child of the emperor: an imperial child, who is blessed by the emperor in a ceremony that bestows upon them the ability to control imperial oaths. Imperial children given this designation may also be selected to serve as padifehl of an imperial territory someday. The blessing ceremony takes place when the emperor deems it time—usually when a powerful child has come into their powers, generally upon an Awakening from age 10-17. Children, like Kaveh ul Fehl, who come into their powers at an early age and show rare amounts of power or extraordinary gifts are blessed at a very young age and are raised accordingly. There are hundreds, perhaps thousands, of imperial children residing in the imperial palace and living in far-flung streets and lands, but the honor of being "blessed" means something far more elite and powerful. The emperor has been decreasing the number of blessing ceremonies and increasing the requirements as more and more of his children are born with great power. The order of blessing does not correspond to the age of the child or their power, it is simply the order in which a child was blessed.

Chrimoa: an elite crafter of decorative glass and ceramic pieces.

crouel: a person with little or no magic.

croupa: a sickness not unlike croup.

farhani: a necklace worn in imperial territories that signifies a magi's power level and has the magi's imperial fealty oaths embedded within. The investigorii can use the oaths to detain individuals in their territories for questioning.

fehlta, fehltan: a unit of currency used across the empire. Prior to its use, "measures" were used: five measures, three half measures, two quarter measures. Fehlta are similar to the Magahda coins used in ancient India. In the Fehl Empire, there are 5 magi coinmasters keyed to the treasury whose responsibility is to create the coins using personal, magical stamps. When a coinmaster dies or retires, another is keyed to take his place. The five stamped signatures have to be correct for the coin to be legitimate. Counterfeiting coins is extremely difficult and punishable by death.

gate medallion: an object which has been imprinted with coordinates to transport a person to a specific place and contains a one-time activation. They are incredibly rare and expensive because they can only be created by a gatemaker or gate relic.

gatekeeper: a magi who cares for and repairs already created gates, and who is able to switch internally embedded coordinates to open through other created gates (connecting already created gates together). A rare ability.

gatemaker: a magi who creates ripgates and who is capable of tethering ripgates to physical objects and locations—making an arch or object with an open interior into a semi-permanent gate between two places. An extremely rare and coveted ability. **See also: ripgate**

imperial names: names given to citizens of the empire. The census requires all magi in the empire to receive designations based on the following name scheme: First Name **al** Power Level **el** Occupation **il** Birth City **ol** Oath Temple **ul** Family Name. These get shortened in informal use to First name **ul** Family Name.

Example formal: Ninli al Six el Healer il Tehras ol Gomen ul Summora

Example informal: Ninli ul Summora

For people living outside of the empire, individual society naming schemes prevail.

imperial professional titles: the professional designation that precedes one's imperial name. Professional titles eschew many of the imperial naming scheme elements brought by the census. Title + Family Name is most often used. If there is more than one person of the same profession with the same family name in the room, the power level is given in the middle. The first name would be added as well if the power level is also the same.

Examples:

Healer Summora

Healer Six Summora and Healer Four Summora

Healer Ninli Six Summora

investigore: head of the law enforcement, similar to a director. Investigore Malik ul Malit when formally addressed.

investigorii: a law enforcement unit or an individual officer (singular and plural).

imperator: title for the head of an army unit.

karogi tiles: tiles used in karogi (a game).

khursifa (**khursifas**): a spell-woven conveyance mat that can connect and use wind enchantments in a city and through its own woven magic. A type of flying carpet. Under the hands and skills of a specialist, they can be made to do wondrous things as a mode of transportation.

Kore: a fictional, powerful eastern dynasty.

layer, layers, layer split: The split of one world into five, each duplicate existing on top of the next. Three creation magi (worldchangers) working together split the Earth into five identical layers of land. Four layers have magic, while one layer (sometimes referred to as "the first") is without. This first layer contains all the humans and creatures born without magic and is protected from the magical worlds by ruthless groups of devout magi. **See also: pentalayerists**. The Fourth Layer was created specifically for beasts, creatures, and hybrid beings and is sometimes referred to as "the land of the beasts." Five layers of the same world, existing each on top of the next. Four steady layers and one of chaos—not fully settled during the event that produced them. One of no magic, two of plenty, one of beasts and power, one of chaos.

magi: a user of magic.

mancaleh: a classic board game, sometimes referred to as mancala.

majex (imperial majex): the wife of the emperor. The high imperial majex is the ruling wife.

narsumina: a pet name Rone calls Taline (used in much the way someone would call another "princess"). The reference is to the beautiful, vestal temple attendants of Narsum, the god of beauty, youth, age, and time.

padifehl: the leader of an imperial territory, usually a child of the emperor.

palmera: a palm spring drink that is highly intoxicating.

pentalayerists: a group who seek to protect and preserve the layers as they were designed. This includes protecting the non-magic world from magical influence. Their goal is to eradicate magi and relics that can open gates between layers. As a precautionary measure, and if given the opportunity, they will also destroy any relic or magi deemed too powerful, who may disrupt the status quo.

Polingsa Manuscripts: manuscripts and scrolls that contain powerful spells created and kept by the Polingsa family. Qara ul Polingsa encourages Nin to steal them so that they can be added to the library for the masses, while still giving Qara a reasoned voice among the elite.

revenant: one of the undead.

ripgate: a temporary gate created by a gatemaker or relic. It is different from a gate, which is a permanent or semi-permanent fixture.

sandrake: a type of sand dragon.

sandpronga: a large worm-like sand creature with immense teeth.

Sanskrine: modified Sanskrit

scholari: the head of knowledge or science in an imperial territory.

scepter chamber: a curved chamber at the heart of the Palace of Tehras that holds the twelve scepters of Tehras. Four per "wall" in the curved chamber.

shadowshaper: one who can use and craft shadows to enhance sensory perception and who can control shadows by pushing their own sensory output through them. A shadowshaper can connect their senses through a shadow to affect whatever the shadow is touching. In this way, shadows become extended limbs of the shadowshaper and are able to do whatever a regular limb can. A thousand shadows could become a thousand separate swords when wielded by a magi whose mind is able to control a thousand different limbs at once. Only two shadowshapers are known to exist. Neither is fully human. It is speculated that a regular human mind is incapable of wielding as many separate entities as shadowshapers have been observed to wield.

stormbrewer: a magi who controls storms.

string: a signature, the feel of a person's magic—how one magi sensitive to it can identify another.

sunmaker, sunchaser, suncatcher, suntaker: a magi who manipulates sunlight or light for specific civic tasks (enforcement, agriculture, leisure, etc.).

Swee: a fictional, powerful northern dynasty.

windcatcher, windmaker, windchaser, windtaker: a magi who manipulates the winds for specific civic tasks (chasing people using wind spells, crafting directional breezes for city travel, routing weather for agricultural means, etc.).

PLACES (story + modern equivalents)

Anarta: a region of ancient India.

Ancyra: the Latin form of Ankara, Turkey.

Antequere: Antequera Dolmens Site in the province of Málaga.

Assaka: a kingdom of ancient India.

Axšaina Sea: the Black Sea.

Babil: Babylon.

Bekli: Göbekli Tepe.

Bilbat: an ancient Sumerian city.

Caire: a district in Tehras noted for gambling.

Campistel: a fictional setting where the Spread of Verdis occurs.

Casp Sea: the Caspian Sea.

Dernholm: the fictional city where Rone and Oralia lived in exile.

Dozine: a fictional place set in ancient Syria.

Ersine: the Continent of Africa.

Fehlaka: the imperial capital. Modern day Failaka Island, Kuwait.

Gerod: a fictional place where the Festival of Marsk is held.

Idiqlat: the Tigris River in Sumerian/Akkadian.

Kailāsa: Mount Kailash in Sanskrit.

Kastoni: a fictional place set in Jordan.

Kiš: Kish, an ancient city in Sumer.

Krokola: Karachi, Pakistan.

Lisso: Lisbon, Portugal.

Magadha: a kingdom of ancient India.

Memfi: Memphis, Egypt.

Purattu: the Euphrates River in Akkadian.

Sarg: a fictional place set in northern Oman.

Tehras: the capital city of Tehrasi. Roughly Tehran, Iran.

Tehrasi: a province of the Fehl Empire that approximates modern day Iran.

Temple of the Scepter: a Second Layer temple that contains three chambers—the key chamber, the lock chamber, and the antechamber. The antechamber contains a gate to the scepter's actual location in the First Layer. The temple is located in the Caspian Hyrcanian Mixed Forests in northern Iran on the southern border of the Caspian Sea. But the scepter itself is in India. The temple gate did not just go through layers, but across them as well, in order to conceal the hiding place.

Telb Mountains: Alborz Mountain Range.

Ur: an ancient city in Sumer.

Uruk: an ancient city in Sumer.

CHARACTERS

Ninli ul Summora, Ninli, Nin: (age 19) healer and thief, gatemaker. Incredibly powerful magically and physically gifted in movement. Is unable to read (pure alexia) due to brain trauma at age 9.

Taline ul Summora, Tal, Tali: (age 20) healer and thief, spellcrafter. Highly intelligent with an excellent memory, but magically weak due to repeated stripping of her abilities when younger. Can recreate the bases and glyphs for spells she sees even a single time but is unable to power them.

Rone ul Valeran: (age 21) relic hunter, gambler, and trickster. The bastard son of two magically gifted lines, Valeran and Fehl. He is blessed/cursed with a distinctive hair color that cannot be magically or physically altered.

Kaveh ul Fehl: (age 22) thirteenth "blessed" child of the emperor, head of all imperial armies, and the emperor's favorite. A shadowshaper who is undefeated in battle, he answers only to the emperor and has ties to no other. He is known as the Shadow Prince, Imperator General, Imperator General of the Empire, Terror of the Battlefront, Nightmare of the Empire, and He Who Has Never Failed.

Ifret: corporeal creature of shadow, companion to Kaveh.

Sher Fehl: (age 52) emperor, The Fehl, Great Fehl, Emperor of All He Touches.

Nera ul Fehl: (age 48) High Imperial Majex, favorite wife of the emperor. Born Nera Erias.

Aros ul Fehl: (age 32) first born of Nera, first blessed child of the emperor, no current territory.

Etelian ul Fehl: (age 31) Padifehl of Tehrasi, second born of Nera, second blessed child.

Carsue ul Fehl: (age 30) Padifehl of Moru, sixth blessed child

Shiera ul Fehl: (age 30) Padifehl of Cuipsin, eighth blessed child, beloved by her country.

Zorus ul Fehl: (age 30) Padifehl of Kemet, ninth blessed child

Urful ul Fehl: (age 30) Padifehl of Shoune, twelfth blessed child

Rayd ul Fehl: (age 28) Padifehl of Bahra, third born of Nera, eleventh blessed child

Baksis ul Fehl: (age 27) imperial prince, twentieth blessed child, no current territory.

Simin ul Fehl: (age 26) imperial prince, eighteenth blessed child, no current territory.

Voiya ul Fehl: (age 24) Padifehl of Fehla-da, fourth born of Nera, fourteenth blessed child.

Omari ul Fehl: (age 11) Padifehl To Be of Cuipsin, hundredth blessed child.

Namir ul Mero: (age 24) Personal Guard of Omari, distant cousin to the Queen of Kush.

Akel: a fifteen-year-old boy who becomes the head of Ninli's "ducklings." Akel is a budding spymaster.

Barrinis: a deceased family line of gatekeepers and gatemakers.

Ber ul Hon of the First Guard: the investigator into Shirsk and Siru ul Teg's death.

Birsa: a "seeker" whose enslavement bonds to treasure hunters was broken by Ninli. Birsa has been living in First Layer India for the past two years. She has been given the name "Luriandur—Devotional of Sea and Storm" in her new community.

Bilen Osni: Crelu ul Osni's son, Bilen was leading a revolution to upset the Carre Dynasty due to Jisarek's increasingly dangerous actions.

Crelu ul Osni was forced to execute Bilen in order to prove his own loyalty.

Crelu ul Osni: Scholari of Tehrasi, worked for and betrayed the Carre Family; now rules Tehrasi from the shadows and hunts scepter lore.

Farrah Osni: Crelu ul Osni's deceased wife, and Ninli's tutor and primary maternal influence.

Kūruš: Cyrus the Great

Goran, First General Goran: one of Kaveh's generals on the battlefront

Gursuf Sule: a villain from Rone's past.

Heba: a master of courtly enchantment, makeup, and dress, and a loyal handmaiden to Ninli. Heba was the handmaiden who wore Zehra Amanan Carre's face when the Carres were killed.

Irsula of Denz: Night Terror of the Land of Darkness, Mistress of Shadows; mother of Kaveh ul Fehl. Born to Darkness and a human woman, she is half-human. Imprisoned, and with no oaths taken, she has no imperial census designation and no surname. Denz is the place of her birth.

Larit ul Polingsa: bondmate of Qara ul Polingsa, healer.

Malik ul Malit: Investigore of Tehrasi. Head of the investigorii—the law enforcement branch of Tehras.

Oralia Valeran: Rone ul Valeran's mother

Pikerens: the family that Oralia Valeran married into after abandoning Rone.

Qara ul Polingsa: an elite of Tehras, politician.

Reyi: a loyal handmaiden to Ninli who was killed in the Carre massacre.

Siran Bey: Taline's birth name.

Siru ul Teg: The First General in charge of the northern section of the front in Kaveh's absence. He was the lead point on Shirsk.

Sora: a loyal handmaiden to Ninli who was killed by Lorsali.

Carre Family (in order of age):

Giran Carre: former King of Tehrasi.

Jisarek Carre: brother of Giran, kidnapper of Nera ul Fehl.

Salare Carre: former Queen of Tehrasi.

Savvan Carre: former crown prince.

Lorsali Carre: former first princess.

Fein Carre: former prince.

Allit Carre: former prince.

Memni Carre: former prince.

Jolan Carre: former prince.

Zehra Amanan Carre: former princess.

PANTHEON

Sehk-Ra: two-faced god of death and chance (shadow wielders, undertakers and embalmers, death rite clerics, touch killers, gamblers, thieves) and god of the sun, rule, order (rulers, head of households, judgment/truth speakers).

When face names are used individually: Sehk for death and chance, Ra for rule and order.

To be Sehk-Ra-blessed is to be in total control = the god of dominion.

Ferra: goddess of birth and health (healers).

Akkan: god of winds, travel, and travelers (port mages, paladins/finders, some weather mages).

Gripna: goddess of domestic matters/hearth/estate/money (homemakers, merchants).

Narsum: god of beauty, youth, age, and time. Depiction varies—sometimes shown genderless, sometimes shown possessing all genders, sometimes shown as an infant, sometimes stooped with a cane. Narsum is the representation of all things experienced in a lifetime—change both physical and spiritual. Narsumina is the title given to the vestal tenders of Narsum's shrines and temples—usually beautiful, young women.

Marsk: god of war and victory (warriors, rulers, politicians, etc.).

Oceana: goddess of all waters, the seas, rivers, rains and snow (fishermen, some weather mages, etc.).

Verdis: god of flora and fauna, forests (hunters, herbists, farmers).

Called upon by imperial citizens, prayer usage varies:

A healer might pray to Verdis to find herbs, but to Ferra to bless a procedure.

A sailor might say: May the winds of Akkan bless us and the waters of Oceana hold us.

Godly names are used as swear words often, especially Sehk-Ra, Sehk, and Ra with any combination of descriptive terms attached. Sehk-Ra-be-damned, Sehk-damned, etc.